The Christmas Cowboy

Rodeo Romance Book 1
by
USA Today Bestselling Author
SHANNA HATFIELD

The Christmas Cowboy
Copyright © 2013
by Shanna Hatfield

ISBN-13: 978-1492805137
ISBN-10: 1492805130

For permission requests, please contact the author, with a subject line of "permission request" at the email address below or through her website.

Shanna Hatfield
shanna@shannahatfield.com
shannahatfield.com

This is a work of fiction. Names, characters, businesses, places, events and incidents are either the products of the author's imagination or used in a fictitious manner. Any resemblance to actual persons, living or dead, or actual events is purely coincidental.

*To those who never
give up on their dreams...*

Books by Shanna Hatfield

FICTION

CONTEMPORARY

Love at the 20-Yard Line
Learnin' the Ropes
QR Code Killer
Rose
Taste of Tara

Rodeo Romance
The Christmas Cowboy
Wrestlin' Christmas
Capturing Christmas
Barreling Through Christmas
Chasing Christmas

Grass Valley Cowboys
The Cowboy's Christmas Plan
The Cowboy's Spring Romance
The Cowboy's Summer Love
The Cowboy's Autumn Fall
The Cowboy's New Heart
The Cowboy's Last Goodbye

Silverton Sweethearts
The Coffee Girl
The Christmas Crusade
Untangling Christmas

Women of Tenacity
A Prelude
Heart of Clay
Country Boy vs. City Girl
Not His Type

HISTORICAL

Hardman Holidays
The Christmas Bargain
The Christmas Token
The Christmas Calamity
The Christmas Vow
The Christmas Quandary
The Christmas Confection

Pendleton Petticoats
Dacey
Aundy
Caterina
Ilsa
Marnie
Lacy
Bertie
Millie
Dally

Baker City Brides
Tad's Treasure
Crumpets and Cowpies
Thimbles and Thistles
Corsets and Cuffs
Bobbins and Boots

Hearts of the War
Garden of Her Heart
Home of Her Heart

Chapter One

"This seat taken?"

Startled by the deep voice speaking close to her ear, Kenzie Beckett glanced up into eyes the color of sapphires and lost the ability to speak.

Shaking her head, she moved her oversized shoulder bag from the chair in question to a space near her feet. The intent gaze of the man made her sit up straight in the chair and fight the urge to lick her suddenly dry lips. She'd noticed the handsome cowboy at the airport many times, but never had the opportunity to be this close to him.

He smelled every bit as good as he looked.

"Mind if I sit down?" he asked, pointing to the empty chair beside her.

Nervous, but with no reason to refuse, she again shook her head. Slowly inhaling a deep breath, she smiled and stuck out her hand as the cowboy folded himself into the seat. He filled the space next to her with an appealing scent that made her think of leather, spice, and rugged masculinity.

"I'm Kenzie."

Pleased when he took her hand and gave it a firm, yet gentle shake, the contact created an unsettling storm of electrical currents to rush up her arm.

"Tate." A white-toothed grin displayed two dimples through the scruffy stubble on his face. "Tate Morgan."

"It's nice to meet you, Mr. Morgan." Tongue-tied and awestruck, Kenzie couldn't believe she sat next to Tate Morgan, rodeo star.

Although ranching and rodeos were no longer part of her life, she kept up with some of the details. The good-looking cowboy sitting next to her was one of the top saddle bronc riders in the world. She knew he was from Washington State, but never connected him to the Tri-Cities area where she lived. She absently wondered if he was from Kennewick, Richland, or Pasco.

He must frequent the Pasco airport as often as she did with his rodeo travels. That was probably why she'd seen him there before and why he was waiting in the seat next to her to board the flight to Denver.

"Where are you traveling today?"

"Tennessee," Tate replied, grateful he arrived late at the airport. The only seat left in the waiting area was the one next to the dark-haired beauty who caught his eye the last few times he flew out of town. "Call me Tate. All my friends do and I certainly hope we'll be friends."

Kenzie narrowed her gaze. She should have known he'd start flirting within seconds of sitting down. Apparently, a pair of boots, a Stetson, and perfect-fitting Wranglers gave a man free license to flirt with any female crossing his path.

"I don't make it a habit of becoming friends with people I randomly meet at the airport." She tore her gaze away from Tate's gorgeous blue eyes. Swiftly closing the fashion magazine she'd been mindlessly reading before he startled her, she stuffed it into her bag and checked her watch again.

"Really?" Tate pushed the brim of his Stetson up with an index finger and revealed a hint of light brown hair. "I figure once names are exchanged and handshakes are given, you're a friend until proven otherwise."

Heat filled her cheeks at his words. Despite his friendly tone and broad smile, she recognized a rebuke when she heard one.

What was it about this man that threw her off her game?

As a corporate trainer for one of the most successful direct sales companies in the country, she could get a room filled with consultants on their feet and enthusiastically following her direction with no problem. She could take on the corporate team, pitch ideas, and win them over to her way of thinking with hardly a blink.

But put her next to a cowboy, especially one as attractive as Tate, and she lost the ability to function with any degree of logic or wisdom.

A voice over the loudspeaker interrupted her thoughts, announcing another fifteen-minute delay for the Denver flight.

Kenzie released a pent-up sigh, opened a zippered pocket on her bag, and pulled out her phone. She sent a text message to the organizer of the regional meeting in Denver she planned to lead later that morning, informing the woman she would probably be late.

Normally, Kenzie liked to arrive the day before an event so she didn't run the risk of being late. It also gave her time to prepare to give her best to the consultants.

The trainer originally lined up to lead the meeting had an emergency and asked Kenzie to cover for him, so she'd only found out she needed to be in Denver the previous evening.

"Is everything okay?" Tate drummed his fingers on the arm of the seat. In spite of his calm facade, he had a tight connecting flight schedule and if they didn't get moving, he was going to miss his plane.

"It will be if we can board and be on our way soon," Kenzie said, tugging on the navy skirt of her business suit. The airport was warm and stuffy, crowded as it was with people waiting for flights, even though it was early May and the temperature outside was pleasant. "I'm leading a meeting in Denver and unless we make up some time in the air, a few hundred consultants will be left waiting for me to get there. I don't like to keep people waiting."

"That's good to know." He grinned again. "What is it you do?"

Kenzie glanced over to see if he was genuinely interested or just killing time. At the inquisitive look in his eyes, she relaxed a little.

"I'm a corporate trainer with Dew." Kenzie took a business card from her bag and handed it to him. "We're a skin care company that's been around since the 1940s."

Tate accepted the card from Kenzie and stared at the logo of a pale blue dewdrop with the word "Dew" embossed in gold across the center.

"Dew?" He thought it was an odd name for a company. "Where's the name come from?"

Kenzie smiled and Tate felt drawn to the light shining in her beautiful brown eyes. They reminded him of the molasses his dad was so fond of eating - dark, rich, and sweet.

"All women want a soft, dewy complexion." She bit her tongue to keep from launching into her usual spiel about the company and their superior products.

"If they hired you to be a walking billboard, you do a great job," Tate said, causing Kenzie to blush again. "So your company is all about stuff women use to preserve their youthful appearance?"

"Basically."

Convinced the outrageously handsome cowboy next to her would not understand the importance of moisturizers, lotions, and exfoliators to the health of aging skin, she nodded her head.

Tate shot her a wicked grin. "So your people go door-to-door peddling goo?"

"No, they don't go door-to-door or peddle goo." Kenzie couldn't stop the smile lifting the corners of her mouth as she removed a catalog from her bag and handed it to Tate.

He browsed through the glossy pages, noticing the company offered more than just lotions and potions. Dew sold a collection for men, spa items, and gift options in what appeared to be a well-thought-out product line.

"How does it work? How do your… what did you call them? Consultants?" At her nod he continued. "How do they get catalogs into the hands of potential customers?" Unfamiliar with the concept of direct sales, if Tate found something he didn't know, he quickly set out to learn all he could on the topic.

"Home parties. People invite friends into their homes and host parties. Consultants give a brief presentation and take orders. The party host receives freebies and discounted product for her trouble and people get together for a fun hour or two while shopping in the comfort of someone's home," Kenzie explained, warming to the subject.

She put herself through college doing direct sales. Her passion for the industry, Dew in particular, was why she was a well-respected corporate trainer at the age of twenty-seven.

"If I invite a bunch of buddies to my house, set out some snacks and have one of your consultants come show us your stuff, you'd give me freebies?" Tate asked, only halfway joking. If he could somehow coerce Kenzie into being the consultant, he'd host a party every month just to be able to see her.

"In theory, that's how it works." She laughed as a visual popped into her head of Tate and his friends sitting around with facials dripping off their stubbly chins. "Of course, the freebies depend on your total orders for the party."

Before Tate could ask more questions, the call to board rang through the airport. Under the assumption it would take a while, Kenzie began to gather up her belongings to make a final trip to the restroom.

Tate put a hand on her arm, drawing her attention. "You can leave your stuff here. I'll keep an eye on it," he said, nodding his head toward the restroom door.

"Well, I…" Kenzie said, surprised by his offer. She didn't know the man and shouldn't trust him, even if he did seem nice.

"I promise not to run off with your stuff or touch anything." Tate held his hand up as if he made a pledge. "Scout's honor. Besides, I'd look ridiculous toting that bright pink bag. It clashes with my shirt."

She'd tried not to notice how well his burgundy shirt fit across his broad shoulders and chest.

"Thank you," she said, getting to her feet. "I'll be right back."

"No need to hurry." Tate glanced at the long line of people waiting to board.

When she returned a few minutes later, Tate stood at the back of the line, both his bag and hers over his shoulder, her suit jacket draped over his arm.

"I thought I better get in line since it's finally starting to move." He handed Kenzie her jacket.

"Thank you." She took her bag from him and slid the strap over her shoulder. Hurriedly digging in a side pocket, she pulled out her boarding pass and checked to make sure everything was just as she left it. Tate seemed like a good guy, but trusting handsome cowboys had gotten her into trouble before.

"What have you got in that thing? Rocks?" Tate teased as they stepped closer to the door.

"No, bricks." Kenzie grinned over her shoulder at him as she handed her pass to the ticket agent.

Tate felt an unfamiliar twinge in the region of his heart as Kenzie took her boarding pass and walked out the door. Regardless of his extensive experience with the opposite sex, he'd never had anyone affect him like the beautiful brunette.

As he gave her a quick once-over, he admired the dark hair piled on her head, her long legs, and trim figure. Her stature intrigued him. He generally preferred smaller women, but in her heels, Kenzie nearly met his six-foot one-inch height.

A hint of something soft and floral tickled his nose while they walked onto the plane and waited to go down the aisle. He leaned closer and breathed in her scent, deciding he'd never smelled anything quite so inviting and feminine.

Out of habit, he tugged his hat more firmly on his head and studied the harried faces on the crowded plane. He hoped the flight would go quickly. It was vital he catch the connection to Nashville where he'd meet a friend to hitch a ride to his next rodeo.

He swallowed back a grin when he located his seat and Kenzie sat across the aisle from him. Suddenly, his day looked brighter. The connecting flight concerns shuffled to the back of his mind.

Instead of worrying, he had a few hours of uninterrupted time to get to know his lovely traveling companion.

After settling in to his assigned space, Tate noticed Kenzie leaning back in her seat, eyes closed, hands gripping the armrest with white knuckles.

He reached across the aisle and placed his hand on hers, watching her eyes pop open.

"We won't crash, you know." He attempted to coax her smile out of hiding.

"I know. I just hate takeoffs. I'm fine once we get in the air." Kenzie offered Tate a tense glance. "It's that awful feeling when your stomach is weightless that gets me every time."

"That's one of the best parts of flying." He waggled an eyebrow her direction.

"It's not surprising a daredevil like you would think so." She squeezed her eyes shut when the plane roared down the runway and lifted into the air. As it gained altitude, she let out the breath she'd held and relaxed.

"How do you know what I do for a living?" Certain they hadn't gotten around to discussing why he was going to Tennessee or his career, his brow wrinkled in question as he looked at her.

"I assumed you're a daredevil by that gleam in your eye and the look on your face that says you love adventure." Kenzie wasn't willing to acknowledge she recognized Tate's name and knew exactly what he did for a living. She refused to admit to anyone, least of all the handsome cowboy beside her, she had even a passing interest in anything to do with the pro rodeo circuit. That was classified information she'd take to her grave. "You appear to be someone who lives life on the edge."

"I guess some people think I do. I ride saddle broncs as a profession. Well, at least I do when I'm not busy ranching." Tate chuckled and shook his head derisively. "What I really should say is when I'm not gone to a rodeo, I stay busy on our family ranch."

"Is that why you're traveling to Tennessee?" Kenzie asked, trying to think what rodeo he'd entered. It had been a long time since she'd kept close tabs on the rodeo circuit.

"Yep. I'm meeting a friend in Nashville and then we're off to the rodeo. We're both competing tomorrow." He removed his hat and placed it on his lap.

Kenzie admired his strong hands as he ran tanned fingers through his thick hair to loosen the band pressed into it from his hat. She wouldn't allow herself to think of that head of light brown hair. Cut short, it was just long

12

enough to have some finger-tempting waves, absolutely meant to torment women.

"Does your friend also ride saddle broncs?" Unsuccessfully, Kenzie tried to keep her gaze from entangling with his.

From experience gained in what seemed like a lifetime ago, she knew saddle bronc riders were artists, of a sort, as well as spectacular athletes. While bull riding and bareback riding were wilder, saddle bronc riding demanded style, grace, and precision.

"Nah, he's a steer wrestler," Tate said, grateful Cort McGraw agreed to swing by the airport and pick him up on his way through Nashville.

Thoughtfully observing him, Kenzie pulled a water bottle from her bag and took a drink. Once she screwed the cap back on, she turned to Tate. "You said when you aren't out on the rodeo circuit, you ranch. Where do you live?"

"South of Kennewick." The ranch his grandfather started back in the early 1900s and his father made successful through unwavering dedication and plain old hard work had always been his home. "If you head toward Umatilla and take the last exit before you cross into Oregon, we're about ten miles off the beaten path on the Washington side of the border."

"I've never driven around much in that area." In the time she'd been in the Tri-Cities, Kenzie hadn't done any exploring. She was rarely home long enough to do more than catch up on laundry and visit her one close friend.

"Are you originally from the Tri-Cities?" Tate asked, wondering where Kenzie grew up. She seemed like the very persona of a fashionable city girl, opposite of the type of girl he thought would someday fit into his lifestyle.

"No, my family lives in Portland." Kenzie brushed imaginary lint from her skirt. She knew the next question Tate would ask and beat him to it. "I moved to Kennewick three years ago because I needed to get out of Portland. My best friend lives near Pendleton and encouraged me to move closer. I chose the Tri-Cities area because it works well with my job. I spend a lot of time traveling and being close to an airport is essential."

"What made you want to leave Portland?" Tate stretched his legs beneath the seat in front of him. He hated flying, not because he was afraid of the plane crashing, but mostly because he felt cramped and uncomfortable the entire time. Whoever designed the seats must not have taken long legs and broad shoulders into account.

"Let's just say the city wasn't quite big enough to keep from running into my former fiancé and his very pregnant girlfriend." A flash of anger fired in her eyes.

At Tate's raised eyebrow, she shook her head. "It really was for the best. We were at the bakery, doing a cake tasting for our wedding, when a woman ran in and started screaming at Sonny, slapping his face. Apparently, she'd just found out she was pregnant. She demanded he tell me the truth, and he confessed he'd been seeing her on the side."

"More than seeing her, I'd say." Indignant on behalf of the woman he'd just met, he thought her ex-fiancé had to be a certified idiot to mess up a future with Kenzie. However, if the man hadn't been an idiot, Tate wouldn't be sitting across from her, enjoying their conversation and hoping he'd see her again.

"Anyway, I ran into them all the time. Since my job isn't based in a specific area, it doesn't really matter where I live. When Megan called and invited me to stay with her for a while, I decided to take her up on the offer. The drive from Helix to the airport in Pasco grew old in a hurry, so I rented an apartment in Kennewick." Uneasy, she glanced at Tate. "Now you know more about me than you ever wanted to."

"Hardly." He wondered if her skin would feel as soft as it looked as he studied her strong cheekbones and creamy complexion. Popping his knuckles seemed the only way to keep from reaching across the aisle and indulging his curiosity by touching her cheek. When Kenzie cringed at the sound, he stopped and gripped the armrest. "Your friend Megan — is she, by any chance, Megan Montgomery?"

"Yes. Do you know her?" Kenzie's voice carried a note of friendly interest.

"Yep. I know her husband, Owen. He purchases cattle from us and we've bought horses from them for years." Tate was surprised he and Kenzie hadn't run into each other before, since the Montgomery clan liked to entertain and often hosted barbecues and dinners. "Megan's fed us more than a time or two."

"Wow. I'll have to tell Megan I met you." She made a mental note to call her friend later that evening. "When you say us and we, who else lives on the ranch with you?"

Tate laughed and the sound resonated somewhere deep and untouched inside Kenzie, drawing out her smile.

"It's just me. Well, me and my foreman, Monte, and the ranch hands. My dad moved into an assisted living facility in Richland about a month ago, so I'm still getting used to rattling around the house by myself when I'm home."

"Oh, I'm sorry. Is your father unwell?" Kenzie asked, wondering what type of ailment required Tate's father to move into a care home.

"Nothing is wrong with Pop except old age. He turned ninety on his last birthday and finally agreed it was time for him to retire," Tate said, chuckling. He loved to see the reaction on people's faces when he told them his father's age.

Determined to be a bachelor his whole life, Tate's father, Kent, didn't know what hit him when he met a beautiful young woman who turned his world upside down.

"I can see by the look on your face, you're trying to do the math and coming up shy a few years," Tate teased with a knowing grin. "I'm twenty-nine. Pop was nearly sixty when he married my mama. She was in her late twenties. Most folks thought it was quite a scandal for them to get married, but they loved each other. I don't think Pop ever recovered from losing Mama. I was about eleven when she had kidney failure and died. We all thought she was in good health, but it seemed to hit her out of the blue. It's been just me and Pop since. He's done remarkably well for his age, but the winter was hard on him and he was ready to move off the ranch and into town once spring arrived. He's in great shape, but I still worry about leaving him home alone. He agreed assisted living was a good option."

"I'm sorry, Tate. I know how hard it is to lose a parent," Kenzie said, not wanting to bare her soul to this stranger. "Do you have any siblings?"

"Nope, but I've got a bunch of friends who are as close as brothers and some cousins, however many times removed, who live a few hours away in Grass Valley." He smiled as they made small talk the rest of the trip.

When the pilot announced the plane would soon land, they both glanced at their watches. They'd made up most of the lost time.

"I've enjoyed this flight more than any I have in a long time, Kenzie. Thank you for talking with me," Tate said as they landed and gathered their things in anticipation of leaving the plane.

"It was nice to visit with you, Tate. I hope you do well at the rodeo." She genuinely wanted him to win. It was hard to remain cool and aloof around such a warm, inviting personality.

Despite the alarms sounding in her head to stay far away from him, Kenzie was grateful she had the opportunity to meet the charming cowboy.

"I do, too. It's a long way to go to not at least place," Tate said with the grin Kenzie was starting to think of as his trademark.

Some irrational part of her wanted to kiss each dimple in his scruffy cheeks.

Together they hurried through the airport. When they arrived at the point where they would go their separate ways, Tate shifted his bag and placed his free hand on Kenzie's arm, pulling her to a stop. Gently taking her hand in his, he smiled, trying to ignore the powerful force surging from their joined fingers up his arm.

"I hope we run into each other again." He sincerely hoped he would see the beautiful girl another time. Although he'd just met her, he knew she would linger in his thoughts.

"That would be nice." Suddenly, she felt very shy. "You never know when we'll meet at the airport."

"Sure don't, since we both seem to travel frequently." Tate raised an eyebrow at Kenzie, giving her a beseeching look while shrugging his broad shoulders. "Wish me luck?"

"Of course." She smiled and squeezed the hand he still held. Thoughts of how nice his palm fit against hers infiltrated her resolve to walk away and not give Tate another thought. "Good luck."

"I meant a good luck kiss." The smile he bestowed on her had charmed many women into doing his will.

"Oh, I… um…" With a slim likelihood of seeing the handsome rodeo star again, Kenzie desperately wanted to kiss him. Before she could talk herself out of doing something crazy and completely out of character, she placed a warm, moist kiss to Tate's enticing mouth then stepped back. Her lips sizzled from the brief contact.

"Ride 'em, cowboy." Flushed, her cheeks burned as she turned and started walking away from temptation dressed in a cowboy hat and snug-fitting jeans.

"Kenzie!" Tate called after her, stunned by the impact of the kiss.

When she stopped and looked over her shoulder, he shot her a teasing grin. "Make them all dewy-eyed, Miss Dewdrop."

Kenzie laughed and waved before racing toward baggage claim. Nearly running through the airport, she caught a taxi and made it to her meeting with five minutes to spare.

Chapter Two

Greeted warmly by the leaders of the regional team in Denver, Kenzie quickly began the meeting, going into motivational mode. It took her only a few minutes to have the room erupting in cheers and the women attending on their feet, filled with excitement and energy.

After the two-hour meeting, she spent another hour shaking hands, visiting with consultants, and scheduling one-on-one appointments for the following day.

Finally escaping to her room for a few minutes of quiet before she joined the regional leaders for dinner, Kenzie traded her plain blouse for one more suited to a dressy occasion then refreshed her hair and makeup.

As a corporate trainer for a company that emphasized how their products could make women feel beautiful, Kenzie strived to maintain a polished image. Dressed in suits with tasteful heels, hair styled into a fashionable updo, and makeup minimal but effective, she was the embodiment of a young, successful executive.

Her current life was opposite of how she pictured herself when she was a young girl, filled with big dreams. Sometimes she wished for the simplicity of the life she had planned, before things changed so suddenly and pushed her in an entirely different direction.

Anxiously plucking her phone out of her pocket, Kenzie kicked off her heels, sank onto the bed, and impatiently waited for her friend Megan to answer.

"Hey, girl, how'd your meeting go?" Megan asked, her cheerful voice making Kenzie smile. The two had been best friends since first grade, when Megan's family moved to town.

"Fine. I thought I was going to be late because the flight out of Pasco was delayed, but I made it in the nick of time." Uncertain how to broach the subject of meeting Tate, she decided to jump right in. "I met one of your friends at the airport."

"Oh? Who?" Megan asked. The sounds of dinner preparations in the background let Kenzie know her friend worked while she talked.

"Tate Morgan." Her thoughts wandered to how good he looked in his boots and Wranglers as he waved goodbye. Cowboys, particularly good-looking, loaded-with-charm cowboys, were a definite weak spot for her and she needed to avoid them at all costs.

A rodeo south of Portland was how she met her former fiancé. His family had a ranch about an hour out of the city where Kenzie enjoyed riding horses and being in the country until she found out about his girlfriend.

Burned more than once by a handsome cowboy, she knew they were nothing but bad news. Still, she couldn't quite stop herself from picturing the intense blue of Tate's eyes, the dimples in his cheeks, or the way the brief touch of their lips completely scrambled her thoughts.

Lethal.

He could be positively lethal to her system if she let her guard down.

"Tate? You met Tate?" Megan asked in surprise. "And...? What did you think?"

"He seemed nice enough." Her feigned disinterest drew a disdainful snort from Megan.

"Nice enough. Did you lose your eyesight on the way to the airport?" The long-suffering sigh Megan expelled confirmed her frustration with her best friend.

She'd tried multiple times to set Kenzie up on a date with the man, but the girl always found some excuse. However, she realized she'd never mentioned his name, just that Owen had a friend she really thought Kenzie should meet. "He's gorgeous, funny, and one of the sweetest guys I've ever met. Are you sure it was our Tate?"

"Suddenly he's your Tate?" The smile on Kenzie's face reflected in her voice. "If he's so important to you, why didn't you ever mention him before? He's more than a little famous in the world of rodeo."

"Because I know how you feel about cowboys, especially rodeo cowboys. I've invited you for dinner numerous times when he was here, but you've always had some flimsy excuse that I let slide because I love you," Megan said with the slightest hint of humor.

"You know I don't want to be set up with a cowboy, any cowboy. Other than Owen, they are all trouble with a capital 'T'." A quick glance at her clock confirmed she had a few minutes before she needed to meet her dinner companions in the hotel lobby. "He did seem nice, though."

"You met one of the hunkiest, all-around good guys on the planet and all you can say is that he seems nice? Did you suffer a bump to the head in your travels today?" Megan sounded exasperated.

"What do you want me to say?" Kenzie stuffed her feet back in her shoes and stood by the bed.

"How about you fell in love with him after one glance and can't wait to see him again?" Megan prompted.

"You need to get off that ranch and out more, my delusional friend." Kenzie laughed derisively. "I didn't fall under his spell although I'm sure, for a cowboy, he is perfectly nice. I enjoyed talking to him, but that's it. Unless I run into him at the airport, the odds are high I'll never see or hear from him again."

"I wouldn't be so sure," Megan said in a tone that meant she was plotting something.

"Stay out of it, Meg. You know where I stand on the cowboy issue, so just leave it alone," Kenzie warned, needing to go. "I'll be home day after tomorrow. Maybe we can have lunch, do something fun."

"I'd like that. Just let me know when you want to get together."

Kenzie disconnected the call, grabbed her evening bag and hurried out the door, shifting into what she called her trainer mentality. Her job was to keep the consultants pumped up and excited about their Dew businesses. The best way for her to accomplish that was to show authentic interest and enthusiasm in their success.

A consultant for many years before she moved into the corporate office, Kenzie's inside perspective on how to be successful, combined with a caring personality, made her a magnet to the consultants she mentored. They all wanted to ask her questions, hear her story, gain some insight into how to do their jobs better.

After offering encouragement and helpful suggestions to the women at dinner and those she met with the following day, Kenzie was grateful for a good night's sleep before she had to fly back to Pasco. She left mid-morning for the airport, more than ready for a few weeks at home before her next regional event.

She breezed through security without any problem. After locating her gate, she bought a cup of coffee and waited for her flight.

With time on her hands, she took out her laptop and finished typing a report for the corporate office about the training meeting as well as the individual appointments she'd held the previous day. She entered notes about consultants she planned to work with over the next few weeks and saved the report before sending it off to her supervisor, who was also the president of the company.

Employed by a family-owned business had many benefits, and being able to communicate directly with the president was one she appreciated.

Finished with her work, she started searching online for rodeo scores, annoyed by her curiosity about Tate's standings. His blue eyes, dimpled cheeks, and charming smile had invaded her thoughts with unrelenting frequency the past few days.

"Fancy meeting you here, Dewdrop." A familiar voice resonated directly above her.

"Tate!" Kenzie said in surprise, looking up into his incredible eyes, wondering how her thoughts of the man made him magically materialize. "How did you do?"

"I took first and I'm giving you all the credit." His engaging smile made dimples pop out in his cheeks and his eyes crinkle at the corners.

"Me? What did I do?" Confused, she stared at Tate as he took the seat next to her.

"I'm pretty sure that good luck kiss was just what I needed to win." Slowly pushing his hat brim upward, he leaned close to her ear and dropped his voice to a deep, rumbling tone. "I might need one before every rodeo."

"Don't be ridiculous." She fought the shiver snaking its way up her spine at his warm breath on her neck. Unwilling to acknowledge her feelings, she instead changed the subject. "You must have been on an early flight to make this connection."

"I generally get up before the chickens," Tate said, leaning back in his seat and resting his arm along the back of Kenzie's chair.

Thrilled and dismayed at the feel of his arm across her back, Kenzie sat up straight, holding herself away from him. She started to say something to him about moving his arm, but clamped her mouth shut when three women close to her age ran up to Tate, begging for his autograph.

Hastily swallowing back a sigh and putting on his celebrity smile, Tate got to his feet and chatted with the women. He gamely signed the magazines they held out for him and even posed for a few photos.

One of the fans, dressed in a revealing top with skintight jeans and spiked heels, pressed herself against Tate and pulled his head down to whisper in his ear. Kenzie watched as he shook his head and stepped away from the woman.

"You girls travel safe and have a great day." Tate waved to his fans as they left then settled into his seat next to Kenzie. The adoration of the women was unwelcome. In truth, he hoped they'd find someone else to ogle and leave him alone.

At first, he'd been flattered by the attention he received from fans but it grew old in a hurry. Some of his fans, with their cloying perfume and hungry eyes, left him unnerved and feeling somehow tainted.

Women chasing after him, throwing themselves at him, and propositioning him was an aspect of his career Tate hated. His father raised him with a healthy respect for women along with a set of strong morals. Besides, he was an old-fashioned guy who liked to do the chasing, not the other way around.

He glanced at Kenzie. By the tense set of her shoulders and the way she tightly pressed her lips together, the women didn't impress her.

"Some of your devoted fans?" Her tone sounded edgy and laced with disapproval when she finally spoke.

"Occupational hazard," Tate said with a flirty grin, trying to make light of the matter.

Annoyed, Kenzie huffed, shutting down her laptop and putting it in her bag. She pretended to ignore Tate as the warmth of his arm brushed against hers. Another shiver raced over her when his delicious scent floated around her and his minty breath blew across her cheek.

"You want your own autograph? Is that the problem?" Curious, he wondered what she'd do if he placed a kiss on her delicate neck. Her skin looked so soft, beckoning to him.

As often as the woman paraded through his thoughts since she kissed him for good luck the other day, he was amazed he'd been able to stay on the horse at the rodeo, let alone ride it as well as he had. Even sleeping, Kenzie's face floated into his dreams, right along with the scent of her alluring fragrance.

"Certainly not," Kenzie said, whipping her head around to find Tate's teasing lips just inches from her own. Unprepared for the desire to kiss him racing from her head to her mouth, she leaned back and glared at him. "I'm not one of your… those… women."

Tate chuckled and took Kenzie's hand in his, giving it a squeeze. "I'd never confuse you with one of them, Dewdrop. You're a fine lady. I was just teasing."

"Oh." In all fairness, Tate hadn't seemed particularly interested in any of the women, sending them on their way as quickly as he could. Deciding to give him the benefit of the doubt, she relaxed against her seat and asked him questions about the rodeo.

Although they didn't sit together on the flight back to Pasco, Tate talked her into giving him her cell number before they boarded the plane. He kept them both entertained with a stream of funny text messages.

A comment he sent about the obnoxious person sitting next to her made Kenzie laugh aloud, drawing the attention of those around her. Tate looked at her over his seat and winked. She shook her head at him, but couldn't keep from smiling.

After they landed, she walked through the Pasco airport to baggage claim and found Tate waiting for her.

Playfully, she smacked his arm and gave him a reproachful look.

"You're awful, you know that?"

"I kept you entertained, didn't I?" Tate asked as they waited for the baggage carousel to start rotating.

"That's beside the point." The heavy bag she carried dropped to the floor as the luggage began to appear on the carousel.

"Which one is yours?" Tate asked as Kenzie watched for her suitcase. "I'll grab it for you."

She stared at him as if he started speaking in foreign tongues. Did gentlemen really still exist?

A bright pink suitcase caught his attention. He grinned when she nodded then lifted it as if it weighed nothing, setting it next to her.

"Thank you." Surprised by his nice manners, she pulled out the handle and draped her shoulder bag over it.

"I knew it had to be the pink one." Tate hefted a large duffle bag off the carousel. Easily hefting his bag over his shoulder, he pulled Kenzie's suitcase toward the door. "Is someone meeting you or did you drive?"

"I'm over in long-term parking," Kenzie said, trying to take her suitcase from Tate. The look he gave her made it clear he was hauling her suitcase to her car.

Rather than voice a snappy comment about managing for herself, she walked beside him, pointing to her car. He placed the suitcase in her trunk and opened the door for her.

Not quite ready to say goodbye, she stuck out her hand and Tate eagerly took it in his. Instead of shaking it, his thumb rubbed soft circles across her palm. Kenzie couldn't ignore the sparks shooting up her arm from the contact.

Tate's fingers felt so big and strong and perfectly right holding hers. She would have pulled her hand back, but it seemed to have a mind of its own as it nestled against his.

"I'm sure glad we met on this trip, Kenzie Beckett." The dimples popped out in his cheeks as he smiled at her.

"It was very nice to meet you, too," Kenzie said, genuinely pleased he sat beside her the other day as they waited for their flight to Denver. It would be so easy for her to fall for the handsome, charming cowboy, but Kenzie didn't intend to make that kind of mistake.

After today, she'd probably never see him again anyway.

"Maybe I'll see you around sometime." Tate didn't want to let go of Kenzie's hand and walk to his truck, but he needed to get on the road home.

"Maybe." Finally mustering the strength to pull her hand from Tate's grasp, she smiled at him. "Good luck with the rodeo season."

"Thanks." He started to walk away then stopped, unable to leave without tasting her lips. Suddenly dropping his bag, he took a step back and put his hands on either side of her face.

Gently rubbing his thumbs across her incredibly soft cheeks, he moved closer until his belt buckle brushed against the front of her suit and peered into her eyes. Fully expecting to see disapproval or surprise, he smiled when he recognized a look of invitation.

He whispered "for good luck," right before his lips settled on hers in a demanding kiss that took her breath away. Unable to think of anything except how right it felt to be with him, she lingered in his embrace.

Lost in the sensations produced by his insistent mouth, her hands wound around his neck, while his wrapped around her waist, pulling her flush against him. Abruptly, reality washed over her and she pulled away.

Stunned for a moment by the impact of the kiss, Kenzie tried to regain her mental footing. Tate dropped his hands and stepped back.

She watched him stride across the parking lot to his truck, making her wish he'd give her another kiss.

When he turned and winked at her, she waved, cheeks blushing a bright shade of pink almost the same color as her bag.

If she had any sense at all, she'd never see him again, banish him from her thoughts. When it came to gorgeous cowboys, though, Kenzie didn't always do the smart thing.

Chapter Three

Tate wiped the sweat off his forehead with the back of his gloved hand and glanced at his watch. He'd have to hustle if he was going to catch his flight on time.

The prospect of running into Kenzie made him grin. Since meeting her the previous month, he'd seen her three times at the airport, and twice they'd been on the same flight.

Thoughts of the lovely city girl filled his head. If he weren't careful, she'd be wrapping herself around his heart.

The fascination he held for Kenzie was something new and completely alien to him. If he didn't think of her as his personal good luck charm, he wouldn't allow himself to get so distracted by her apple cheeks, expressive dark eyes, and soft lips that quirked up at the corners like she was about to laugh or had some secret she was keeping.

Kenzie was intelligent, funny, and sweet, as well as professional and driven. She was everything Tate never realized he'd been looking for in a woman.

From their conversations, he knew she had two half-sisters, twins, who were ten going on twenty. She adored her mother, liked her stepfather, and talked with fondness of her friend Megan.

He also knew she seemed to despise cowboys in general, although he sensed her warming toward him a little at their last encounter.

Each time he stole or charmed a kiss from her for good luck, he placed first at the rodeo where he competed. If he could, he'd kiss her before each ride, and not because he thought it would help him win.

Tate entirely liked the idea of Kenzie kissing him for no reason at all, other than to feel the jolt of electricity that shot between them when they got within touching distance.

Expertly pounding the last staple into the post, he made sure the barbed wire stretched tight along the fence he mended. Tate gathered the fencing supplies, started the four-wheeler, and headed back to the house.

The ranch foreman, Monte, waved as he crossed the ranch yard. Tate reminded him that he needed a ride to the airport. He didn't like the idea of leaving his truck unattended in long-term parking when he'd be gone for more than a week. Monte would drop him off at the airport then pick up a load of supplies at the feed store before making the drive home.

In a rush, Tate took a shower and shaved then slapped on cologne in hopes of seeing Kenzie. He sent her a text message yesterday to see if she had any upcoming travel plans, but she hadn't replied. In the past month, they texted back and forth any number of times, but she often took a few days to respond.

Tate tried not to think about the fact the one woman who captured his attention didn't seem to be attracted to him.

If he'd merely been seeking companionship, he could have his pick of any number of girls from his fans. Schmoozing with them was something he dreaded after the rodeo.

Rather than put up with their flirting, he and a few of the other guys often employed covert maneuvers that kept them out of sight until they could make an escape from the arena to the safety of their hotels or vehicles. Despite the many offers available, none interested him.

Tate double-checked the bag holding his gear as well as his carry-on bag, settled his hat on his head and strode out the door. Monte waited at the end of the walk with the air conditioner running in the pickup.

Mid-June and already blazing hot, Tate dreaded to think what it would be like in August. In all likelihood, he wouldn't be home for most of the month.

It was a good thing Monte was very capable at managing things while he was gone, otherwise he'd never be able to pursue his dream of being a world-champion saddle bronc rider.

On the way to the airport, they discussed ranch details. Monte dropped him at the door with a promise to pick him up in a few weeks. Tate had plans to ride in several rodeos, traveling with his friend Cort. He'd arrive home for a few days of rest before driving to a series of rodeos that would begin with the Fourth of July rodeo in St. Paul, Oregon.

Routinely checking in his duffle bag, Tate stood in line at security, emptying his pockets, removing his belt, and tugging off his boots. An all-too-familiar scent settled over him. Slowly turning around, he looked into the warm brown eyes that filled his dreams.

"Hey there, Dewdrop." Tate gave Kenzie's cheek a quick peck, wishing he could kiss her lips.

A becoming shade of pink blossomed across her cheeks. She hid her pleasure at seeing him by picking up a couple of the plastic containers to go through security and taking off her shoes.

"How are you, Tate?" Kenzie asked as she placed her electronics in one of the bins and removed her watch.

31

"I'm doing great. Although I'll be even better if you tell me you're going to be on my flight today," Tate said before being motioned to proceed through security.

Quickly gathering his belongings, he threaded his belt back through its loops when Kenzie stepped beside him, stuffing her laptop into her bag and snapping her watch into place.

When she tried to balance on one foot to put on her heel, Tate took her arm to steady her. Appreciative of his help, she quickly put on her shoes then waited while he tugged on his boots.

"If you're flying to Denver, you're in luck," Kenzie said, checking to make sure she had everything back in her bag as she walked toward two empty seats.

"Once you get to Denver, where are you headed?" Denver was most often a connection point to somewhere else for them both. Depending on their destination, it was either there or Salt Lake City.

"Santa Fe." She sat on one of the plastic seats to wait for the call to board.

"Is that right?" A grin spread across his face. Kenzie would be his traveling companion for the whole trip this time, since he was going to Santa Fe for a rodeo. Cort would compete with him there then they would drive to Texas for a round of rodeos.

"That's right." Kenzie fussed with her skirt, adjusting the hem. The way Tate looked at her with an intense light in his eyes left her flustered. "Why?"

"No reason." He set his carry-on bag on the seat next to Kenzie then walked to the counter at the gate. A few charming smiles and some fast talking resulted in the agent giving him a new seating assignment next to Kenzie.

Tate returned to his seat grinning like an idiot, thrilled at the notion of spending several hours in her company.

"What's got you looking so pleased with yourself?" Kenzie asked as he placed his arm along the back of her seat.

"Nothing, Dewdrop." He picked up her hand and held it in his. The contact made his pulse accelerate, and he breathed deeply of her fragrance. It always brought to mind a bouquet of summer flowers.

Kenzie started to say something then changed her mind. The familiar way Tate held her hand made her think thoughts she knew would only lead to trouble.

In need of a distraction, she took her wallet from her bag and left Tate to go to the coffee shop. She returned with a bottle of water for her and handed him a bottle of Mountain Dew.

Tate accepted the soda pop, unscrewed the cap and took a deep swallow. It pleased him that Kenzie remembered his favorite beverage.

While they waited for the flight, they talked about places they'd traveled in the last few weeks and discussed plans leading up to the Fourth of July holiday.

"What are you doing for the Fourth?" Tate asked as the seating area filled to overflowing.

"I haven't decided yet." She rooted around in her bag until she found a tube of sheer lip gloss. As he watched her apply it, Tate was sorely tempted to kiss it away. Instead, he focused his attention on the passengers impatiently waiting to board.

"What are the options?" Tate asked as they got to their feet and stood in the slow-moving line.

"I could stay home and relax before I have to fly to Omaha for our annual convention or I could spend the holiday with Mom, Steve, and the girls." Kenzie handed her boarding pass to the agent at the gate.

"If you go see your family, what would you do? Do you have any traditions?" Tate asked as they walked onto the plane.

"We'd probably have a barbecue, watch fireworks, you know, the usual stuff." She looked for her row then slid into her window seat. Her jaw dropped when Tate stowed his bag in the overhead compartment and sat down beside her.

"You'll start catching flies if you aren't careful," he teased as she snapped her mouth shut and buckled the seatbelt.

"How did you finagle your way into this seat?" She wondered if there was anything Tate couldn't manage if he wanted it bad enough.

"All you have to do is learn to ask nicely." A jaunty smile highlighted his dimples.

Kenzie wanted to kiss each dimple and then linger on Tate's tempting lips. Since it was the first time she'd seen him clean-shaven, she spent a moment studying his face until an inexplicable pull tugged her toward him.

She busied herself digging in her bag to keep from reaching over and running her hand over his taut, tan cheeks.

"I think it has more to do with your ability to charm the female agents with your smile and good looks," Kenzie observed, pulling a magazine from her bag before stuffing the oversized catchall under the seat in front of her.

"So you think I'm charming and good-looking." He took the magazine from her hand and frowned at the fashion periodical she frequently read.

"I… um…" It was hard to think coherently with him sitting so close and smelling so delicious.

Tate laughed and took off his hat, running his hand through his hair to loosen the hat ring around his head. "I'll let you off the hook this time. Now, let's talk about these ridiculous magazines you read."

"What about them?" Kenzie glanced at the cover of the trendy publication Tate handed back to her. She thought many of the articles were frivolous and outrageous as well, but she liked to keep on top of what people perceived as trends, popular styles, and what personal care products were on the current recommended list.

Occasionally, Dew's products were featured and she always made sure to buy extra copies of the magazine to share with consultants she mentored. It gave them a boost to see national publications recommend the company's products.

"I don't really see you as the kind of girl who takes this stuff seriously." Tate pointed to an article in the magazine about how to create perfectly pouty lips.

"What type of girl do you see me as, exactly?" Kenzie asked, her tone teasing and light.

"A very beautiful girl who is driven, smart, and successful," Tate said, making her blush. "One who is funny and kind, with a terrible aversion to cowboys."

She appreciated Tate's compliments and hoped he was sincere. A part of her couldn't help but wonder if he was just flirting. He was correct about her aversion to cowboys, though.

"Don't look at me like that, Miss Skeptic. I'm telling it like I see it." As he leaned back in his seat, he took Kenzie's hand in his. "If you ever decide to quit being a corporate trainer for Dew, I envision you doing something like modeling for Victoria's Secret or maybe one of those makeup commercials."

He leaned back and narrowed his gaze, pretending to study her critically with his hands poised like a camera. "I could totally see you rocking a runway look for a swimsuit company."

Kenzie turned to glare at him, realizing he thoroughly distracted her during takeoff. Spared the part of flying she hated most by Tate's joking comments, she relaxed as the plane gained altitude.

"Your devious plan worked and I appreciate it," Kenzie said, squeezing his arm. Shocked by the rock-hard strength of his bicep beneath her fingers, she'd have liked nothing better than to leave her hand lingering there for a while. Instead, she picked up her magazine and started thumbing through it. "So where does your connection in Denver take you?"

"With you." Leaning his head back, he turned the full voltage of his brilliant gaze her direction. Desperate to kiss her, he fought down the urge although the look on Kenzie's face made it incredibly difficult.

He couldn't believe his good fortune in having the same itinerary as her for the entire trip. What were the odds they would be traveling to the same city?

"With me? You're going to Santa Fe?" Kenzie asked, looking pleasantly surprised. "Are you riding there?"

"Yep. Tomorrow. If you want to watch, I'll get you a ticket." All of a sudden, he wanted more than anything for Kenzie to watch him ride.

Kenzie shook her head. "As much fun as that would be, I have a dinner meeting tomorrow and even if I could go, I don't have any clothes appropriate for attending a rodeo. Thanks for the offer, though."

"If you change your mind, I'd be happy to have you as my guest." He pondered if he could say or do anything to change Kenzie's mind. Instinctively, he knew pushing her to do something would have the opposite effect and drive her in the other direction.

They chatted about any number of topics, sidestepping the suggestion of her attending the rodeo.

In Denver, they ate a quick lunch before boarding the flight to Santa Fe. He somehow managed to sit beside her again and Kenzie was thrilled at his companionship despite her repeated mental warnings to stay far away from Tate Morgan.

She had never experienced such an all-encompassing attraction to a man, and that included her two-timing former fiancé. It was more than attraction, though. It was like some piece of their hearts connected, some place in their minds aligned. They fit together so perfectly, as if they'd always known each other.

The welcome familiarity she felt with him was why she had to be on guard. It would be too easy for her to fall for him and she knew if she lost her heart to Tate, it would be forever lost and forever broken when he behaved like she was convinced he eventually would.

Cowboys weren't a faithful lot. After a while, he'd find a new skirt to chase then she'd be left alone and devastated.

Gathering her thoughts along with her things as the plane landed, she renewed her resolve to guard her heart around him.

Tate discovered Kenzie's hotel wasn't far from his as they exited the airport. As they shared a taxi, some quick talking convinced Kenzie to have dinner with him since she didn't have any meetings until the next morning.

Smug with his success, Tate checked into his hotel room, called his friend Cort to go over details for the following day then pumped the hotel concierge for some ideas on where to go for a romantic dinner.

With a nervous feeling completely out of character for him, Tate dug through his clothes trying to find something to wear to a nice restaurant. He really needed a dinner jacket and made another call to the concierge who arranged to have one rented and delivered to Tate's room.

He jumped into the shower and shaved for the second time that day. Tate took extra care combing his hair, slapping on his aftershave, and making sure his boots were polished.

Mindful of the time, he caught a taxi and found Kenzie waiting in her hotel lobby wearing a little black dress that accented every succulent curve of her figure. The dress was a pleasant surprise, since he'd never seen her in anything except business suits.

Tate kissed her cheek as he took her elbow in his hand and escorted her out the door to the waiting cab.

"You look amazing, Kenzie," he said as he helped her in the car. He would have paid big money to see her hair down, although the softened updo she wore was still very appealing. A few curls danced around her face and gave her an utterly feminine appearance.

Inhaling her summery scent, Tate took her hand in his and rested their clasped fingers on his thigh.

"You look pretty good yourself." The dark gray dinner jacket Tate wore accentuated the breadth of his shoulders. A black button-down shirt with the collar open, a newer pair of pressed Wranglers, and a polished pair of boots completed his look. His hair, carefully combed into submission, begged her to run her fingers through it and tousle it in the way she was used to seeing him.

The smell of his aftershave mingled with Tate's unique scent, making her knees weak while the feel of his hard thigh beneath their hands caused heat to flood up her neck and into her cheeks.

Inwardly groaning, she realized she should have refused to have dinner with him. The struggle to keep her growing interest in the hunky cowboy under control was hard enough when she randomly saw him in the airport.

It was nearly impossible on a date with him. Tate's appearance and his courteous behavior made it perfectly clear this wasn't just two friends getting together for dinner. A wild and fiery attraction blazed between them. One even Kenzie couldn't ignore.

"I took the liberty of making a reservation," Tate said as the taxi stopped in front of a busy restaurant. The adobe exterior gave a definite Southwestern vibe to the building.

Kenzie admired the architecture as Tate escorted her inside and provided his name to the host. After checking the reservation, the host smiled at him then motioned for someone to see them to their table.

Seated in a private corner, any lingering doubts Kenzie had that this was just a casual dinner between friends disappeared before they even opened the menu. The looks Tate continued shooting at her with his hot blue gaze had her gulping ice water and wishing for a fan.

The man was completely disconcerting. And distracting.

"Have you eaten here before?" Kenzie asked as she looked through the menu without really seeing the words printed on the page in front of her.

"Nope. Usually, I hang out with the guys and grab a burger or a sandwich. If we're feeling extravagant, we might order a steak." Tate contemplated what he wanted to order.

"I hope you aren't missing out on something by being here with me," she said, sincerely concerned about disrupting his routine. "You really didn't have to do this, Tate."

"I know I didn't have to invite you to dinner, Kenzie. I wanted to. Very much." His voice was deep and husky. "I've been trying to work up the nerve to ask you on a date since the first time I saw you in the airport months ago. I sure wasn't going to pass up the opportunity when it practically landed in my lap today. This will be the first real meal we've eaten together because airport food absolutely doesn't count."

Kenzie laughed and the warm sound cut through the tension and helped them both relax. "Well, when you put it like that…"

After the waitress took their orders and brought them drinks, Tate raised his glass to hers. "A toast to new friends, new adventures, and new opportunities. I'm really, really glad we met, Dewdrop."

"Me, too." Her voice was soft while her eyes shimmered with emotion.

If Tate didn't know better, he'd think Kenzie was just as attracted to him as he was to her. The sight of her dressed in something other than a suit did funny things to his head and heart.

He wanted, so very badly, to get her alone and pull the pins out of her hair. He wondered if the dark, silky locks were as long as he envisioned. His fingers itched to find out.

Tate looked around the restaurant and pointed out some of the art pieces to Kenzie, sparking a discussion about their varied tastes. Despite the unmistakable yearning dancing between them, threatening to throw them both off-kilter, they managed to keep up a lively conversation through dinner.

Not in a hurry to end their evening, Tate asked Kenzie if she'd like to go for a walk since the restaurant was located in an area with an array of interesting shops.

Strolling hand in hand, they looked in store windows, watched people, and meandered down the sidewalk, unwilling to think about the time when they'd have to say good night.

As the sun sank and the evening shadows grew long, Kenzie glanced at her watch and sighed.

"If I don't get some sleep, I'll be useless tomorrow for my meetings. As much as I've enjoyed this evening with you, Tate, I really do need to return to my room." She wished she had hours more to spend with the handsome cowboy.

He'd been well mannered, thoughtful, and kind. She was beginning to think that maybe she shouldn't generalize all cowboys based on the bad experiences that haunted her past. Maybe she should give Tate a chance.

On that thought, she moved closer to him as they waited for a taxi.

Tate dropped his arm around her shoulders and tucked her against his side, surprised when she didn't pull away.

Delighted, he hoped he was starting to wear down her resistance. Up until that evening, she'd done her best to keep him at arm's length no matter how hard he worked to breach her defenses.

When they arrived at her hotel, he walked her to the elevator then decided she needed an escort to her room. "You never know what kind of riffraff you might run into in the hallway," Tate said, trying to sound serious.

"I'm pretty sure the most dangerous person I'm going to encounter is already holding my hand," Kenzie teased as they stepped off the elevator and walked down the hallway to her room. Hesitant to open the door, she didn't want Tate to get the wrong idea.

She pressed a quick kiss to his cheek. "Thank you for a lovely evening. I don't know when I've enjoyed myself quite so much."

"I had a good time, too, Dewdrop." While he leaned one arm against the doorframe, he brushed his fingers across Kenzie's smooth cheek. "Thank you for going to dinner with me."

"You're welcome," she whispered, her eyes glued to Tate's lips. She watched the corners of his mouth tip up in a smile.

"Do I still get a kiss for good luck?" Tate asked, slowly running one callused hand down her bare arm to her wrist. The jolt of something fierce and unknown rocked through him from his head clear to his toes.

"Sure." Completely rattled by Tate's touch and heated look, she pressed her mouth lightly to his. Before she could pull away, his hands encircled her waist, holding her against him as he deepened the kiss.

Fiery bursts of light exploded behind her eyes. She looped her hands around Tate's neck for support since her wobbly knees threatened to give out on her as the kiss intensified.

Finally drawing back, Tate took a deep breath. He brushed his thumb across her just-kissed lips and flashed his dimples, further muddling her already distracted thoughts.

"If you change your mind, the rodeo starts at seven. I'll save you a seat." Tate turned and walked down the hallway. He waited until he was on the elevator to pump his fist in the air. Walking into the lobby, he realized he probably looked a little deranged with the goofy smile plastered on his face.

After that bone-dissolving kiss with Kenzie, he felt helpless to do anything but grin.

Chapter Four

"Do you think she'll come?" Cort asked Tate as he stretched behind the chutes at the rodeo.

Determined to center his focus on the upcoming ride, Tate struggled to block out thoughts of Kenzie.

If he hadn't been in love with her before last night, he certainly was now.

He kept picturing how tempting she looked in the candlelight at the restaurant, how her skin felt so soft beneath his fingers, how much that one amazing kiss had him wanting hundreds more.

"Probably not." Tate stretched his legs, making sure the adjustment on his stirrups was just right.

"You sent a ticket to her at the hotel, didn't you?" Cort leaned against the fence and chewed on a toothpick.

"Yeah, but that doesn't mean she'll be here," Tate said, annoyed and out of sorts for reasons he couldn't explain and didn't want to examine.

More than anything, he wanted Kenzie to watch him ride tonight. He knew she had a meeting, but from what details he gathered, it should be over at seven. If she really wanted to see him ride, she'd have time to get to the rodeo.

His current state of irritability derived from the thought that she honestly wasn't interested in him.

Cort's chuckles caused him to look up with a cool glare.

"What's so funny, man?" Tate asked, looking around for the source of his friend's amusement. Finding nothing out of the ordinary, all he could see was a bunch of other cowboys getting ready to compete.

"You." Cort shook his head as he waggled a finger at Tate. "I've never seen you so worked up about a girl before and I've seen you with a lot of girls."

"Yeah, well most of them weren't of my choosing, you know. I can't help who is in the recent circle of biggest fans or stalkers," Tate said, continuing to stretch his muscles as he brushed aside a niggling concern over one fan that wouldn't leave him alone. He was convinced the woman was certifiably insane.

"Whatever." Cort waved a dismissive hand at Tate. "Admit it, man. She's under your skin."

"I'm not admitting anything," Tate said, knowing Cort was right. Kenzie was under his skin, wrapped up in his thoughts, with an ever-tightening hold on his heart.

If he wanted to win the event, let alone stay on the horse he'd drawn, he was going to have to concentrate on the ride ahead and quit speculating about Kenzie and her feelings for him, or the apparent lack of them.

Later, they sat on a fence watching the grand entry of the rodeo. Cort nudged Tate so hard he almost fell backward off the top rail.

"Is that her?" Cort motioned to the bleachers as Tate regained his balance. Although he hadn't met Kenzie, his friend shared several photos he took of her with his phone.

Tate's gaze followed Cort's pointing finger and his eyes widened in surprise. Kenzie maneuvered her way to her seat dressed in a navy suit and heels.

Quickly jumping off the fence, Tate jogged toward the stands. Kenzie looked around, getting her bearings, as he hustled up the steps and squatted down beside her.

"Dewdrop, I didn't think you'd be able to make it." He took her hand in his and squeezed her fingers. The warmth in her eyes as she gazed at him made his heartbeat kick into overdrive. Maybe she cared about him more than she wanted to admit.

The jubilant smile on his face made her glad she raced through her presentation, ran through the hotel as if the building was aflame, and pleaded with the taxi driver to put some hustle in it so she'd arrive at the rodeo on time.

Kenzie smiled at Tate, savoring the feel of his big, rough hand against hers. A bright light twinkled in his blue eyes while the grin on his face was both charming and engaging.

"My meeting wrapped up early so I decided to come. I realize, though, I am probably the only person here in a business suit, so don't make fun of me," Kenzie warned good-naturedly.

"No, ma'am." Tate kissed her cheek before taking a seat on the steps beside her. He'd reserved a seat for her on the end of a row with some of his friends in hopes if she did come, he could sneak in a few minutes with her. "I'm really glad you're here."

"Me, too," Kenzie said with a sincerity Tate could hear in her voice.

"Is there anything you need me to explain to you?" Tate asked, as they watched the end of the grand entry.

"This ain't my first rodeo, cowboy." The western twang she inflected into her voice made them both laugh.

"Okay," Tate said in surprise. He wondered what else he had to learn about the beautiful woman who just made everything right in his world by showing up to see him ride.

When the bareback riding began, Tate whipped off his hat to hide their faces and gave Kenzie a kiss that made her wonder if her shoes would melt right off her feet.

"For luck." He stood and settled the hat on his head as those around them laughed or hollered.

"Ride 'em, cowboy." Kenzie grinned at Tate with flushed cheeks. Thoroughly embarrassed, his attention also pleased her immensely. He'd just made it known to anyone watching that she was off limits and that was fine with her.

Tate hurried down the steps and behind the chutes with Kenzie's eyes glued to his jean-covered backside.

A little girl sitting beside her watched her observation of Tate.

"Is he your boyfriend?" the little girl asked.

Kenzie looked down at the blond hair in pigtails, red flowered T-shirt, and jeans tucked into bright red cowboy boots. The cherubic face staring up at her made her smile.

"Not exactly," Kenzie said, not wanting to discuss her feelings for Tate with a six-year-old.

"Either he is or he isn't," the wise child said, staring at Kenzie with tiny arms crossed over her chest and an impatient look on her face. "Grammy says you've got to learn to make up your mind."

"Your Grammy sounds very smart." Kenzie watched as Tate disappeared into the sea of cowboy hats barely visible behind the chutes from her seat.

"Is Tate your boyfriend?" the cherub asked again. "He's really nice, and all the girls think he's cute."

"He is nice and very cute." Although she replied to the child, her thoughts remained lost in the kiss Tate planted on her in front of everyone. Normally, she would be mortified at such behavior, but somehow, tonight, it seemed perfect.

"If you let him kiss you like that, don't you think he's probably your boyfriend?"

"Probably." Kenzie held out her hand to the child, deciding an introduction was in order. "My name's Kenzie."

"I'm Katie Jo Powell, but everyone calls me Katie," the little girl said, enthusiastically shaking Kenzie's hand. "That's my mommy, Mara, and my brother, Hunter, and my sister, Breelin. We call her Bree. My daddy went to get us some snacks."

"It's very nice to meet you, Katie," Kenzie said, then smiled at the little girl's mother who held a wiggling toddler on her lap while a little boy who looked to be about four bounced on his seat next to Katie.

"How come you're dressed like that?" Katie pointed to Kenzie's suit.

Kenzie didn't have time to change even if she'd had something appropriate to wear. The clothes she packed for the trip consisted of business suits, blouses, and the black dress she'd worn last night to dinner. She refused to buy jeans and boots just so she wouldn't stick out like a sore thumb.

Due to the heat, she removed her suit jacket and draped it over the back of her seat. The slight breeze blowing across her bare arms brought welcome relief. Her sleeveless silk blouse wasn't the coolest thing she could wear on a hot summer evening, but it was all she had to wear.

"I came here right from work so I wouldn't miss Tate's ride," Kenzie said, watching as Tate's friend Cort successfully wrestled a steer.

"Do you know what Tate rides?" Katie asked, sitting on her knees in her seat.

"He rides saddle broncs." Kenzie watched as team ropers raced into the arena.

"Yep. That's almost as good as bulls," Katie declared with a nod of her head.

"Almost," Kenzie repeated, trying to hide her smile. The precocious child next to her was really something. She was about to ask Katie more of her thoughts on the rodeo when the girl's little brother almost took a head dive off his seat. Kenzie grabbed his arms in time to keep him from falling and his mother looked at her in gratitude. Hunter began to cry, but the woman had her hands full with the baby.

Kenzie stretched over, offering to take the chubby toddler while Mara consoled Hunter.

The baby eyed her warily but when Katie patted Bree's hand and told her the pretty lady was a friend, she smiled and jabbered at Kenzie, bouncing on her lap. The little one was soon squealing with delight, as Kenzie made funny faces and talked nonsense. When Kenzie took her tiny hand and blew on her fingers, Bree kicked her feet and giggled, making Katie laugh.

She was still holding the baby when Katie stood on her seat. "Here comes Daddy."

A wiry cowboy with a cardboard box full of food made his way up the steps to their row. He tipped his head at Kenzie, surprised to see a stranger holding his daughter, as he sat in Hunter's vacated seat.

"Daddy, this is Kenzie." Katie jumped down as she waited for her father to pass out the food. "She's Tate's girlfriend, sorta."

"Tate, huh?" The cowboy offered Kenzie a friendly smile. "Isn't that an interesting development?"

Suddenly, Katie's last name registered in Kenzie's brain and she realized she sat with the family of a world champion bull rider. No wonder Katie thought riding bulls was superior to broncs.

"It's nice to meet you, Mr. Powell." Kenzie shifted the baby to stick out a free hand.

"Call me Huck," the cowboy said, taking his sniffling son in one arm while passing the box of food to his wife so he could shake Kenzie's hand. "It's nice to meet the woman who finally turned ol' Tater's head."

Blushing, Kenzie wasn't quite sure what to make of Huck's statement. She didn't have time to give it more thought as the saddle bronc riding began.

While the Powell family ate hotdogs and slurped cold pop, Huck pointed to the third chute and told Kenzie to keep her eye on the gate if she wanted to see Tate ride.

Tate nodded his head, the gate swung open, and his horse ran out in a burst of motion that lifted all four feet in the air.

The horse twisted and turned as he bucked, giving as great a performance as the man on his back.

Awestruck, Kenzie stared at Tate. Graceful and limber, he executed each move with a smooth finesse that made what he was doing seem like an art form.

Holding her breath as he rode, she realized Tate was not only a well-trained athlete and very good at what he did, he was also magnificent to watch. Time seemed to slow as she took in every movement he made from his hand in the air, his legs spurring front to back, to his body as it rocked in rhythm to the animal beneath him.

When the buzzer announced Tate made it for the eight-second ride, Kenzie finally exhaled with relief as he swung behind the pickup man and slid off the far side of the horse, waving his hat at the crowd. Turning, he executed a quick bow and pointed his index finger her direction before disappearing behind the chutes.

"Are you sure he's not your boyfriend?" Katie asked with a hotdog-filled grin, followed by a sweet childish giggle.

Chapter Five

The knowledge that Kenzie sat in the stands gave Tate a certain peace of mind while simultaneously sending his blood zinging through his veins. Pumped up on adrenaline, he was ready to ride for all he was worth.

The bronc he drew didn't get the name Twister because he was an easy ride. Tate somehow managed to center his thoughts on the horse and visualize himself on the back of the animal, taking each twist and turn in stride.

Slowly easing into his saddle on the back of Twister, Tate adjusted his seat and tightened the bronc rein in his left hand.

Tugging down his hat, he nodded his head and Twister exploded out of the chute like he'd been shot from a cannon.

While all four hooves were still in the air, the horse lived up to his name as he writhed and turned with a swiftness intended to unseat Tate.

Focused on maintaining his center, he blocked out everything but the horse beneath him. His heartbeat thumped loudly, the sound echoing in his ears, as he anticipated Twister's next move then the next. Rapidly moving with the horse, Tate kept his free hand high in the air with the rein held tightly in the other.

When the buzzer sounded, he left his free arm up for just a second longer then dropped it to the rein, hanging on while catching sight of a pickup man in his peripheral vision. He leaned over, caught the guy's arm and swung across the back of his horse, landing on the ground on the far side.

Triumphantly waving his hat, he turned to the crowd. All he could see was Kenzie sitting in the stands, smiling at him with a baby on her lap. His legs grew rubbery as the adrenaline from his ride ebbed, replaced by a sense of something waiting for him in the future. Tate took a deep breath and hurried out of the arena behind the chutes.

"Ladies and gentlemen, that is what I'm talking about!" the announcer boomed into his microphone. "That cowboy knows how to get 'er done. I've never seen a ride quite like that before. What do you say to a ninety-one point ride for Tate Morgan!"

Tate couldn't believe he scored that high. The sound of the crowd erupting in cheers propelled his feet forward as he gathered his gear and stuffed it into his bag.

Slapped good-naturedly so many times by guys he'd known the past few years since he entered the rodeo circuit, he thought he might have permanent handprints embedded in his back.

"Man, that was something. You rocked it." Cort gave Tate a victorious fist bump. "Maybe you need to bring your good luck charm with you to every rodeo."

Tate grinned as he removed his protective vest and stowed it with the rest of his gear. "I would if she'd cooperate, but that isn't going to happen. Not even a chance. And I'm pretty sure she'd pitch a fit at being tied up and thrown in the back of your truck if we decided to kidnap her."

"You have to admit since you met her, you've had consistently high scores and haven't messed up on a single ride." Cort walked with Tate toward his pickup to store their gear. They planned to leave that night and drive straight through to the next rodeo in Texas.

"I know, but this is just a fluke. The odds of us ending up in the same city at the same time again are slim to none," Tate said as they walked back to the arena. "Want to meet her?"

"Sure." Cort adjusted his hat and grinned. "You better be careful, though. She might be so taken with my good looks and charm, she'll forget all about ol' Tater."

"I'm not overly concerned." Tate frowned at Cort as they made their way up the steps to where Kenzie sat visiting with Mara, Huck, and their kids. Caught up in conversation, she didn't see him approach.

Tate bent down and kissed Kenzie's cheek while she talked to Mara. She turned and smiled at him. Sparks flickering in her eyes lit a flame in his.

Huck got to his feet and pumped Tate's hand. "That was a kick-…"

A not-so-gentle nudge from his wife prompted Huck to alter his choice of words. "That was an awesome ride, man. Congratulations."

"Thanks." Tate stepped back as Huck scooted past Kenzie and stood on the step next to Cort. "I've got to get ready for my ride. See you guys later."

"Ride good, Daddy," Katie hollered at her father's retreating back. Huck lifted a hand in acknowledgement then hurried out of sight.

Kenzie stood, still holding the baby, and looked from Tate to Cort, waiting for an introduction. Cort finally elbowed Tate. He appeared to have forgotten there was anyone else around beyond the brown-eyed beauty standing beside him.

"Sorry, Kenzie, this is my buddy, Cort," Tate said, placing his hand on Kenzie's back as she shook hands with his longtime friend. "Cort McGraw, meet Kenzie Beckett."

Cort grinned and took off his hat. "Ma'am, it's a bona fide pleasure to meet you. This guy has done nothing but sing your praises for the last several weeks. Despite that, he didn't properly convey what a gorgeous girl he's been chasing around the airport."

Kenzie blushed and sat down, adjusting the baby on her lap. She'd been around enough cowboys to know they were full of meaningless flattery, although Cort seemed nice.

"I'm gonna go wait with the guys." Cort tipped his hat to Kenzie then Mara. "It was really nice to meet you, Kenzie."

"You as well." Kenzie smiled as Cort turned and jogged down the steps. Tate picked up Katie and tickled her sides before setting her in the seat her father vacated, leaving the seat next to Kenzie open for him.

"Tate, you took my seat. I want to sit by Kenzie." Katie gazed at him with big blue eyes.

"I want to sit by her, too, and you've had her all to yourself since the rodeo started," Tate reasoned with the child.

Katie thought about what he said for a minute and finally nodded her head. "Okay. But you have to behave. Kenzie said she's not sure if you're her boyfriend or not, so you better be extra nice to her."

"I will," Tate said with a serious expression on his face. He turned to Kenzie and winked as he took her hand in his.

They were watching the barrel racers when Tate recognized some of his die-hard fans strolling by, trying to find him among the crowd. One in particular had recently moved from fan to stalker status.

Sliding down in the seat, he pulled the brim of his hat low then swept Katie onto his lap, placing her so she blocked his face.

"What are you doing?" Kenzie asked, intrigued by his odd behavior. If she didn't know better, she'd think Tate tried to stay out of sight.

"He's hiding." Katie clapped her hands as the announcer pumped up the crowd for the bull riding to begin. Apparently, she was used to the routine because it didn't seem out of the ordinary to the little girl.

"Hiding? From what?" Kenzie asked, confused as she looked from Tate to Mara to Katie.

"From them." Katie pointed to a group of scantily clad women wandering along, appearing to search for someone. "My daddy has to hide from them sometimes, too. Mama says they are just a bunch of tr-…"

"Katie Jo! That is enough." Mara reached over and placed a hand over her daughter's mouth.

Katie giggled and swung her feet on Tate's lap. "But Mama, I heard you tell Daddy…"

"You just never mind, young lady." Mara rolled her eyes. Leaning around Tate, she shrugged at Kenzie with a resigned look on her face. "They come with the territory, whether the guys want them around or not. Some of them, like Tate and Huck, have gotten quite skillful at outmaneuvering their fan club."

"Really?" Kenzie asked, feeling her neck muscles tense. Isn't that why she'd been avoiding a relationship with Tate all along? Because there would be an endless supply of women chasing him, pelting him with propositions and proposals. Because she was certain at some point he'd leave her brokenhearted while he turned his attention elsewhere.

"Huck said Tate is particularly masterful at getting away unscathed," Mara said, handing Kenzie a cloth to wipe the baby's chin while giving Hunter a look that made him settle down. "That's why we're all excited to hear about you. He never gives any female the chance to get too close to him."

Tate glanced at Kenzie, sensing her reluctance to believe he really was a good guy who avoided involvement with women looking for something he wasn't willing to give. He was certain nothing he could say would convince her and decided his actions would have to speak louder than his words.

Katie squealed as the bull riding started and they all turned their attention to the arena. When Huck rode, both Hunter and Katie jumped up and down shouting, "Go, Daddy!" Huck made the ride, earning an eighty-seven score.

"That's awesome." Tate grinned at Mara as she and the kids cheered and clapped.

"He's hoping to hold onto the title this year," Mara said as the kids settled down.

"He'll do it." Tate stood and pulled Kenzie up with him. "Cort and I have got to hit the road, but we can drop you off at your hotel."

"Oh, okay." Surprised by his plans for an abrupt departure, she wished she could spend more time with Tate. She should have realized he and Cort would be heading out to the next rodeo.

Kenzie turned to the Powell family and told Mara how nice it was to meet her. She kissed the baby on her downy head and passed her back to her mother. After ruffling Hunter's hair, she hugged Katie and thanked the little girl for the privilege of sitting next to her.

Tate held her suit jacket while she slipped her arms in the sleeves then placed a hand at the small of her back as Kenzie carefully made her way down the steps of the stands in her heels. He tucked her hand in the crook of his arm as they strode out of the bleachers and toward the back parking area where Cort waited.

On their way to the pickup, they ran into several people Tate knew. The men took one look at Kenzie and insisted on introductions. Tate wanted to punch more than a few of his so-called friends when they settled their roving eyes on the lovely woman holding onto his arm.

Finally, they made it away from the arena and started toward the area where trucks and trailers parked. Kenzie carefully picked her way through the gravel and dirt in her heels, trying to keep her balance and not ruin her shoes.

"Sorry," she said, looking at Tate with humor in her eyes. He had an arm around her waist and held her hand in his, offering his support. "These shoes are definitely not regulation rodeo gear."

Tate laughed. Before Kenzie could take another teetering step, he swung her into his arms and carried her toward Cort's pickup.

"Tate, put me down," Kenzie ordered. Her protest was halfhearted at best as she draped her arms around his neck. "You'll break your back and then how will you ride?"

"Dewdrop, you don't weigh as much as a bale of hay, so just never mind," Tate said, trying to remember how to walk with Kenzie's face so close to his. He could see a warm glow in her beautiful brown eyes and her rosy lips taunted him. The deep breath he inhaled filled his nose and flooded his senses with her enticing summery fragrance. Tate bit back the groan working its way up his throat.

Before he lost his head and gave in to the urge to kiss her until they were both breathless, he arrived at the pickup.

Cort swept off his hat with an elegant bow. "Your chariot awaits, milady."

Kenzie smiled as Tate set her down and helped her into the pickup. He was particularly appreciative of the view provided as Kenzie climbed into the truck in her slim skirt.

"You two are something else," she said, sitting between them on the front seat. "I appreciate the ride, but if it's too far out of your way, I can call a cab."

"Nope. You're stuck with us," Tate said, looking at Cort, who nodded in agreement. "We'll drop you off then be on our way."

The three of them discussed how many stops Cort and Tate would make in the next few weeks. Tate would fly home the first part of July then head off for a round of west coast rodeos before meeting Cort in Wyoming for a few weeks of travel. He planned to be home at the end of August to participate in the Big 4 Rodeos, running consecutive weeks beginning in Kennewick and ending with the Pendleton Round-Up.

Cort pulled the pickup to a stop in front of Kenzie's hotel and parked, but didn't move to get out of his seat. He tipped his hat to Kenzie and gave her a smile that had a reputation of bending women to his will.

"It was a real pleasure to meet you, Miss Kenzie Beckett. Hope to see you around again soon." Cort gave her a flirtatious wink.

She offered him a warm smile and stuck out her hand to shake his.

"It was very nice to meet someone I've heard so much about," Kenzie said, her eyes twinkling with a mischievous gleam. "Everything Tate said about you is completely untrue. You seem intelligent enough, haven't drooled at all, and I'm glad to see you not only have all of your teeth, but they would make any dentist proud."

Tate snorted with laughter at Kenzie's teasing while Cort shot a narrowed glare his direction.

"I should have known he would fill your head full of stories," Cort said, waving at Kenzie as she slid out of the cab. "Have a safe flight home."

"Thanks for the ride, Cort. I really appreciate it."

Tate took her hand and walked with her inside the hotel. Not wanting to say goodbye in a lobby full of strangers, he escorted Kenzie to her room. Since there were a few teens loitering in the hallway, she opened her door and held it as Tate followed her inside.

"I hope you know I never, ever let rodeo cowboys, or any men for that matter, come to my room," Kenzie said, the corners of her lips quirking up in a grin.

"The only reason you did right now is because you know Cort will honk the horn or pound on the door if I'm not back down there in five minutes." Tate removed his hat and tossed it on the bed.

Kenzie watched his hat land on the white duvet and decided she should have called a cab to pick her up after the rodeo instead of riding with Tate and Cort.

The handsome cowboy staring at her with fire in his blue eyes was about to obliterate her resolve to never again get involved with a man, especially one so incredibly attractive.

"Kenzie..." His deep, rough voice made heat pool in her belly and her limbs feel languid. "I wish I didn't have to leave tonight, Dewdrop."

"I wish you didn't have to leave, either," Kenzie admitted, taking a step toward him.

That step was all he needed as assurance Kenzie would welcome his kiss. Wrapping his arms around her, he pulled her to his chest and pressed his lips to hers.

Flames of heat engulfed him as he deepened the kiss and Kenzie's very essence soaked into his soul.

When he finally raised his head, they both drew in a ragged breath.

"Tate, I... you..." Kenzie said, unable to form coherent thoughts, much less complete sentences.

"Yeah, I know." He rested his forehead against hers then playfully rubbed their noses together. "Thanks for coming tonight, Kenz. It meant a lot to me to have you there."

"Thanks for inviting me." Firmly grasping Tate's muscular biceps in her hands was the only thing that kept her standing since her legs refused to hold her after that kiss. "I really enjoyed watching you ride and meeting Cort as well as the Powell family."

"Huck's bunch is pretty special." Tate grinned, grateful Kenzie fit in so well with his friends.

"You've got some really good friends, Tate. I'm glad for you." She breathed deeply of his unique scent blended with the smell of horses and leather. Since he'd be on the road the rest of the summer with no hope of seeing him before fall, she wanted to memorize every detail about him, from his thick hair and electric blue eyes to his enticing, spicy cologne.

"They are pretty great. It makes all this travel not quite so hard and lonesome," Tate said, realizing he needed to leave or he was going to find it too challenging to say goodbye. "I'll keep in touch. If it works to be in the same city at the same time, or even meet briefly in an airport, let me know. I don't want to wait until September to see you again."

"Just keep me posted where you are and we'll go from there," Kenzie said, wishing her schedule wasn't quite so hectic.

Quite often, her travel plans came together at the last minute, when she was called to lead a pop-up meeting or fill in when another trainer couldn't make it. Coupled with the meetings already on her schedule, her summer was going to be extremely busy. No matter how much she wished she could spend time with the cowboy standing beside her, she knew she wasn't going to see him for a while.

"Be safe, Tate, and keep showing them how it's done. Your ride tonight was amazing. I'm so proud of you."

Tate picked his hat up off the bed, filled with a deep sense of accomplishment at her praise. It meant a lot to him to have his peers tell him what a good ride he had made, but for some reason hearing the girl who captured his heart say it meant even more.

"It's because my good luck charm was sitting in the stands cheering me on. Or maybe it was that sizzlin' kiss before my ride." A devilish grin filled his face. "You could jump in the truck and come along with us. Cort and I would enjoy having you."

Kenzie laughed then brushed at a nonexistent speck on Tate's shirt, seeking any excuse to touch him one more time. "You and I both know that isn't going to happen, but thanks for the offer."

"One of these days you might take me up on it." Although his tone was teasing, the words were sincere.

"One of these days I might." Desperately wishing she'd met Tate long before her heart had been trampled beneath the boots of two-timing cowboys, she hated to say goodbye. Sorely tempted to throw caution, her career, and good sense to the wind and go with him, Kenzie knew she couldn't.

"Have a great summer." He took Kenzie's face in his hands and gave her one last, tender kiss.

"You too." She released a sigh filled with longing and regret. "Ride 'em, cowboy."

As he swooped in for another kiss, his cell phone rang. Noisily smooching Kenzie on the cheek, he grinned. "I've got to run if I don't want to ride in the back with the horse the whole way."

"Cort wouldn't do that." She walked Tate to the door and gave him a warm hug followed by another quick kiss.

"You have no idea." Tate tipped his hat to her as he stepped into the hall and quickly disappeared around the corner.

Kenzie was still standing in the door when he poked his head back around the corner and blew her a kiss. "Take care, Dewdrop."

Catching the kiss, Kenzie smiled and held her hand to her heart as she backed into her room and closed the door, thinking September was a long, long time away.

Chapter Six

A glance at his watch confirmed seventy-eight days, eighteen hours, and twenty-six minutes had passed since he last set eyes on Kenzie.

By now, Tate should have forgotten about the beautiful girl, her scent should have stopped invading his senses, her presence should have vanished from his dreams.

Instead, she consumed his thoughts.

Every dark-haired, tall woman dressed in a suit Tate encountered as he traveled made him do a double take, just to make sure it wasn't Kenzie.

They stayed in touch through phone calls and text messages, but she'd been as busy with her travel schedule as he'd been with his.

In mid-July, she attended Dew's annual convention for its consultants, monopolizing more than a week of her time in Omaha.

While he rode in rodeos across the Northwest, he missed seeing her when she spent a few days at home before flying to a series of meetings on the East Coast.

Tate competed in Wyoming and Montana while she was in the south, ramping up consultants for a strong fall and holiday season.

With the Labor Day weekend behind him, Tate was finally home for a few weeks, anxious to ride in the Pendleton Round-Up. He'd participated in the Horse Heaven Round-Up in Kennewick, followed by the Walla Walla Fair and Frontier Days, taking his dad to both events.

He also entered the Lewiston Round-Up in Lewiston, Idaho. Tate rode well but didn't earn a high score.

The previous evening he returned to the ranch from Lewiston. He spent the day catching up on happenings at the ranch. Thanks to Monte and his crew, the place ran like a well-oiled machine.

The only thing that would make his life any sweeter was to have Kenzie back. She left for a series of trainings in Utah and Colorado the day before he returned home for the Big 4 Rodeos. Because of her sincere dedication to those she coached, she worked closely with a group of consultants trying to achieve leadership levels before the end of the year.

As he showered and shaved, Tate mentally counted the hours until he could see her again. She promised to be home in time to watch him ride at the Pendleton Round-Up next week.

Swiftly donning his favorite blue shirt and a pair of newer jeans, Tate called to check on his dad before he headed to Owen and Megan Montgomery's house for a barbecue.

Between the three rodeos he participated in the past three weeks and getting caught up at his ranch, Tate looked forward to an evening to relax with Owen and Megan and their friends.

Tomorrow was the official kickoff of the weeklong Pendleton Round-Up festivities. Tate attended every year since he could remember because his dad always liked to watch the festivities. He wondered if Kenzie ever attended the famous event.

Tate waved to some of the hands across the ranch yard as he pulled away from the house. He thought about how impractical it was to consider a long-term relationship with the driven career woman.

One, if not both of them, were always on the road, gone for days and sometimes weeks at a time. It was insane to try to rationalize how a future together could work, but Tate had thought of little else since he arrived home.

The more he got to know Kenzie, the more convinced he became that she was the girl for him. Even with her fancy city girl clothes and career, he couldn't picture any other woman fitting into his life, fitting him as well as she did.

As impossible as it seemed, she had engaged every one of his senses, sometimes into overdrive. She made him laugh and smile, challenged his mind, and encouraged his dreams.

He hoped after the Round-Up they'd have a few days to spend together before one of them had to take off again. If they planned to have any kind of relationship, they really needed to be together, at least occasionally.

Talking on the phone or texting couldn't compare to face time, and that's what Tate really wanted.

Face time, lip time, heart pounding wildly against heart time.

Mindful that those thoughts would cause his temperature to spike and his mind to wander, Tate directed his attention to his rodeo career.

Right now, he was at the front of the standings with a solid shot at taking the world champion title. He'd never experienced so many good rides as he had since meeting one very beautiful business executive. He was certain a large part of his success was due to Kenzie, or at least the effect she had on him.

With his thoughts circling back around to the lovely go-getter, Tate drove down the Montgomery's driveway and parked his truck with a few others in front of the big ranch house.

He wandered around to the side yard. Owen stood at the barbecue while Megan hurried over to him, balancing their baby, Aiden, on one hip.

"Tate, we're so glad you could come." Megan stretched up to kiss his cheek. "We haven't seen you in half of forever."

"Thanks for the invite." Tate tickled the baby beneath his chin, eliciting a happy gurgle.

When Aiden held out his arms, Tate didn't hesitate to take the baby from his mother. Aiden stared up at him with wide eyes, babbling in his own language. The baby plucked at the button on Tate's shirt pocket and waved one little fist in the air.

"He's sure grown since I last saw him," Tate commented to Owen as he walked over to where he flipped burgers on the grill.

"Like a weed." Pride was evident in both Owen's eyes and voice as he looked at his son. "You ought to try that whole settling down with a wife and having a baby thing. It's a lot more fun than anyone lets on."

"Huh," Tate said, not willing to say anything that might sound incriminating. Despite his best intentions, he couldn't stop from asking about Kenzie. "Speaking of a wife, has yours heard from Kenzie lately?"

Owen grinned and nodded his head. "As a matter of fact, she has."

"She has?" Tate asked, shifting the baby from his right arm to his left. Aiden grabbed a handful of Tate's collar and pulled while pumping his legs.

"Yep. Just a few minutes before you arrived." Unable to contain his mirth, Owen chuckled.

"And?" Tate asked, wanting more detail. Baffled by what Owen found funny, Tate gave his friend a questioning glance.

"She seems to be fine." Owen looked toward the house and tipped his head that direction. "Why don't you see for yourself?"

"See for myself?" Tate turned as Kenzie walked out the back door carrying a large bowl of potato salad.

At least Tate thought it was Kenzie.

This woman had on jeans that fit her to perfection, scuffed boots, and a summery cotton blouse. A curtain of dark hair fell in waves around her shoulders and down her back.

Tate nearly dropped the baby as he watched her walk across the yard and set the bowl on the picnic table. Owen grabbed Aiden as Tate moved away, eating up the distance separating him from the woman he loved.

"Kenzie?" Tate asked, wondering if his eyes were playing tricks on him. "Is it really you?"

"Yep, cowboy, it's really me." Her brown eyes twinkled and her smile lit her entire face as she grabbed his hand and squeezed it gently.

About to make a scene in front of a yard full of guests who would never let him live it down, Tate ushered her inside the house. Megan looked up at the slamming of the screen door and pointed toward the office where Tate dragged Kenzie and shut the door behind them.

Yanking off his hat and tossing it at a chair near Owen's desk, Tate crushed Kenzie to his chest, burying his hands in her luxurious hair and breathing in her enthralling perfume.

"Baby, you have no idea how much I missed you," Tate said in a raspy whisper, overwhelmed by the rush of emotions that slammed through him upon seeing Kenzie. Convinced he had to be dreaming, he ran his hands up and down her arms, memorizing the feel of her soft skin against his work-roughened fingers.

"Maybe half as much as I missed you." Thrilled Tate seemed happy to see her, Kenzie was inordinately pleased his first thought was to hold her instead of ravaging her with mind-boggling kisses.

Before she could wonder if he would get around to kissing her, he tilted up her chin and melded their lips together with such heat and longing the connection scrambled her thoughts and made her knees wobble.

"Tate," she whispered, leaning into him, absorbing his warmth, breathing in his masculine scent. Not wanting to admit it, she had counted the minutes until she could see the handsome cowboy again. She'd missed his smile, his seductive voice, and his incredible blue eyes as well as his quick wit and good-natured teasing.

"Let me see you." He pushed her back far enough he could get a good, long look. The girl who haunted his thoughts, danced through his dreams, and kept him on his toes the past several months didn't appear at all like he remembered. That woman was all business with her tailored suits, tidy upswept hair, and moderate heels.

The country girl currently gazing at him with passion sparking from her eyes and laughter lingering around her very kissable mouth looked relaxed and comfortable in worn jeans and boots with her hair hanging loose. If he stared too long at her snug-fitting jeans, there was a good chance he'd lose the ability to hang onto what little sense he had left.

After admiring her from head to toe, he returned to her head where he ran his fingers through the silky strands of her hair. "I've never seen your hair down before, Dewdrop. It's gorgeous, just like you."

"Thank you." She relished the feel of Tate's hands in her hair. It was one thing to dream about being with Tate and fantasizing how he'd react to seeing her with her hair down, dressed like a country girl. It was something else entirely to experience his satisfied reaction.

He pulled her against his chest, wrapped his arms tightly around her, and held on for a few minutes, knowing he'd found the one woman meant to be there.

"I thought you were going to be gone for almost another week," Tate finally said, inhaling the floral aroma of her hair. She smelled so luscious he could hardly think straight.

"I was, but when I realized you were actually home and not off to some other rodeo, I begged one of the other trainers to take over my Colorado classes. I've covered for her twice this summer, so she was willing to repay the favor." Drawn into Tate's hot blue gaze, she rubbed her hand along his smooth jaw.

His skin was taut, tan, and begging for her lips to press a hot kiss against it. She resisted the urge and instead laced her hands behind Tate's neck, drawing nearer to him. "I got on the first flight headed for Pasco and arrived home just a couple of hours ago. When Megan told me you'd be here tonight, I got here as fast as I could."

"I'm so glad." He kissed her until they both fought a nearly insatiable desire for each other.

Kenzie finally drew back and smiled, "We better get out there or Owen will start asking questions, quite loudly, about what we are doing in here."

"True. He's got those overprotective, cavedweller tendencies, you know." He placed his arm around her waist and pulled her close to his side, stealing another kiss as they walked outside.

Casually strolling over to where Megan and Owen stood talking by the barbecue, Aiden held out his arms to Kenzie. She picked him up, blowing on his neck and making him laugh.

Tate watched her for a moment, realizing she seemed to like kids. Since he someday hoped to have a few of his own, he was pleased to see the loving way she interacted with Aiden. Kenzie looked at ease as she held him while talking to Megan. Unfamiliar feelings flopped around inside Tate's chest at the sweet picture she made with a baby in her arms.

Later, sitting side by side on a bench at the picnic table while they ate, Kenzie asked Tate if he wanted to go riding with her after dinner. He readily agreed and helped clean up the dishes so they could head out to the barn faster.

"Owen said you can ride Buster." Kenzie approached a stall in the barn and held out a carrot. A beautiful palomino mare nuzzled the treat then nodded her head at Kenzie. "Goldie gets excited to go out for a run," she said, putting a bridle on the horse and leading her out of the stall.

"Yours?" Tate asked as he saddled Owen's horse. The discovery that there was much more to Kenzie than he knew left him edgy and confused. Part of him was thrilled his city girl had a country side. The other part of him was thoroughly disappointed she hadn't told him before now.

Never, in a million years, would he have pegged Kenzie as a girl who would ride a horse, let alone own one. Curious what else she'd kept from him, he was of a mind to be mad at her. And he would have been, except he was too happy to see her again.

"Yep. I bought her as soon as I moved back. Megan and Owen are kind enough to let me keep her here. Megan and some of the hands ride her so she keeps in shape between my sporadic visits." Kenzie adjusted the cinch on her saddle. "I bet you didn't know this city girl corporate trainer had a little bit of country in her."

"No clue," Tate admitted, fighting down his irritation. How, in all the things they'd discussed the last several months, did the topic of her having country ties never enter the conversation?

Incorrectly assuming Kenzie grew up in Portland, Tate realized he should have asked more direct questions about her past. "I guess your love of country music should have been a hint. If I didn't know better, I'd say you've been holding out on me, Dewdrop. Those cowboy boots aren't new and those jeans are obviously worn in all the right places. The way they fit, you're seriously making it hard for me to look at anything else."

Tate's comment made her blush. "I haven't always been a city girl." She knew she should have been upfront with him from the start. She hoped if he really got to know her, he'd eventually find out she spent the first fourteen years of her life on a ranch, she loved horses, and was really a country girl at heart.

Rather than volunteer the information, she'd waited to see where their relationship was headed, or if they even had one. "I grew up on a ranch not far from here until my parents divorced."

Comments Kenzie made during their conversations should have tipped him off to her upbringing, if he'd paid attention. With her knowledge of rodeo, ranching, and country life, he should have put two and two together instead of making ignorant assumptions.

It must have occurred to her at some point during the last four months they'd known each other to tell him about her background. Realizing she carefully avoided discussing her father or her parents' divorce, he suddenly wanted to know what really happened.

"What made you change, Kenzie? What happened to the ranch? Why did you leave?"

"When my parents divorced, my mom moved me to Portland, as far from the ranch life I loved as she could possibly get. Dad didn't handle our leaving well and started drinking. When he died, we sold the ranch to pay off his bills and moved on with our lives."

"What happened to your father? You never talk about him." Tate studied Kenzie as they mounted the horses and rode out on a trail behind the barn, past the fields of recently harvested wheat.

"He died a year after the divorce," Kenzie said, not making eye contact with Tate, focusing instead on the trail ahead.

"I'm sorry, Kenzie. It's incredibly hard to lose a parent." Close enough he could reach over and put his hand on her leg, he gave it a gentle pat.

The comforting gesture almost brought Kenzie to tears. Swallowing down her emotion, she changed the subject, asking Tate about his standings and how he thought he'd place in the rankings after the Round-Up.

Tate knew she was trying to distract him from asking more questions and decided to let her for now. Someday, though, he'd get the full story out of her about what had happened to her father, why she was so wary of cowboys, and what made her leave behind ranch life.

As they rode along the ridge behind the Montgomery's ranch house, Tate breathed deeply of the hay-scented air and smiled. He would never have pictured himself riding out here with Kenzie and decided just to enjoy the surprise of her not only having a rural background, but also being a very good rider.

"You look beautiful on a horse," Tate said as they stopped to watch the sun start its evening descent. "Not many people ride with such grace and ease."

"Thank you." She'd thought the same thing about Tate the first time she watched him ride a bronc. "You don't look too bad yourself."

"Do I look good enough for a kiss?" Tate gave her a come-hither smile, wanting to forget there were still unanswered question between them and enjoy the moment they shared.

"Maybe." Her eyes automatically focused on Tate's inviting lips. His tempting smile brought out his dimples and rendered her incapable of doing anything but surrendering her mouth to his when he leaned over, kissing her long and deep.

"Kenzie, I wish..." Tate started to say, but was silenced by another breath-stealing kiss. She tasted like every sweet thing he'd ever experienced, only better.

After a few more kisses that left them both trying to gather their composure, Kenzie turned Goldie back toward the barn and they rode the rest of the way in silence.

While they unsaddled the horses, they discussed plans for the coming week and agreed to meet at the parade the next morning in Pendleton. Tate tried to talk Kenzie into letting him pick her up, but she refused, saying it wasn't necessary for him to drive that far when she was perfectly capable of driving herself.

After returning to the house, they thanked Megan and Owen for dinner then walked out to their vehicles.

Kenzie leaned against the side of her car and squeezed his hand, looking at him with regret.

"I owe you an apology, Tate."

Surprised by her words, he stood unmoving. "For what?"

"For not telling you about my past, for letting you think I spent my life living in town." Her gaze dropped to her feet. "I didn't lie to you, but I didn't exactly tell you the truth, either. I'm sorry."

"Why didn't you tell me?" Tate was glad Kenzie brought up the subject. He'd been blindsided when she walked outside earlier, looking like she'd stepped out of one of his fantasies.

"I was afraid," she whispered, swirling the toe of her boot in the dirt.

"Afraid?" Tate couldn't keep his hands to himself any longer and pulled her into his embrace. "Of what,

Dewdrop?" She relaxed against him as she let out her breath.

"Of you. I was afraid you'd like me more because I was raised on a ranch. You think that type of girl fits into your life better than one from the city." Kenzie spoke against his neck, with her head resting on his shoulder. "I didn't want my background to matter."

"Kenzie, that's ridiculous. I like you for you." Soothingly rubbing his hands along her back, he kissed the top of her head.

At first, her country roots might have made a difference, but then again, she'd attracted and held his attention for months without him knowing if she even owned a pair of blue jeans.

Never mentioning his preference for a country girl, he puzzled over how she could have known he initially thought her city girl ways would never mesh with his lifestyle. That was before he got to know her and long before he came to love her.

"Would you like me as much if I was afraid of horses, refused to get my shoes dirty, and had no idea how to drive a stick-shift?" Kenzie asked, still not raising her head to meet his gaze.

Lifting her chin with his finger, he smiled at her, love filling his bright blue eyes. "I'd like you no matter what. I'm not gonna lie to you, though. The fact that you're a great rider, can drive a stick, and right now have more muck on your boots than I do is kind of a turn on, Dewdrop."

Kenzie's lips tipped up in a smile and he brushed his mouth against each corner then kissed her forehead.

"Going forward, let's be completely, totally, and thoroughly honest with each other. You already know all my secrets and I look forward to discovering the rest of yours."

"What makes you think I've got more?" Kenzie asked, kissing his chin.

"You're a complex and complicated woman of mystery." Theatrically, he waved a hand in the air. "Of course you've got more. Just don't hold out on me with the big ones, please. They're a little hard to recover from."

"Deal." She stepped back and held out her hand for Tate to shake. Instead, he wrapped her in his arms again, swinging her around and raining kisses on her neck, making her giggle.

Lost for a time in a lingering kiss, he finally helped Kenzie into her car with a promise to see her the next morning in Pendleton.

At the thought of spending the coming week with her, he wondered how he'd ever get any sleep, especially dreaming about Kenzie dressed in those snug fitting jeans.

>◇<

Kenzie parked her car several blocks from the parade route and popped her trunk. She didn't have a chance to get out before Tate was there, holding the door open and pulling her to her feet. He gave her a warm hug and a warmer kiss before turning her loose and stepping back to offer her an admiring glance.

"Looking good, Dewdrop." Tate spun her around to take in her dark jeans, boots, and summery blouse. The sparkle on her belt caught fragments of the sun's rays and shimmered around them. "You make everything you wear look amazing but I'm telling you, Kenz, you could be a model for those jeans."

"Your idle flattery will get you nowhere." Despite her casual tone, fiery cheeks gave away her pleasure at Tate's comment.

"I just tell it like I see it, and I really like what I'm seeing," Tate said, taking the foldable stools Kenzie dug out of the trunk in one big hand. "What are these for?"

"To watch the parade." Kenzie shut the trunk and took Tate's other hand in hers. "I realize you rough and tough cowboys don't mind standing for hours on end watching the parade, but I'd prefer to have somewhere to sit. These stools will put us up high enough we can see over the rest of the crowd."

"Good idea." He steered Kenzie through traffic and across the street. Quickly walking to the parade route, they found a place to sit behind a row of folding chairs. "Just don't tell the guys I had a seat for this thing."

"My lips are sealed." Before she took a seat on one of the stools, she glanced at the crowd gathering around them.

She tried not to shiver when she felt Tate's presence behind her and his fingers brushing the hair away from her neck. His breath warmed her ear when he leaned close and she could smell the minty aroma of his gum.

"Don't seal them too tightly. I've got plans for those delectable lips later." His low, suggestive voice made her shiver in delight before he placed a teasing kiss beneath her ear.

"Tate," Kenzie whispered, feeling butterflies burst into motion in her stomach while her cheeks flamed with heat again. "Behave."

"What fun is that?" He looped his arm around her shoulders as he stood behind her. Not one to stay still for long, he soon gave Kenzie a kiss on her cheek with a promise to return soon. When he reappeared ten minutes later, he carried two steaming cups of coffee.

"How'd you know I could use a caffeine jolt?" she asked, taking the cup he offered and sipping the dark brew.

"Great minds think alike." Tate sat down next to her. "Besides, we've traveled together enough I know you like black coffee in the morning to get your blood pumping."

Kenzie didn't bother to tell Tate that seeing him, with his teasing smile and hinted promises of things to come, had her blood pumping more than a triple shot espresso.

Instead, she calmly sipped her coffee while they talked before the parade started. Once it began, they clapped and cheered, waved and watched, enjoying the variety of entries.

Afterward, they returned the stools to Kenzie's car then walked downtown where they wandered through vendor booths and shops, including the town's iconic western store.

After grabbing a quick bite to eat, Tate looked at his watch. Kenzie promised to go with him to the concert that night featuring one of her favorite country artists. It wouldn't start for several hours, so Tate thought about ways to pass the time.

"Want to see my ranch, Dewdrop?" Tate asked as they glanced in a store window featuring a display of vintage saddles and boots.

"Your ranch?" Kenzie asked, turning to look at him.

"We've got several hours to kill and I don't know about you but I'm only good for so many stores full of tourists elbowing me in the side. We could go out to the ranch, throw some steaks on the grill for dinner and be back in plenty of time for the concert," Tate said, thinking he had devised a great plan.

"Sure." Pleased at the idea of seeing the Morgan Ranch, she nodded her head.

"Do you want to bring your car and then you can ride back with me tonight?" Tate hoped Kenzie would say yes. Situated between Pendleton and Kennewick, a drive from the ranch and back again guaranteed he'd have more time with Kenzie after the concert if she agreed.

"Okay," she said as they walked back to where they parked. Tate gave her a kiss and held her door until she buckled her seatbelt, then hurried to his truck and led the way out of town and onto the freeway. Taking the exit for the Tri-Cities, he drove several miles before turning off the road onto a private lane.

At the head of the driveway, Tate parked his truck in front of the large farmhouse, complete with a big porch and gingerbread trim. Painted a creamy shade of yellow with pale blue and white trim, the house looked neat and inviting.

Tate held Kenzie's hand as she got out of her car and looked up at the lovely house.

"Tate, it's wonderful," Kenzie said, surprised by how much the place resembled the one she'd always fancied as the perfect house. Although the picture had only been in her head, the house in front of her was just how she envisioned the home of her dreams.

"Come inside and I'll give you the grand tour." Tate took her hand and led her down the walk and up the front steps. As he opened the door, he was glad he'd taken time that morning to straighten up after himself. He had a housekeeper who came in once a week to clean. Tate was especially glad she'd been there the previous afternoon to dust, vacuum, shine, and polish.

"Oh, my," Kenzie said as they stepped into the foyer where a grand staircase descended in a sweeping curve. "This is amazing."

"My grandfather built this house for my grandmother. When I was a kid, I used to love sliding down the banister." He ran his hand along wood smoothed from the fingers of his family.

"I can just picture you sliding down this when you thought no one was watching." She envisioned a young Tate with freckles on his nose, unruly hair, and an engaging smile.

77

"I did it even when Pop was watching," Tate said with a laugh, recalling good memories from his childhood. He escorted Kenzie into the formal parlor, then the dining room, his office, the kitchen, and a big space he'd converted into a media room with a large screen television and comfortable leather chairs. Directing Kenzie up the back stairs, he showed her the multiple bedrooms and bathrooms, saving the master suite for last.

A king-sized bed, covered in a light gray and cream striped comforter, dominated the room. Pale gray walls and antique bird's-eye maple furniture caught Kenzie's attention. Although the room was simple in its décor, it was inviting and surprisingly neat.

"That furniture is gorgeous." She stepped farther into the room, running her hand over the top of the dresser. The artistic lines of the piece drew her admiration.

"It was a wedding gift for my grandmother," Tate said, pleased Kenzie seemed to cherish the same things that were important to him. "Pop said his dad had it special made for his new bride."

"That's a wonderful story and legacy." She turned to find Tate staring at her with an odd look on his face. Rather than contemplate what put it there, she wandered back out the door and down the big stairs to the front entry.

Tate watched Kenzie walk from the room, trying to pull his thoughts together. Seeing her in the master suite made him realize how much he wanted her there permanently — in his life, in his house, in his arms, in his bed.

Hastily shaking his head to clear his wayward thoughts, he hurried down the stairs, leading her back to the kitchen where they began preparations for dinner.

Later, they sat outside at a table on the back porch, eating steak and baked potatoes while discussing plans for the upcoming week of festivities.

Kenzie wasn't surprised when Tate said Cort, Huck, and a few other friends would be staying with him.

"Will Mara and the kids come with Huck?" she asked, taking another bite of tender beef. It had to be one of the best steaks she'd ever eaten.

"No, they don't travel with him much. It's too hard on the kids." If he planned to pursue Kenzie and make her a part of his future, he wouldn't keep traveling. Not if she waited for him at home.

Tate joined the rodeo circuit just for fun but when he did so well at it, he decided to pursue it as a career. Although he loved to ride, he was getting tired of the travel, tired of the women chasing him, tired of never feeling settled.

After experiencing the best year of his career, Tate entertained the idea of making the following year his last. If his relationship with Kenzie continued the way it was currently headed, he'd have every reason to retire from rodeo sooner rather than later.

Recently, he noticed a big change in her attitude toward him. She no longer seemed to be keeping him an arm's length away. With a little more effort on his part, he might break through all the barriers she'd erected around her heart.

Aware that her cheating former fiancé had done a number on her, he still couldn't comprehend why she was so against dating a cowboy. He supposed she'd get around to telling him someday.

For now, though, he planned to enjoy every minute of being with her while their schedules cooperated.

Once they finished dinner and washed the dishes, they headed back to Pendleton for the concert. The two of them visited with people they both knew as they enjoyed the performance then returned to the ranch. Tate asked Kenzie to come in for a while but she declined, walking to her car.

From their early morning parade-watching to the end of the concert, Kenzie enjoyed every single minute of her day spent with Tate.

He made her feel special, cherished, beautiful, and like she was the most important thing in his world. She'd never felt like that with anyone before and something in her heart whispered she never would again.

"Thanks for an amazing day, Tate." She gazed at him with a soft light in her warm brown eyes, hoping he knew how much he had come to mean to her.

About to fall into her dark eyes, lit with an inner spark, Tate knew if he did he had no hope of finding his way back out. Tenderly wrapping his arms around her, he kissed her slowly and thoroughly until she trembled against him.

When he lifted his head, he watched a dreamy look pass across her face before she slid into her car.

"I need to get home," she said quietly, frantically grasping at her unraveling composure before she lost all her good sense. When Tate shut her car door and leaned down for another kiss, she reached through the open window and brushed her hand along his jaw.

"Thanks for hanging out with me today," Tate said, not ready to tell her good night, but knowing she needed to leave. If she didn't head down his driveway soon, he wasn't sure he'd be able to let her go. "If you don't have plans tomorrow, I'm picking up Pop and taking him to church, then out to lunch. You're welcome to join us."

"I'd like that." Kenzie looked forward to meeting Tate's father. "Where should I meet you?"

"How about Pop's place?" At Kenzie's nod, he gave her directions and kissed her cheek. Before stepping away from the car, he bid her good night and his heart goodbye.

Chapter Seven

"I like her, Tate. She's something special," Kent Morgan said as he and his son stood outside the care home, watching Kenzie pull out of the parking lot. "You better not let her get away."

"I'm working on it, Pop." Tate tipped back his hat and watched until Kenzie's car disappeared around the corner.

"Work faster, would you, son?" Kent said with a teasing light in eyes that were still a bright shade of blue. "I'm not getting any younger, you know, and I'd surely like to hold a grandbaby in my arms before you bury me six feet under."

"Pop!" Tate shook his head at his father as they slowly walked back inside the facility and toward Kent's room.

"Well, it's true. If you think you can wait another thirty years to get hitched, you better think again, boy." Kent shuffled into the room and hung his hat on a hook by the door. He sat in his recliner while Tate pulled out a straight-backed chair and straddled it.

In his prime, Kent Morgan had been every bit as tall and athletic as his strapping son. Even on the other side of ninety, Kent still carried himself well. His steps slowed and his shoulders tended to stoop, but he was still stronger and in better shape than most men twenty years younger. His mind was clear, although occasionally forgetful, and his wit sharp.

Tate didn't want to think about what life would be like without Pop. His father had always been more than a parent. He was a friend, confidant, and partner.

"That Kenzie is not only a beautiful girl, but sweet and funny," Kent said, not telling Tate anything he didn't already know. "She won't take any sass off you either. Yep, she's a keeper. In some ways she reminds me of your mama."

"She does?" Tate was surprised to hear Pop mention his mother. "How so?"

"Your mama was a beauty, too, but she could set me on my ear without me even knowing what happened. She was full of spunk and life, but also had a gentle kindness that was bone-deep." Kent's voice caught as he dug out a snowy white handkerchief from his pocket and swiped at his nose. "I sure miss that woman, even after all these years."

"Mama was one of a kind, wasn't she, Pop?" Tate knew his father had never gotten over his beloved wife dying so young and leaving him alone to raise their son.

"She was for sure." Kent took a deep breath and returned the handkerchief to his pocket. "But I'd be willing to bet Kenzie is too. I hope you'll bring her around again soon."

"I'll try, Pop. She travels even more than I do, so it's been challenging to be together," Tate said, getting to his feet and preparing to leave.

"Figure it out, Tater. You mark my words, this is one girl you don't want to let get away." Kent's laugh followed Tate out the door.

><><

"He did not!" Megan squealed in Kenzie's ear as she sat folding laundry on the couch, nearly making her drop the phone.

"He did. Tate took me to meet his dad," Kenzie said, trying not to smile at how well the day progressed.

Earlier that morning, Kenzie arrived at Kent Morgan's care facility as Tate and his father sauntered out the door. Tate so closely resembled his father, Kenzie would have been able to pick the older man out of a crowd, even though they definitely looked more like grandparent and grandchild than father and son.

With a head full of snowy white hair, eyes that were still bright, and a smile every bit as engaging as Tate's, Kenzie marveled that Kent managed to stay single until he was almost sixty.

Kent placed a warm kiss on her cheek and bestowed several compliments on how she looked like an "angel dropped down from heaven." Kenzie realized Tate got his charismatic personality from his father.

Initially nervous at meeting him, the kind old gent quickly put her at ease and they were soon both teasing Tate. Kenzie sat between the two at the church service. Afterward, Tate had to do some fast maneuvering at the restaurant they went to for lunch to keep his dad from taking the seat next to her.

Content as she thought back over the day, Kenzie liked Kent Morgan. If she could have picked a grandfather, since both of hers passed away years ago, he would have more than fit the bill.

"Kenz, that is huge." Megan's voice sounded high-pitched and excited. "It's bigger than huge, it's... colossal."

"Enough with the drama." Kenzie laughed as she folded another bath towel, adding it to her growing pile. "No big deal. His dad is very nice and Tate said I got the seal of approval."

"Of course you did. Does this mean you are finally willing to give Tate a chance?"

"Maybe." Kenzie didn't have any other choice. Her heart wouldn't let her walk away now, even if she wanted to. Truthfully, walking away was the last thing she wanted to do. Running into Tate's arms and staying there forever seemed to be a much better idea.

Somewhere between sitting by him at the airport for the first time and going to see him ride in Santa Fe, she'd fallen in love with the handsome cowboy.

Although she and Tate hadn't spent a lot of time together, Kenzie felt like she'd known him all her life.

Gracious, kind, fun, teasing, and gentle were all traits she associated with Tate. He was driven, intelligent, loyal and, as far as she could tell, honest.

It was that last trait that finally caused her to admit not every cowboy was like her ex-fiancé or her father.

"He's a really great guy."

Megan sounded very pleased with this admission from her best friend. "Have I ever steered you wrong?"

"No, not so far," Kenzie admitted. "Look, I've got to go, but I'll see you guys tomorrow at the bull riding event. Tate got us tickets."

"Great, I'll be watching for you. I'm so glad you could be home for the Round-Up this year. You know you're welcome to stay here instead of driving back and forth, if you want."

"Thanks, but I'll pass. You always have extra company as it is and I don't need to take up one of your guest beds when I can drive home." Kenzie set the folded laundry into a basket to carry back to her bedroom.

"Suit yourself, but the door's open if you change your mind. I think Tate was in shock when he saw you here the other night." Megan giggled as she recalled the stunned look on Tate's face at the barbecue. "You should have given him warning."

"It's good to keep him guessing," Kenzie said with a laugh. "Night, Meg."

"Good night."

Kenzie disconnected the call, still amused by the look of complete surprise on Tate's face when he noticed her at Megan and Owen's barbecue. Watching him in an airport or even at the rodeo was so different than seeing him at home with her friends.

The way he gazed at her with those striking blue eyes often left her light-headed and weak-kneed. His kisses... Kenzie tried not to think about what they did to her because then she'd never get to sleep.

Engaged to Sonny, her cheating former fiancé, for several months, he'd never made her feel like she did with Tate.

The slightest touch of Tate's lips made her hot and cold, thrilled and frightened, filled with a passion and wanting so intense, it was beyond her ability to fathom.

Kenzie flipped through some silly photos on her phone she'd taken of him one day while they were waiting for a flight. Looking at them always put a big smile on her face. She realized Tate did that. He made her smile, made her laugh, made her so happy.

Resigned to putting aside her biased thoughts about cowboys in general, Kenzie went to bed with a light heart, looking forward to spending the next week really getting to know Tate.

><><

"You ready for this?" Kenzie asked as Tate took a deep breath beside her. With the leading score for saddle bronc riding at the Pendleton Round-Up for his performance earlier in the week, Tate was going for the title in the final round. She was proud of him and of how well he'd ridden.

"As ready as I'll ever be." Tate needed to get down to the chutes and prepare for his ride. If he had another great score, he'd secure the first place position as well as take home some great prizes. "I need a kiss for good luck, though."

"Of course you do." Her eyes sparkled with teasing and something more, something that made Tate's temperature kick up a notch on the warm September afternoon.

Tate would have liked a little privacy to kiss her properly, but settled for putting his arm around her back and shielding their faces with his hat. Their impassioned kiss drew many stares and more than a few comments. Beside them, Owen hooted with laughter and Megan giggled.

"Ride 'em cowboy," Kenzie said, uttering the phrase that went along with the good luck kisses she'd given him since the first one they shared in the Denver airport.

"Show 'em how it's done," Owen called as Tate hurried down the steps of the stands and waved a hand over his head, quickly disappearing in the crowd.

Megan set Aiden on Kenzie's lap to keep her distracted while they waited for the saddle bronc riding to begin.

As she held the baby, Kenzie felt a deep sense of gratitude for the wonderful week she experienced with Tate. After spending every day together, she was more in love with the wonderful man than she ever thought she could love anyone.

The first day Tate rode, she brought his dad to watch and then took him home afterward. The senior Morgan seemed thrilled with the chance to see his son ride as well as spend time with Tate's girlfriend.

Pleased with the opportunity to get to know the elderly man better, Kenzie felt content and happy seeing the pride on his face as he watched Tate compete. Kent hinted, more than once, that he was in a hurry for Tate to settle down and produce some grandbabies. He seemed to think Kenzie was the girl who could make it happen.

She didn't know if there was any truth to the old man's wishes, but she liked to dream about someday becoming Mrs. Tate Morgan.

Earlier in the week, Tate hosted a barbecue for his friends at the ranch and asked Kenzie to play the role of hostess. While she greeted guests and helped prepare the food, Tate grilled steaks and joined in the good-natured joking going on between the guys. The way they worked together, so naturally and intuitively, it was easy to pretend she really belonged there.

While her thoughts trickled over the last several days, Kenzie couldn't remember when she'd enjoyed anything more than just being with Tate.

They'd wandered through the dozens of vendor booths set up in town for the festivities and Tate surprised her that morning when he gave her a necklace she'd admired the previous day.

His fingers lingered against her skin as he fastened the silver chain around her neck then placed a kiss on the clasp, making a shiver work its way up from her toes.

She fingered the necklace as she brought her thoughts back to the present. Kenzie looked down at Aiden's happy little face and smiled. Although she thought all hope for a family of her own died with her broken engagement a few years ago, she liked the idea of starting one with Tate.

When the announcer let the crowd know the saddle bronc event was about to begin, Kenzie handed Aiden back to Megan, wanting to focus her full attention on Tate and his ride.

He was in the chute, adjusting the rein in his hand and tugging his hat down on his head. When he was ready to ride, he gave a brief nod and the horse burst out of the gate, bucking wildly. Kenzie didn't think she'd ever tire of watching Tate perform.

He was all grace and smooth motion, making what he did look so simple and yet so amazing.

The buzzer sounded, signaling the end of another successful ride. Kenzie joined the crowd in clapping and cheering. Cort and Huck leaned over the fence, waving their hats and hollering in excitement.

"How about that, folks?" the announcer asked in his booming voice. "Tate Morgan could walk away the winner with his eighty-nine point ride. Let's hear it for Tate!"

The crowd cheered again and Kenzie smiled broadly. Eager to offer her congratulations, Owen told her where to find Tate behind the chutes and she hurried out of the stands.

On her way there, she bumped into some of Tate's friends from the circuit and briefly stopped to visit with them. After bidding them goodbye, she hurried on her way behind chutes.

She rounded a corner and saw Tate talking to Cort. Kenzie smiled and took a few more steps toward him as a woman tapped his arm to get his attention. When he turned to see who it was, the woman planted a kiss on his lips, pressing her body against Tate.

Unable to watch a second longer, Kenzie spun around and started to stomp off but ran into Huck.

"Whoa, Kenzie! Where are you going in such a hurry?" Huck asked, steadying her with a grip on her elbows.

Anger burned up the back of her throat, rendering her unable to speak. Barely able to see through the haze of her tears, she shook her head and took a step back.

Huck looked behind her and saw Tate trying to disentangle himself from a woman who'd been quite fervent in her pursuit of him all summer.

"Oh, man." Huck grabbed Kenzie's arm before she could run off. "Kenzie, I know this looks bad, but it isn't what you think. Tate can explain."

"I'm sure he can," Kenzie managed to spit out before jerking her arm away from Huck and running toward an exit, away from Tate and her broken dreams for the future.

Hurrying to her car, she got in and drove out of town, ignoring the ringing of her cell phone. Finally turning it off, she tossed it on the passenger seat, knowing she should have stuck with her plan to stay away from faithless cowboys.

An hour later she arrived home, slammed the front door, and kicked off her boots. She sat on the couch staring at a blank television screen long enough for the afternoon light to pick up the soft edges of twilight.

Her home phone rang with consistency. Every fifteen minutes it jangled and the answering machine would pick up. Tate and Megan left numerous messages, but she ignored them. She hadn't turned her cell phone back on and decided if her home phone rang one more time, she'd unplug it.

When it rang a few minutes later, she got off the couch and disconnected it from the jack in the wall.

Kenzie ventured into the kitchen, poured herself a glass of juice, and sat at the small table trying to decide what to do.

Tate was too good to be true. Like the other smooth talking men in her past, he told her what she wanted to hear and worked his way past her defenses. He was just another good-looking, fast-talking, two-timing cowboy. Just like the other cowboys who betrayed her.

Unlike her fiancé, whose deception was hurtful and shocking, Tate had truly captured her heart and left it broken.

Slowly sipping her juice, she didn't feel like eating, didn't feel like anything. She was too numb and cold inside. Eventually, she returned to the couch, pulled a fleece throw off the back and snuggled into it as she rested against the soft cushions.

Her mind spun in a hundred directions yet her eyes began to drift shut when the doorbell rang.

A deep sigh worked free from her lungs. She got to her feet and glanced out the peephole. It wasn't a surprise to see Tate standing on her doorstep. Although he hadn't been to her apartment before, he certainly had her address and knew how to find her.

She turned around to hide in her bedroom until he left, but he pounded on the door.

"Kenzie, I know you're home." His voice was loud enough for her and half the neighborhood to hear. "Open the door."

Intentionally ignoring his request, Kenzie willed him to give up and leave. The thought of facing him was more than she could handle with her heart shattered in so many pieces.

The bell rang several more times and Tate pounded on the door again. "Look, I don't know what you think you saw, but you don't know the whole story. Nothing happened. I promise. Please, Kenz, open the door. Please?"

He sounded hurt, angry, and worried as he pleaded with her. Twice, Kenzie's hand hovered on the knob, ready to open the door.

Forcing herself to be strong, she leaned her forehead against the cool wood and placed her palm against the place where Tate knocked. If she opened the door to him, she'd listen to what he said, no matter what lies he told, because she wanted to be with him more than anything.

"Give me a chance to explain. It isn't what you think. That woman... I've had problems with her before." Tate's voice held frustration and a hint of desperation. "If you won't talk to me face-to-face, will you at least pick up your phone? Please, Dewdrop?"

Tears burned her eyes as they rolled down her cheeks and splashed to the floor. She wanted to believe Tate. She wanted it to be a simple misunderstanding, but she couldn't allow herself the luxury of giving him a chance to sweet-talk his way out of what happened.

The flash of recognition on Tate's face when the woman wrapped herself around him was unmistakable.

Another loud rap at the door along with a final plea from Tate had her holding both hands over her mouth to keep from calling out to him. She listened to his footsteps stomping down the walk followed by the sound of his pickup engine starting.

"Goodbye, Tate," Kenzie whispered. Sobs wracked through her as she slid to the floor and used the door for support.

The room was dark when Kenzie rose to her feet and went to bed. After a fitful night of sleep, she got up, took a shower, and packed her travel bag. A quick call to corporate had her taking over a training meeting in Chicago with several other stops in the Midwest.

She packed her suitcase and grabbed a trench coat then locked her apartment with plans to be gone for several weeks. Maybe by the time she returned, she'd be able to take a breath without each one causing pain to shoot through her chest.

If she kept busy, she wouldn't have time to think about Tate or the huge hole he left in place of her heart.

No good would come from dwelling on what would never be. Kenzie straightened her spine and drove to the airport.

Some people might run away from their problems, but she would fly.

Chapter Eight

"Man, you've got to get your head back in the game. We've still got a few rodeos to get through before the finals and you're gonna screw up everything if you don't pull yourself together," Cort said, sitting across the table from Tate in some backwater diner on their way to the next rodeo.

Although he took first place in saddle bronc riding at the Pendleton Round-Up, it was the last rodeo Tate placed in at all. After losing the only woman he'd ever truly loved, he also seemed to lose his edge and drive to win the championship title.

On a day when he should have been celebrating his victory, he instead fought against the brutal force of Kenzie's rejection as it flooded over him in crushing waves. His frantic trip to her apartment to try to set things right ended with him being so angry he nearly wrecked his truck twice on the way home.

A picture of his future without Kenzie in it seemed like a long stretch of bleak darkness. Nothing mattered if he couldn't share it with her.

Thoughts of the infuriating woman made his chest hurt so badly he had difficulty breathing. She'd become his world and he needed her more than he ever thought he'd need anyone.

Clearly, the feeling wasn't mutual.

From information he pried out of Megan, Kenzie flew out of town the day after the Round-Up and hadn't returned.

Miserable knowing she thought he cheated on her, it wounded him to the core that she believed the worst of him.

Maybe she never really loved him. Even though they hadn't said the words, he thought their feelings for each other were obvious.

The wonderful week they spent together in Pendleton convinced him, beyond a doubt, that Kenzie was the girl he wanted beside him forever.

Apparently, though, he was just an interesting diversion for her. Otherwise, she'd give him a chance to explain what really happened.

Tate sighed and ran his hand through his hair, ignoring both the sandwich on the plate in front of him and Cort's concerned looks.

Cort had been a trooper the last few weeks. His friend had done everything to bring him out of his funk from offering unwavering support to picking a fight with him. Nothing seemed to help draw him out of the hole he'd crawled into when Kenzie so abruptly shut him out of her life.

Fast on his way to losing his focus heading into the finals, if Tate couldn't get his head on straight, he might as well not even compete in Las Vegas.

"Look, you've got to let Kenzie go or you're going to blow this," Cort said, looking at him with a pointed glare as he finished his sandwich. "There isn't a single thing you can do to change her mind and moping around isn't helping you at all. Snap out of it or go home!"

Genuinely liking Kenzie, Cort thought she'd been good for Tate. Regardless, he was angry about what she'd done to his best friend. She could pretend all she wanted that Tate didn't matter to her. Cort knew better and so did half the people on the circuit.

It didn't take a genius to see Tate and Kenzie were completely loopy for each other. That was why Cort couldn't begin to fathom what was going through Kenzie's head.

How could she just turn her back on the once-in-a-lifetime love Tate offered and pretend he didn't exist?

"I'm not going to blow it," Tate grumbled, realizing Cort was right. He wasn't doing himself any favors by constantly dredging up what had happened with Kenzie. He had to get his mind back on his goal and move forward. He'd worked too long and too hard to throw away his shot at coming out on top for the year.

Tate renewed his resolve to win at the finals, sat up in his chair, and ate his sandwich. Later, as he and Cort walked out of the diner, he thumped his friend on the back.

"Thanks, man." Tate looked at Cort.

"Whenever you need a kick in the pants, I'm happy to help." Cort dug an elbow into Tate's side, making him grunt.

"Friends like you are rare, indeed." For the first time in weeks, Tate offered him a genuine smile. "Come on, let's hit the road."

Any time his thoughts turned to Kenzie in the following days, Tate reined them in and forced himself to go into internal optimist mode, giving himself numerous pep talks.

The positive attitude he adopted seemed to work, since he placed at the next three rodeos where he competed.

After Cort placed the high score at a rodeo in California, they sauntered out to his pickup and heard someone calling their names. Fearful it might be some members of their obsessive fan club, they turned, expecting the worst. Grins creased their handsome faces as they watched Megan and Owen Montgomery hurrying toward them.

"What are you two doing here?" Tate hugged Megan and shook Owen's hand, pleased to see two friendly faces from home.

"We brought some horses to a sale. We heard you two were competing and decided to take in the rodeo before we leave tomorrow," Owen said, slapping Cort on the back.

"You guys did awesome," Megan said, patting Tate on the arm. "Are you heading out already?"

"In the morning," Cort said, readjusting his hat and leaning against the driver's side door of his pickup. "We're staying at the roadside dump on the way out of town."

Megan laughed then gave her husband a pointed look.

"What do you say to eating dinner with us?" Owen asked. "We're starving and it would be our pleasure to buy dinner for two champs."

"When you ask like that, how can we say no?" Tate grinned, happy to see his friends.

A few more people joined them as they walked to a restaurant near the rodeo grounds. By the time they found seats, their party was at an even dozen and conversation around the table was loud and lively.

When everyone seemed caught up in a story Cort shared, Megan bumped Tate's elbow to get his attention as he sat next to her.

"Are you really doing okay, Tate? I'm worried about you," Megan said, looking at him with searching eyes. He'd lost a little weight, looked a little tired, and seemed a little depressed.

Tate could see true concern on her face and hear the compassion in her voice when she spoke.

"I love Kenzie like a sister, but I'll tell you point-blank, she's being a pigheaded idiot right now and I'm plenty riled at her." Megan surprised Tate with her words.

"I appreciate that, Megan, but I know she's your best friend. She needs you and I don't want to be the reason anything comes between the two of you." Tate shrugged his broad shoulders then released a sigh as he sat back in his chair. "I care a lot about her, but I guess she didn't feel the same."

"Oh, yes, she did — she does. That whole debacle at the rodeo with your zealous fan threw her for a loop, though. I've talked until I'm blue in the face trying to convince her you didn't do anything wrong." Megan pushed fries around on her plate. The numerous times she tried to discuss the situation with Kenzie in the last month resulted in them both being extremely aggravated. "Once that girl gets something in her head, it's nearly impossible to change her mind."

"What exactly does she think happened?" Tate asked, hoping Megan could shed some light on the situation.

What Tate knew was one of his fans turned into a stalker, forcing him to get a restraining order against her when she attacked him after a rodeo in July. She showed up in Pendleton and caught him by surprise, kissing him before he realized what was happening. By the time he got her peeled off, he looked up to see Kenzie running away.

Huck tried to tell her what happened, but she refused to listen. While Cort got security, Tate ran after Kenzie but she was already gone.

Since he was the winner of the saddle bronc competition Tate stayed for the awards ceremony after the rodeo although he tried calling her multiple times. When Kenzie wouldn't answer her phone or the door, he knew she had jumped to all the wrong conclusions. It was impossible to understand why she wouldn't give him a chance to explain or listen to anyone else trying to give her the facts.

"She thinks you have a girl at every rodeo and she's just another diversion among many," Megan said, not able to look Tate in the eye as she took a sip of hot tea.

"That's insane!" Tate's raised voice drew the attention of those seated close to them. Curious gazes cast his direction made him soften his tone. "That is completely untrue."

Megan put a calming hand on his arm. She gave Owen a look and a nod, grabbed her coat and asked Tate to take a walk with her outside.

Soon, they strolled down the sidewalk in the nippy autumn air.

"Did Kenzie ever tell you about her ex-fiancé?" Megan asked as leaves crunched beneath their feet.

"She said she was engaged to a jerk and broke things off when his girlfriend turned up pregnant," Tate said, angry all over again on Kenzie's behalf.

"Did she mention he was a cowboy?" Megan asked, hoping she could make Tate understand why Kenzie ran from him.

"No. She left out that little detail." Tate shoved his hands deeper into his coat pockets, annoyed to discover one more secret Kenzie kept from him. What happened to their deal to tell the truth? She told him most of the details about her broken engagement, just not the part about the loser being a cowboy.

"I see." Megan decided to forge ahead, now that she had Tate's attention. "Did she tell you about her dad?"

"Just that he had a ranch near yours and that he died after the divorce." He wondered what her father had to do with Kenzie's inability to believe the truth about him.

When they came to a bench, Megan sat down. Tate took a seat beside her, leaning forward with his elbows resting on his knees.

"What didn't she tell me, Megan? I get the idea there is more to this story." The look he leveled at her was both imploring and wary.

"Growing up, Kenzie and her dad, David, were super close. Like two peas in a pod, they both loved ranching and that whole way of life. Kenzie's dad doted on her and she loved him right back." Megan watched the breeze blow a trail of dried leaves across the street.

Chilled, she wrapped a scarf around her neck. She took a deep breath and looked at Tate, wishing Kenzie had told him the story of her past so she wouldn't have to.

"When Kenzie was eleven, her dad started competing in local rodeos, team roping with a friend. They competed in rodeos on the weekends and worked their ranches during the week. The following year, her dad wanted to go pro, so he left the ranch in the hands of a foreman and Kenzie's mom, Susan, then hit the road. He competed for a few years and did okay. Susan and Kenzie cheered him on when he competed anywhere close to home. One weekend, they decided to surprise him. They flew to the rodeo, watched the performance then went to find him. What they found was David involved with some woman he'd just met. Apparently, he'd been cheating on Kenzie's mother since he went pro and the woman there was just one of many affairs."

Tate groaned and took off his hat, running his hand through his hair. No wonder Kenzie had a thing against cowboys, particularly rodeo cowboys. "Go on."

"Susan booked the first flight she could back home, packed their bags, drove to Portland, and started over. Kenzie was devastated. Not only had her dad lied and cheated on her mother, he'd betrayed her trust as well. Since Kenzie was their only child, David had been grooming her to take over the ranch."

Megan cleared her throat and gave Tate a guarded look. "Kenzie lived and breathed ranch life. Susan's abrupt move to the city was doubly hard on her. What David did was so wrong, so unforgivable; no one blamed Susan for leaving. David realized right away he still loved his wife and daughter but losing them was the price he paid for his philandering. He begged Susan to come back, but she refused. Dropping out of rodeo, he tried to drown his problems in alcohol. One night he got drunk, took out a pistol, and ended his life. Susan had to sell the ranch to settle his debts and a year or so later, she remarried. Kenzie abandoned her dreams of ranching and forged a new path for her life. When she agreed to marry Sonny, I think she was trying to recapture a little of what she'd lost with her dad even though she never loved him. She's had major trust issues, especially with men and particularly cowboys, ever since."

"I can understand the reasoning behind her not trusting me, but I'm not like that." Unable to fathom the pain Kenzie had gone through at such an early age, he glanced at Megan. "I would never cheat on her or hurt her."

"I know that, Tate. I think Kenzie knows that, too. But she's scared and having a hard time admitting good guys really do exist, especially after being burned twice by cheating cowboys." Megan placed her hand on his back and rubbed it like she would for a distraught child. "Just give her some time. She'll come around. I know for a fact she misses you terribly and she's completely miserable without you."

"She is?" The tidbit of information offered him encouragement

"As her best friend, I shouldn't tell you this, but she's cranky and sleep-deprived and can't seem to get past the fact that she ran away from the best thing that has ever happened to her," Megan said with a grin.

"Interesting." A glimmer of hope shined in his eyes. "I don't suppose you know where she's at right now?"

"I do, but I also know she's not ready to talk to you. She's still trying to convince herself you're guilty of everything on her list of accusations." Megan stood and smiled at Tate. "You can't push her in this. Don't try to force her to talk to you because you'll drive her further away. Kenzie is going to have to come to the conclusion she can't live without you in her own good time, so give her some space and be patient, even if she is acting like a dork."

"I'll try, but it's hard." Tate stood then they ambled back toward the restaurant.

Megan stared at Tate's handsome face, clouded with misery, and caved a little. "Her birthday is Tuesday and she'll be in Boston, but that's all I'm spilling."

The smile Tate gave Megan made her understand exactly how Kenzie had fallen under his spell. That trademark Morgan grin was all male charm and caused women to want to do whatever he asked.

"Thanks, Megan. I don't suppose you know where she's staying?"

"I just happen to have that information." Megan pulled out her cell phone and tapped in a quick text message, sending it to Tate. "And now you do too. But she better not find out it was me who tipped you off."

"You're the best." He gave her a one-armed hug as they walked back to their table.

><><

After speaking at two meetings and leading a training session, Kenzie was exhausted. Even though it was her birthday, she was miserable.

Utterly drained by keeping up a cheerful pretense, she was ready to go to her room, soak in a hot bath, and pretend she'd never met Tate Morgan. She hadn't been this depressed since her dad died.

In some ways, she felt like she was grieving, mourning a future she dared to dream that would never, ever happen.

Finally free for the evening, she returned to her room, kicked off her shoes, removed her suit jacket, and flopped back on the bed. She must have dozed because a light tapping on her door startled her awake.

Hurriedly rising, she peered through the peephole into the hall. All she could see was a huge bouquet of bright pink and white flowers.

"Miss Beckett?" the hotel staff member moved the bouquet so Kenzie could see his face and verify he was a hotel employee she'd spoken with earlier in the day.

"Yes?" Kenzie opened the door and stared at the flowers as if she'd never before seen roses and stargazer lilies. The aroma of the bouquet drifted into her room, filling it with a pleasant scent.

"Delivery for you," the bellman said. "Would you like me to set them inside somewhere?"

"No, I can take them." Kenzie accepted the flowers and placed them on the desk in the room before pulling a few dollars from her skirt pocket for a tip. "Thank you."

"Oh, I almost forgot. This is for you, too." The young man handed Kenzie a small box from a gourmet sweet shop rumored to have amazing candy.

"Thanks," Kenzie said, watching as the door closed, leaving her alone in the room with a gorgeous bouquet and a small box of chocolate truffles.

The simple message on the card she found in the flowers brought tears to her eyes:

Happy Birthday, Dewdrop. Hope you are well. Tate

How did he know where to find her? Why did he send her flowers? How did he know it was her birthday?

The only answer floating through her mind was that her supposedly best friend had turned into a traitor. If she weren't so happy to receive the flowers and candy, she'd never again speak to Megan, that meddling busybody.

Kenzie opened the box of candy and stared at the decadent pieces of chocolate, trying to decide if, in good conscience, she could keep them. The practical side of her won and she popped a piece of candy in her mouth, letting the rich chocolate melt on her tongue as she sat on her bed staring at the beautiful flowers.

Hungry for a good meal, she ordered room service and indulged in some of her favorite foods, savoring each bite. After that, she treated herself to a long soak in the tub then put on her pajamas and robe.

She sat on the bed, gazing at the flowers and thinking about Tate. A call from her mom and sisters roused her from her musings. A few friends called or sent texts with their well wishes, filling her lonely evening with cheerful messages. Their sentiments made her feel special and loved.

Megan was the last to call.

When Kenzie accused her of sharing confidential information, Megan neither denied nor confirmed it, although she did point out that anyone browsing Dew's corporate website could see what meetings she would lead. It would be easy to assume the hotels where the trainings took place would also be where Kenzie stayed.

Somewhat mollified by that information, Kenzie settled in for a good chat with her friend and was soon in a better state of mind.

"How is he, Meg?" Kenzie suddenly asked as their conversation wound down. She didn't have to say Tate's name for Megan to know whom she meant.

"He's okay, Kenz, but he's hurt and sad, and he really misses you," Megan said honestly. If she could reach through the phone and shake Kenzie, she'd do it so fast the woman's head would spin. She didn't know what it would take to get her to believe Tate was innocent of any wrongdoing, especially since the girl wouldn't listen to anything regarding the topic of Tate.

"Oh." Kenzie didn't know what else to say. She assumed Tate would have a new girlfriend, forgetting all about her.

"If you were inclined to call or send him a message, I think he'd be happy to hear from you." Megan encouraged Kenzie to do the right thing. "If you don't believe Tate, look up the police records. He really did have a restraining order taken out against that woman you saw. Huck and Cort were there when it happened."

"He did?" Kenzie asked, distracted by the word restraining order. Had anyone mentioned that detail before? So angry at the thought of Tate's betrayal, she hadn't really listened to a word anyone said in his defense.

"Kenz, you really should give him a chance to explain everything before you lose out on a wonderful guy and the chance for true happiness," Megan said then hung up the phone before Kenzie could offer any argument.

Chewing her lip as she sat on her bed, trying to decide what to do, Kenzie didn't like to think she let the bad experiences from her past cloud her ability to rationalize what really happened with Tate in Pendleton when she saw that woman kissing him.

Finally, she typed a text message to the cowboy, thanking him for the flowers and candy, hitting send before she could change her mind.

Kenzie went to sleep feeling better than she had for several weeks. The next morning, she checked her text messages before she even got out of bed, anxious to see if he replied.

His name stood out in the list of many texts she'd received. Rather than give in to the desire to read his, she hurried through the rest of them, saving his for last.

Not sure what to expect when she read his, the message gave her a moment of pause:

You're welcome. Safe travels.

The fact that he sent her such a brief and impersonal message bothered her more than if he'd sent a lengthy plea to see or speak to her again. Where was his profession of undying love and devotion? What happened to her being the center of his world?

Safe travels?

What kind of response was that?

Maybe he was over her. Maybe he was moving on. Maybe Megan didn't know as much about Tate as she implied. Why did she really care what he thought, anyway?

With a deep sigh, she shut down thoughts of Tate and shifted her focus to the day ahead.

Several days later, Kenzie flew home, half-hoping she'd run into Tate along her travels. However, she realized he was probably at his ranch for a few weeks until the finals in December. She knew from discussions during the Round-Up he planned to travel to Las Vegas with Cort.

The website she frequently checked for scores and news reported Tate was among those who'd be competing, along with Huck and Cort.

After spending time catching up on mail and assuring her neighbors everything was fine, she went to the grocery store, ran a few errands, and returned to her apartment with nothing to do.

Caught up on paperwork, she had no more out-of-town trips scheduled for the rest of the year, except for the annual corporate retreat in December. She wouldn't report to work until mid-January when Dew launched their new year with a new catalog and product line.

Restless, she decided to go for a drive. Kenzie found herself pulling up at Kent's care facility. Clueless as to what compelled her to visit the elderly man, something had urged her to see him.

No matter what happened between her and Tate, she really liked his father and enjoyed spending time with him.

Softly knocking on his door, she was saddened when no one answered. Aware that Kent was a little hard of hearing, she knocked with more force and waited. Disappointed, she started back down the hall to leave. Suddenly, Kent rounded the corner from the dining area and looked at her with delighted surprise.

"Kenzie, darlin', what are you doing here?" Kent looped his arm around hers as he kissed her cheek.

"I came to visit you." Glad to see the old man, he looked as good as he had the last time she'd visited him in September.

"Well, a visit from you calls for a celebration," Kent said, leading the way to the dining room. He got them both a cup of tea and charmed the staff into bringing them a plate of cookies as they took a seat at a table by a sunny window overlooking the courtyard. "How are you, honey?"

"I'm fine." She mustered a smile while swallowing down tears. Tate looked so much like his dad, it made her heart hurt to see the old gent. The two Morgan men shared the same smile, the same jaw and chin, the same blue eyes, although Tate's were much more intense than his father's eyes.

In some bizarre way, though, seeing Kent made her feel better, too. "The question is how have you been? You have to fill me in on who you've terrorized around here since the last time I visited."

Kent snorted and slapped his leg, taking a sip of his tea before regaling Kenzie with a round of stories that made her laugh until her sides hurt.

"Kent, you are too much. How did the folks here get along before you moved in?" Kenzie asked with a teasing smile.

"I don't know. It almost wears me out trying to keep them all on their toes." A broad grin wreathed his face as he took another cookie. He asked Kenzie about her travels as well as her plans for Thanksgiving. Although he carefully avoided any mention of Tate, she would have eagerly gobbled up any information about him the old man offered.

They visited a while longer before Kenzie decided Kent looked tired and offered to walk him back to his room. He shuffled along beside her, talking about some of the different residents on the way to his room.

At his door, she gave him a kiss on his weathered cheek and patted his arm.

"If you think you can stand my company, I'd like to come visit you again." Kenzie offered him a saucy grin.

"I'd sure like that, darlin'." Kent placed his hand on her arm. "You're like a breath of sweet, fresh air. I'd be happy to have you come anytime."

"It's a date, then." She let Kent know the next time she'd plan to see him.

As she turned to go, he took her hand and squeezed it. His fingers, shaped so much like Tate's, made her swallow hard as she gazed down at his gnarled hand. Moisture flooded her eyes as she looked up at him.

"He misses you, honey. More than you know." Kent went into his room and closed the door.

Kenzie took a deep breath and stared at the ceiling a moment, waiting for the tears to clear from her eyes before walking out to her car.

After returning home, she started baking treats for the holidays out of boredom. She rarely watched television, didn't feel like reading, and had nothing better to do with her time. She stored the goodies in resealable bags and plastic containers, placing them all in the small freezer in her laundry room. Just before Christmas, she planned to take the treats out and share them with friends.

In need of a distraction from her thoughts of Tate, she couldn't find or create enough activities to keep her mind from lingering on him.

Desperate, she left a few days later for Portland. Her plan had been to spend four days with her family for Thanksgiving, but now her trip was going to be closer to two weeks. She knew she could count on her twin sisters to keep her mind occupied with thoughts that didn't involve one devastatingly gorgeous cowboy.

Chapter Nine

Kenzie tugged her suitcase off the luggage carousel, straightened her suit jacket, and tucked an errant curl behind her ear.

Surrounded by cowboy hats everywhere she looked, she smiled. For nearly two weeks in December, Las Vegas became a playground for people who spent the majority of their time ranching and farming for a living. When the rodeo finals rolled around each year, the city got a little bit country as hordes of cowboys arrived.

She hurried toward the line for taxis and tried to keep from looking around in hopes of spying Tate or one of his friends. At the Pasco airport, as she arrived for her flight to Las Vegas, her eyes widened at the number of men wearing cowboy hats waiting in the security line.

A quick scan over the crowd confirmed Tate wasn't among them, filling her with an odd mix of disappointment and relief.

A dimple-chinned cowboy tipped his hat and held the door for her, forcing her to concede most cowboys had nice manners, even if they couldn't be trusted any farther than she could throw them.

Kenzie slid into a taxi and couldn't help but stare out the window as they drove down the strip. Despite the many trips she'd made to Las Vegas, the city never failed to make her gawk like a first-time tourist.

After paying the driver and climbing out of the car at her hotel, she took just a few steps before another handsome cowboy held the hotel door for her and offered to carry her suitcase. She declined his help with her luggage, but thanked him with a smile, aware he watched her walk away.

A tall woman dressed in heels and a business suit most likely wasn't something people working on a ranch saw every day.

Kenzie barely had time to set down her bag in her room when her phone rang. Quickly answering the call from one of her coworkers, she agreed to meet for dinner thirty minutes later.

Thoughts of the week's activities drew out her sigh.

The president of Dew, grandson of the couple who started the company, was obsessed with all things western. Since he took over the company, the annual corporate retreat that always happened at the end of the year moved to Las Vegas so he could go to the rodeo and take his top staff along.

Meetings, trainings, and brainstorming sessions were held for four days, starting early Tuesday morning with everything wrapping up Friday afternoon. The corporate staff and trainers attending the meetings knew the expectation was for them to show up in full-on business mode during the day.

Evenings were open, but all of them had a standing invitation to sit in the corporate suite at the rodeo.

Kenzie had avoided going in the past because watching the rodeo reminded her too much of her father, but she knew she had to go this year. It was impossible for her to be in town and not watch Tate ride.

Loath to admit it, she was actually looking forward to seeing the rodeo again. Her parents brought her when she was twelve and she remembered it being an amazing experience.

Hastily touching up her makeup and hair, Kenzie grabbed her purse and headed down to the hotel's lobby to meet a few of her coworkers. The women greeted each other with hugs and friendly conversation then decided where to go for dinner and piled into a taxi.

A delicious meal kept them lingering in the restaurant much longer than they planned. It was late when the group finally wandered outside to catch a cab.

A sea of cowboy hats and boot-clad feet milled through the crowds on the sidewalk in front of the restaurant. Kenzie took a step in the direction of the waiting taxi and watched Tate walk by with a lovely redhead on his arm.

Frantically ducking behind a potted plant, she remained unseen as she followed Tate's progress down the sidewalk. She'd somehow forgotten how good he looked in a pair of blue jeans and boots. Heat climbed up her neck to her cheeks as her gaze lingered on his backside.

"Good heavens, Kenzie! Do you know him?" her friend Michele asked, staring at Tate.

"Yes," Kenzie huffed, embarrassed as people around them looked from her to Tate's departing form.

"Well, why haven't you mentioned him before?" Michele asked as they got in the taxi to return to their hotel.

"There's nothing to talk about." Kenzie cut off her friend before she started asking more questions. Desperate to change the subject, she threw out a topic she knew would grab Michele's attention. "Do you know what guest speaker is lined up for the luncheon Thursday? Mitch said he heard it was going to be Jack Canfield."

"No. The speaker Thursday is…" Michele launched into a discussion of the agenda for speakers, since she was on the planning committee.

Kenzie didn't run into Tate again during the day. At night, she donned her boots and jeans and joined her coworkers to cheer him on from their private suite. There was no way Tate would know she was there.

During the team roping at Friday night's performance, Kenzie excused herself to go to the restroom and ran into Mara and Katie Powell.

"Kenzie!" Katie yelled, throwing her little arms around Kenzie's legs, greeting her with a friendly smile. "What are you doing here? Are you here to see Tate? Will you watch my daddy ride?"

"Katie, don't overwhelm her with questions." Mara hugged Kenzie and whispered in her ear. "He's not been the same since you two broke up. He really misses you."

"So I've heard." Kenzie recalled the bombshell redhead he'd been with the other evening and shook her head. "I saw for myself how much he misses me."

"What do you mean?" Mara gave Kenzie an odd look. She knew for a fact Tate hadn't been on a single date or shown any interest in anyone other than Kenzie.

"I saw him the other night with a very beautiful woman on his arm. He didn't look like he was suffering too greatly." Uncertain why she was telling this to Mara, she admittedly liked the entire Powell family the first time she met them.

"Oh," Mara finally managed to say. Surprised by this bit of news, she figured Tate probably had a good explanation for it. Besides, she couldn't blame him for not wanting to be alone. Kenzie had left him high and dry back in September.

"Will you guys be here until the bitter end?" Kenzie asked as Mara tried to keep an excited Katie from running off.

"Until the very end. How about you?" Mara thought Kenzie looked sad and tired, not at all like the girl they'd met back in Santa Fe who was excited and full of life.

"I fly out Sunday morning, so I guess I'll probably be here." It would take a natural disaster to keep her away at this point. Tate had a shot at coming out as the winner and Huck and Cort were both holding their own as well. She wanted to see if all three of them would place first.

"There's an empty seat if you want to join us," Mara offered, as she started stepping away from Kenzie due to Katie's insistent tugging on her hand. She told Kenzie what section to look in to find them.

"Thanks for the offer. I might tomorrow night, but for now, I better stay with the group," Kenzie said, quickly explaining about the corporate suite.

"Well, if you get tired of sitting in the comfy seats with your own private TVs and catered food, you're welcome to join us." Mara grinned before walking off with Katie.

Kenzie would have loved to sit with Mara and the kids, but she worried Tate or one of his friends would see her and she might end up having to deal with him face-to-face.

If that happened, she couldn't maintain her aloof demeanor. She certainly wasn't prepared to make a scene in front of everyone and she had no doubt there would definitely be a scene if she saw Tate.

At least she thought throwing her arms around him and kissing him until they both were breathless constituted a scene, because that is exactly what she could foresee happening.

Every time she saw him ride, a mixture of awe and fear cast some sort of spell over her. The opportunity to watch him every night had effectively rendered her incapable of doing anything but thinking about his next ride and hoping he'd take the top score.

As much as she'd tried to convince herself she didn't care a thing about Tate, her heart kept telling her otherwise.

><><

Tate watched wave after wave of humanity walk by the table where he sat at a Christmas vendor show, held in conjunction with the rodeo. He and a few other competitors were at a table along with a pretty girl serving as Miss Rodeo signing autographs.

In the past week, Tate signed more autographs than he had in the previous years of his career. Although his hand cramped from writing his name so many times, he still had another hour to go before his shift ended.

Tired of signing autographs and schmoozing fans, he was ready to be finished with the duty. Normally, he would have enjoyed visiting with people, but since today was the last day of the rodeo, the crowds were crazy as they filled the convention hall.

He barely managed to keep from rolling his eyes when a couple of women Cort referred to as "flouncing floozies" stopped by the table and requested he add his autograph on their chests.

Tate refused. Instead, he signed a photo for each of them and offered an impersonal smile as he sent them on their way.

As they sauntered off in what he labeled man-hunting gear of short skirts and tacky boots with low-cut, too-tight shirts, Tate glanced up to see Kenzie and an older woman glaring at him. Kenzie's eyes narrowed in disgust before she walked off.

"Kenzie!" Tate called, coming to his feet as she tried to hurry away. Trapped behind the table by all the people waiting for autographs, Tate jumped over the top of it and pushed his way through the crowd until he caught Kenzie by the arm and grabbed her hand.

"What are you doing here?" he asked when she swung around, branding him with a searing look.

"Shopping," she said brusquely. She held up a few bags in the hand that Tate hadn't captured in his.

"Not here at the show, I meant here in Vegas." Tate noticed Kenzie's friend giving him an approving glance.

"Our corporate retreat is here this week." Kenzie yanked her hand away from Tate. It took all her willpower not to wipe it on her jeans, as if she'd touched something filthy. Finally considering the idea that she may have been wrong about calling him a cheating skunk, the sight of him with his adoring fans renewed her anger and her resolve to stay away from him. "Now if you'll excuse us…"

Tate stepped in front of them, blocking their departure. "I haven't met your friend." He gave Kenzie a charming smile before turning it toward her friend and holding out his hand. "I'm Tate Morgan."

"Mr. Morgan, Michele Ponti. It's a pleasure to meet you. We watched you ride all week and we'll be cheering you on tonight." Michele wondered how Kenzie knew Tate and why she wasn't falling all over the cute cowboy who seemed to hold more than a passing interest in her.

"Thanks, Miss Ponti." Tate smiled, courteously touching the brim of his hat.

"Michele, please. Call me Michele," the woman gushed, in awe of the gorgeous rodeo star smiling at her.

"I appreciate the support, Michele. It's going to come down to the wire to see who takes the title." Tate offered an arm to Michele and held the other out to Kenzie. "If you'd like to come back to the table, I'll sign a photo for you."

"I'd like that very much," Michele said with a giggle. Fifteen years older than Kenzie, she had a fun-loving outlook that sometimes made her seem like the younger of the two. "It looks like you're quite popular today."

"I guess." Tate took two photos from the stack on the table and signed one for Michele before offering the other to Kenzie.

Dramatically sighing, she snatched it from him and stuffed it in the pink bag slung over her shoulder. "Are you sure you wouldn't rather sign some part of my anatomy?" Kenzie bit out, glowering at him.

"Darlin', I'd be happy to later, in private, if you'll meet me after the rodeo so we can talk, but I can't do that here. It goes against my personal policy of only signing photos." Much to his satisfaction, the heated look he gave her made her fidgety.

"Point taken." She dipped her head his direction. "We better let you return to your fans."

"I suppose I should get back to it," Tate said, wanting to ditch his duties the rest of the afternoon and walk around with Kenzie. "Have you visited all the vendor booths?"

"No, we're just getting started." Kenzie edged away from Tate's table.

"In that case, I won't keep you." Tate tipped his hat to Michele and then Kenzie. She'd only taken a few steps when he called to her. She stopped and looked back over her shoulder as he approached her. "Would you mind taking a look at this booth and letting me know if you think Pop would like one?"

"One what?" Kenzie took the vendor map that he held out to her, noticing a booth number circled in red.

"You'll see when you get to the booth," Tate said with a grin that made her nod her head in agreement. "Please, I'd really like your opinion. I know Pop's taken quite a liking to you."

"The feeling is mutual," Kenzie said, unable to keep herself from smiling when he mentioned his father. "Your dad is wonderful. I'd be happy to check out whatever this is and let you know what I think."

"Thanks." Although people walking by bumped him on both sides, Tate watched Kenzie and Michele until they disappeared into the crowd.

SHANNA HATFIELD

Kenzie could feel Tate's gaze on her back and turned down a side aisle as quickly as possible, tugging Michele along with her.

"You just hold it right there, missy." Michele pulled Kenzie to a stop in front of a booth selling metal wall art. "We aren't taking another step until you tell me all about that very handsome cowboy who seems quite taken with you."

"There's not much to tell," Kenzie said, pretending interest in a welcome sign cut from metal and juniper wood. "We met at the airport in May. We often catch the same flights. I thought we might have a future together until I caught him kissing some trollop at a rodeo. End of story."

Michele looked stunned for a moment then gathered her composure. "Was he kissing her or was she kissing him?" Michele eyed Kenzie. She'd known the woman for years and she'd never seen her worked up like she was around Tate Morgan. It was plain to see the strong attraction and chemistry sizzling between the two, whether either of them wanted to admit it.

"What does it matter? The point is, I caught him with her and he knew from the get-go that kind of stuff wouldn't fly with me." Kenzie ambled toward another booth.

"Kenzie, I've been married, quite happily I might add, for almost twenty-two years," Michele said, giving Kenzie a knowing look. "I have a pretty good idea of what love looks like and you both are wearing it. Not to mention the sparks you can practically see flying between you two."

Despite her annoyance with Michele, Kenzie couldn't keep from grinning. "You really are dramatic, you know that? And a little crazy. Maybe even something of a hopeless romantic."

Looping her arm around Kenzie's, Michele tugged her toward a clothing booth. "Possibly, but you have to admit, I keep things lively for you."

"That you do," Kenzie said as she picked up a blouse she knew she had to have.

Two hours later, Kenzie sat on a bench outside, keeping watch over a pile of shopping bags, while Michele was in the restroom. While she waited for her friend to return, she sent Tate a quick text message telling him she fully approved of the vintage milk cans painted with farm and ranch scenes he liked for his dad.

He sent back a message asking if she was still there and she replied that she was about to take a taxi with Michele to their hotel.

She'd barely closed her phone and stuck it in her purse when Tate burst out the doors and hurried her direction.

Surprised to see him, his sapphire blue gaze pulled at her, drawing her into a place she wasn't sure she'd ever want to leave. She hated to admit it, but she'd missed him these past few months with an intensity that was nearly crippling at times.

"Hey." Her voice sounded soft and breathless as she got to her feet.

"Hi there." Tate took her hand in his and twined their fingers together, studying her face for a reaction.

Kenzie thought about yanking her hand away, but Tate's callused palm against hers felt too familiar, too right.

"I'm glad I caught you before you left." The smile he gave her made her knees as feeble as her resolve to ignore him, forcing her to sit on the bench. He hunkered down in front of her, still holding her hand. "Would you have an early dinner with me before the rodeo or can I see you afterward? Please, Kenzie? I would really appreciate the opportunity to speak with you."

"I… um… I just don't…" Kenzie wavered between what her head told her to do and what her heart wanted to do. The look on Tate's face pushed her heart ahead as the winner.

"Please?" Tate pleaded.

As he gazed at her with an overpowering intensity, she knew there was no way she could possibly refuse, even if she could have forced the word "no" past her traitorous lips.

"Okay," she said, nodding her head. When he kissed her cheek, his familiar scent filled her nose, stimulating her senses, and making heat ripple through her midsection. "I'll see you after the rodeo. I don't think you should let yourself get distracted before."

"What are you planning that would distract me?" Tate asked with a cocky grin and twinkling eyes.

"Nothing and you know it, Tate Morgan! Why, I should…" Kenzie jerked her hand away from his.

"Give me a good luck kiss before I ride tonight," Tate interrupted, winking at her as he got to his feet and pulled her up with him.

Kenzie looked at him for a long moment before she smiled.

"I suppose I could do that." Kenzie realized kissing him was likely to wreak havoc on the carefully constructed pretense of normality she'd built since September.

"Great. I'll come find you before I ride." Once again taking her hand in his, he squeezed it gently. "Where are you sitting?"

"Dew has a corporate suite at the event, but Mara Powell invited me to sit with them. I thought I'd take her up on the offer tonight." She looked forward to seeing Mara and the kids, sitting with them as they cheered on Huck, Tate and Cort.

"Perfect. I know exactly where to find you." Tate tipped his hat at Michele as she walked up beside Kenzie.

"It was very nice to meet you, Michele. And you, Dewdrop, I'll see later."

Michele and Kenzie, along with a few other women, watched Tate walk off with a swaggering step.

"Dewdrop?" Michele finally asked, giving Kenzie a teasing look. Raising an eyebrow, she took note of the girl's flustered state. "You've got to tell me how you acquired that nickname."

"Oh, just get in the cab." Kenzie nudged her friend toward the taxi's open door.

Back at the hotel, Kenzie was too wound up to rest before the rodeo. Instead, she repacked her suitcase, gathering her training materials and stowing them in her oversized bag before taking a long shower.

After dressing in a new blouse and her favorite jeans along with a pair of cowboy boots, she spent twice as long as usual styling her hair. She recalled how much Tate liked it hanging long and loose, leaving it down in soft curls. Mindful of how much she wanted to feel his hands in it again, she almost gathered it all up into a knot. At the last minute, she couldn't quite talk herself into doing it.

Since she still had time to kill, she dug around in her bag for a notebook to write down some training ideas. Instead of the notebook, she pulled out the photograph of Tate.

Although it was black and white, she could imagine the intense blue of his eyes, the golden tan of his skin, and the light brown of his wavy hair. He leaned against a fence with his hat tipped back, leather chaps over his muscled legs, looking way too sensuous for Kenzie's raw emotions to handle.

Tenderly tracing her finger along his face, she released a sigh and carefully put the photo back in her bag between two training workbooks to keep it from being wrinkled or damaged.

She sank down on the couch and decided to keep an open mind when she talked to Tate later. Maybe there was some truth to the story that he hadn't been cheating on her in Pendleton. If it was true, if he really did have a stalker, she owed him the world's biggest apology.

After gathering her purse and phone, she went down to the lobby to wait with Michele and a few others for the shuttle that would take them to the rodeo.

A while later, after arriving at the center where the rodeo was held, Michele convinced Kenzie to wander one last time through the booths set up outside. They purchased hot, doughy pretzels and cold drinks then strolled inside to meet the rest of their group.

Kenzie settled into her seat in the corporate suite and hung out there with her coworkers prior to the rodeo starting. When she finished her pretzel, she told Michele she was going to sit with a friend.

"Make sure you say hello to Tate for me." Michele gave Kenzie a taunting smile.

"Tate? Tate Morgan?" Tom Bridgeland, president of the Dew Corporation, leaned around his wife to pin Kenzie with an inquisitive stare. "You know Tate Morgan?"

"Yes, sir," she said, trying not to feel like a kid caught with her hand in the cookie jar.

"You've been holding out on us, Kenzie." Although his tone sounded scolding, his bright smile revealed his delight at discovering a link to one of the rodeo stars.

"Yes, sir." Kenzie noticed all eyes in the suite suddenly turned to her.

"Do you think I could meet him?" Tom asked in a tone just short of pleading.

"I can ask him." Kenzie hoped Tate wouldn't mind meeting her boss.

"That would be great." Tom excitedly slapped his hat against his leg. "Let me know what he says."

Kenzie sent Tate a quick text message. He promptly replied that he'd be happy to shake hands with her boss. After giving him directions on where to find the corporate suite, she sat back down and waited.

When he arrived a few minutes later, Cort and Huck accompanied him. All three signed Tom's program, as well as the programs of several other people.

Kenzie could hardly take her eyes off Tate as he laughed and talked with her boss and peers.

He was one good-looking man, especially with his light brown hair peeping out from the brim of his black hat, a charming smile, and broad shoulders that looked like he could handle anything. The shirt he wore intensified the blue in his eyes while a pair of jeans that looked like they were custom-made for him drew more than one set of female eyes to his fine rear end.

Lost in her thoughts of how good he looked, Kenzie was surprised when Tate took her elbow in his hand, bringing her to her feet. His unique scent tantalized her senses while sparks shot up her arm at his touch.

"You all won't mind if we steal Kenzie away for a while, will you?" Tate asked, his eyes sparkling like bright jewels and dimples dancing in his handsome face.

"Not at all." Tom shook Tate's hand again. "It was a true pleasure to meet you boys. Good luck tonight."

"Thank you, sir." Tate tipped his hat to the group before he took Kenzie's hand in his, following Cort and Huck out of the suite and over to the section of seats where Mara and the kids waited.

"Look who we found hobnobbing with the bigwigs," Huck said as Katie jumped up and threw her little arms around Kenzie.

"Kenzie! You came!" Katie enthusiastically tugged Kenzie into the seat next to hers. Huck picked up Hunter and held him on his lap while Mara held the baby.

"It'll be nice to catch up with you," Mara said with a warm smile. "I'm so glad you came to sit with us, Kenzie."

"I'm looking forward to catching up with you, too." Kenzie smiled as Katie climbed onto her lap and traced the glimmering sequins on the yoke of her shirt.

"You're so pretty," Katie said in a singsong voice as she wiggled one foot, clad in a bright red boot. "Just like a princess."

"That she is." Tate winked at Kenzie as he took Katie's seat next to her.

Cort squatted down on the edge of the aisle to visit for a moment then headed off to prepare for the last round of competition.

"You better get down there, too, man," Huck said, nodding his head toward Tate. "You want to be ready to take the title tonight."

"I'm more than ready." Tate picked up Katie and bounced her wildly on his legs before setting her on her feet. Her giggles echoed around them as Tate removed his hat and put it up to block the view of anyone watching.

He intended to give Kenzie a quick, chaste kiss. However, the sparks sizzling between them exploded and the kiss rapidly escalated into something driven, demanding, and utterly amazing. His free hand wrapped around the back of her neck, burrowing beneath her hair, and she leaned into his chest.

Tate finally pulled back, slapped his hat on his head and kissed Kenzie's cheek. While he appeared to recover quickly from the intensity of the kiss, Kenzie had a hard time regaining her mental balance as she stared into his eyes. They sent her messages she was afraid to interpret but couldn't ignore.

"How could I lose with a good luck kiss like that?" he teased, satisfied their kiss put the bright blush on Kenzie's cheeks and left her looking slightly dazed.

"Good luck," Kenzie finally managed to say, still trying to gather the frayed edges of her composure together after that earth-shattering melding of their lips. "Ride 'em, cowboy."

"You can bet I will, Dewdrop." Tate hurried down the steps and out of sight.

"Kenzie, why is your face all..." Katie started to ask, but was cut off by her father's hand over her mouth.

"You just never mind, kiddo." Huck shot Kenzie a knowing grin that made her flush an even brighter shade of red.

As the rodeo began, Kenzie was grateful Huck traded seats with her so she and Mara could visit.

They laughed and chatted until Cort competed in the steer wrestling. He placed first and the score put him in second place overall for the event.

When the announcer declared it time for the saddle bronc riding to begin, Kenzie grinned at Mara. She turned her attention to the chutes, waiting to catch a glimpse of Tate.

Drawing Twister, Tate was the fourth to ride. Kenzie recalled watching him master the horse in Santa Fe. She hoped he would earn as good a score tonight as he had then. If he did, it would move him far ahead of the competition.

The horse charged out of the chute in a burst of fury, swiveling and bucking wildly.

In what seemed like slow motion, Kenzie felt a shiver slide down her spine as she watched Tate. She loved to see him ride, to watch his smooth, fluid movements on the horse.

The fringe on his chaps flew up and down. She imagined she could hear the slapping sound it made each time it connected with his leg. His left hand tightly gripped the rein while his right hand danced in the air with each buck of the beast beneath him.

Twister executed a rapid turn before jumping high into the air. He whipped his huge body around on the way down and the velocity of the action caused him to roll over on his back, on top of Tate.

The horse quickly gained his feet as the buzzer sounded and raced around the arena while Tate sprawled in a motionless heap.

Screams gave way to hushed silence as Kenzie surged to her feet. Cort and a few other cowboys rushed out to Tate, but he remained unresponsive and unmoving on the arena floor. Her breath came in tight, sharp gasps as she prayed he would be fine.

Huck set down Hunter, grabbed her hand, and they hurried out of the stands, running through the masses of people in the corridor toward the medical area.

Nothing could happen to Tate.

It just couldn't.

In spite of every effort to keep from admitting it, she was completely and hopelessly in love with him.

Chapter Ten

Still trying to recover from the shock of discovering Kenzie was not only in Las Vegas, but also at the rodeo watching him, Tate couldn't wipe the cheesy grin off his face. He'd been sporting it for several hours — ever since he ran into Kenzie that afternoon.

He'd taken plenty of flak for it the past thirty minutes as he stretched and worked his muscles, waiting for his turn to ride.

His friends all knew he'd gone through a rough time during autumn when his girl left him, but it was easy to see Tate was on top of the world as he waited for his final ride in the rodeo.

Although he experienced a great season on the rodeo circuit, two other riders had done equally well. They were all so close in their ranking, who walked away the winner was going to be anybody's guess as it came down to this last ride.

While he tried to center his thoughts on taking the championship title, a pair of warm brown eyes and rosy lips disrupted his focus.

In the weeks since Kenzie ran away from him, he'd been plagued by a constant pain in the region of his heart. Even after renewing his commitment to taking the title, the pain remained, eating away at him. Right up until she smiled at him at the Christmas vendor show.

Seeing Kenzie again made it perfectly clear to Tate he needed her. Without her, his life seemed so empty and incomplete. In the short time they spent together that afternoon, he'd suddenly found a part of himself that had been missing since September.

From the way she looked at him earlier, he hoped they had a chance of resuming their relationship and moving forward together.

The kiss they shared made him think he still had a shot at winning her heart. If it rattled her half as much as it had him, there was definitely something undeniably powerful between them.

"You ready to do this?" Cort asked, slapping Tate on the back as he stepped beside him, rousing him from his visions of Kenzie.

"What do you think?" Tate adjusted the buckle on his chaps, floating on adrenaline and hope.

"I think you're ready to take home the title and then see about chasing after one very attractive business skirt." Cort referred to the suits Kenzie usually wore. "For the record, she also makes a smokin' hot cowgirl."

Tate gave Cort a cautionary look then thumped him on the shoulder. "Just keep in mind she's already taken, man."

Cort grinned then hustled off to compete. Tate stood on a gate and cheered when Cort took the high score for the night, placing him second overall.

Returning his attention to getting ready for his ride, it wasn't long before he walked up to the chutes and prepared to mount Twister. Tate hoped history would repeat itself tonight, considering the score he got the last time he rode the horse.

Softly talking to the animal, Tate asked him to give the ride his best. When the horse bobbed his head, Tate took that as agreement on his part.

Intent on blocking the other riders and their scores from his mind, he took a series of cleansing breaths, slid on the back of the horse, and found his center. After tightening the rein in his left hand, he pulled down his hat, took one more deep breath and nodded his head for the gate to open. "Let's do it!"

Right out of the chute, something inside Twister seemed to snap as the big animal leaped and contorted beneath Tate. It took every ounce of concentration and skill on his part to stay in the saddle. He tried to anticipate what the animal would do next.

Twister suddenly shot up in the air then flung his body to the side. The force of the action carried him completely over. Before Tate could jump out of the way, Twister crashed on top of him and the world went black.

When he came to, Tate heard voices close around him, although the words sounded muffled. As he struggled to gather his thoughts together, the last thing he remembered was Twister coming over backward and the fear he'd be crushed beneath the horse.

Since the gritty taste of dirt filled his mouth and he could smell horses, manure, and sweat, he went with the assumption that he was lying on the ground in the arena.

Quickly taking stock of his aches and pains, his head throbbed, it was hard to breathe, and his left arm felt like someone clamped it in a vise. His left knee also hurt, though not with the intensity of his arm.

Hesitant to open his eyes and visually assess the damage, he finally pried one eye open then the other. Cort hovered above him, worry etching lines across his face.

"You okay, man?" Cort's voice was laced with concern as he removed Tate's mouth guard so he could talk.

"Depends," Tate managed to say through the jaw he clenched against a wave of pain, noticing several other faces above him.

"On what?" Cort moved back slightly to allow more room for the medical team.

"Did I score?" Tate asked, hoping the horse didn't go down until after he'd ridden the required eight seconds.

"No." Cort shook his head. He retrieved Tate's hat from the arena floor and slapped it lightly against his leg, dislodging a cloud of dust. "The buzzer went off just as Twister got to his feet. I think they'll give you a re-ride if you can manage it."

"Whether he gets one or not, there is no way he's riding again tonight," one of the medic team said. "From the way you look, I'd say missing the re-ride is the least of your problems."

"Just tape me up and I'll be fine. Tell the judges I'm asking for a re-ride." Tate battled the urge to be ill right there in the arena. His head pounded in rhythm with his heart and each beat made him dizzy and nauseous. When it became apparent he couldn't get to his feet and walk out of the arena, Tate was loaded on a stretcher and hauled out. He waved to the crowd with his good hand and received a roaring round of applause.

"Let Tate know what you think about all his hard work here at the rodeo, folks. It's gonna be hard for that cowboy to end the year like this," the announcer said, encouraging more clapping and cheers as Tate was carried through a gate and out of sight.

After rushing him to the treatment area, the medics removed his protective vest, chaps and shirt then split open the leg of his jeans. The doctors probed his side when he heard Huck's voice outside the door.

"She's family, just let her in." Huck sounded aggravated. He strode into the room with Kenzie beside him and stopped next to Cort.

"Hey, Dewdrop," Tate said, trying to muster a grin which looked more like a grimace as pain wracked through his body. Despite everything, her presence had a calming effect on him. "I might need to take a rain check on our dinner tonight."

"You think?" Kenzie smiled around the tears threatening to spill from her eyes.

A fine coating of dust from the arena covered Tate's hair along with his face, which looked unnaturally pale beneath the dirt. His eyes were glassy and he clenched his jaw so tightly, she could see the cords stand out in his neck.

Somewhat unnerved by his bare torso, Kenzie moved to stand by Tate's head and hold his good hand. Huck quietly said something to Cort then ran out the door to get ready for his upcoming ride.

The doctor let out a relieved sigh following an examination and X-rays. "You've got a mild concussion, fractured arm, three cracked ribs, and a wrenched knee." The doctor crossed his arms over his chest. "Considering how that horse fell, you're lucky he didn't do more damage. We'll splint your arm, brace your knee and ice your ribs. Other than that, there isn't much else we can do for you, son."

Tate tried to sit up and sucked in a gulp of air as his ribs protested. Kenzie watched as the doctor helped him into a sitting position. "I need to…"

"You aren't going back out there. There is no way on God's green earth you can ride anything else tonight, and not for several weeks until your injuries mend." The doctor gave Tate a stern look.

"But if I don't ride again and score, I'm…"

Cort shook his head at Tate, cutting off whatever else he planned to say. "Still going to place, it just won't be first."

Disappointment settled over Tate like a wet blanket.

"I'm sorry, man." Cort started to thump his shoulder then thought better of it, dropping his hand to his side.

Tate kept his mouth shut, clamping his lips together to fight both his pain and his anger. Not a single person in the room, including his best friend, would let him get back on a horse.

Before he could further reflect on his misfortune, the doctor put a splint on his arm. Unable to do anything but endure his ministrations, the pain medication kicked in and his body relaxed while his eyes began to droop.

"Just rest awhile, Tate." The doctor helped him recline on a narrow bed then walked Cort and Kenzie toward the door.

Tate raised his head and looked at them with a pleading gaze. "Tell Huck to nail it."

Cort nodded his head and walked out the door with the doctor and Kenzie.

"We'll hold him here for a while, make sure we didn't miss anything, and keep an eye on that concussion. You two might as well go watch Huck ride. When you come back, we'll discuss getting Tate home as quickly and with as much comfort as possible."

"Thanks, sir." Cort took Kenzie's arm and guided her back to the arena. Returning to where Mara and the kids sat, they answered her questions and waited anxiously for Huck to make his ride.

Kenzie watched in wonder and admiration as Huck not only had an incredible ride, but also stayed on the bull long past the time the buzzer sounded, his hand waving in the air triumphantly.

The crowd surged to its feet, whistling and shouting their approval, knowing Huck rode the extra time for his injured friend.

As a reporter shoved a mic in his face a few minutes after the ride that garnered him the championship title, Huck looked in the camera and smiled, answering the reporter's numerous questions. Asked about riding the bull the additional time Huck simply said, "that's for Tate," touched his fingers to the brim of his hat with a brief tug and walked off.

Kenzie certainly hoped someone recorded the rodeo or had shot a video of Huck's ride to share with Tate. She could probably find it on YouTube in a day or two.

As she mused over modern technology, her phone rang with a number she recognized belonging to Tate's father.

"Hi, Kent. This is Kenzie," she said. The old cowboy was no doubt sitting up watching the rodeo on television. She plugged her other ear with her finger in an attempt to cut down on the surrounding noise then pressed the phone closer, trying to hear what Tate's father said.

"How's my boy?" Kent asked, his voice sounding worried and raspy.

"He's going to be okay." She adopted a cheerful tone. "He's got a broken arm, a few cracked ribs, a wrenched knee, and a concussion. The doctor said he'll be fine once everything mends."

"That's a relief." Kent released a sigh. "Where's he at now?"

"With the medic team. They gave him some painkillers and he's resting." Curious how Kent knew she'd be with Tate, she asked. "How did you know to call me?"

"Tate called earlier to say he ran into you today and was planning on taking you out to dinner later." Kenzie could hear the smile in his voice. "That boy was pleased as punch to see you again."

"I was happy to see him, too," Kenzie admitted as much to Kent as to herself. "I'll let you know if there's anything new to report, but from what they've said so far, he'll be just fine. He's plenty mad about not getting his re-ride, though."

Kent chuckled. "I'm betting he's more than mad. He probably thought they could tape him up and turn him loose."

"Something like that," Kenzie said, realizing Kent knew his son well. She imagined Tate probably inherited some of his tenacity from his father.

"Keep watch over that boy of mine, honey, and let me know how things look tomorrow," Kent said, his relief carrying through to Kenzie that she was there for Tate.

"I will. Good night, sir."

"Good night, sweetheart." Kent disconnected the call.

The Powell family and Kenzie cheered enthusiastically as the winners entered the arena. Kenzie fought back her tears, knowing how hard Tate worked to be there with them, how close he came to taking the title. Sniffling, she turned a watery smile to Mara who nodded her head.

While Huck spoke with more reporters, Cort picked up Hunter. Mara carried baby Bree, leaving Kenzie to hold Katie's hand as they walked out of the stands. Huck met them at the door, taking his son from Cort and shaking his hand.

"That was quite a ride, Mr. Powell." Cort grinned at Huck, slapping him on the back. "Congrats on winning the title again this year."

"Thanks, man. Some congrats are in order for you, too. Second place is nothing to sneeze at." Huck kissed Mara and his two girls before accepting Kenzie's hug and words of congratulations.

"So what do we know about Tate?" Huck asked as he followed Kenzie and Mara to the medical center.

"That he'll be fine but it's going to take some time to heal." Cort looked at Huck and shook his head as they entered the medical center. Tate wasn't going to be happy about being laid up with injuries when he would no doubt be ready to tackle a new year on the circuit and come out on top.

Huck looked thoughtful a moment before responding. "We're all sorry for Tate. He worked so hard for the title and to lose it at the last second seems so unfair."

"Yes, it does." Kenzie ruffled Katie's hair when the little girl leaned against her, wrapping her arms around her leg and holding on.

"Did you see my daddy ride?" Katie asked, still wound up from all the excitement.

"I sure did." Kenzie knelt down so she was on eye level with the child. "He did a great job, didn't he?"

"Yep. My daddy's the best," Katie said, puffing up with pride. "Everybody said so. He gets the trophy and everything!"

"Congratulations again, Huck. You certainly deserved it." Kenzie smiled at the champion bull rider then stood when the doctor entered the room and offered them an encouraging smile.

"Tate's a lucky man, considering what happened. I can think of a few dozen ways this could have gone much, much worse. His concussion should be fine in a day or two, and his ribs should be better in a week to ten days. His left arm has a fracture with some swelling. We put a splint on it but as soon as the swelling goes down, his doctor will most likely cast it. His knee has a slight tear in the cartilage. Nothing that needs surgery. Some rest, ice, and a compression bandage should take care of it. I'd like him to see his regular doctor in a day or two, just to make sure everything is on the mend."

A collective sigh of relief echoed through the room and the doctor again smiled. "There really isn't anything further we can do for him. Was he planning on driving or flying home?"

"Driving." Cort was privy to Tate's travel plans. "He was supposed to leave with me tomorrow."

"Where are you boys headed?"

"Boise, Idaho." The ten-hour drive wouldn't be good for Tate. Even after they reached Boise, Tate would still need to get to Kennewick from there.

"I'd rather he waited a few days, but I've already concluded that won't happen. It would make me much more comfortable releasing him if we can get him on a flight home. The sooner he can be restful, the faster he'll start his recovery." The doctor looked around the room. "He's going to be pretty sore and tender for a while and will need some basic care, like getting ice for his knee, arm and ribs, keeping an eye on his concussion, making sure he doesn't try to lift anything."

"I can try to get him on my flight," Kenzie heard herself say as she looked at the doctor. "I was going home tomorrow anyway, but my flight leaves early in the morning."

"See if you can get him a ticket," the doctor said, knowing the sooner they could get Tate on his way home, the better for everyone. The trip would be unpleasant at best, but knowing cowboys as well as he did, he knew Tate wouldn't laze around a hotel room until he felt well enough to travel. "You'll need a wheelchair for him. Be sure to let the ticket agent know that when you call. I'll give you a list of things you can do to help ease his travel experience as well as provide care for the next week."

"Kenzie, are you sure you want to do this?" Mara asked, placing a hand on Kenzie's arm, giving her an uncertain glance. Considering the fact she hadn't even been speaking to Tate twenty-four hours ago, they all looked at her with apprehension.

"I'm sure," Kenzie said, determined to help the wounded man as best she could. "I'm flying the same direction anyway."

"I could park my truck and fly him home then come back to get it." Cort ran a hand through his already disheveled hair.

"There's no need for that." Adamantly, Kenzie shook her head. "I can get him home. I promise."

"If you're sure…" Huck held a sleeping Hunter against his chest. "We can make other arrangements if you'd rather not mess with this."

"I wouldn't call helping out a friend 'messing with this.' You can trust me to get him home." Kenzie smiled reassuringly from Huck to Cort. "It'll be fine. No problem."

Huck and Mara left to put the kids to bed before Huck had to attend the award ceremony held at one of the hotels while Cort and Kenzie went over a list of suggestions from the doctor that might help Tate feel more comfortable.

Finally rousing Tate and checking him one more time, the doctor handed Kenzie his pain pills while Cort went to get his truck. With Tate's arm in a sling, they draped his shirt around his shoulders and helped him into a wheelchair. The doctor wheeled Tate outside and Cort helped hoist him into the pickup.

"Good luck to all three of you," the doctor said, shaking his head as he took the chair back inside, knowing they'd all need it. He'd seen enough injured cowboys to know the "suck it up" mentality made them quite a challenge for a caregiver to handle.

Chapter Eleven

Cort parked the truck at the hotel's front entrance then hurried around the truck. He took the wheelchair one of the hotel staff brought out, moving it close to the passenger door.

Kenzie had called ahead and asked the concierge to have a chair ready when they arrived. She climbed out on Cort's side of the truck and ran around to offer her assistance.

Tate's face was a shade somewhere between green and gray as they helped him into the chair and wheeled him inside. Cort handed Kenzie his room key and ran back out to move his truck while the bellman pushed Tate's wheelchair to the elevator.

When they reached his floor, Kenzie was thankful the room wasn't far down the hall. She swiped the key and held the door as the helpful young man wheeled Tate into the room.

Fully expecting a messy space with clothes and guy stuff everywhere, the room was surprisingly neat.

"Which bed is yours, Tate?" Kenzie asked as the bellman helped Tate to his feet. He pointed to the one closest to the door. Kenzie hurried to fold back the covers and turn down the sheet then glanced at Tate's dirt-covered clothes. For one night, it wouldn't really matter if he went to bed dirty, she tried not to think about the grime in his hair and coating his jeans.

Using what little strength his legs had, Tate slid onto the bed and would have continued to the floor if Kenzie hadn't grabbed his good arm and held him upright.

"Come on, cowboy, stay with me just a little longer," she said, watching sweat break out on his upper lip and trickle along his forehead as he tried to scoot further back on the mattress.

"Can I get anything, miss?" the bellman asked, helping settle Tate on the bed.

"Ice. Can you please get us some ice? And maybe a stack of hand towels?" Kenzie asked over her shoulder, dropping her purse on Cort's bed.

She turned back to Tate and divested him of his hat and boots. Carefully removing his shirt, she looked at the variety of bruises beginning to discolor his skin. A large one on his side marked the spot of his cracked ribs. Every breath Tate breathed, every movement he made had to hurt.

Tate collapsed against the pillows, groaned and swallowed hard, looking like he was about to be ill. Kenzie rushed into the bathroom and got him a glass of water along with a damp washcloth.

Gingerly, she held up his head while he took a drink then wiped his face with the cloth.

Cort arrived, followed by the bellman carrying a bucket of ice and towels as well as some resealable plastic bags.

"I thought these might be helpful," he said, handing her the bags and setting the ice and towels on the stand by the bed.

"Thank you so much." Kenzie began digging in her purse for a tip, but Cort paid the man then asked him to make sure they had the wheelchair available for Tate to use bright and early in the morning.

When the bellman left, Cort walked over to the bed. "The doc said to give him another dose of meds then let him sleep." Cort refilled Tate's glass and held his head while Kenzie shook out pills and put them in Tate's mouth. He drank enough water to swallow then seemed to lose consciousness.

"I hate to ask this, Kenzie, but I've got to go to the awards ceremony." Cort offered her an imploring look. "Can you stay with him awhile? I promise I'll hurry."

"It's fine, Cort. I know you need to go." She smiled at Tate's faithful friend. "Go on and don't worry about us. With the way he's out of it, I'm sure things will be quiet until you get back."

"Are you sure you don't mind?"

"Not at all." She eyed Cort's dirt-streaked pants and shirt. "You might want to change, though."

"Good idea." Cort rummaged through a suitcase then took clothes into the bathroom, closing the door behind him. Kenzie heard the shower running and Cort emerged a few minutes later in clean clothes, toweling the last of the water from his hair. "I'll be back as quick as I can."

"I know you will." Kenzie tipped her head at him and grinned. "Have fun, just don't enjoy yourself too much."

Cort laughed and finger-combed his black hair, settling his hat on his head and pulling on a pair of polished boots. "I really will hurry back as soon as I can." He tossed a concerned look Tate's direction before hurrying out the door.

"Well, cowboy, looks like it's just me and you." Kenzie removed Tate's sling so he could rest more comfortably. She stepped into the bathroom and ran hot water over the cloth she'd used earlier on his face. Quietly returning to the bed, she sponged off his exposed skin, wiping away dirt and sweat. She started with his head and worked until his hair was clean then continued down his neck, across his shoulders and along his chest to his jeans.

Tate would rest more comfortably without them on, but she refused to be the one to remove them.

She did unfasten his belt buckle, hoping it made him a little more comfortable. After spreading open the ripped leg of his jeans, she wiped the skin of his hard thigh down to his shin, then removed both his socks and wiped his feet.

A wry grin curved her lips upward as she stared at the ruined jeans. It was a shame to see them destroyed when they fit Tate to perfection.

Hurriedly slamming the brakes on her thoughts before they drifted somewhere she didn't want them to go, she grabbed extra pillows off the closet shelf and placed them beneath Tate's arm and knee. After filling resealable bags with ice, she covered Tate's skin with hand towels then gently set the ice against his ribs and knee.

The next hour was spent getting Tate a ticket on her flight and arranging details to ensure his travel would be as painless as possible.

Not knowing what else to do, she sat down in the one armchair in the room and grabbed the TV remote. She muted the volume and flipped through the channels until she came across a news report showing Tate's ride. The crash looked even worse on television. She sent a prayer heavenward, grateful he was still alive with relatively minor injuries.

Exhaustion overtook her. Her eyes wouldn't stay open so she decided to rest them for just a minute. The next thing she knew, Cort stood over her, grinning.

"Told you I'd hurry," he said, glancing at the clock. He'd been gone less than two hours and part of that time was fighting his way through traffic then escaping a group of ardent admirers.

"How's he doing?" Cort gave Kenzie a hand as she got out of the chair and walked closer to Tate's bed.

"He's been asleep since you left," she said, running a hand over Tate's head. He looked peaceful as he slept. The pills the doctor gave him really knocked him out, which was probably for the best.

"Looks like you cleaned him up." Cort observed Tate no longer looked or smelled as if he'd wallowed in the dirt. "Too bad he wasn't awake to enjoy his sponge bath."

Kenzie flushed as she picked up her purse, glaring narrowly at Cort.

"I'll keep watch over him tonight. Do you want me to run you over to your hotel?" Cort asked as she stepped closer to the door.

"No. I can walk. It's just across the street." Kenzie gave Tate one last glance. "I'll leave putting on his jammies to you." Kenzie shot Cort a sassy grin.

He chuckled and shook his head. "Party pooper."

Swiftly slinging the strap of her purse over her shoulder, Kenzie laughed and opened the door. "I'll be ready to go at four if you can pick me up so I don't have to drag my luggage through traffic."

"I'll be there. You sure you don't want me to walk you back to your room?" Cort wasn't convinced she should be out alone that late at night.

"I've got pepper spray and I know how to use it. I'll let you know when I get to my room. If you don't hear from me in fifteen minutes, tell Tate I left him the pink tote bag in my will."

Cort chuckled again and waved as she walked down the hall and stepped into the elevator. Kenzie hurried through the lobby and across the street. She was safely in her room in less than ten minutes. Quickly calling Cort, she let him know she was fine, and then responded to a call from her boss. He wanted to make sure Tate was going to be okay.

Thanking him for his concern, she climbed into bed exhausted and set her alarm for three-thirty, giving herself just a few hours to sleep.

She stepped outside the hotel at four the next morning as Cort pulled up to the curb. He hustled around his pickup, placed her luggage in the back seat of his truck then held the door for her.

Since she was officially off duty from work and traveling with a wounded man who needed care, she decided to forgo wearing her traditional suit. Instead, she donned jeans, boots, and a soft cream-colored sweater.

"Are you sure you want to do this?" Cort asked as he drove across the street to his hotel.

She eyed him a moment then offered a reassuring smile. "I promise to get Tate home in one piece. I know things between us have been… um…" Kenzie struggled to find the right words and finally gave up. "Really, it'll be just fine."

"I'm not worried about you taking care of him," Cort said, winding through the parking lot to the front entrance. "I'm more worried about him being impossible to handle and making you want to parachute from the plane. He's not the most fun guy on the planet to be around when he's injured or sick."

Kenzie laughed and relaxed against the seat. "I can handle it." She hoped that would prove to be true since her experience in giving care derived from handling cranky, out-of-sorts women, and not angry, disgruntled men.

After entering the room Tate shared with Cort, she watched as he opened his eyes when the door shut behind them.

"Hey, what's going on?" he asked, groggy and not quite awake. He tried to pull his thoughts together, to recall what happened the previous evening, and think of the reason why Kenzie was with Cort in their hotel room.

Suddenly remembering the horse falling on him, he sucked in a breath that made pain wash over him from his aching head to his throbbing knee.

"No worries, man. Your ol' buddy Cort is on top of things." With a forced brightness, Cort smiled at his friend. "Let's get you up and dressed."

"What're you doing here?" Tate turned his attention to Kenzie, noting she looked fresh and pretty for it being so early in the morning. A glance at the clock confirmed that it was barely past four.

"Helping," was Kenzie's short reply as Cort motioned for her to turn on the bathroom light.

"Why are you both up so early? Aren't we leaving closer to noon, Cort?" Tate asked, sure he hadn't forgotten their departure time. He groaned as Cort helped him sit up then noticed he still wore a pair of dirty, torn jeans.

"Yeah, well, some plans had to be made and um…" Cort hesitated to share the rest of the details with Tate because he knew his friend would balk at the plans.

Kenzie waited for Cort to tell Tate he was traveling with her, but the coward stared at the floor as if it was the most fascinating thing he'd ever seen.

"Oh, good grief," she said, stepping next to the bed and planting her hands on her hips. "You're flying home with me this morning, cowboy, so you better get a move on. We've got an early flight to catch."

Maintaining her bravado, even at the stunned look on Tate's face, Kenzie pointed to the suitcases across the room. "Help him get dressed. I'll be back in a minute." She snatched his room key off the desk and marched out the door.

Tate watched her leave the room with his mouth hanging half-open. He tried to stop the spinning in his head as Cort helped him out of bed and into the bathroom. They were both bad-tempered before Tate was satisfied he looked presentable.

"I need to pack my stuff," Tate growled as Cort assisted him back to the bed. He sat on the edge while Cort helped him put on his boots, since he couldn't bend over without gasping in pain.

"I've already got your stuff packed and ready to go," Cort said, not making eye contact with Tate. "You really should be grateful Kenzie is willing to travel with you. Between your cheerful attitude and delightful smell, this isn't exactly going to be a walk in the park for her, you know."

Tate shot Cort a cold glare. Smart aleck comments from the peanut gallery were unwanted and unwelcome. He just wanted to be home where he could lick his wounds in peace.

"Did you get all my gear?" Tate asked as Kenzie tapped on the door and walked in pushing a wheelchair.

"Yep. It's all in my truck." Cort packed the last of Tate's belongings in his suitcase then gathered his own things. He'd taken their bags of gear to his truck when he went to get Kenzie, now he just had to get Tate and the suitcases loaded.

After settling Tate in the wheelchair, Kenzie took the handles, pushing it out the door while Cort lugged the suitcases and two smaller duffle bags. Once Tate was situated and the suitcases loaded in his truck, he ran inside to the front desk and checked them both out of the room, returning the wheelchair.

Tate sat in stony silence next to Kenzie on the truck's front seat. She did her best not to be intimidated by the trip ahead or the sullen man beside her.

Cort slid behind the wheel, looking around her at Tate's dour expression. "He's still grumpy, but at least he shouldn't embarrass you too badly on the way home." He gave Kenzie a teasing smile.

At Tate's narrowed look, Cort and Kenzie both laughed, trying to ease the tension.

Unable to find anything to laugh about, Tate frowned. Rather than indulging in a pity party on his way home, he would have to put some effort into trying to be a tolerable traveling companion for Kenzie.

Irritated they made plans without his consent, he was grudgingly grateful to be going home sooner rather than later. He just wished he wasn't traveling with Kenzie. Appearing weak and helpless wasn't exactly how he planned to woo his way back into her good graces.

At the airport, they pulled up at the outdoor ticket counter to find a wheelchair waiting along with an attendant to see them to their gate.

"Thanks for everything, man." Tate stuck out his hand to Cort once he sat in the wheelchair.

"Anytime, Tater." Cort leaned down to whisper to his friend while Kenzie spoke with the ticket agent. "Be good to Kenzie and don't give her too much sass. She didn't have to be your personal nurse or make arrangements for you to fly home with her."

"I know," Tate said quietly while Kenzie finished checking their luggage and getting their boarding passes. "I'll do my best to behave."

"See that you do." Cort winked at Kenzie as she turned to study the two men.

Both very handsome in their own way, the one in the wheelchair had the ability to make her knees feel like jelly and her stomach flutter wildly.

Cort placed a hand on Tate's shoulder. "I'll check in with you later and make sure you made it home in one piece."

"Thanks again, bro," Tate said to Cort as Kenzie gave him a parting hug.

"Take care of my travel partner," Cort said as he returned her embrace. "We've got to come back stronger than ever next year, you know."

"I know." Aware of how driven the two rodeo cowboys were to take titles next year, she smiled warmly. "Safe travels home, Cort."

"Thanks." He tipped his hat to her then climbed back in his truck and drove off.

"I think we're ready to roll," Kenzie said to the attendant who would push Tate's wheelchair to the gate.

Kenzie paid to upgrade to priority screening. They breezed through the security line and were soon at their gate with plenty of time to board.

"Do you need any further assistance, ma'am?" the attendant asked as Kenzie took a seat next to Tate's wheelchair.

"I think I can get it from here. Thank you." She tipped the attendant and sent him off with a smile. When she turned to Tate, fatigue rimmed his eyes and pain rode the tense line of his jaw. "Would you like something to eat or drink? Coffee or a bagel? Anything?"

"Tea would be great, Dewdrop. I don't think my stomach is up to coffee this morning." All he wanted was to fall into his own bed and sleep for hours on end, but he mustered a smile. "If you promise you won't tell anyone I ate a bagel, just a plain one would be good."

"Your secret is safe with me," Kenzie whispered confidentially. She dug around in her bag, searching for her wallet but looked up as Tate waved a twenty-dollar bill in her face.

"Let me buy breakfast, please." He held the bill out to her. "It's the least I can do after being such a burden to you today."

"Let's get one thing straight right now, cowboy." Kenzie took the money while giving him a look that made him open his eyes a little wider. "You aren't a burden, or an inconvenience, or whatever else you've convinced yourself you are. Let's just say it's a friend helping a friend and leave it at that. If the boot was on the other foot, would you help me get home?"

"Of course, but…"

Kenzie cut him off with a dismissive wave of her hand as she got to her feet. "No buts. No arguments. Just sit there and try to stay out of trouble until I get back."

Tate looked up at her and nodded his head, swallowing his wounded pride.

It took her almost twenty minutes to purchase mint tea, bagels, and bananas. Kenzie tamped down her annoyance when she returned to the gate to find three inappropriately attired women surrounding Tate, chatting away.

From the ashen tone of his skin, Kenzie could see him fighting both exhaustion and pain, but the women didn't appear to have a clue.

"How nice of you ladies to keep Tate company while I was gone." In her sweetest tone of voice, she broke up the circle they made around him. "He's a little worn out from his adventure yesterday, so I hope you'll excuse him while he has some breakfast and prepares for his flight."

Kenzie somehow managed to set the box holding their breakfast on Tate's lap, escort the women away from him, and send them off with a friendly wave before he even realized what happened.

"Can't seem to stay away from the floozies, can you?" Kenzie took the box of food and handed Tate a plain bagel, sliced open and toasted.

"It's not like I invited them over here." Tate bit into his bagel, willing his stomach to settle down before the flight. The doctor gave him some medicine to take after he ate that would cut the pain. He hoped it kicked in before they boarded because he was ready to crawl into a hole and die. The parts of his body that didn't ache pounded with acute, sharp pain.

"I suppose not." She sipped her tea.

"What's that supposed to mean?" he asked sharply, stopping his bite of bagel halfway to his mouth.

"It means that no matter where you go women like them are always going to be fawning over you." As much as she wanted to ignore their existence, seeing them with Tate really got to her. How could they have a relationship when she would constantly be worried about women chasing after him?

In truth, it wasn't so much the women chasing after him as the thought of him not running away that bothered her.

"And?" Tate asked, finishing his bagel in two bites and washing it down with the soothing mint tea. He accepted the banana she peeled and handed to him.

"Not everyone would want to compete with your ardent fan club."

"Not everyone would think they need to compete," Tate said in a voice that turned hard and flat. Kenzie's inability to trust him or believe in him combined with the pain from his injuries was about to push him over the edge. He was tired of waiting for her to see reason and in no mood to put up with her insinuations that he was a skirt-chasing snake. "Not everyone would jump to conclusions, assume the worst, and lump me in with a bunch of two-timing losers."

Instead of responding, Kenzie picked up their trash and dumped it in a nearby garbage can, giving herself a moment to think about what Tate said. Not willing to get into an in-depth discussion in the busy airport, she instead asked him if he'd called his dad.

"Not yet. I didn't want to wake him up." Tate studied Kenzie and decided to resume their conversation another day when he didn't feel like he'd been slammed to the ground by a thousand-pound load. On second thought, that was exactly what happened when he considered the weight of the bronc that crashed on top of him.

Kenzie glanced at her watch, wondering what time Kent usually started his day. If she was ninety, she might be excited to get up and greet each day, happy to be alive. "Is he an early riser?"

"Most of the time." Tate took out his phone and called his dad. A brief conversation assured the old man that he was fine, on his way home, and all would be well.

Kenzie tried to hide her smile when she heard Tate reassuring his dad he would behave himself.

With an announcement that boarding would soon begin, Kenzie wondered how offended Tate would be if she asked him if he needed to go to the bathroom. He saved them both the embarrassment by asking her to push him to the nearest restroom.

She paid a quick visit to the women's restroom then stood near the men's restroom, waiting for Tate. He emerged pale-faced with sweat running down his neck. Kenzie handed him a bottle of water and the medication the doctor prescribed. Tate took it without saying a word.

When they returned to their gate, the plane was starting to board. An attendant stood ready to push Tate onboard.

"All ready to go?" Kenzie asked, forcing a friendly smile.

"Yes, ma'am," the attendant said, pushing the wheelchair while Kenzie followed along behind, carrying both her purse and Tate's small duffle bag that wouldn't fit in his hastily packed suitcase.

Once they were on the plane, Tate sank onto a front row seat, giving him room to stretch out his leg. The brutal force of the throbbing made him both queasy and bad-tempered.

"How'd you score these seats?" Tate asked as Kenzie stowed his bag in the overhead bin and sat beside him.

"My boss was quite impressed with you. When he heard about your injury, he offered to pay the difference to upgrade us to first class." Kenzie took a book out of her bag before stuffing the bright pink catchall under the seat. "Normally, I would have objected, but I thought this would make the flight more comfortable for you."

"I'll have to remember to thank him." Tate removed his hat and leaned his head against the seat. He closed his eyes and tried to relax. Even though the flight was only a couple of hours, he had an idea it would seem like half of eternity unless his pain medication kicked in soon.

"So what's your plan when we get to Pasco? Is your truck at the airport?" Kenzie asked, taking Tate's hat from his lap and standing to put it in the overhead storage. He opened one eye and looked at her before closing it again.

"No. Monte will pick me up. He won't know I'm flying in today, though. I was going to spend a few days with Cort and his family in Boise before going home." Tate dreaded the hour or two it would take Monte to get to Pasco from the ranch once Tate let him know he was at the airport. He should have called and let him know he'd be landing in a couple of hours when he had the opportunity.

"I see. Who's going to take care of you for the next week or so? You know the doctor said you need to keep your leg elevated and iced, and stay off it. Then there's the whole concussion and cracked rib thing, not to mention your arm. You're lucky you're right-handed." Kenzie studied Tate. He looked absolutely miserable even though he worked at pretending he was fine. "Do you have someone at the ranch that can take care of you until you're feeling better?"

"I'll manage," Tate said through clenched teeth. He felt sick to his stomach again. Between a splitting headache and his other aches and pains, he wasn't sure flying was the best idea after all. The alternatives, though, were even less appealing. He couldn't imagine feeling like he did, holed up in a hotel room for days on end. The thought of riding home stuck in the cab of Cort's truck made him shift uncomfortably in his seat.

Maybe everyone did have his best interest at heart in trying to get him home as quickly as possible.

"Right." She mulled over the idea of Tate trying to manage without any assistance. Most likely too stubborn to admit to his crew or his friends he needed help, the thought of him suffering alone didn't set well with her. "You could always share a room with your dad until you feel better. I'm sure the nursing staff would be happy to take care of another charming Morgan."

"Funny. Real funny." He opened his eyes long enough to give her a halfhearted smile that still managed to bring out his dimples and make her heart skip a beat.

Of all the men on the planet, why did Tate have to be the one who made her fall head over heels in love? Why couldn't she have gone for a banker, an insurance salesman, or even the FedEx guy?

It just had to be the most handsome cowboy she'd ever laid eyes on or kissed. Tate was an undeniably great kisser.

As the plane taxied down the runway and took off, Kenzie noticed he held the armrest in a death grip.

"That's my move, you know." She pried Tate's right hand from the armrest and grasped it between both of hers.

"I thought I'd borrow it this trip." His jaw clenched against the churning in his stomach and the pain rolling over him in waves.

He would not be sick on the plane. And he most definitely would not be sick in front of Kenzie.

It wasn't going to happen.

Sucking in a deep breath that made him remember his cracked ribs, he tried not to crush Kenzie's delicate fingers in his as she held his hand. He allowed himself to inhale a whiff of her fragrance, to let it penetrate past the pain and sickness, and bring him a sense of calm.

Amazingly, she smelled like a field of summer flowers even though it was now December. Her hands were soft and he remembered the feel of her skin beneath his hands from the past times he'd touched her.

As he pictured her eyes full of warmth and compassion, he let his mind drift to her high cheekbones flushed pink from something he'd said to make her blush, her lips curving up as they most often did like she was about to smile or trying to keep a secret. He thought about how tall and poised she always looked, her keen intelligence, and how she could make him laugh when she wasn't driving him crazy.

The pain meds finally kicked in, allowing him to sleep and dream of Kenzie.

As his breathing evened out, his grip on her hand loosened. Kenzie knew Tate slept. She released the breath she'd been holding, relieved he could rest.

Eagerly picking up the holiday romance she'd started reading, she lost herself in the love story and was surprised when she heard the announcement their flight would soon arrive in Pasco.

A glance at Tate confirmed he continued sleeping. No doubt, he would wake up when they landed.

Hurriedly shoving her book into her bag, Kenzie was surprised when Tate continued to sleep right through the landing. When the flight attendant leaned over to wake Tate, Kenzie stopped her and asked if they could get off the plane last.

Once the few remaining passengers exited the plane, Kenzie gently nudged Tate. He opened his eyes and gave her a disoriented look.

"Kenzie?" he asked, seeming confused about where he was and why she was there.

"Hope you had a nice nap, sleeping beauty, but it's time to get your carriage and leave the plane." Kenzie stood to retrieve Tate's hat and carry-on bag from the overhead storage compartment.

The flight attendant waited with a wheelchair and between the two of them, they settled Tate in the seat.

Kenzie plopped his hat on his head and draped their bags over her shoulder, taking the handles of the wheelchair in her hands.

"Thanks so much, I can take it from here," she told the attendant with a smile. She rolled Tate's wheelchair down the ramp, into the airport, and toward baggage claim.

Tate fished his phone out of his pocket and called his ranch foreman while Kenzie watched for their luggage to appear on the carousel.

"Hey, Monte," Tate said, trying to sound upbeat, but coming across as half-drugged and pain-ridden. Kenzie looked over her shoulder at him and shook her head.

"Yeah, that wreck was something else, all right. Listen, I'm..." Tate's conversation ended unexpectedly when Kenzie grabbed his phone from him.

"Monte, this is Kenzie. Remember me from last fall?" Kenzie stepped far enough away from Tate he couldn't hear her conversation. "Look, Tate's going to need some care and I know you guys aren't set up for that there. He's going to stay with me until he can at least walk. The doctor thought he should be up and around in a few days. He'll give you a call when he's ready to come home. If you get any random calls from him in the next two or three days insisting you come get him, please ignore him. He's being a little stubborn about the extent of his injuries and he's on a lot of painkillers."

Tate couldn't hear what Monte or Kenzie said, but by the smile on Kenzie's face, she found the conversation amusing. He scowled as she disconnected the call and gave him back his phone. "That wasn't necessary. I'm perfectly capable of speaking to Monte."

"I know you are." Kenzie snagged their suitcases and Tate's bag of rodeo gear, setting everything by his wheelchair. "I told him not to worry about coming to get you. You're going home with me."

Chapter Twelve

Convinced his pain medication made him loopy, Tate thought he heard Kenzie say she was taking him home with her, but it had to be a mistake.

Less than twenty-four hours ago he thought she wanted him out of her life for good and now she planned to take him home to her apartment. It didn't make any sense.

Not only was he drugged, he could add hearing issues to his list of troubles. Maybe that was a result of the concussion.

"Did you hear what I said?" Kenzie asked as she pushed him toward the door, trying to drag their luggage behind her.

"Not exactly." Tate looked at her with pain-glazed eyes. There was no way he was going to her apartment and let her care for him like an invalid until he was well enough to walk out of there.

Not happening.

If he had to call a taxi to drive him out to the ranch, he'd do it. He'd offer bonus pay to whichever one of the hands would stay in the house and play nursemaid for a few days.

"I said you're going home with me until you're back on your feet. The doctor said it would only be a day or so before your knee will bear weight again." Kenzie positioned a suitcase on either side of Tate then set his bag of gear near his feet. She slid her hot pink bag off her shoulder and rummaged through a zippered pocket.

While she dug through her purse, Tate pulled his phone back out and started searching for the number of a taxi service.

"What are you doing?" Kenzie asked, still riffling in her bag.

"Calling a taxi." Quickly finding a number, he placed a call. Kenzie snatched his phone away and shut it off.

"Stop being ridiculous. I promise I'll take good care of you." She studied him, trying to decide if he was lucid and stubborn, or dopey from his medication. Since he was always upbeat and optimistic with a smile on his face, his surly behavior was enough to give her reason to pause,

"I'm not worried about that." Tate dropped his gaze to his knee. If he stared hard enough, he was sure he could actually see it throb. "I just think I better go home."

"Nope." Finally fishing her car keys out of the bag, she leaned down and looked in his face. "I've got some time off, I'm more than happy to help, and you've got no better prospects. No more arguing. Besides, the doctor in Vegas said you need to see your doctor and you might have to do some therapy on your knee soon. You can't exactly drive yourself since your truck has a clutch."

"Fine," Tate said, still scowling. Apparently, Kenzie was trying to figure out how to get him, the luggage and herself out to the car. The wind whipped violently and it looked freezing outside. Chilled sitting in his shirtsleeves near the big sliding doors, he wished he had on his jacket. Then again, it would be a challenge to get it on without help and he'd rather be frostbitten than ask Kenzie for assistance.

"How about you wait right here while I get my car and bring it to the door? I think that will be easier than trying to get you and our stuff to the far side of the parking lot in this wind," Kenzie said, taking a step toward the door.

Tate nodded his head and resigned himself to sitting in the wheelchair looking like an invalid while everyone stared at him as they walked by. A few people stopped, offering their condolences on his injuries and losing the championship title, doing little to bolster his already low spirits. He didn't know so many people recognized him. Maybe the cowboy hat, arm in a sling, and bandaged knee tipped them off.

Curious what took Kenzie so long, he started to call to check on her when he remembered she kept his phone.

Words his father wouldn't be happy to hear filled his thoughts as he fought to control his anger.

That infuriating woman was doing her best to make it impossible for him to arrange a ride out to the ranch.

Part of Tate wanted nothing more than to hang out at Kenzie's and spend time with her. He wanted to see if they could resurrect the relationship they'd been building until she jumped to the wrong conclusion last fall.

The other part of him, the part that felt cheated, angry, and broken, just wanted to go home where he could mourn the loss of the championship alone and mope as long as he liked.

Left sitting in a wheelchair unable to move while she ran out in the cold to get the car wasn't helping his already dark mood. If he could have walked more than two or three halting steps, he'd have chased after her despite his pounding head, throbbing arm, and aching ribs.

He glanced outside and saw Kenzie hop out of her car. She raced back inside, wearing a dark green wool coat that highlighted her glossy brown hair. Transfixed by her beauty, for a moment Tate could do nothing more than stare at her.

"It's cold out there." Kenzie hustled toward him with a plaid fleece blanket draped over her arm. Gently placing her hand on his back, she urged him to sit forward and draped the blanket around his shoulders. As she pulled it together in the front, she stepped back and smiled. "It's not a coat, but warmer than just your shirt."

"Now I've got the lap robe to go with my wheelchair," Tate commented dryly, embarrassed beyond reason to not only feel like an invalid, but to look the part. "Maybe you should take me over to stay with Pop, like you mentioned earlier. If I had a set of false teeth, I'd fit right in."

"Not quite." She laughed as she wheeled the two suitcases out the door and put them in the trunk of the car. She came back and retrieved Tate's bags, setting them in the back seat.

Finally, she was ready for Tate.

"I'll try to help you in as quickly as I can, but be prepared for the bite of the wind. It'll steal your breath away," she said as she pushed him outside.

Tate shuddered, despite the warmth of the blanket. Gathering all the strength he had left, he used his good arm and leg to get out of the chair and into the front passenger seat of the car. The heat blasting through the vents delivered welcome warmth.

After pushing the wheelchair inside, Kenzie returned, sliding behind the wheel and heading out of the parking lot.

"I'll get you settled then make a run to the grocery store." They entered the freeway and drove toward Kennewick and her apartment. Tate was glad she lived on the bottom floor of a fourplex because he couldn't make it up any steps. Concerned how he'd manage the few steps from her car inside the apartment, worry churned in his stomach, pushing his queasiness to an unbearable level.

Kenzie continued glancing at Tate out of the corner of her eye and saw him clench his jaw along with the armrest. Although she acted confident about taking care of him, the prospect of being his caregiver frightened her.

It had been a long time since she'd nursed anyone and the thought of having Tate so close for an extended period made her feel unsettled and jumpy. To compensate, she put on a bright smile and bluffed her way along, trying to keep upbeat.

When she pulled into her parking space at the apartment complex, she noticed Tate's fingers turned white from his death grip on the door handle.

"Can you sit tight for just another minute or two?" Kenzie asked. She didn't wait for a response before jumping out of her car and running up the steps to the apartment above hers.

Her neighbor worked nights and was a friendly sort of guy. They'd gone out a few times, as friends, but she'd never had a romantic interest in the man.

Anxiously ringing the doorbell, she waited and rang it again. She'd have to do something nice for Paul in exchange for waking him up and begging for his help. She prayed he hadn't gone to sleep yet. Impatiently waiting another moment, she rang the bell again and knocked on the door.

Paul's door swung open as she started down the steps. He stuck a sleep-tousled head outside.

"Hey, Kenzie. What can I do for you?" Paul asked, rubbing his hand across his eyes, trying to come fully awake.

"I'm so, so sorry to bother you, but I could really use your help." She rushed back up the steps. "I've got a friend who's hurt and needs a few days of care before going home so he's staying with me. He can't really walk without assistance and I was hoping you could help get him to my guest room."

"Sure, just let me put on some shoes." Paul disappeared into his apartment and returned wearing slippers. He slipped on a sweatshirt as he followed Kenzie down the steps.

"I'll run in and make sure we've got a clear path," Kenzie said, unlocking her door. She quickly pushed a chair out of the way then ran into the guest room, pulling the decorative pillows and quilt from the bed before turning back the covers.

When she returned outside, Paul had a strong arm braced around Tate, helping him to his feet while talking about the rodeo finals.

"Dude, I saw you crash last night on TV. That wreck was wicked," Paul said as he shifted an arm around Tate's back and helped him shuffle toward Kenzie's door. "You're lucky you aren't in the hospital, man."

"Lucky. Yep, that's me." Tate ground his teeth against the pain that seared him with every step. Somehow, Kenzie managed to offer support on his injured side as he hobbled along. Despite the pain, it took just a minute to get him to the guest room, half-carried as he was by Kenzie and her friend. He sank down on the bed and let out the breath he'd been holding.

While Paul talked about rodeos and cowboys, Kenzie removed Tate's hat and boots, followed by his sling, then helped him peel off his shirt.

"I think Paul better help you with your jeans," Kenzie said, blushing as she hurried out of the room.

"That's okay. I can get it," Tate said, mortified at the thought of a complete stranger helping him take off his pants.

"Hey, no worries." Paul backed toward the door.

"Thanks, man. I appreciate your help." Tate watched Kenzie's neighbor step into the hallway.

"Anytime, dude. Take care." Paul offered a friendly wave before disappearing down the hall.

One-handed, Tate fumbled with his jeans and managed to remove them then climb into the bed. Although the room was cool and the sheets chilly, the soft mattress beneath him felt wonderful.

Even though he couldn't distinguish the conversation, the rumble of voices floated down the hall. Tate closed his eyes. The front door shut and moments later he sensed Kenzie's presence nearby. Her summery scent filled his nose and he would have breathed deeply if it didn't make his sore ribs hurt so badly.

A light caress of fingers across his forehead surprised him. He remained unmoving, kept his eyes closed, and savored Kenzie's touch. Her hair brushed against his cheek as she bent to kiss his forehead.

"Rest well, cowboy," she whispered before leaving the room, closing the door softly behind her.

Outside the guest room, she leaned against the wall and took a deep breath, followed by another.

She'd fallen in love with a happy-go-lucky rodeo cowboy who was charismatic, strong, and on top of his game.

Seeing him wounded, hurt, and deflated did funny things to her. His vulnerability made her want to champion him while stirring up soft, tender feelings in her heart. She loved the hero image of Tate she'd built up in her head as well as this all too human side of him.

She could only imagine how hard it was for him to lose the championship title he'd worked so hard all year to win. If only that darn horse hadn't fallen back on him, Tate would have claimed first place with points to spare.

Since she couldn't do anything to change what happened, she began making plans as she walked toward the kitchen. She had a few ideas on how to put a smile back on his face.

><><

Caught in a dream that a horse reared over on him, Tate awoke with a startled gasp and pain gripping his side. Swiftly opening his eyes, he realized he was in an unfamiliar bedroom.

Was he in a hotel room? Still in Vegas?

The room appeared too homey to be a hotel.

Where was he?

As he struggled to remember, his gaze shot to the door. It opened and a beautiful brunette walked inside.

Kenzie.

He was with Kenzie at her apartment in Kennewick.

Relaxing his grip on the sheet knotted in his fist, he let out a sigh. His tongue felt heavy and thick, and every inch of his body ached.

At some point while he slept, Kenzie placed a pillow so it would support his arm. She carried another with her now, along with a glass of water and a bottle of pills.

"Time for some more drugs." Kenzie grinned, handing Tate a pill followed by the glass of water. He drained the glass and reached to set it on the nightstand by his bed, gritting his teeth at the strain it put on his ribs.

"Let me get that." She took the glass from him then stuffed the pillow under the covers near his knee and slid it beneath his leg.

Tate settled back against the pillows. His eyes grew heavy again and he let himself fall asleep.

The next time he awoke, he could tell from the lack of light sneaking around the blind at the window it was probably late afternoon. The clock beside the bed confirmed it was almost five.

"You doing okay, son?" a familiar voice asked from across the room, startling him.

"Pop?" Tate turned his head to see his dad sitting in a chair in the corner. "What are you doing here?"

"Kenzie thought I might like to see for myself that you're alive, if not well," Kent said with a grin. He worked himself out of the chair and walked to the bed. Carefully sinking down to the edge of the mattress, he patted Tate's good leg and nodded his head. "That is quite the girl you've found, Tater. I think you better hang onto her."

"I've tried, Pop, but I'm not so sure she wants to be held." Attempts at analyzing what happened with Kenzie in Las Vegas left him even more confused. It seemed as though she suddenly decided he was no longer the enemy and was open to being friends. He hoped much more than friends.

With his brain still sluggish from his medication and unable to think things through clearly, he turned his attention to his dad. "How'd you get here?"

"Kenzie picked me up after she ran to the grocery store." Kent chuckled. "Nearly insisted I come over and stay for dinner. From what I can surmise, we're having soup and homemade bread."

Tate could smell something yeasty in the air and his stomach responded with a growl. He was no longer nauseous, and looked forward to putting something in his empty belly.

Slowly lifting back the covers, he tried to decide how he was going to walk to the bathroom to take care of some other basic needs, even if he had no clue where it was. Although Kenzie spent time at his house on the ranch, he'd never been inside her apartment.

"Where you headed?" Kent stood and stared down at Tate.

"Bathroom." Tate set both sock-covered feet on the floor and hoped his knee would bear his weight.

"Hang on." Kent walked across the room and grabbed a cane. He handed it to Tate and grinned. "Kenzie said you'd probably need to use this for a few days."

Apparently, Kenzie had been busy while he slept. Tate glanced around and noticed a door in the guest room that looked like it connected to a bathroom. As he shuffled across the floor to the door, he felt every bit as old as his father.

Shocked by his reflection in the bathroom mirror, Tate cringed at the dark shadows beneath his eyes. His hair pinwheeled every direction and a growth of stubble covered his face.

Opening the bathroom door, he called to his dad. "Pop, is my suitcase in there?"

"Sure is. You need something?"

"My shaving kit." Tate looked around the door. His dad opened the suitcase resting on a small, upholstered bench by a cherry wood dresser. Kent dug around and retrieved the case, carrying it to Tate.

"I don't think you need to worry about a shave right now, son. She'll overlook your whiskers considering the circumstances," Kent said with a teasing light in his eyes.

"I'm not worried about a shave, Pop, but I'd like to brush my teeth and comb my hair." Tate dug around in the case with his good hand. When the effort of getting toothpaste onto his toothbrush proved more than he could handle, his dad did it for him, making him feel useless. It reminded him of being a little boy when his dad taught him how to take care of himself.

He managed to comb his hair without Kent's assistance and even used one of the soft, fluffy washcloths rolled into a basket by the sink to wash the grit from his eyes. Somewhat refreshed, he hobbled to the suitcase and shuffled items around with his right hand until he found a pair of black lounge pants. By sitting on the edge of the bed, he managed to get the pants on without asking his dad for help.

"You're looking almost bright-eyed and bushy-tailed now." Kent patted Tate on the shoulder, watching as he scooted back on the bed until he could lean against the headboard.

With his right hand, Tate tried to adjust the pillows behind his back. Not having much success, he was about to give up when Kenzie breezed into the room.

"I thought I heard some noise in here," she said, going to the bed and arranging the pillows for Tate until he could comfortably rest against them. "Are you hungry?"

"Yes, ma'am," Kent said, winking at Tate. "It sure is nice of you to have me stay for dinner."

"There's nothing nice about it." Kenzie got down on her knees and slid a card table from beneath Tate's bed, setting it up in front of Kent's chair. "If you're here, you can keep an eye on this guy. It gets me out of nursing duty."

Unsure if she was teasing or serious, Tate worried about being a burden to her. Lost in his thoughts he failed to see the sassy look she turned his direction before disappearing out the door. She soon returned with a dishcloth and wiped off the table then dropped a tablecloth over the top of it.

Her next trip back to the room, she carried a large tray with glasses of milk, bowls of steaming chicken soup, and thick slices of homemade bread dripping with butter. She set a glass of milk, bowl of soup and a plate with bread in front of Kent, put her dishes on the table then placed the tray across Tate's lap.

Again, she exited, returning with a kitchen chair. She set it at the card table beside Kent.

"I think we should give thanks for this fine meal," Kent said, bowing his head and offering a short but heartfelt prayer.

Half-starved, Tate enjoyed every bite of the filling soup. The bread was warm and aromatic, as only made-from-scratch bread can be. "Thanks, Kenzie, for this wonderful meal."

Kenzie looked up from her soup, surprised Tate would thank her for such simple fare. Her grandmother always made soup and bread whenever Kenzie felt down when she was a young girl and needed some comfort food.

"You're welcome." Nodding her head, she returned her attention to the meal. Kent's hand on her arm caused her to look his direction.

"It's very good, honey. Some of the best bread I've had in years," Kent said, reaching for another piece. "A beauty who can cook, Tate... you don't come across that every day."

"Pop…" Tate's voice held a note of warning, not wanting to know what ideas danced through his father's head.

"Just saying, Tater." Kent laughed before taking a bite of bread. While Kenzie ate her soup, Kent winked at Tate.

"How did he get the nickname Tater?" Kenzie asked, enjoying the teasing going on between Tate and his father.

"It could have been that he was always grubbing around in the dirt or that he never cleaned behind his ears and we'd tell him he was going to start growing 'taters' back there," Kent said with a jovial smile wreathing his weathered face. "But it's probably from the ranch foreman we had when Tate was a little boy. He was forever saying 'Tate, 'er ya gonna…' so we all started calling him Tater."

"I like it." The saucy grin she shot Tate caught him off guard. "Do we need to check behind your ears before we let you go back to sleep? I don't want any taters growing in my guest bed."

"No," he grumbled. Despite his gruff tone, he was pleased at the way his dad and Kenzie interacted with such ease. He knew Kenzie had been to see his dad a few times even after she dumped him in September. He didn't realize they were quite so chummy, though. In light of the way his dad and Kenzie both liked to tease, it could mean trouble for him.

A good kind of trouble.

Mostly.

While he mused over the possibilities, Tate's eyes once again grew droopy. Kenzie walked over to the side of the bed and handed him another pain pill. Once he took it, she moved the tray off his lap, rearranged his pillows and pulled his covers up.

Her efficient care for him put a huge dent in his ego, but he was too exhausted and sore to do anything about it at the moment.

"Looks like we're losing him to dreamland, Kent. Shall we move our party elsewhere?" Kenzie asked with a smile as she loaded dishes onto the tray and walked out of the room.

"I'm right behind you, honey," Kent said as he followed her to the kitchen.

Kenzie talked with Kent about the Morgan Ranch while she washed dishes and put away food. After she placed a handful of cookies in a resealable bag for him to eat later, he talked about what Tate was like as a little boy.

"He was always a happy kid," Kent said, sitting at Kenzie's small kitchen table sipping from a cup of hot tea. "Nothing ever got him down for long, so don't worry about him overmuch. He just needs a few days to get his feet under him and he'll be back to his old self."

"I'm glad to hear that." Kenzie hoped what Kent said was true. It made her heart hurt to see Tate in his current maudlin state. Suddenly, she wondered what drove him to get involved in the rodeo in the first place. From what she knew, it was only his third year in a pro career. "Why did he decide to go pro with the saddle bronc riding?"

"He was always good with animals, loved the horses." Kent sat back in his chair, looking thoughtful. "When he got old enough that I didn't think he'd get the stuffin' knocked out of him, I let him start working with the untrained horses on the ranch. He came alive when he climbed on the back of a bucking horse. Something about the thrill of taming it, I guess. His friend Cort, have you met him yet?"

At Kenzie's nod, Kent continued. "Cort and Tate were thick as thieves growing up but they were about thirteen when Cort's folks moved to the Boise area. The boys would visit back and forth summer vacations. Anyway, Cort started steer wrestling several years back. Told Tate he had fun and made good money at it. Ol' Tater wasn't interested in steer wrestling at all, but he liked the idea of riding broncs. He went to one of those rodeo schools and learned all he could then spent the rest of that year practicing before he felt ready to take on the rodeo circuit. In no time at all, he'd gone pro."

"Why does he do it? I don't get the idea it's for the money." She sat down next to Kent at the table, tracing her finger over the plaid pattern in the tablecloth.

"No, it was never about the money." That would be the last reason his son would participate in the rodeo. "It's a challenge for him. His plan was to quit once he earned a world champion title. Unfortunately, he thought that might happen this year. Looks like he'll have to decide if he's going to give it another go or hang up his spurs. He's a solid boy, Kenzie. He made sure the ranch was in good hands with Monte managing it before he ever decided to get involved in the rodeo. I think the hardest thing for him was trying to decide how to keep an eye on me and be on the road so much. When I agreed to the care home, it took a load of worry off his shoulders. I don't mind living there, although sometimes it's nice to see something besides the inside of that place."

"We'll have to get you out and about more often, then." Kenzie stood and gathered their coats. "For now, though, I better get you back or someone will think you've been kidnapped."

Kent laughed, pushing himself up to his feet. "Now wouldn't that be something."

Kenzie ran out to start her car and let it warm while Kent snapped his coat and put on his hat. Although the wind had died down, it was still bitterly cold outside.

She grabbed Kent's bag of cookies and held onto the old man's arm, helping him out the door, almost walking into Paul.

"Hey, how's your friend?" Paul asked, stepping back as Kenzie and Kent moved toward her car.

"Doing okay. Thanks for asking," Kenzie said, smiling at her neighbor. "This is Tate's dad, Kent Morgan. Kent, this is my neighbor, Paul Jones."

Paul shook hands with the elderly man and smiled. "Nice to meet you, Mr. Morgan."

"You, too, son," Kent said, giving the man a quick once-over. He looked like a decent sort and acted respectfully toward Kenzie.

"Well, I gotta run or I'll be late for work," Paul said with a wave as he rushed to a big SUV and drove away.

"Paul helped me get Tate settled this morning when we got home. I couldn't quite manage by myself," Kenzie explained as she helped Kent into her car.

"That was nice of him," Kent said, wondering if a little jealousy on Tate's part might spur him into action where Kenzie was concerned.

His son was taking much too long to get down to the business of courting the lovely girl. Kent wanted to see a grandbaby before he died.

Forcing himself not to rub his hands together in anticipation of stirring up Tate and prodding him into doing something about his feelings for Kenzie, Kent realized he hadn't had this much excitement for a long while.

Chapter Thirteen

Worn out from the events of the past few days, Kenzie awoke to light peeking around the edges of her bedroom drapes.

Lazily rolling over in bed, she stretched, letting her thoughts wander to the handsome cowboy in her guest room.

After taking Kent back to the care home the previous evening, she returned to find Tate sleeping peacefully.

She watched him for a long moment, drinking in the sight of his face, looking so boyish in slumber. Gently pulling the covers up over one muscled shoulder, she gave in to the desire to run her fingers through his hair then bent to softly kiss his cheek.

His masculine scent filled her senses and the warmth of his stubbly cheek made her lips tingle, leaving her incapable of settling down for the night.

She cleaned her already neat apartment, baked a pie, and readied her Christmas cards for mailing. Finally forcing herself to go to bed, she fell into an exhausted sleep.

Mindful she needed to check on Tate, she made herself get out of bed when she could easily spend a few more hours sleeping.

Since Tate seemed inclined to think he could go to the ranch and take care of himself, she still hadn't returned his phone. Kent thought it was funny she'd taken it away and told her she had matters well in hand.

Cort and Huck both called to check on their friend and she'd given them an honest report. Cort said he'd update anyone who needed to know about Tate's condition and chuckled when she told him why Tate didn't answer his phone.

After yanking on her workout clothes, she peeked inside Tate's room. Soundly sleeping, she left him alone and closed the door.

She hurried outside and jogged to the fitness center available to members of the apartment complex. Grateful for the close location of the gym, Kenzie went through her standard workout then jogged through the freezing temperatures back to her apartment.

When she returned inside, noise from the guest room let her know Tate had discovered the remote control for the television in his room.

Quietly opening the bedroom door, she was pleased to see him sitting up, looking more alert than he had the previous day.

"Good morning," she said. Suddenly remembering she didn't have on a speck of makeup, her hair was in a messy ponytail, and sweat ran down her neck, she hovered in the doorway, wishing she'd taken time to shower first.

"Hey," Tate said with the easy grin she loved, although it looked a little forced. It made her stomach flutter when his dimples popped out in his cheeks.

She fought the urge to fidget when Tate attempted to look her over. "Working out?"

"Yes. The apartment complex has a fitness center." Kenzie stuck her head far enough into the room to see Tate watched the news.

"Handy." He continued staring at what he could see of her around the door she used as a shield.

"I'm going to clean up. If you want to take a shower, I can help you wrap your arm to keep it dry." Kenzie thought it might help Tate feel better to take a shower. The modified sponge bath she'd given him after his accident hadn't really gotten him clean. There hadn't been time, even if he was able for him to take a shower the previous morning. "I'll just be a minute."

"Okay."

Kenzie backed into the hall, leaving the door open. It seemed odd that Tate offered such short sentences. She realized it had been many hours since his last pain pill and he was probably hurting.

She rushed to the kitchen, got him a cold glass of water and a banana, then returned to his room.

As she bustled into the bedroom, he tightly twisted the sheet in his right hand.

"Why didn't you say you were hurting?" Kenzie asked, handing him the banana. He ate it in a few quick bites then took the glass of water and medication she held out to him. "I'm not very good at mind reading, so you'll have to let me know what you need, Tate."

"Thanks." He reached out and grasped her hand in his, giving it a light squeeze. "I'm not very good at this being helpless stuff."

Kenzie smiled and squeezed his hand in return.

"I guess we'll have to learn together." She walked over to the door. "I'll be back in a few minutes."

Kenzie took a quick shower then hurried to dress. She left her hair to air dry, but took a minute to give her eyelashes a few swipes of mascara and apply sheer lip gloss.

Vanity made her roll her eyes in the mirror. Quickly, she made her bed then picked up her dirty clothes, carrying them to her little laundry area off the kitchen and tossing them into the hamper. Armed with garbage bags and a roll of duct tape, she returned to Tate's room.

He looked irritated as he watched the news, clenching his jaw.

As she listened to a reporter talk about Tate's accident, it didn't take long to figure out why he was upset. "Although he seems to have gone missing after his accident, sources say he is expected to have a full recovery. It remains to be seen if this Washington State cowboy will make another run for the championship next year."

"Tate, you don't…" Kenzie started to say, but a cool glare cut her off.

A clip of Huck riding the bull the final night of the rodeo flashed across the screen. The reporter said something about Huck dedicating his winning ride to his wounded friend.

"Nobody told me Huck rode the extra time," Tate said. Reproach colored his voice as he shut off the TV and dropped the remote on the bedside table.

"He did it for you." Kenzie approached the bed. She wasn't sure if Tate was mad at her for basically kidnapping him and stealing his phone, mad because of losing the championship, or mad at the world in general.

"He's a good friend." Tate turned his blue gaze to Kenzie. "It's odd none of them have called."

"They have. I talked to Cort and Huck last night." Unable to pull her eyes away from Tate's, she felt only marginally guilty for keeping his phone from him. "They're both worried about you and Cort said to tell you he made it home just fine."

"I see." Aggravated Kenzie treated him like a misbehaving child, she had no right to take his phone even if she thought she had reason. "Do you think, perhaps, I can have my phone back today?"

"Of course." Kenzie needed to say something, even if Tate wouldn't like hearing it. "Look, Tate, I'm sorry I took your phone from you, but I really don't think it's in your best interest to go home alone. I realize you might not want to be here with me in light of what happened in the past. If you still insist on going home, I'll take you to the ranch today right after your doctor's appointment."

"What appointment?" Tate searched through the fuzzy corners of his mind trying to remember a doctor appointment.

"The doctor in Vegas said you should see your family doctor in a day or two and your dad told me who to call. You've got an appointment later this morning," Kenzie said, placing the garbage bags and tape on the nightstand by the bed. "If he says it's fine for you to go home alone, I'll make sure you go today. If he thinks you need to have someone look after you for a few days, then you'll agree to stay here. Fair enough?"

"No." Wincing in pain, he flipped back the covers and swung his legs over the side of the bed. "It's not fair to you. No matter what happened between us, I would never expect you to be my personal nurse. It's not right."

"Just think of it as me helping out a friend I care about very much." Kenzie studied the splint on his arm, saying more than she intended.

Intently staring at her, Tate absorbed her words. Although he'd rather hear her declarations of undying love, admitting she cared about him as a friend was a good start. Her actions the last few days also spoke volumes.

She wouldn't give up her valuable time to just anyone and the fact that she'd gone out of her way to bring his dad to visit made it clear she cared about him more than she might be willing to admit.

"I think we can wrap the bags around your arm and tape it here." She pointed to a spot above his elbow. "It should keep the water out."

Without waiting for him to comment, she diverted her gaze from his muscled chest and stomach by focusing her attention on wrapping his arm. Once she finished, she pushed up the leg of his lounge pants and removed the compression bandage from his knee.

"You're on your own from there, cowboy," Kenzie said with a cheeky grin, handing Tate his cane and watching him get to his feet. She walked ahead of him to the bathroom, flipped on the lights, laid out towels, and stepped back into the bedroom.

"Do you need anything else?" She asked as Tate shuffled into the bathroom.

"Nope."

"If you do need anything, just shout." Kenzie backed toward the hallway. "I'll make some breakfast while you shower."

Tate didn't say a word as he closed the door.

Kenzie hurried to remake his bed with clean sheets. She put the others in the washing machine and turned it on.

As she made French toast and coffee, she worried about Tate. He seemed so unlike himself, even more so than yesterday.

Maybe she could bring Kent back for another visit after lunch, if Tate was still staying with her. She'd take him home if that was what he really wanted, but she didn't think it was a good idea.

With one ear tuned down the hall, Kenzie listened for the shower to stop running. When it did, she heated maple syrup, poured steaming coffee into two mugs, put the toast on plates and loaded everything on a tray. She carried it to Tate's room and pushed the door open with her foot.

He stood in front of his suitcase, clad only in his underwear, holding a pair of jeans in his hand.

"Oh!" Kenzie turned around as quickly as she could with the loaded tray and stepped into the hall. "Sorry about that."

"No big deal." The humor in his voice also showed on his face. He was glad she'd given him time to get his briefs on before she barged right in.

Tate dropped the jeans back in the suitcase, pulled out a pair of blue plaid lounge pants and limped over to the bed. He managed to tug them on with his one good hand before scooting back against the pillows.

"I'm decent. You can come back in," he called, hiding his smile as Kenzie returned to the room. Her hair was still damp on the ends, curling in a thick mass around her shoulders and down her back. He swallowed hard, fighting the urge to bury his hands in the silky strands.

Her fresh, floral scent washed over him as she leaned over him to set down the tray. He had no idea what bath products she used, but he was sure the label had to say something about being guaranteed to drive men wild.

"I'm so sorry, Tate. I'll knock next time." Her cheeks stung from the heat of embarrassment. Things between them were uncomfortable enough without her barging in on him nearly naked.

"It's fine." Hungry, Tate looked at the coffee and golden brown French toast.

When Kenzie took his hand in hers and offered thanks, he was somewhat chagrined to hear his stomach growl loudly, declaring his hunger.

Able to cut the toast with his fork one-handed, he took pleasure in being able to do something for himself.

Kenzie pulled a chair close to the bed and chatted while they ate. When they finished, she took the tray to the kitchen and returned with ice packs. She placed one on his ribs, one on his arm, and the last one on his knee.

"I completely forgot to ice you yesterday," she said, adjusting his leg so his knee rested on a few pillows before she settled the pack on it. "I'll try to do a better job of playing nurse today."

"You're doing a good job," Tate said, experiencing a mixture of gratitude and resentment. He was thankful for Kenzie's attentive and gentle care, yet irritated and annoyed that he needed anyone to take care of him.

Accustomed to doing things for himself and lending a hand to others, he didn't like being on the receiving end of assistance.

It rankled him.

Almost as much as losing the championship.

In all honesty, Tate felt cheated. He'd busted his tail the entire year, traveling the country, giving one hundred and ten percent, to lose it all at the very last second. Well, point-nine seconds if the video clip he'd seen on the news was accurate.

Determined not to quit until he won, Tate knew he'd do it all over again in the coming year. Just as soon as his arm healed, he could walk normally, and his ribs no longer ached. It wouldn't be the first time he'd had to dig deep and forge ahead and he was sure it wouldn't be the last.

He glanced at the woman who forced him into her care. She looked feminine and entirely too lovely for his drug-addled mind to handle. He hadn't yet adjusted to seeing her in something other than business attire.

Her dark blue jeans, berry red sweater, and brown boots gave him the idea she was ready for some holiday fun. Given a choice, he liked seeing her best in her jeans and boots, looking like a country girl. Although he did dream about what she'd look like wearing something lacy and silky with a lot more skin exposed.

As his temperature climbed, he reined in his thoughts and brought them back to the day ahead.

"What time did you say we're going to the doctor?" he asked, trying to remember if she mentioned a time earlier.

"At eleven," she said, wondering what she could do to make Tate feel better. He looked miserable. She couldn't help but think some of it was from his acute disappointment. "You can rest for a while or watch TV or I can find you a book to read. What sounds good to you?"

"Rest, I think." Tate was already tired of sleeping and staying in bed. He was a man of action, not sitting still for long. How was it, then, that it was all he could do to keep his eyes open long enough to see Kenzie nod her head at him and smile?

As she settled the covers over him, he turned his head toward her hand where it brushed his cheek. "Thanks, Dewdrop," he whispered before succumbing to his weariness.

The next time Tate awoke, the first thing he noticed was a huge bouquet on the dresser. Filled with red flowers and holiday greens, it was festive and cheerful, reminding Tate Christmas was just around the corner. The scent of the flowers carried a hint of the pine branches tucked artfully into the vase.

A tap at his door drew his attention away from the bouquet.

"Come in," he said, grinning at the thought of Kenzie finding him in his unmentionables earlier.

"We've got about half an hour before we need to leave for your appointment." Kenzie walked over to the bed. "I thought you might want to get dressed and comb your hair."

"Yep." Tate sat up, ignoring the pain the movement created in his ribs. They were tender and it was hard to miss the large bruise on his side when he got out of the shower earlier. "Who sent the flowers?"

"My boss." Kenzie fished ice packs from beneath the covers where they slid while Tate slept. "He called this morning to see how you were doing and the next thing I knew, the florist delivered these."

"He didn't need to do that. I'm already indebted to him for the upgrade on our plane seats." Humbled by the man's kindness, Tate was grateful Kenzie worked for someone who obviously valued people.

"Tom loves all things western, particularly rodeos. It was so nice of you to bring Cort and Huck to sign autographs. You definitely made an impression on him the other night." Kenzie helped Tate move his knee off the pile of pillows on the bed.

"It wasn't a big deal." He waited for his head to stop spinning before he attempted to get to his feet.

"It was to him. If you wouldn't mind having him visit your ranch sometime, I think he'd love to spend a day with a real cowboy." Kenzie studied Tate. He seemed more talkative, although his face was still pale and he looked a little shaky.

"I wouldn't mind at all. I'll figure out a weekend, once the weather is nice, when I'll be home and invite him to come."

"He'd love it." She held her hands at her sides as Tate used the cane to leverage himself off the bed. He was getting adept at it. "Why don't you comb your hair and do whatever else you need to do, then I can help you put on your shirt and boots."

"Okay." On his way to the bathroom, he snagged a pair of jeans out of his suitcase. He refused to think about leaving the house in his lounge pants. It was bad enough he had to wear them in front of Kenzie, but he sure wasn't going out in public wearing his pajamas.

Although it took some work on his part, Tate managed to get his jeans on, teeth brushed, and hair combed.

When he opened the bathroom door, Kenzie leaned over his bed, tucking in a blanket. He admired the view of her long legs and the way her jeans fit so perfectly.

She turned around at the sound of the bathroom door opening and her thoughts ran together in her head.

Tate stood in the doorway wearing his snug-fitting jeans. The sight of his bare torso and hair still damp from his efforts to comb it into submission made her mouth go dry and she swallowed hard.

"Shall we finish getting you dressed?" she asked brightly, trying to hide her flustered state as she walked over to his suitcase. Tate told her to grab the shirt on top of the pile, so she did, thinking the light green and black plaid western shirt looked quite festive.

Carefully helping him work his broken arm into the sleeve, she smoothed the fabric across his shoulders. A jolt of heat arced between them.

Kenzie fastened the snaps and assisted him with his sling then motioned for Tate to sit down on a chair. She put on his socks, followed by his boots, and looked up at him with a smile that made his heart thump rapidly.

He wanted to take her in his arms and kiss her senseless. Instead, he pecked her cheek and grinned. "I think I'll skip the belt today and leave the shirt untucked."

"Good plan." She took his phone out of the back pocket of her jeans and handed it to him. He picked up his wallet from the bedside stand and stuffed it into his pocket then dug one-handed in his suitcase for his jacket. He hadn't packed a warm coat, but the jacket was better than nothing at all. Kenzie helped him put it on then went out to start her car.

When she came back in, Tate slowly made his way toward the door.

"Are you going to decorate for Christmas?" Tate asked. The apartment didn't have so much as a wreath or poinsettia anywhere in sight.

"Probably not." Kenzie slipped on her coat and picked up her purse.

"Why?"

Kenzie seemed like the type of girl to go all out for the holidays. He knew she was a Christian and observed the real reason for the seasonal celebration, not just the commercial trappings.

"Let's get you out to the car and see what the doctor has to say." Kenzie avoided his question as she waited for him to shuffle out the door. Expertly backing the car out of her parking space, she asked Tate about past injuries and how long he'd known Dr. Renwick as they drove to the doctor's office.

She sat in the waiting room with him until a nurse called him back to an examination room. After giving Kenzie a curious look, the nurse asked if she wanted to come along and Tate answered with an emphatic "no."

"I'll wait here." Kenzie hid her grin. "Thanks."

Eventually, the nurse returned and asked Kenzie to follow her to the doctor's office. He stood behind a large desk as she walked into the room and offered her his hand. Kenzie took it, immediately liking the man's firm handshake and friendly smile.

"Tate tells me you've been taking care of him the past few days." Dr. Renwick sat down and leaned back in his chair, studying Kenzie. The woman sitting across from him was beautiful and confident, but he also sensed a gentleness in her.

"Yes, sir," Kenzie answered, wondering why she was in the doctor's office.

"He said you practically kidnapped him and refuse to let him leave unless I give the go-ahead," Dr. Renwick said, watching the surprise register on Kenzie's face.

"Well, I... um... It isn't exactly..." Kenzie fumbled, trying to find the best words to explain the situation. Everything happened so fast since Tate's accident, she still felt a little out of balance. "He needed some help getting back from Las Vegas and I just didn't think it was a good idea for him to go home alone. He can't even put his socks on by himself."

The doctor laughed and wagged his finger at Kenzie. "I like you, Miss Beckett. You're good for Tate. That boy is entirely too independent and full of himself. I can say that because I've been treating him since he was eight."

Kenzie smiled at the doctor.

"That was a good call on your part, not letting him go home alone. He does need a few more days of care and then, if he feels like it, he can go back to the ranch. In the meantime, keep doing what you've been doing. Rest is the best thing for him right now, along with nourishing food. Ice his knee, arm and ribs periodically for the next few days. I'd like him to get in a couple of therapy sessions for his leg. As soon as the swelling goes down, we'll get that splint off and put a cast on his arm for a month or so, then do some therapy on it as well. The nurse is setting up his appointments right now so when you leave you'll have the dates and times," Dr. Renwick said, jotting down some notes.

The doctor looked back up at her. "His concussion is taking care of itself. All things considered, his ribs look good. He'll be able to use the hand of his broken arm once we cast it and the pain lessens. Let's cut back the pain meds and have him take them at night before he goes to bed. If you can get him to take it easy another day or so, then I'd say he could go back to the ranch by the weekend."

"Okay." Kenzie refused to think about how quiet and lonely her apartment would seem when Tate left. Maybe she'd surrender to her mother's pleading and travel to Portland to spend the holiday with her family.

"Tell me, Miss Beckett, why are you taking care of Tate?"

"We're friends. He needed some help and I was available," Kenzie said, matter-of-factly, not wanting to delve any deeper into her reasons than that of friendship.

"I see," the doctor said, seeing much more than Kenzie realized. After questioning Tate, he knew the young people were involved in a relationship for several months. "Have you ever nursed anyone before?"

"Not for a while." Many times, she'd bandaged her dad when he got hurt. Her mother fainted at the sight of blood, but it hadn't bothered Kenzie.

Her dad used to walk inside the house with a wound and yell, "I need help, Nurse Kenzie!" She'd gather up supplies and treat him. They both enjoyed the routine. Only the last wound her father received, the one he inflicted himself, was beyond anyone repairing.

"You do an admirable job," Dr. Renwick said, giving her another smile. "If Tate seems a little grumpy, just ignore it. As he starts to heal, he'll be more like himself."

The doctor stood and walked her to the nurse's station where she received a list of Tate's appointments. She'd barely sat down in the waiting room when the doctor escorted Tate out and told them to have a great day.

Kenzie decided to forgo any outings and instead drove straight home. Tate shuffled inside and sank down on the soft cushions of the couch in the living room, reclining his head against the overstuffed back.

"Mind if I hang out here for a while?" he asked as Kenzie hung up her coat then helped him out of his jacket.

"You can hang out here as long as you like." Kenzie went to the kitchen to warm up leftover soup for lunch. She returned carrying the now familiar tray and set it on the coffee table in front of Tate.

She placed pillows behind him so he could easily sit upright, then they enjoyed the simple meal. Tate's energy began a rapid decline. He couldn't bring himself to think about trekking back to the guest room.

Aware of Tate's exhaustion, Kenzie pulled off his boots and rearranged the pillows as he swung his legs onto the couch, letting himself relax.

When she draped a throw over him, he caught her hand and kissed her palm. "Thanks, Dewdrop."

"You're welcome, cowboy."

><><

Silently watching Tate sleep from her seat in the rocking chair across the room, Kenzie nursed a cup of tea.

The man stirred myriad emotions in her, but she wasn't sure what to do about those feelings.

She knew she loved Tate, admitted she was in love with him. It was the fact that she wasn't completely sure she could trust him that held her back.

Did he share her soul-deep feelings or was she just another diversion? From things his dad and Cort hinted at, they seemed to think Tate's feelings for her were something new and incredible, absolutely genuine.

Still uncertain, Kenzie rose from her chair and went to the bedroom she used as an office. After turning on the computer, she checked her emails and responded to a few questions from consultants, replied to an email from her sisters, and sent a message to Megan with an update on Tate's doctor visit.

As soon as Tate had settled in the previous morning and fell asleep, she called to give her friend the latest scoop. Megan gushed in response to the news.

"Kenz, having Tate dropped in your lap is a sign you're meant to be together."

"Just don't go planning anything," Kenzie cautioned her exuberant friend. "He's only here for a few days."

"I know, but anything can happen." Megan sounded entirely too gleeful for Kenzie's liking. "It's Christmas, the season of miracles."

Kenzie shook her head thinking about Megan's opinions.

Finally ready to get some answers to her questions about Tate, Kenzie searched online for his name and soon found details in a newspaper article about the restraining order he took out on some woman who attacked him at a rodeo.

Apparently, the woman had ripped his shirt, clawed his arm, and tried to yank out some of his hair before Cort and Huck pulled her away. Kenzie had noticed a newer-looking scar on Tate's upper arm and wondered if that was it. More searching brought up a photo of the woman, the one she'd seen kissing Tate in Pendleton.

Remorse and regret washed over her in a sickening wave, making her slump in her chair. Because of her stubbornness, her willingness to jump to conclusions that weren't true, she'd hurt Tate and denied herself the pleasure of spending the last few months with him.

Kenzie thought back to the week they spent together in Pendleton.

She was deeply in love with Tate. Even when she thought he'd been two-timing her, her heart still belonged to him.

Sighing, she rubbed her temples. She owed Tate an apology.

No wonder he acted so bewildered and upset when she refused to see or talk to him. He'd done nothing wrong. Nothing at all.

The betrayal she experienced from her father and Sonny had altered her perception. Kenzie wondered if she could allow herself to trust a man, get over her petty jealousy, and have a real relationship.

Was she willing to give it a try? Would Tate even be willing to give her a second chance?

If so, she had a lot of groveling to do.

Chapter Fourteen

The apartment was quiet when Tate awoke from a nap. He took as deep a breath as he could with his injured ribs and recalled falling asleep on Kenzie's couch.

As he opened his eyes, he took in a fire crackling in the gas fireplace across the room. Slowly sitting up, he looked around but didn't see Kenzie anywhere. No noise came from the kitchen so he got to his feet and used the cane to work his way down the hall.

Not paying attention earlier, he now took time to look in open doors as he passed them. The first door opened to a small office with a big desk, filing cabinet, and storage cupboards. The room sat beside a bathroom quite similar in design to the one in his room. He assumed this was a guest bath but Kenzie's summery scent floated in the air and he knew it must be her bathroom.

Continuing his self-guided tour, the next door revealed a lovely bedroom, complete with a deep burgundy satin comforter on a king-sized bed and dark walnut furniture that looked like it belonged in an antique display. The bedroom was smaller than the guest room and it was obvious there was no private bath.

Some photos on the dresser showed Kenzie with an older woman who closely resembled her, along with twin girls. The photo that really got his attention was one of

Kenzie with an attractive man. She looked to be about thirteen or so, smiling so brightly the camera captured the sparkle in her warm molasses eyes. Horses were visible in the background and Tate assumed the man must have been her dad. He grinned at the hot pink boots on Kenzie's feet. Evidently, that was her favorite color even then.

Tate left the bedroom and worked his way down the hall. He briefly wondered if Kenzie had given him her room, but the smaller bedroom was obviously the room she used.

As he hobbled back into the living room, the front door opened and Kenzie hurried in with her hands full of grocery bags.

"Hey, you're up," she said, breezing past him into the kitchen. He followed, wondering what he could do to help.

She motioned him to the table, where he sat and watched her. He liked that she worked with efficient movements as she put things away. In no time at all, she sat beside him with a cup of tea, scooting a plate of cookies his direction.

He took a drink of the hot tea and liked the blend of spices. "This is good. Tastes like Christmas." He took another swallow, savoring the rich flavors.

"It's Christmas tea." Kenzie sipped her own drink. "I only make it this time of year."

From her earlier avoidance of his question about Christmas, he was under the impression she didn't celebrate it at all.

He looked up from the cookie he'd just bitten into when Kenzie cleared her throat.

"Tate, I… um…" She stared at her hands before looking at him with tears filling her eyes. She inhaled a ragged breath, let it out, and licked her suddenly dry lips. "This is harder than I thought it would be."

She stopped and swiped at the tears starting to roll down her cheeks. Tate wondered if she was ready for him to leave. As much as he'd fought being there, he didn't like the idea of her wanting him gone.

"What is it?" he asked, placing his warm hand on her cool one. He turned her hand over and meshed their fingers together. It felt so right to intertwine them and he'd missed that simple touch so much since September. "What's wrong?"

"I'm so sorry, Tate," Kenzie said in a rush, still wiping at her tears with one hand while the other clung to his. "I jumped to conclusions, judged you unfairly, and I'm sorry. When I saw that woman kissing you, I assumed the worst then refused to listen when anyone tried to explain what really happened. I don't know how you can ever forgive me, but I hope someday you will."

It would have been easy for Tate to hold onto the anger and sense of injustice plaguing him since the moment Kenzie pushed him away. However, he was ready to move on and leave the past mistakes and hurts behind them. He had a feeling they wouldn't be repeated.

"Kenzie, all is forgiven. Okay?" Tate wanted to hold her, kiss her, and let her know how glad he was she finally acknowledged he'd done nothing wrong. Instead, he brought her hand to his lips and kissed the back of it, giving her a smoldering look as his eyes turned from a brilliant clear blue to a darker, stormier shade.

"But, Tate, I…"

Tate let go of her hand and placed his fingers on her lips, silencing her. Electric currents danced between them at his intimate touch. "You don't need to say any more. The fact that you're sorry is good enough for me."

"But I've been so awful to you." Kenzie worked to curtail her tears before she turned into a sobbing heap of hysterical female. Convinced Tate was in no shape to deal with that, she took a calming breath. "I don't deserve your forgiveness, Tate. I'm just so very sorry."

"I know you are, Dewdrop." Soothingly, Tate cupped her cheek and gazed into her eyes. "If I wasn't so thoroughly incapacitated, I'd show you exactly how glad I am to hear it."

His comment made her smile, as he knew it would. She sniffled, wiping away the last of her tears.

"You're pretty terrific, you know that?" Kenzie rose from the table and refilled their mugs with more hot tea.

"So I've been told," Tate said, doing his best to look arrogant and conceited.

"And you're so modest, too." She grinned as she sat back down, scooting the mug of hot tea across the table to him.

"You know it." He winked, taking a drink of the spicy tea.

Later that evening, after eating the chicken casserole Kenzie made for dinner, they sat on the couch with the fire blazing merrily, drinking hot chocolate laced with a liberal dollop of peppermint whipped cream.

Tate sighed in contentment with his head resting against the soft cushions of the couch and his knee supported by a pile of pillows on the coffee table.

"Now this is what I call domestic bliss." He turned his head to stare into Kenzie's eyes. Firelight flickered in the warm brown orbs, drawing Tate into a place he didn't ever want to leave.

Kenzie sat close enough to him her arm brushed his right side. The only thing that would make the evening better would be the ability to wrap both arms around her and hold her close. Instead, he leaned over and kissed her lips, savoring the taste of chocolate with a hint of peppermint and Kenzie's unique, sweet flavor.

She blinked and looked at him with questioning eyes. "What was that for?"

"For this chocolate," Tate said with a broad grin. "I won't admit it if asked, but I love hot chocolate and the peppermint makes it even better."

"Good to know." Mentally filing that detail for later use, she took another sip of her drink.

"Are you really not going to decorate for Christmas?" Tate tried to grasp the idea that people could go through the holiday season without adding some festive cheer to their home. Even he and his dad had decorations they got out and put up every year.

"I usually don't." Kenzie stared into the fire. How could she tell Tate that Christmas held too many reminiscences of her father and was one of the hardest seasons to get through? She didn't know how to make him understand the painful memories the season always dredged up. It was long past time to let go and move on, but it was so difficult.

"What do you usually do, then?" Curious what spoiled the holiday season for Kenzie, he hoped there was a way to help her enjoy it this year.

"Keep busy with work. Sometimes I volunteer at the senior center. If she begs long and hard enough, I sometimes spend it in Portland with Mom. My stepdad's family goes all out for the holidays but I don't feel right intruding on their family celebration," Kenzie admitted, staring at the flames dancing in her gas fireplace.

"I'm sure they love having you. Steve's been married to your mom quite a while, not to mention your sisters sort of tie you all together." Tate was surprised Kenzie didn't see herself as part of the family.

"I know, but despite their best efforts to make me feel welcome, I still think of myself as an outsider. I always spend Thanksgiving and New Year's with them, so my Mom doesn't think I'm ditching her entirely." The faraway look on her face made her seem almost lost. "Most of the time I spend Christmas at home and have a quiet day."

"That sounds pitiful and no fun at all." Sadly shaking his head, he stared at her. When she gave him a narrowed look, he grinned. "You aren't staying home alone this year."

"I'm not?" Kenzie asked, wondering what Tate had in mind.

"If you aren't going to Portland, then you'll come out to the ranch or we'll bring the party to you." Already making plans, Tate liked the idea of celebrating the very special holiday with Kenzie.

"You do realize Christmas is next week, don't you?"

"Yep, which is the reason we need to start making plans." He sounded more eager and interested in something than he had since his accident. "I won't take no for an answer."

"Fine." Kenzie released a long-suffering sigh, although pleased Tate wanted to spend Christmas together.

"Don't act like you'll enjoy it or anything." His sarcastic tone revealed his wounded feelings by her lack of enthusiasm. He hoped she'd be excited at the thought of spending Christmas with him.

"Sorry," Kenzie said with a small smile. She set down her now empty mug and leaned back against the couch cushions. "It's just… Christmas has been hard since my dad died."

"What makes it hard?" Tate wanted Kenzie to talk about what really bothered her.

"Daddy and I were always super close, you know. Not that I didn't love Mom just as much, but Dad understood me. We always clicked." Kenzie immersed herself in her memories. "He was so much fun and he went all out for the holidays. We'd go to the woods and get a tree then he and I would decorate it while Mom made sugar cookies. We'd sit together eating cookies and drinking hot apple cider, talking about special ornaments and making plans for the holiday season. Dad and I would hang the lights, help Mom decorate the house, and we always worked together on some secret gift for her. He just made Christmas so special and magical. When he and Mom split up, it was as if all the magic died. Christmas hasn't been the same since."

"You know some of that is just growing up, don't you?" Tate asked, setting down his mug and taking Kenzie's hand in his. When she looked at him with a quizzical expression, he continued.

"As kids, Christmas is magical and wonderful and full of special surprises. Once we grow up, some of that wonder disappears. It doesn't mean Christmas still can't be special. It's just different. No matter how hard you try, nothing ever quite recaptures the magic of Christmas like when you were a child. It's just the way it is. I'm sorry about your father, Kenzie. It's a hard thing to lose a parent. But don't you think he'd want you to move on? When my mama died, Pop made a huge effort to make Christmas special that year. It wasn't the same, never will be, but he put enough love into it that we moved forward and each year it got easier to celebrate without her."

"I'm sorry, Tate. I sometimes forget you've lost a parent, too. I suppose that maybe it is time to put the past behind me and look toward the future," Kenzie said wistfully, wishing it could be as easy as it sounded.

"What do you think your future holds?" Fervently wishing she would include him in her plans, he rubbed his thumb across the palm of her hand.

"I don't know, but I'm hoping this really hot, completely frustrating cowboy will want to be a part of it." Kenzie gave Tate a flirty smile.

"Is that right?" Tate ignored the pain in his side and leaned over to kiss Kenzie with a thoroughness that left them both breathless. He couldn't believe she'd just said she wanted a future with him in it. Mindful of not pushing the issue, he let her comment slide. "Before your dad died, how did you envision your life? What were your dreams?"

Kenzie was quiet so long Tate didn't think she would answer. Finally, she let out a sigh and rested her hand on his leg.

"As my father's only child, he groomed me from the time I was old enough to walk and talk to take over the ranch. I went everywhere with him, learned everything he knew about ranching, cattle, and horses. Up until Mom left him, I knew my future was going to be ranching. I loved every inch of our place and didn't have any other dreams. Even after the divorce, I thought eventually I'd end up back at the ranch with Dad. Then he died and we had to sell the ranch. I gave up my dreams and went with what was practical."

"I'm sorry, Dewdrop. No one should have to let their dreams go like that." Tate wrapped his good arm around her and kissed the top of her head.

When she tilted her head back and locked her eyes to his, he couldn't help but surrender to the need to kiss her. Several breath-stealing moments later, he felt completely ensnared by the emotions Kenzie stirred inside him.

"I think you better behave for the time being," Kenzie whispered against his lips as he tried to keep from groaning with pain.

"Maybe you're right." Cautiously leaning back against the cushions, he fixed his gaze on her face. "If I promise to be good, will you at least think about putting up a few decorations?"

"I'll think about it." The impish look she gave him made his heart trip in his chest.

><><

The next morning Tate opened his eyes and stretched, feeling much improved.

His head didn't hurt, he could wiggle the fingers of his broken arm, and his knee barely throbbed.

The tempting aroma of coffee and bacon wafted beneath his door, making him ravenous for breakfast.

Quickly grabbing the cane next to his bed, he got up and hobbled to his suitcase. Certain everything he owned was dirty, he opened the lid to discover Kenzie had washed his clothes. They sat neatly folded in his suitcase, ready to wear. After picking up a pair of lounge pants and a T-shirt, he went to the bathroom to take a shower then remembered he needed to cover his arm.

Slowly limping across the bedroom, he opened the door and started toward the kitchen but stopped short when he got to the living room. Christmas decorations filled the room and familiar carols played in the background.

This was quite a change from yesterday.

He admired a hand-carved nativity set, smiled at some decorations obviously crafted by a childish hand, then studied the holly garlands draped over the doorways and along the mantle.

In the kitchen, he watched Kenzie for a moment as she fried bacon. A cheery red apron covered her dark green sweater. With her gleaming hair pulled back into a ponytail, she looked like a lovely ornament. He listened to her hum along to a popular Christmas carol and watched her sway slightly to the music.

"Happy Holidays, Dewdrop," Tate said in a teasing voice.

"Oh, Tate, I didn't hear you." She spun around, looking a little chagrined at his catching her humming a holiday tune.

"I see one of Santa's elves escaped from the North Pole and vandalized your house last night." The grin on his handsome face did great justice to his dimples and made Kenzie's knees weaken.

"Something like that." She smiled at Tate, wondering how he could look so enticing with his hair sticking up every which direction around his head and a crease from the pillowcase on his cheek. "Thanks for last night. I appreciate what you said and I'm going to make an attempt to grow up and move on."

"So far so good," Tate said, noticing a plump snowman cookie jar on the counter. "Where did all this stuff come from?"

"It's mine." Hastily wiping her hands on a dishtowel, she pulled some garbage bags out of a drawer. "Mom didn't want any of the decorations when she left Dad, so she saved them for me. When I moved here, I brought them along. I couldn't bear the thought of throwing them away, even if I wasn't ready to use them."

"I bet each piece has a story behind it," Tate said, pointing to a resin reindeer wearing a happy smile as it sat next to the toaster.

"Most of them do. I'll share the best ones with you." Quickly wrapping the garbage bags around his arm, she fastened the ends with tape. "After you went to bed, I decided to get this stuff out and stayed up way too late reminiscing, but I wanted to surprise you this morning."

"Mission accomplished. I'm totally surprised." Tate kissed her cheek then looked into her much-loved face. "Thank you, Kenzie, for everything."

"You're welcome," she said, pointing toward the doorway. "You better hurry it up or I'll eat all this bacon by myself."

"Don't even kid about a thing like that. Bacon is serious business." Tate limped out the door, looking forward to spending the day with Kenzie.

After eating a filling breakfast of bacon, toast, and eggs with juice and coffee, Tate decided to check the messages on his phone. Overwhelmed by the sheer number of messages people left for him, it seemed everyone wanted to know where he was, how he was doing, and if he had plans to continue the pro rodeo circuit in the coming year.

Going back to his room, he called Cort and visited with him for a while then talked to Huck.

Exhausted by the time he hung up from a call with his dad, he fell asleep with the phone still in his hand. He woke up when it buzzed. It took him a moment to realize what was making the annoying noise.

When he answered the call, he was surprised to find one of the local television personalities on the line, inviting him to make an appearance on the morning news program a few days before Christmas. They wanted him to talk about his rodeo career and plans for the coming year. Tate agreed and hoped he'd be able to walk on the set without his cane by then.

He rose from the bed and made his way to the living room. A scent redolent of Christmas tickled his nose, making him grin.

"What are you making, Dewdrop?" he asked as he rounded the corner to the kitchen.

"Gingerbread bars," Kenzie said, turning to look at him over her shoulder.

Tate almost laughed at the sight she made, along with the upheaval in her normally tidy kitchen. Baked goodies or sweets in the making covered every counter surface. As she squeezed a drizzle of frosting over a big pan of bars that smelled amazing, flour dusted her chin and highlighted one of her cheeks.

"Have you done quality control on those? Need a taste-tester?" Tate asked, hoping he could get a taste sooner rather than later. He'd lay the charm on extra thick if he had to in order to get a sample of the goodies.

"You can eat as many as you like, within reason, after you have some lunch," Kenzie said, setting her ground rules for his cookie consumption. "I thought we could have sandwiches, if that's okay with you. I got a little preoccupied this morning."

"Sure." Tate glanced around to see if he could do anything to help then decided he had no idea where to start.

"If I put the sandwich stuff on the table, can you make them?" Kenzie finished with the frosting and rinsed her hands.

"You bet." Suddenly anxious to be done with lunch, he wanted to move on to the sweets. He swiped a pinch of cookie dough from a bowl when he thought Kenzie wasn't looking. It was buttery with a rich cinnamon flavor.

"Snickerdoodles, you snitch." Kenzie took lunchmeat and cheese from the fridge.

Tate decided with her superpowers of being able to see behind her back, she'd make a great mother someday.

The desire to be the father of those children hit him square in the heart, making him catch his breath. Rolling the idea around in his head and liking it more with each passing second, he felt a new sense of longing and purpose.

Abruptly sitting at the table, he realized his feelings for Kenzie were the forever kind. The settle down, have a family, and grow old together kind of feelings that drove a man to think of proposals, weddings, and babies.

He let his mind wander, considering the possibilities.

By the time she set the sandwich ingredients on the table, he'd once again composed his thoughts.

"Hope you like turkey and ham," she said, setting out two plates and silverware along with a bowl of pasta salad.

"Two of my favorite sandwich ingredients." Tate assembled sandwiches, helped himself to a scoop of pasta salad, and waited for Kenzie to come to the table. She placed a glass of water in front of him and he offered her a smile of thanks.

He was taking a bite from his sandwich when the oven timer dinged. Kenzie jumped up to take out a sheet of cookies then popped in another one.

"What are you going to do with all that?" Tate asked, inclining his head toward the overflowing counters when she returned to the table.

"Give it away," she said, taking a bite of pasta salad.

Tate choked on his sandwich and washed it down with a gulp of water. "What? Why?"

"I always make up tins of treats to give to people who might not have any homemade goodies, like Paul, and some of the elderly neighbors, a few people at church. I'll make sure to put together some treats for your dad. Is there anything he likes in particular?"

"Everything," Tate said with a grin. His sweet tooth came directly from his father. "He'll eat anything you take him."

"Great." Kenzie didn't mention her plans to send Tate home with an ample supply of treats when he left. Thoughts of his leaving made her sad, so she mentally switched gears.

"Are you finished with your Christmas shopping?" Kenzie asked as Tate made himself a second sandwich.

"Shopping?" Tate repeated. He hadn't purchased anything other than the vintage milk can in Las Vegas that would ship directly to his dad. He typically sent gift cards or gift baskets to friends. He needed to get something nice for Huck and Mara's family as well as something for Cort. A trip to the bank for cash bonuses would take care of his ranch hands. "I haven't exactly started yet."

Kenzie looked up at him with a raised eyebrow.

"I'll see what I can find online." A trip to the mall was pretty much out of the question.

After clearing the lunch dishes out of her way, Kenzie went back to her baking project, giving Tate tastes of whatever he wanted. With a glass of milk in front of him and his second gingerbread bar in his hand, he was happily full and unbelievably content.

While he still held some lingering disappointment about what happened at the finals, he knew brooding wouldn't change anything and decided to focus on his plans for next year.

Depending on how long it took his arm to heal, he would most likely miss several weeks of competing.

Many cowboys sidelined with injuries could find themselves in a financial bind before returning to the rodeo. Thanks to a crisis fund, those with serious injuries could receive assistance until they got back on their feet.

Tate felt fortunate his injuries were relatively minor and the rodeo wasn't his sole source of income. Between good insurance and the ranch, his finances wouldn't experience an impact, even if he did have to wait a month or two to get back on the rodeo circuit.

Determined to ignore the what-ifs flying through his thoughts, he decided any major decisions about his career could wait until after the New Year.

Surrounded by the smells of holiday baking, the sight of a beautiful woman with flour streaking her cheeks, and the sounds of Christmas carols in the background, Tate slipped right into the holiday spirit.

"You're a terrific cook." Tate took a hot snickerdoodle right off the cookie sheet as Kenzie pulled it out of the oven. He tossed the cookie up a few times in his hand until it cooled enough to handle and hobbled back to the table.

Kenzie gave him an indulgent grin. "I don't cook all that often, but I do like to bake for the holidays." She washed an empty bowl then put away a canister of flour. "If you're under the delusion that I'm domestic, you might want to rethink that. I just do enough to get by because I'm really not home that much."

"That is so not true." The look he shot her said he knew otherwise. "I do enough to get by which is nuking stuff out of boxes or cans and barbecuing meat. You can actually cook, and quite well from what I've tasted."

"Thanks." The unexpected praise made her blush. She busied herself storing cooled cookies in a resealable bag. "My mom is a good cook and I learned a lot from my grandma before she died."

"Where did your grandma live?" Tate couldn't recall Kenzie mentioning a grandparent before.

"Portland. It's where my mom was from originally. She and Daddy met at college and you know the rest of that story. When we moved to Portland, we lived with Grandma for a few years until Mom got back on her feet. By then, she was seeing my stepfather. It wasn't long until they married and we moved to a new house. Grandma was always in the kitchen baking or cooking and it helped me get through an incredibly tough time being with her. There was something comforting about cooking together."

"I'm glad you had your grandma to help you." He was also glad the woman shared her cooking skills with her granddaughter. He didn't think he'd ever had so many delicious sweets in all his life.

"Grandma was a gem." Her gaze fell to the snowman cookie jar on the counter, remembering when her grandmother gave it to her, full of her favorite treats after Kenzie had a particularly rough day at school. "Most of my furniture belonged to Grandma."

"She had some great antiques." It was nice to know Kenzie valued the pieces she inherited from her grandmother. With the money she made as a corporate trainer, she could afford to purchase anything she wanted for her apartment, but instead she used the pieces that had sentimental value.

"Thanks, I'm pretty partial to them." She slid the last pan of cookies into the oven.

As he finished his glass of milk, Tate glanced around the kitchen, letting his gaze rest on Kenzie. It required a considerable effort on his part to keep his hands, and lips, to himself, despite his aches and pains.

"Is there anything I can do to help you?" he asked. He assumed his best option was staying out of the way.

"No, but thanks for offering," Kenzie said, loading the dishwasher with what would fit and starting to hand-wash the rest.

Tate noticed Kenzie didn't have a lot of fancy gadgets or equipment in her kitchen, just the basics, including a rolling pin that looked like it had been used for many years. "I'm surprised you don't have all kinds of kitchen toys. Don't great cooks like to keep up on the latest inventions to make their lives easier?"

"Great cooks might but I'm not one. Even if I was, I'm not home enough to justify the expense or use of space for that kind of stuff." She dried a baking sheet and stored it in a skinny cupboard.

"If you were home more and could justify it, what one thing would you get?" he asked, curious as to what type of kitchen tools drew Kenzie's attention.

"One of those stand mixers. I've always wanted one, but there's no point in buying it when I'm rarely home. It's not like I entertain much or have a lot of company." The look on her face told Tate she would love to have one of those mixers.

"Speaking of company, if you rarely have any why do you have such a nice guest room? I couldn't help but notice it's much bigger than your room and has the private bathroom."

Kenzie briefly wondered when he'd seen her room, but knew she'd left him alone a few times while she ran errands. He must have been looking for her. "I'm not here that much so it's no biggie. When I do have company, I want them to feel welcome and comfortable. So far, my longest-staying guests have been my little sisters. They usually spend a week with me right after school gets out for the summer."

"Isn't that your busiest time of year?" Tate asked, not at all surprised Kenzie would take a week off to spend with her sisters. He remembered her mentioning something about them visiting not long after they met.

"One of the busiest, but it's the only time they can come stay for a full week. I do some work from home those days and everything works out." Quickly finishing the dishes, she wiped down the counters.

"I can't wait to meet them." If the twins were like their big sister, they'd be full of life and fun.

"They'll be over the moon to meet you, but I won't subject you to their effervescent personalities anytime soon." She dried her hands and hung the towel on a hook, offering Tate a teasing grin.

He laughed then asked Kenzie if he could use her computer for a while. She told him to knock himself out then looked sheepish, considering he recovered from a concussion.

Full of too many cookies and not enough pain medication, Tate sat at the computer posting on his blog, responding to Facebook messages, tweets, and answering emails from friends. Offering reassurances he was doing fine, he let everyone know he looked forward to seeing them in the coming year on the circuit.

When he finished with that, he began shopping online for gifts. He found a gift basket perfect for Huck's family, purchased Cort a gift certificate to his favorite ranch supply store, and ordered some books and puzzles for his dad. He ordered gift cards for his other friends and a couple of surprises for Kenzie. Everything should arrive in time for Christmas.

Feeling good about his shopping, Tate went back to the guest room and soon fell asleep, dreaming of the way

Kenzie looked coated in flour with a special light gleaming in her dark eyes.

Chapter Fifteen

Kenzie sat by the fire in the rocker, letting the chair move back and forth in a comforting rhythm. For the first time since she'd moved in, her apartment looked festive. The only thing missing was a tree.

It felt good, unbelievably good, to allow herself to embrace the holiday spirit this year. She had Tate to thank for the positive change.

Thoughts of him made her stomach flutter and her heartbeat increase in tempo. He was handsome and funny, gentle and wonderful. He made her laugh, challenged her, and encouraged her. The way he looked at her with those smoldering blue eyes made her feel beautiful and wanted.

Kenzie refused to think about how empty her life would seem when he went home. She knew it was wrong to wish it, but she hoped he wouldn't feel like leaving anytime soon. Even though he was in no shape to do more than hold her hand and steal a kiss or two, she cherished the time she spent with him, getting to know him better.

Tired in a happy, good way, Kenzie let her thoughts drift to the upcoming holiday. The realization she hadn't yet purchased a gift for Tate sent her mind spinning into overdrive.

She wracked her brain, trying to think of something special to get him, something that would let him know exactly how much he meant to her. Lost in her thoughts, she looked up when he hobbled into the room.

It appeared he'd attempted to comb his hair, although the cowlick on the left side of his head refused to cooperate.

The sight of it made her smile at him with such warmth, Tate momentarily worried both legs would give out on him before he seated himself on the couch.

"What?" He ran a self-conscious hand over his head. Not used to her looking at him so intently, he found it both disquieting and fascinating.

"I was thinking about you, and suddenly here you are," she said with saucy grin, sending Tate's temperature up a notch. When he continued to stare at her, not speaking, she wondered what ran through his mind. Unable to read his thoughts from the look on his face, she scrambled for a safe topic.

Lazily turning so her legs dangled over the arm of the chair, she wiggled her feet and let out a contented sigh. "I don't know about you, but I've indulged in too many treats today. Could you choke down a salad for dinner?" Kenzie asked, hoping Tate wouldn't mind eating something light.

"That sounds fine." The firelight caressed Kenzie's dark hair, making it glow with a rich vibrancy, drawing his attention. Instead of giving in to his longing to bury his hands in it and kiss her until they both lost their ability to reason, he nodded toward the kitchen. "Can I help with anything?"

"Sure." Kenzie got to her feet and held out a hand to help Tate stand. He used his cane to limp the few steps to the kitchen, following behind her.

After pulling a variety of veggies from the fridge, she rinsed them before setting the produce on the counter. She placed a cutting board and knife in front of Tate then turned around to grate some cheese and wash a head of lettuce.

As they worked together, she asked about his online shopping and he quizzed her about other things she planned to bake before Christmas. They ate salad and laughed at funny memories they shared from past holidays.

Kenzie told Tate how her sisters decided to set a trap for Santa one year. She helped her stepdad make it look like they caught the jolly old elf and wrote a note admonishing the two little live wires to be good.

Tate admitted to pulling a few pranks that nearly got his presents revoked, like setting a video camera in the fireplace to record Santa's entry, and trying to rig a duck blind on the roof to watch Santa land without being caught.

After dinner, they snuggled on the couch to watch television.

Tate, who absolutely loved everything about Christmas, was glad Kenzie wanted to watch *The Polar Express*. It was a cute movie, although he was much more interested in having her cuddled up to his side than what was on television. Partway through the show, he looked over to see Kenzie swipe at the tears trickling down her cheeks.

"What's wrong, Dewdrop? I thought you were enjoying this." Dumbfounded by her tears, he wiped them away with his thumb. She remained relaxed against him, not giving any signal that something bothered her.

"I am," she sniffed, offering him a watery smile. "I'm sorry, but those two little kids singing their hearts out always make me cry. It's just so sweet."

Tate didn't expect the rush of love for this amazing woman to engulf him at that moment. He knew behind her cool and confident business persona was a sappy girl who probably cried during greeting card commercials.

"Sweet," Tate repeated, cupping the back of Kenzie's neck with his good hand and pulling her head toward his. When their lips connected, the jolt rocked Tate all the way to his toes. Resting his forehead against hers, he grinned. "You're sweet and something else altogether, Miss Kenzie Beckett. Something very special."

"Tate," she whispered, pressing her lips to his then resting her head on his shoulder while he slipped his right arm around her. They watched the rest of the movie and started watching another one when Tate glanced down to find Kenzie asleep. She had to be completely exhausted from taking care of him, decorating her apartment, baking, and doing all the other things she'd accomplished the last few days. She could run circles around him even when both his legs worked properly.

Tate turned off the television and basked in the simple pleasure of having Kenzie so close to him. Drowsily, he watched the fire flicker and felt his eyes grow heavy. He knew they needed to go to bed or they'd both end up asleep on the couch with cramped muscles before morning.

"Kenzie," Tate said, gently shaking her shoulder. "Time for bed."

When that didn't rouse her, he leaned over and nuzzled her neck.

"Oh, Tate, that's nice." The sultry tone in her voice brought him instantly wide-awake. His gut clenched and the temperature in the room suddenly turned tropical.

He moved from nipping her ear to kissing a hot trail down her jaw, ending with her lips. She wrapped her arms around his neck, toying with the back of his hair above his shirt collar, leaning into his chest.

Tate ignored the protests from his cracked ribs and held her close, kissing her with a fervor that brought her from half asleep to fully participating in the passionate encounter in a matter of seconds.

"I think we better call this good night," Tate finally managed to say after giving himself a moment to catch his breath and rein in his errant thoughts.

"Probably." Kenzie took a deep breath and rose to her feet. After making sure the front door was locked, she turned off the fire while Tate stood and ambled toward the guest room. Kenzie followed him and turned down his covers, helped him take off his shirt and brought him a glass of water so he could take a pain pill.

Tenderly kissing his cheek, she gave him one last, long gaze that left him overheated before walking out of the room and shutting the door behind her.

Unable to relax in the big comfortable bed, Tate kept thinking about the affectionate, tempting woman in the other room who had worked her way thoroughly and completely into his heart.

Despite his fatigue, sleep was a long time coming.

"Rise and shine, cowboy," Kenzie said in a cheery voice as she breezed into Tate's room. She pulled back the drapes and turned the mini blinds so sunshine filtered through the windows. "We've got places to go and people to see."

"What?" Tate asked, shielding his eyes from the bright morning light by putting a pillow over his head. "What time is it? Where are we going?"

"It's after eight and you've got a nine-thirty appointment with the physical therapist today. You better move that cute keister of yours out of bed." A sassy smile tossed over her shoulder drew his gaze as he watched her turn on the bathroom lights then come back to the bed.

"You think my keister is cute?" Tate asked, a sleepy grin spreading across his face that left Kenzie with quivering knees.

"Never mind." Before handing him his cane, she focused her attention on wrapping his arm in garbage bags and tape.

Instead of limping to the bathroom, he turned his bright gaze on her and the heat of it seeped into her very bones.

"What else do you think is cute? Any other details you want to share?" Tate asked with a bold smile as he got to his feet.

"No." She motioned him toward the bathroom. "Put some hustle in it or you're going to be late."

"If you're worried about me being late, why didn't you wake me up earlier? Or remind me to set an alarm last night?" Tate asked as he hobbled to the bathroom door.

"If you must know, I'm also guilty of sleeping in this morning. You're always awake early and I didn't even think about an alarm. So there." She stuck her tongue out at him then flounced out of the room.

Amused by her childish gesture, Tate shut the bathroom door. Quickly showering, he vowed to make time later for a shave. His face itched and if he had the opportunity to kiss Kenzie, he didn't want his stubble to scratch her soft skin.

When he emerged from the bathroom, she'd already made the bed. He appreciated that she kept things neat and orderly.

He dug around in his suitcase and found a pair of basketball shorts and running shoes he'd used during his daily workouts in Las Vegas. He managed to get his socks on by himself but needed help with his shoes and T-shirt. If he was going to therapy, he assumed workout clothes would be the best thing to wear.

With his cane in hand, he limped to the kitchen where Kenzie pulled a pan of muffins from the oven.

"That was fast," she said, glancing up to see his T-shirt draped over one shoulder. Swiftly setting down the muffins, she wiped her hands on a dishtowel then stepped around the counter to help Tate with his shirt.

It required an enormous effort to drag her thoughts away from his broad chest and shoulders, covered as they were with impressive muscles. After helping him dress the past few days, she thought she should be immune to seeing his bare upper torso, but she wasn't. The site of it made her mouth go dry and her stomach flutter.

"You told me to hurry it up, boss." A jaunty grin brought his dimples to the forefront. "Are you going to let me eat before you take me off to be tortured?"

"Of course." Kenzie poured glasses of juice and handed them to Tate to put on the table. She placed the muffins on a plate, scooped up the eggs she scrambled, and forked fried ham out of a skillet.

As they sat across from each other at her little table, Kenzie split open muffins and buttered them, setting two on Tate's plate.

"I'm going to ask you something, Dewdrop, and I want a straight-up honest answer." Tate stared at Kenzie over his glass of orange juice.

"Okay." Whatever he was going to ask sounded serious and she wasn't sure she wanted to start out the day with that type of conversation. She folded her hands on her lap and waited for him to speak.

"You've spent the last few days taking great care of me. I appreciate it more than you can know, but what about your life? Is having me here disrupting what you'd normally do? I can go home or find somewhere else to stay if I'm throwing off your schedule."

Tate looked at her with such sincere concern on his face that tears pricked her eyes. She loved him so much. More than he probably could guess, especially since she hadn't gotten around to actually saying those three little words to him.

The notion of him anywhere other than right there with her was unthinkable. She cherished the time they spent together, where she could see him anytime she wanted. It was easy to pretend they belonged together and he'd never leave when it was just the two of them.

She glanced at Tate with her brown eyes simmering like warm, rich molasses. He fell into their depths without a single thought of resistance.

"As a matter of fact, you've thrown me all out of whack. My routine has been completely disrupted." The serious, irritated tone of her voice made her sound quite displeased although she was only teasing.

At Tate's crestfallen look, her lips lifted in a grin. "I've missed catching up on the soap operas, cleaning the lint out of the dryer, scrubbing the grout in the tub, and at least three or four great naps. I just don't know how you'll make that up to me."

"Kenzie, I'm serious," he admonished, although the dimples in his cheeks said otherwise. He let out the breath he didn't even realize he'd held at her cheeky reply. "I really do want to know if I'm in your way."

"Never, cowboy. Not ever." She leaned over to kiss his cheek. Tate turned his head at the last second so her kiss landed on his lips instead. He wished he'd gone ahead and taken the time to shave when she pulled back after a potent kiss with her face red from his whiskers.

"Honest?" Tate asked, still not certain what Kenzie hinted at. He rubbed his fingers gently over the red skin around her mouth before returning his attention to his breakfast.

"For sure," she said, taking a bite of her muffin. "Now hustle it up or we'll be late."

"Yes, ma'am." Tate gulped his juice and stuffed the last of his muffin in his mouth. He rose from the table and hobbled back to his room to brush his teeth and grab his jacket.

Kenzie watched him leave the table and shook her head. Did everything about him have to be amazing?

Kind and thoughtful, funny and sweet, he also had a great pair of legs to go along with the rest of his killer physique. It was a good thing he was mostly incapacitated by his injuries.

With the direction her mind kept venturing, she couldn't allow him to stay if he was at one hundred percent physical condition.

Kenzie rushed to do the dishes while trying to capture her runaway thoughts. When she finished, she dried her hands and ran out to start her car. She stood by the door buttoning her coat as Tate reappeared, carrying his shoes. After helping him put them on, they hurried out the door.

At the physical therapy facility, Kenzie helped him inside then left to run errands. She mailed a few packages at the post office then hurried to the dry cleaners to pick up her business suits. At the grocery store, she loaded a cart while her mind spun around, trying to think of a gift for Tate.

Finally returning to the facility ninety minutes later, Tate waited for her, looking drained and spent.

"How'd it go?" Kenzie asked, holding the door for him as he walked out into the cold to her car. Covered in a light sheen of sweat, she worried about him getting sick in the chilly temperature.

"Fantastic," Tate said derisively. "The doc set me up with some crazy woman who seems to think it's her personal mission to whip me back into shape. Evidently, she'll be working on both my leg and arm."

"Oh, you poor wittle thing." She spoke to him as she would a pouting child. Carefully patting his leg, she started the car and backed out of the parking space. "Did the big bad woman scare wittle Tater?"

Tate scowled at her then focused his attention out the window. He knew therapy would be painful and unpleasant, but he had no idea how much so. His doctor told him he could let his knee heal by doing exercises at home. However, since he was an athlete with an active career to return to, he suggested an accelerated course of therapy to help him get back on track.

If the therapist didn't kill him, his knee would be in great shape before long. Kenzie's teasing made him annoyed instead of lightening the mood as he knew she'd hoped it would. He continued glaring out the window, ignoring her.

"I'm sorry." A glance at Tate revealed his frown as he stared out the window. "I shouldn't have teased. I know therapy can be awful. I broke my elbow when I was in high school and had therapy on it for a few weeks. It was one of the most painful things I've ever experienced."

"How'd you break your elbow?" Tate pulled himself from his dark thoughts, curious if Kenzie played sports in school. He couldn't remember her mentioning any sport activities.

"It was stupid." Her cheeks turned pink at the memory.

"I know all about stupid." Remorsefully glancing at his arm, he gave her an inquisitive look. "What did you do?"

"Megan invited me to spend the summer with her before we started our senior year of high school. We were acting stupid like seventeen-year-old girls are prone to do, driving around in her dad's old pickup. Megan had a crush on a boy, so we drove past his house twice then she decided to drive by again. We practiced looking cool, with our arms resting on the rolled down windows. Erroneously, we thought we had it all going on. Megan got so excited when the boy looked up as we went by, she didn't pay attention where she was driving. I was watching her ogle him and didn't see the mailbox until she drove too close and smashed it with my elbow. My mom was not the least bit happy to have me come home in a cast."

"He must have been a really cute boy to distract you two so much," Tate said, giving Kenzie a taunting grin.

"Megan thought so since she married him." Her eyes twinkled with mirth as she smiled at Tate. "Check out the mailbox the next time you go to the Montgomery's ranch. The dent by the flag, that's all mine."

Tate chuckled and shook his head, trying to picture Kenzie as a carefree girl. He assumed she was probably always very responsible and mature. "I'd give Megan a bad time about that, but obviously her efforts paid off."

"Obviously," she agreed, pulling into her parking space at the apartment complex.

After carrying in groceries and setting them on the counter, Kenzie wrapped his arm again and he hobbled off to take another shower. Once she put everything away, she decided to go pick up his dad. She left Tate a note that let him know she'd be right back.

When she returned with Kent, Tate stood at the stove, stirring a pot that smelled surprisingly good. He looked over his shoulder and smiled both at her and his dad.

"Wondered where you ran off to." Tate gave his concoction a stir. "How are you, Pop?"

"Fair to middlin'. Can't complain." Kent took a seat at the table after Kenzie helped him remove his coat.

"I thought you two might like to visit this afternoon." Kenzie carried the dry cleaning she'd tossed over a chair back to her room. Quickly returning to the kitchen, she got out plates, set the table, and poured glasses of water. Somehow, Tate managed to dress in jeans and a shirt that snapped, although he didn't have on any shoes. His cheeks were freshly shaven. The combination of his aftershave with his masculine scent made her mouth water.

"So what did you make for lunch?" Vainly, she tried to distract herself from thoughts of how desperately she wanted to press her lips to his smooth, taut cheeks.

"Just this noodle stuff Pop taught me to make, but it's usually pretty good and filling. I think we've got leftover salad from last night, don't we?" Tate spooned noodles cooked with hamburger and a creamy sauce into a serving bowl. Kenzie carried it to the table then took the leftover green salad out of the fridge along with some salad dressing.

Kent asked the blessing then they ate the meal with a lively conversation about trouble he got into as a boy.

Kenzie loved hearing him talk about things that had happened almost a century ago. No wonder Tate was so active and full of life. Apparently, he inherited his liveliness from his father.

While the men ate more than their share of cookies, Kenzie cleaned up the table then turned on the fire in the front room.

The men talked about the ranch for a while and Tate surprised her when he discussed in detail what was going on at the ranch that day. Despite not being there, he was very involved in the day-to-day operations. She liked that he kept on top of what was happening and took full responsibility for the Morgan Ranch.

Kenzie excused herself to her office where she checked emails, responded to questions from consultants, and sent a weekly report to the corporate office.

Even though she considered herself on vacation, she still liked to keep in touch with the consultants assigned to her to mentor, as well as the home office. Her boss didn't expect her to work during the weeks she had off, but she felt obligated to stay on top of her career. It made it easier to get back into the swing of things when mid-January rolled around.

When she finished her work, she wandered back to the front room where Kent and Tate engaged in a good-natured argument about the type of bull Tate should look for at a bull sale he planned to attend in February.

Kenzie made hot chocolate and poured three mugs full, adding a dollop of whipping cream laced with peppermint to each before carrying them to the living room.

While Kent sipped his appreciatively, Tate gave Kenzie a wink that was all male flirtation.

She made a silly face at him then turned her attention to his dad.

"Do you like to play games?" Kenzie glanced from father to son.

"What kind of games?" Kent asked, wondering what the intriguing girl had planned.

"Board games, like Clue or Scrabble."

"Sure, honey. What've you got? Can we team up against Tater?" The older man's blue eyes danced with a zest for life his age had not dimmed.

"How about Sorry? You can knock his pieces off the board on your way to victory." Kenzie opened the door to the front entry closet and took a game off the shelf.

"Hey!" Tate protested while his dad laughed.

"I like the way this girl thinks, Tater." Kent scooted his chair forward so he could reach the coffee table where Kenzie set up the game.

An hour later, all three of them laughed as Kenzie retrieved Tate's latest piece from the floor where Kent knocked it off the board.

"I can't believe you beat us both, Pop." Tate stared at his dad. "Are you sure you didn't cheat?"

"How would I cheat? I could barely make a move with you two watching me like hawks," Kent said, stretching his legs amid much creaking. "As fun as this has been, I better get back to the center. I promised to play checkers with one of the fellas after dinner. He gets antsy if I'm not right on time. And tonight is meatloaf with gravy so I can't miss that."

"Are you sure, Kent? I'd be happy to have you stay for dinner." She put away the game then took her coat and Kent's from the closet.

"I'm sure, but thanks for the offer. I enjoyed this afternoon. Thank you for bringing me over." The old man got to his feet and gazed fondly at Kenzie as she helped him with his coat. "You be good to this girl, Tater, or you'll answer to me."

"Sure, Pop." Tate grinned as he stood.

"Wanna go with us?" Kenzie asked, turning her attention to Tate. "You could put on your boots while I warm up the car."

"I'd like that." He limped to his room and returned wearing his boots and jacket.

As Kenzie helped Kent out to the car, she looked over at Tate with a smile that made him catch his breath. Her cheeks were rosy from the cold and her dark hair spilled over the hot pink peacoat she wore. It was a good thing he was out of commission or he could be in all kinds of trouble where she was concerned.

Tate hobbled out the door and closed it behind him, wondering what stories his dad would tell on the way to the care home.

He wasn't disappointed as Kent talked about the holidays when he was a boy and things he remembered as being special treats.

"Bet you wouldn't be too happy, son, if you found nuts and an orange in your stocking. You always wanted those action figures and bubble gum." The mischievous grin on Kent's face as he looked over his shoulder at Tate in the back seat was so like the one his son often wore. "If I were a betting man I'd place money on you hoping for something a little more exciting under your tree this year. Or maybe I should say someone."

"Pop!" Tate's warning tone only made his father cackle with laughter.

Kenzie looked at Tate in her rear-view mirror. She raised an eyebrow in his direction. Her look let him know she didn't take his dad too seriously, even though her flushed cheeks gave away her embarrassment at Kent's teasing.

After walking the old man inside and back to his room, Kenzie returned to the car to find Tate in the front seat, drumming the fingers of his right hand on his thigh as he listened to some rousing Christmas tunes.

While *Run, Run Rudolph* played on the radio, Kenzie drove a scenic route toward home that took them past houses glowing with Christmas lights. One street featured nine houses all lit up so they sat in the parked car for a few moments taking it all in.

Not quite ready to end their holiday light tour, she drove through some neighborhoods known for great decorations in Pasco before crossing the big blue bridge to Kennewick and driving through residential areas to see the lights.

"I've never done that before, but it was awesome." A broad grin lit his face as they got out of the car at the apartment complex. "Thanks, Dewdrop."

"You've never driven around and looked at lights?" Kenzie asked as she unlocked her door and went inside. Tate limped in behind her.

"Not really. It wasn't like there were many lights out at the ranch, other than the ones Pop put up. If we came to town, it was usually during the day. When we'd go to Christmas Eve services, we'd be in a hurry to get back home, not drive around in strange neighborhoods," Tate said, grateful for Kenzie's help removing his jacket. "Do you always look at the lights?"

"I haven't for a few years. We used to when I lived in Portland." She turned on the fire in the living room and took out her phone. "I'm ordering pizza for dinner. If I remember correctly, you like yours meaty with extra cheese."

"That's right." Tate sat on the couch and patted the spot beside him. When she sat down, he placed his right arm around Kenzie's shoulders and kissed her cheek. "But I'm buying. I feel like I need to pay you for room and board as it is."

"Stop, already." She rolled her eyes as she ordered the pizza. While they waited for it to arrive, she turned on a Christmas comedy. They were both laughing when the doorbell rang with the pizza. Tate handed her the cash he'd taken out of his wallet earlier to pay for it. She took it but gave him a look that let him know he was hopeless as she answered the door. After leaving the pizza on the coffee table, she went to the kitchen to get plates, napkins and drinks.

"Don't you want to eat this in the kitchen?" Tate asked, looking from Kenzie's pale carpet to the light tan couch.

"It's fine right here." She placed a piece of pizza on each of their plates then handed him one.

"But what if I spill something?" Tate asked, afraid of ruining the couch or the carpet.

"What if you do? I'll clean it up. Don't worry about it." Kenzie shrugged her shoulders and turned her attention to the movie.

The woman was a complete mystery to him.

One he hoped he'd have a lifetime to figure out.

Chapter Sixteen

"What do you mean you're still at Kenzie's? Are you hurt worse than you let on? I thought you'd be home long before now." Cort drilled Tate with more questions than his sleep-fogged mind wanted to process.

"Slow down, man. I'm barely awake and my head's all fuzzy from the pain meds this early in the day." Tate worked himself into a sitting position in bed.

Under normal circumstances, he would have been up and around a couple of hours ago. Since he was stuck in town and injured with a need for extra sleep, he hadn't worried about getting up at the usual pre-dawn hour to which he was accustomed. If he didn't get back into his regular routine, though, he was going to go soft.

Exactly what Cort loudly proclaimed in his ear. "Is she holding you hostage or something?"

The words rankled even though Tate knew his friend spoke them in jest.

"Don't be an idiot." He started to run his hand through his tousled hair and stopped midair when the splint prevented his arm from bending like he wanted. "My doctor has me doing therapy and it's easier to stay in town. I still can't walk great and the doc didn't think I should be home alone."

"Do you need me to stay with you?" Cort wondered if Tate's injuries were more extensive than he thought. It would be just like his friend to make light of something serious.

"Nah, man, everything's good." Tate changed the subject by asking Cort about his plans for the holidays, how his sister and parents were doing, and if he'd finalized his rodeo schedule for the coming year.

Before they hung up, Cort asked for Kenzie's address, saying he wanted to send her a thank you note for taking good care of his travel partner. Tate seriously doubted Cort had ever written a letter of thanks in his life, but gave him the address all the same.

After his first therapy session, he knew not to bother taking a shower before he went.

As they ate breakfast, he asked Kenzie if she'd let him borrow her car and drive himself. Her car was an automatic and he felt recovered sufficiently to handle driving himself the few miles to therapy.

Reluctant to turn him loose without accompanying him, she finally agreed and handed him her keys without saying anything other than, "good luck with your torture today."

She watched him drive away, hoping he really felt as improved as he implied. If he believed himself up to driving to therapy, that meant he'd be ready to go home soon.

Swiftly blocking thoughts of him leaving her alone right before Christmas, she checked her emails then finished making her Christmas gift for Tate.

She hadn't been able to work on it much with him there. Taking advantage of her time alone, she completed the project, wrapped it, and hid it in her closet.

The previous afternoon she ran by the ranch supply store and picked up a few things for him she thought he would enjoy like a new shirt and a pair of soft leather gloves.

It was her homemade gift, though, crafted with a heart full of love, she hoped would make him smile and let him know how much she cared.

Kenzie glanced at the clock and felt a niggling sense of worry Tate hadn't yet returned. Not wanting to make him feel like she was checking up on him, she decided to wait another thirty minutes before panicking.

Twenty-nine minutes later, she took the phone out of her pocket to call him. Before she could place the call, he walked through the front door carrying a huge poinsettia and wearing a big smile.

"Since you don't have a tree, I thought you could use something festive in here." He handed Kenzie the plant and kissed her cheek.

"This is beautiful, Tate. Thank you." She set the poinsettia on a side table and admired its deep red color. "I take it your therapy went well today."

"Yep. She didn't even make me cry," Tate said in mock seriousness as he followed her to the kitchen. After wrapping his arm, she studied him as he limped toward his room. He moved with more ease than he had up to that point.

While Tate showered, Kenzie made lunch. After they ate, they discussed fun traditions their families had when they were kids. Suddenly, she remembered something amusing she and her dad did during the holiday season.

"Do you sing?" Kenzie asked, as Tate lounged on the couch next to her, their hands clasped together and resting on his thigh. She'd heard him sing the few times they'd gone to church together, and thought he had a good voice.

"Like opera or professionally?" Tate turned his vivid blue gaze her direction. His carefree grin nearly rendered her speechless. "Then nope, I don't sing."

She rolled her eyes at his teasing. "I meant along to the radio, that kind of singing. Like a normal person."

"There's not a whole lot normal about me, Dewdrop."

The slow, thorough once-over she gave him left them both overheated. Kenzie nodded her head in agreement. "So I've noticed."

"Why do you want to know?" Curious as to what inspired her to ask the question in the first place, Tate desperately needed to focus his attention on something other than their attraction for one another. Otherwise, things could get out of control in a hurry.

"My dad and I used to make up lyrics to Christmas carols. Mom hated it, but we had so much fun messing with the words." She recalled how much she and her dad enjoyed the tradition he started when she was about four. Thanks to Tate, the memories no longer hurt, but brought a sweetness she never thought she'd feel again.

"I think I need an example to get a solid understanding of what it is you mean." His imploring gaze lingered on her face. "Maybe you can do a practice song. Show me how it's done."

She shot him a skeptical glare then broke into a rousing rendition of *Sleigh Ride*, changing all the words to a mishmash of craziness.

Tate laughed so hard, he had to hold his side to keep his ribs from aching too badly.

"I think for the next one you need to add in some fancy dance moves," Tate said when he finally caught his breath enough he could talk, holding his hand to his tender ribs. "Let's see you work your magic on *Deck the Halls*."

"Nope. It's your turn." She slid away from him to give him plenty of room for his performance.

Tate looked at her like she'd lost her mind. Unless he was at church, alone in the truck, or in the shower, he didn't sing.

"Time's a wastin', cowboy," Kenzie drawled, giving him an alluring pout and batting her long, dark eyelashes at him. "Be a good boy and sing for your supper."

"If I get fed based on my singing talent, I'll starve. Maybe I better call Monte and have him come get me," Tate teased, taking his phone out of his pocket. Kenzie snatched it away from him and held it behind her back. "You aren't doing anything except singing me a song."

"Fine. Have it your way," Tate said, quickly thinking of a song. "Just keep in mind I'm new to this."

After taking a deep breath, he began to sing:

All I want for Christmas is my Kenzie's kiss,
my Kenzie's kiss, my Kenzie's kiss!
Gee, if I could only have my sweetheart's kiss
then it would be a Merry Christmas.

It seems so long since she loved on me,
Months and months devoid of affection.
Gosh, oh gee, how happy I'd be
If she'd offer no objection…

All I want for Christmas is my Kenzie's kiss,
my Kenzie's kiss, my Kenzie's kiss!
Gee, if I could only have my sweetheart's kiss,
I'd wish you a very Merry Christmas.

The exaggerated kissy-faces Tate made while singing his song to the tune of *All I Want For Christmas Is My Two Front Teeth* left Kenzie giggling hysterically.

"You win. Stop, stop!" Kenzie begged, as she tried to curtail her uncontrollable laughter, wiping tears from her eyes.

Tate chuckled at her response to his efforts. As he studied her, he found himself lost in her dark eyes.

"Kenzie," he growled, leaning over so his lips were just a breath from hers.

"Did you really miss my kisses?" she whispered, her eyes focused on his all-too-enticing mouth.

"Like you miss air to breathe and water to drink." Tate's provocative voice forced a shiver to race up her spine. Slowly lowering his lips until they melded to hers, they kissed deeply, ardently, making up for lost time. Burying his right hand in her hair, Tate nuzzled her neck and inhaled her summery scent.

His fingers slid down the column of her throat then he captured her lips again.

Tate could hear ringing in his ears from the intensity of the kiss and wondered how he'd ever existed without the warmth of Kenzie's presence in his life.

"Tate, let me up so I can get the door." Kenzie gently pushed against his shoulder.

"Huh?"

She pushed at him again. He sat back as Kenzie got to her feet, tugging down her disheveled sweater and fluffing her hair as she hurried to answer the door.

The ringing Tate heard was just the doorbell. All sorts of uncharitable thoughts about whoever rang the bell infiltrated his head.

When Kenzie opened the door, he was surprised to see the man who stood on the front step.

"Wow! What you are doing here?" Kenzie gave Cort a hug as he grinned at her. "Come in out of the cold."

"I heard you had an unwelcome visitor who just won't go home. I came to see if I could get rid of him for you." Cort walked inside and pointed at Tate.

"Man, didn't I just tell you on the phone this morning I'm okay?" Tate asked with a broad smile as he shook Cort's hand and got to his feet. "What the heck are you doing?"

"I wanted to make sure you were fine." From Tate's guilty grin and Kenzie's just-kissed lips, Cort determined he was definitely interrupting something. Carefully studying his wounded friend, he decided Tate was fine, maybe too fine if the way Kenzie couldn't keep her eyes off him was any indication.

"Practically good as new." Tate ignored the roll of Kenzie's eyes before she went to the kitchen.

She returned with mugs of hot chocolate and a plate of cookies, immediately stirring Cort's interest.

"Did you make all these?" Cort asked, sampling his third cookie.

"I needed something to do while playing nursemaid to the cowboy." She settled on the couch next to Tate and gave him a sassy smile.

"He didn't mention you were a good cook," Cort said, shaking his head at Tate. "Holding out on me, weren't you? Afraid I'd steal her away from you?"

"Right," Tate said, helping himself to another gingerbread bar. The treats were addictive. Rather like Kenzie's kisses.

One was never enough, two just left him wanting more, and from there he lost the ability to think rationally.

"Did you really drive all the way here to check up on me?" Tate asked Cort.

"Why else do you think I'd brave driving the horrendous roads through Ladd Canyon and Deadman Pass between here and Boise? It isn't because I like taking my life in my hands on ice-covered mountain passes, man." Cort took a sip of his hot chocolate and grinned at Kenzie.

"Were the roads really bad?" She'd driven I-84 to Boise several times, but only when the roads were good, and never in the winter months.

"Actually, no. Since I traveled midday, they were mostly clear. Just a few spots of ice," Cort said, taking another cookie.

"I'm glad you came. It's nice of you to check up on him and it'll be fun to visit with you. How long can you stay?" Her mind raced with ideas of what to make for dinner and where Cort would sleep.

"I thought I'd hang out for a day or two just to make sure Tater is okay. My folks would kill me if I wasn't home for Christmas and Celia would pitch a royal fit." Cort leaned back in the rocking chair by the fire. The inviting atmosphere made it easy to relax. He was thrilled to see his friend looking so content, if a little worse for wear.

"How is Celia?" Tate asked.

Nine years younger than Cort, Celia kept her big brother on his toes.

"As feisty as ever." Cort shook his head in feigned disgust. "We thought she might finally have found a guy who could tolerate her, but she scared him off after the third date."

"I need to meet this girl." Kenzie gave Tate a sideways glance. "Maybe she can give me some tips on getting rid of unwanted suitors."

"Don't even think about it." Tate lifted her hand and pressed a kiss to her palm.

"Do you and your sister look alike, Cort?" Kenzie asked, making both men laugh. Cort's dark hair and gray eyes drew the attention of many women. If his sister shared his coloring, she'd be stunning.

"Not a bit. I think my folks really shook up the gene pool to get two kids who don't resemble each other at all." Cort took out his phone and pulled up a photo of his sister. He handed it to Kenzie and watched her eyes go wide.

Celia, Cort's sister, was the beautiful redheaded girl she'd seen with Tate in Las Vegas. "I saw you with her in Vegas." Kenzie glanced at Tate.

"When?" Celia wasn't at the Christmas vendor show where he ran into Kenzie and she wasn't sitting near the Powell family the night he got hurt because she had to return to Boise before the final night of the rodeo.

"On the strip. You were walking with her." Kenzie recalled how much it hurt to see Tate with another woman, especially one so young and attractive.

Tate grinned, detecting a little jealousy from Kenzie. "We were all having dinner together and Cort decided to stay out late. Celia didn't want to walk back to the hotel alone, so I made sure she got there in one piece."

"Always the hero." Cort batted his eyelashes at Tate while holding his hands folded beneath his chin in an exaggerated pose.

Kenzie laughed. "She's gorgeous."

"She likes to think so." Cort winked at Kenzie. "Seriously, she's a pretty good kid and not even too miserable to have as a sister, just don't tell her I said that. I'll deny it to my dying day."

"Got it," Kenzie said, smiling at Cort as he brought Tate up to speed on rodeo news as well as what was happening with his family.

They talked about Kent and the Morgan Ranch, Tate's therapy, and plans for the coming year. Cort asked Kenzie about her job as a corporate trainer for Dew.

A quick peek at the clock brought Kenzie to her feet. She had no idea it had gotten so late. It was well past time for the evening meal.

"Any requests for dinner?" she asked picking up the empty chocolate mugs and cookie plate.

"Let's go out to eat. No need for you to cook tonight." Tate gave Cort a look that told him to agree.

"I'm in the mood for some good Italian food." Cort picked up on Tate's signal. "Where should we go?"

"Are you two sure you'd rather eat out?" she asked, getting their coats out of the front closet.

"Absolutely." Cort held Kenzie's coat while Tate managed to pull on his jacket.

Cort insisted on taking his pickup and Tate tried to get Kenzie to sing another crazy Christmas song on the way to the restaurant. When she refused, he and Cort launched into a rowdy rendition of *Jingle Bells* that had all three of them laughing.

After Cort dropped Tate and Kenzie at the front of the restaurant, he parked his truck and hurried back.

Since he refused to use his cane, Tate limped to the table, ignoring the reproachful looks Kenzie sent his way.

Laughter filled their meal and Cort agreed to stay for a couple days. Kenzie smiled as they discussed doing a few fun things before he returned home in time for Christmas.

"Why don't you have a tree?" Cort asked as the server removed their plates.

"I didn't want a miniature tree and a big one won't fit in my car," Kenzie said. Tate hadn't asked, assuming she wouldn't want to deal with the hassle and mess of a real tree.

"Want to swing by a lot on the way home?" Cort offered as Tate paid the bill.

"You wouldn't mind?" Kenzie grew excited at the thought of having a real tree once again.

"Heck, no." Cort left Tate and Kenzie at the door while he went to get his pickup. It didn't take long to find a tree lot still open. Cort and Kenzie walked around looking at trees while Tate sat on a bench, either shaking his head or telling them to keep looking. Finally, Kenzie settled on a beautiful fir tree and Tate gave it two thumbs up. Quickly paying for the tree, they loaded it and headed back to Kenzie's apartment.

She dug a box of ornaments out of her storage closet. While the men untangled lights that looked like a snarled ball of twisted wire, she baked a batch of sugar cookies, complete with holiday sprinkles on top.

Once the lights were in working order and draped on the tree, they got down to the business of adding the sentimental decorations.

There were ornaments that belonged to Kenzie's grandparents, some she'd made in grade school, and a handful her mom and dad had given her. The tree-topper was a traditional star that lit up when plugged in. Strands of cranberry-colored beads and candy canes gave the tree an old-fashioned look.

The scent of the tree mingled with freshly baked cookies and filled the apartment with a wonderful, nostalgic fragrance all three of them appreciated.

After turning off all the lights except those twinkling on the tree, they watched a holiday comedy, ate cookies, and drank hot cider.

Kenzie began to yawn before the movie was close to ending but Tate and Cort seemed to be feeding off each other's energy.

"If we won't bother you, Cort and I'll stay up awhile." Tate didn't want to disturb her, but he wasn't yet ready for bed.

"You won't bother me, but I was planning to sleep on the couch and let Cort have my room." Kenzie carried empty mugs and leftover cookies to the kitchen.

"No way." Cort got to his feet. "It's bad enough Tater's probably eaten you out of house and home, not to mention being a royal nuisance. There is no way I'm taking your bed. I'll sleep on the couch. Considering some of the places I've slept out on the road, this is practically luxury accommodations. If you tell me no, I'll go find a hotel."

"I'm too tired to argue with either one of you, so do what you like." She smiled at the two friends who were so much alike with their teasing and some unspoken code of gallantry she had not yet deciphered.

She disappeared down the hall and soon returned with a pile of bedding and pillows, leaving them on the floor by the couch. Tate grabbed her hand and pulled her down for a kiss.

Embarrassed, yet delighted by the display of affection in front of Cort, she wished them both good night then escaped to her room.

Particularly pleased with the way her day ended, it didn't take long for Kenzie to fall asleep with visions of Tate filling her head.

Chapter Seventeen

Cort took Tate to visit Kent the next morning. After lunch with the elderly man, they planned to visit the mall to do a little shopping before Tate's appointment to see the doctor about getting a cast on his arm in place of the splint.

With free time on her hands, Kenzie finished her shopping, caught up on laundry, and called her mother to let her know she was definitely not driving to Portland for Christmas.

Although they'd discussed the fact she wasn't planning to make the trip a week ago, she knew her mother still hoped she'd change her mind.

When her mom practically begged, Kenzie finally told her she was taking care of a friend and wasn't sure how long her help would be needed.

"Why didn't you mention it before, honey?" Susan sounded concerned.

"Because it's no big deal." Her mother was not going to let this go as easily as she had hoped.

"Who is this friend? It's not Megan, is it? Is the baby fine?" Susan fired off questions faster than Kenzie could answer them.

"No, Mom. You haven't met this friend."

"Care to enlighten me?"

Kenzie heard a note of warning as well as censure in her mother's tone. "Not really."

"Kenzie Amelia Beckett, what is going on?" When her mother used her full name, Kenzie knew she was about to receive an earful.

Deciding to get it over with, she spilled the news to her mother as quickly as possible using a few brief details. "I met a cowboy last spring, we fell in love, he got hurt, and he's staying here while he's having therapy."

Silence greeted her on the other end of the line. Kenzie counted the seconds until the explosion rocketed through her phone. She was only at three when it hit full force.

"What? Kenzie! A cowboy? A cowboy! Have you taken leave of your good sense? What are you thinking? Oh, honey, how could you let this happen?"

"I didn't exactly let anything happen, Mom. We traveled on the same flights out of Pasco several times and he invited me to a rodeo in Santa Fe. By then I was already a goner." She rushed to defend Tate. "Mom, he's sweet, and kind, and amazing, and he's so good with his dad. He's in a care home here in the Tri-Cities. His friends are great. You'd really like him. Please don't judge him because of what happened to you, to us, in the past. I made that mistake and almost lost him."

Susan's reply was to let deafening silence linger between them. Kenzie would have assumed her mother hung up on her, except she could hear the disapproval crackling across the connection loud and clear.

"How did he get hurt?" Susan asked after a lengthy pause.

"He... um... well, he rides saddle broncs and was at the finals. He would have won, but the last night the horse fell on him right before the buzzer. He'll be okay, but he had a concussion, cracked ribs, a broken arm, and twisted knee. They're doing therapy on his knee and the doctor didn't want him home alone until he could get around better. He doesn't have any siblings and his best friend lives in Boise, so I had to help him out." A fortifying breath prepared her to continue. "I love him, Mom, and I'm pretty sure he feels the same about me."

"I can't believe you fell for a rodeo cowboy. Didn't you learn anything from my mistakes? Of all the available men on this great big planet, why did you have to pick a cowboy, Kenzie? Why this one?"

"I don't know, Mom. I asked myself that question a thousand times, but it's like I've known him forever. He makes me laugh and think. I'm so happy when I'm with him and my heart actually hurts when we're apart." Her voice softened and she looked at her ceiling to keep the tears stinging her eyes from spilling over. "This isn't like it was with Sonny. This is so much different, so magical and magnificent, and so very right. He's special, Mama. I never dreamed of feeling like this with anyone. With him, I know I'm loved and cherished."

Another awkward silence seemed to last hours instead of seconds.

Finally, Susan spoke, "And this cowboy's name is…"

"Tate. Tate Morgan," Kenzie said, love and pride evident in her voice. "His family ranch is south of here, just before you cross into Oregon."

"I think your father used to mention a Morgan Ranch on occasion." Kenzie heard her mother sigh in resignation. "You do what you need to do, but I want to meet your young man soon. Will you come for New Year's Eve?"

"If the weather cooperates and Tate feels up to traveling, we'll be there. I'll check with him on his plans and let you know." Pleased her mother let her off the hook without a more in-depth interrogation, she smiled. "Thanks, Mom."

SHANNA HATFIELD

"I only want you to be happy, honey, and I can honestly say when you talk about him, you sound deliriously so. But I still want to meet him."

"Okay." She exchanged details with her mother about gifts she mailed for her sisters before hanging up.

She spent a few minutes answering work emails, called to chat with Megan, and made a chicken potpie for dinner. She was crimping the edges of the crust when Tate and Cort walked inside, carrying overflowing bags of brightly wrapped packages.

"Did you two buy out the mall?" Kenzie wiped her hands on a towel and watched them set everything on the couch. They both dug through the bags and placed a few packages beneath the tree before carrying the rest to Tate's room.

When they returned to the living room, she had the fire going, the tree lights twinkling, and Christmas music playing.

"This is downright domestic." Cort walked into the kitchen where Kenzie assembled a green salad. "I might need to fly the coop before I catch something that could do permanent damage."

Kenzie playfully slapped Cort's arm then grinned at Tate as he leaned against the counter, staring at the new cast on his arm. Cort had already signed it with a flourish and Kenzie threatened to add her signature after dinner.

The doctor told him he made great progress and asked how things were at the ranch. When Tate told him he was still staying with Kenzie, the man gave Tate a long look then muttered something about him being more than capable of going home, if he wanted. The problem was that he wanted to stay with Kenzie indefinitely.

Fully aware that he needed to leave, Tate avoided thinking about it. He couldn't when the time he spent with Kenzie made him happier than he'd ever been.

234

For years, he'd dreamed of finding a girl who would capture his heart. He never hoped to find one who fit into his life so well, one who genuinely liked his friends.

Cort and Kenzie continued teasing each other, unaware that Tate turned quiet and reflective.

Maybe getting hurt and losing the championship title was worth it if it meant he had the opportunity to spend time with Kenzie. He wondered if she would have welcomed his presence so willingly into her home or her life if he'd showed up on her doorstep uninjured.

Rather than mulling over what might have been, he embraced the blessings he'd received, let go of the past, and joined in the conversation while Kenzie finished preparing the meal.

"You really didn't need to cook for us," Tate said, helping set the table.

"I know. I wanted to." Kenzie gave him a warm, private smile.

Thankful she was a decent cook despite the fact she spent more time gone than at home, Kenzie liked having a reason to be in the kitchen preparing something special.

The men sitting at the table appreciated her efforts and made her glad she'd decided to cook dinner instead of going out to eat again.

Lavished with compliments on the meal she prepared, Kenzie listened to their friendly banter as Tate and Cort helped pick up after dinner. They acted as if they rarely ate a home-cooked meal. Like her, the majority of their meals were eaten on the go.

Once the dinner dishes were finished, the two men turned on the news while Kenzie dug through her storage closet for a game the three of them could play.

"No way, man. Look at you." Cort chuckled as a teaser for the morning news show aired. Kenzie hurried around the corner so she could see the television. A glossy photo of Tate filled the screen.

"Tune in for a special interview with local rodeo cowboy Tate Morgan. He'll tell us all about his experiences on the pro rodeo circuit and his plans for next year, following his injuries at the finals."

"Tate, I had no idea." She sat next to him, wondering when he'd talked to the television station. "Are you really going to be on the morning news?"

"Yep. Want to come with me?" Tate asked as he took Kenzie's hand in his. He liked the idea of having her there for support.

"Are you sure I wouldn't be in the way?" Kenzie didn't want to intrude on something that was clearly very important to Tate.

"Dewdrop, you could never be in my way." He kissed her temple. "Please, will you come? I'd really like for you to be there."

"Make him beg a little more." A big grin creased Cort's face as he sat by the fire.

"I don't want to make him suffer too much," she said, squeezing Tate's hand. "I'll be there."

"Now, tell her what time you have to be at the station." Cort raised an eyebrow at his friend.

Tate glared at Cort. "I was getting around to it." He turned to Kenzie. "I have to be there by five-thirty that morning."

"Okay." Kenzie shocked Cort with her ready agreement to rising at an early hour.

He gazed at her with a dubious expression.

She pointed an index finger at him. "Ha! Bet you thought I wouldn't roll out at that time of day, didn't you? I'll have you know, Mr. McGraw, I'm an early riser."

"Yes, ma'am." Cort ducked his head, trying to look chastised around his broad grin. Although Tate mentioned Kenzie wasn't quite as citified as they originally believed, he still couldn't picture her as a girl who took on the day bright and early in the morning. She always looked too polished and professional to be a crack-of-dawn country girl.

"Don't mess with her, Cort. You'll lose every time," Tate warned, kissing Kenzie's cheek.

"Speaking of messing with me, that autographed photo you gave me at the vendor show was way too impersonal. I demand a new one." The look she gave Tate dared him to argue.

"How about I just sign my autograph somewhere more personal?" Tate nuzzled her neck.

Kenzie squirmed and smacked lightly at his good arm. "Behave yourself." The teasing comment had made her blush, especially since he made it in front of Cort. "Where did you get your photo taken? It's really very nice."

"Cort's sister is a photographer. She does rodeo photography along with senior photos, that sort of thing," Tate explained. Cort nodded his head in agreement.

"She does excellent work." Kenzie shot Tate a jaunty grin. "She even made you look halfway appealing."

Cort laughed and a round of good-natured joking ensued. When the guys finally quieted down, they played a card game before everyone decided it was time for bed.

Early the next morning, the sound of deep voices talking and doors shutting interrupted Kenzie's dreams of Tate. Hastily scurrying out of bed, she wrapped herself in a warm robe, shoved her feet into slippers, and hurried out to the living room to see what caused all the commotion.

Tate stood near the couch trying to fold Cort's bedding.

"What's going on?" Surprised the men were up when it was barely five in the morning, she couldn't imagine what forced them out of bed when they had no pressing plans for the day.

"There's a storm coming in and Cort wants to get on the road home before it hits. He's going to drop me off at the ranch on his way back to Boise." Tate held out his good arm to Kenzie.

As she pressed against his broad chest, she soaked in his warmth and masculine scent. She would sorely miss having him around all the time. Aware that Tate had to go home eventually, she wasn't ready for it to happen. She'd hoped he would stay until after Christmas.

"I've got the TV interview tomorrow, so I'll be back. If you don't object, maybe we could take Pop out to lunch," Tate said.

At Kenzie's slight nod of agreement, he stroked her back and kissed the top of her head, smiling at her disheveled appearance with hair tumbling every direction.

Soft and all womanly curves in his arms, he could hold her the rest of the day and night and never grow tired of it.

The very last thing he wanted to do was leave, but Cort was right. He couldn't stay at Kenzie's forever and he really did need to go check on things at the ranch.

"I'd like that," Kenzie whispered, trying to talk around the lump in her throat. She wasn't one normally given to outbursts of emotion, but this morning she wanted to stamp her foot and cry.

Christmas was just a few days away and she hoped to spend all the time between now and then with Tate.

"Can I make breakfast for you guys before you go?" Kenzie asked as Cort hurried inside, bringing a blast of cold air with him.

"No thanks. We'll grab something on the road." Cort took Tate's bag with his equipment out to his truck then returned to give Kenzie a warm hug and a kiss on the cheek. "Thanks for taking care of this troublemaker, Kenzie. I'm extremely glad you two are back together. Have a Merry Christmas."

"Thanks, Cort. You too, and drive safely." Kenzie walked to the door with the two cowboys. "Let me know you made it home in one piece."

"Will do and thanks for the hospitality." Cort went out the door to give Tate a moment to say goodbye to Kenzie in private.

"If I don't get out there, he's likely to wake up everyone by honking the horn on that truck." Tate gave Kenzie another long hug and kiss, leaving her flustered. "I'll be back before you know it, so don't forget about me."

"That would be impossible, cowboy." She buried her face in his neck and memorized everything she could about being in his arms. "I'll miss you."

"Not as much as I'll miss you." He kissed her one last time. "Go on back to bed and spend the day doing something just for you. I'll call you later to see how things are going."

She sniffled, but nodded her head. Tate opened the door and started toward Cort's truck. Cort waved one last time before giving Tate an impatient look.

Kenzie ran to the kitchen and grabbed two tins of treats she'd packed to give away. Hurrying outside, she made a beeline for the big pickup. As Tate slid into the passenger seat, she handed the cookies over him to Cort.

"Something for the road," she said, patting Tate on the leg and giving him another quick kiss. "Be safe out there."

"We will. Now, get inside." Tate kissed her cheek before she stepped back and he pulled his door shut. Cort drove off as Kenzie stood outside in the freezing temperatures watching them go.

Sleep would be impossible with her emotions spinning around, so she worked out, took a shower, and dressed. She'd just sat down to eat breakfast when Tate called to let her know he'd arrived at the ranch and Cort was back out on the road.

"I miss you already." Husky and low, his voice made warmth spread through her.

"You'll be so busy getting caught up on ranch stuff that you won't even remember who I am." She tried to keep her tone teasing although she missed Tate more than she would have imagined possible. When he left her house, he took a huge piece of her heart with him.

"I'd have to be in a coma for that to happen, and I'm pretty sure even then I'd dream of you," he said, making her smile. "I'll be there bright and early tomorrow to take you to the TV station."

"I'll be standing in the door holding a welcome sign." Kenzie thought she just might do it, too. "Did you know you left your suitcase here?"

"Yeah. We were about ten miles out of town when I remembered it was still in your guest room. There's nothing in there I need right away. Enjoy your day. Relax and do something fun, pamper yourself a little."

"I'll give your suggestion some consideration." A trip to the spa sounded tempting. "Let me know if you hear from Cort."

"I will. The big storm he predicted looks like it's going to miss us, but he still might hit part of it before he gets home."

"He'll be fine," Kenzie said reassuringly. "Now, go take care of your ranch business, cowboy. I'm sure they're all glad to see you."

"Bye, Dewdrop." Tate disconnected the call. He wanted so badly to tell her he loved her, but decided to bide his time. He had something very special planned for that particular moment.

Chapter Eighteen

Unable to focus on anything but how much he wanted to be with Kenzie, Tate drove back to town late that afternoon. He knew he'd see her the following morning since she'd promised to go with him to the television interview, but he'd been so lonesome for her, Monte practically kicked him off the place, telling him to go see his girl.

Tate drove one of the ranch trucks with an automatic transmission so he wouldn't have to work the clutch in his pickup.

Excited to surprise her, he stood on her front step and rang the bell. He listened to her footsteps hurry toward the door.

When she opened it, the smile on her face forced him to catch his breath.

"Hey! What are you doing here?" Kenzie asked, kissing his cheek then stepping aside so he could come in out of the cold.

Curiosity got the best of her when he stared at her, his good hand still behind his back. She tried to look around him, but he turned so she couldn't.

"What are you hiding?" she asked, her eyes warm and inviting when he stepped inside and nudged the door shut behind him with his boot.

"I couldn't help but notice you're missing a very important component of proper Christmas décor." Tate did his best to sound full of holiday wisdom.

"What could I possibly be missing?" Kenzie glanced behind her and swept her arm toward the living room that did look particularly festive, thanks in part to Tate. "I've got a poinsettia, a beautiful Christmas tree, garlands, pine boughs, sugary treats, and a blazing fire. Did you bring me some chestnuts to roast? If you did, I've got no clue what to do with them, so you're out of luck."

Tate chuckled then raised his arm and held a bunch of mistletoe over their heads. "It seems to me this is the most important decoration of all."

"Possibly." Kenzie reached out and looped her arms around Tate's neck, pulling his head down to hers. Gentle and teasing at first, their kiss soon gained momentum until he dropped the mistletoe on the table near the door and she pressed as close against him as his thick coat would allow.

With a quick breath, she unfastened the snaps on his coat. She slid it off his shoulders, over his injured arm, until it dropped to the floor.

He tossed his hat on the little chair Kenzie kept by the door while a groan escaped his throat. Tate took in every feature of her face, the mouth-watering summery fragrance surrounding her, and the softness of the hot pink sweater she wore. Her favorite color currently matched the shade of her flushed cheeks.

Slowly lowering his head to hers again, Tate wrapped his good arm around her waist and backed her toward the living room without breaking the connection of their lips.

"I missed you," he whispered against her mouth as he guided her to the couch.

When her knees connected with the edge, she sank down on the soft cushions, still holding onto Tate.

He went down with her, ravishing her neck with sizzling kisses that made her whisper his name in a throaty tone, sending blood surging through his veins.

Several passionate kisses later, Tate lifted his head and melded his hot sapphire gaze to her sweet molasses-colored eyes.

"Tate, I think we better... um..." Kenzie tried to remember what she was going to say as Tate once again captured her lips. His hand crept under her sweater and lightly traced the most sensational circles on her stomach and sides. Unable to think or speak, she was glad they were on the couch because she knew her legs would have given way beneath her several kisses ago.

"We better what?" Tate asked, finding the exact spot beneath her ear that made wild shivers race from her head to her toes.

Afraid things were about to go too far, Kenzie pushed against Tate's chest.

"Stop," Kenzie finally managed to say, abruptly sitting up and bumping Tate. He held his side and tried to swallow back the pain, although a grunt escaped. "Oh, Tate, I'm sorry." She placed her hand to his side.

"Serves me right for my amorous mood." He caught his breath as he leaned back into the couch cushions. "My apologies. You just looked so tempting, I couldn't quite help myself."

She gave him a disbelieving stare and rose from the couch. "I'm wearing a chunky sweater and jeans. How could that possibly be tempting?"

"On you, a gunny sack and rubber boots would be tempting." Wickedly grinning, he followed her to the kitchen. He put his arm around her waist and pulled her back against his chest, kissing her neck. "You feel so good, Kenzie. Was it just this morning Cort made me go back to the ranch? It seems more like months."

"I missed you, too." Kenzie gave him a gentle hug, mindful of his healing ribs. "How about I make some hot chocolate and you can tell me all about what's going on at the ranch? How are Monte and the guys? Did they put up any decorations? How are the horses? When do you think calving season will start? You never did say what you're doing here."

"My, you're full of questions, aren't you?" Tate kissed her neck one more time before taking the cup of hot chocolate she handed him and following her back to the couch.

They sat and talked for a while. When the afternoon shadows gave way to evening, they decided to go to a popular Mexican restaurant for dinner. Kenzie offered to warm up her car, but when she opened the door, the beginnings of an ice storm greeted her.

"Looks like we're staying in."

Tate stepped behind her and they watched little pellets of ice ping off windshields and walkways. The last ice storm to hit the area left a thick layer of ice coating everything, making the roads completely treacherous for two days.

"I guess I won't drive home tonight." Pleased at the prospect, Tate was glad the weather kept him trapped with one very beautiful, very tempting woman. He was open to any excuse to stay with her and Mother Nature helped him out quite nicely.

"Absolutely not." She closed the door and hung her coat back in the closet.

"I bet in another ten minutes the roads will be slicker than..." Tate cut himself off at Kenzie's raised eyebrow. "Well, they'll be slick."

"Agreed." Kenzie took his hand and led him back to the kitchen. "Since we aren't going out to eat, you can help me make dinner."

"I thought I was a guest and now you're putting me to work." Tate watched her bend over to dig in the freezer section of her refrigerator. He enjoyed the view entirely too much and missed a question she asked.

"Earth to Tate." Kenzie grinned at him over her shoulder.

"What's that, Dewdrop?" Tate asked shamefaced, although he didn't lift his gaze from her jean-clad derrière.

"I said if you'd rather sing for your supper, you can sit here and entertain me with your repertoire of holiday tunes."

"I'll pass. Hand me the green stuff, I can make the salad."

Periodically looking outside, Tate was glad he drove into town to visit Kenzie. There was no way he would have attempted the drive from the ranch in the morning on the ice-covered roads. Kenzie's apartment wasn't far from the news station and that early in the day the streets should be empty.

After giving each other a long, involved kiss good night that left them both struggling to walk away, Kenzie went to bed thrilled Tate had returned so soon.

If he missed her even half as much as she missed him, they were going to have to make some decisions about the future of their relationship. It was fine to play house while Tate healed from his injuries and remained out of action for the most part, but what happened when his ribs healed and he no longer wore the cast on his arm?

Determined to worry about it another day, Kenzie went to sleep dreaming of a future with her handsome cowboy.

><><

Extra early the next morning, Tate rose to discover Kenzie had once again washed all the clothes he'd inadvertently left behind when he forgot his suitcase. He pulled out his favorite bright blue shirt, emblazoned with the names of his sponsors. A pair of jeans, boots, and his hat would complete the outfit.

A knock on his door reminded him that he had a full day ahead and would spend it all with his best girl.

He opened the portal and grinned at Kenzie. She stood in the hall smelling so heavenly, his heart began to race as he inhaled her familiar fragrance. Her hair was damp, but she wore a pair of black slacks and satiny green blouse that set off the rich color of her hair and eyes.

"I thought you might need some help with your arm," Kenzie said, studying Tate's bare chest. In the days she'd been taking care of him, she'd memorized every freckle, every scar, and every rippling muscle of his upper physique.

Right now, her gaze fixated on the mole right above his heart. She wondered what he'd do if she leaned over and kissed it. Rather than find out, she started shaking out a garbage bag to wrap his arm.

"Thanks, but I've got that waterproof cover for my cast to use in the shower." Tate kissed her cheek as she wadded up the bag.

"Sorry, I forgot." She backed toward the door. "Do you want breakfast or just some coffee?" She stepped into the hallway before she did something crazy, like push him down on the bed and kiss every inch of his deliciously exposed skin.

"Coffee and a piece of toast, if it isn't too much bother." He crossed the floor to the bathroom door. "I'll take you out for a nice breakfast after the interview."

"Sounds good, cowboy." She looked forward to spending another day with Tate.

Excited for him to have the interview, she hoped it went well. With his sidelined status, she knew it bothered him that he might look injured, even if he was. Already walking much better, in another week or two no one would notice the injury to his knee. His ribs also healed quickly. He'd be back on the circuit before he knew it, even if he thought it would kill him to miss competing the first month or so of the new year.

After putting the coffee on to brew, Kenzie returned to the bathroom and dried her hair. She left it down, knowing it would please Tate. Her thoughts wandered to how good it felt to have his big hands buried in her hair, and the deep sound of his voice as he whispered in her ear telling her she was beautiful.

Forcefully rousing herself from her musings, she spritzed on perfume and touched her cheeks, nose and forehead with a dusting of powder before returning to the kitchen and popping bread in the toaster.

As she looked out the window, she noticed ice covered every surface. It would take a little work to get one of their vehicles thawed out and decided to forgo wearing heels for some sensible flats that would give her a little traction on the ice.

The sound of the toaster popping up drew her thoughts back to breakfast. She buttered the warm bread then poured two cups of steaming coffee. Tate appeared as she pulled the creamer from the fridge.

"Thanks for making this." He took a long drink of the hot brew before biting into his toast. "I appreciate you going with me this morning."

"Thanks for asking me." Kenzie sipped her coffee. Tate's shirt accented the blue of his eyes and her gaze fastened on his freshly shaved cheeks along with his tousled hair. Her temperature climbed as she imagined her lips on his cheeks and her fingers trailing along his strong jaw. Desperate for a distraction, she stared into her coffee cup. "Does your dad know to watch this morning?"

"Of course," Tate said with a laugh. "I think he's told everyone at the center they have to get up early to catch the news this morning."

"He's something else." Genuine affection for the old gent made her glad to know him. She was constantly amazed at how well he did for someone his age. Sometimes she forgot he was in his nineties since his mind was sharp and his body strong.

"I'm glad you think so." Tate kissed her cheek. "He thinks you're just the 'sweetest little gal,' as he puts it, and I'd have to agree."

"You two obviously don't know me very well," she teased, placing their mugs in the sink then wiping up crumbs from the toast.

"I'm working on that, you know." Tate winked before going back to the guest room to finish getting ready. He emerged a few minutes later, pulling on his coat and settling a black cowboy hat on his head.

"You look like you should be in some kind of western commercial." Kenzie tugged on the collar of Tate's coat, adjusting it. "A little snowfall and a horse walking beside you and you could sell ice to Eskimos, at least all the females."

"Apparently you get delusional when you're rousted out of bed too early." The affectionate grin he gave her softened his words as he opened the door. "I'm going out to start the truck. No need for both of us to freeze."

"I'll help you." She pulled on a long black wool coat and gloves then wrapped a scarf around her neck. "It might take some work to get all that ice off and I don't want you to feel rushed this morning. Besides, you'd better be careful out there. One slip and you'll end up undoing all that therapy you've suffered through."

"Kenz, I don't want you getting half frozen for no reason." He frowned as she followed him outside.

"I'm not a delicate flower, buster. Who do you think brushes off the snow or gets ice off my car when you aren't around? I manage just fine." She used the scraper she brought along to go to work on the pickup's door, trying to carefully remove enough ice they could get it open.

When she'd chipped through a little of it, Tate grabbed the door handle and gave it a hard tug using his right hand. It opened with a loud crack and they both breathed a sigh of relief.

After starting the truck and turning the defroster on high, Tate and Kenzie slid their way back inside her apartment.

"It's slick, and I mean slick, out there." Grateful Kenzie lived close to the television station, Tate was glad he gave in to his urge to drive into town the previous afternoon before the storm hit.

"We've got plenty of time and it's only a mile or so to the station." Kenzie glanced at her watch.

"I'm not worried. We'll be there early." He wrapped his arm around Kenzie and kissed her cheek, rosy from the cold. "Have I mentioned this morning how beautiful you look?"

"No, but thank you." She gazed into his intense eyes and fell into the tempting blue pools. Stretching up, she kissed him full on the lips then pulled back. "Have I mentioned how much I like having you around?"

"You haven't, Miss Beckett, but you can tell me that as many times as you like." Tate hugged her again before squeezing her hand. "Shall we see if we can slide our way to the station?"

"Lead on, cowboy," Kenzie said, taking Tate's good arm as they went out to the defrosted truck. Cautiously driving to the station, they made it with no problem, arriving fifteen minutes early.

Escorted inside, they waited in a conference room where they could watch the news being broadcast and were offered cups of coffee.

Tate passed, already wired because of the interview, but Kenzie accepted one. They sat side-by-side waiting for his interview. He wove their fingers together and rested their joined hands on his jean-clad thigh.

"Nervous?" she asked, giving him a look filled with such love and warmth Tate felt a part of himself melting into his chair.

"A little." Slightly nodding his head, he let out a sigh. "I always am."

"How many interviews have you done?" Kenzie realized she'd seen online interviews with Tate before she knew him, when he was just another good-looking cowboy who seemed to do well in the rodeo circuit.

"Dozens." Tate shrugged. The local news station had interviewed him shortly after he turned pro and he often gave interviews at rodeos after a winning ride.

If someone walked up to him and stuck a mic and camera in his face, he didn't have time to worry about what he would say or how it would sound.

The interviews scheduled ahead of time made him stew over what questions they might ask and left him nervous. Once he got in front of the camera, he was fine. Today was no exception as he anxiously jiggled the foot of his right leg.

"Do you need to be distracted?" Kenzie asked with a flirty grin, raising one eyebrow as she studied him.

With a clenched jaw, the fingers of Tate's right hand drummed a beat on the arm of the chair in rhythm to the bouncing of his foot. At her question, he went perfectly still and focused his attention on her.

He leaned close to her ear. His minty breath on her neck made a shiver race through her when he spoke in a low, raspy voice. "What'd you have in mind, Dewdrop?"

"Apparently not what you do." Although her insides were a churning mass of liquid heat, she kept her tone light. In need of a diversion from Tate, she started digging around in her bag.

His eyes glowed like twin sapphires and his masculine scent made her feel lightheaded each time she took a deep breath. When he flashed his dimples and wiggled his eyebrow her direction, her blood began to heat despite the cool temperature of the room.

Finally unearthing a paperback novel from her purse, she held it out to Tate. He took it from her and shook his head. "If you think I'm gonna sit here and read some sappy love story, you better think again." He handed the book back to her and looked around for a magazine or newspaper.

"Your loss," Kenzie said, opening the book and flipping to where she had a bookmark. She leaned back in her chair and held the book over far enough that Tate could read the page as well, if he was of a mind to.

Evidently, he was because when she was slow to turn to the next page, he nudged her hand. When she gave him a smug look, he grinned at her. She quickly turned the page and they continued reading until Tate received the call to prepare for his interview.

Invited to go along, Kenzie held Tate's coat along with her own and stood back while they put a microphone on his shirt collar, directing him where to stand.

"Are you okay to stand for a few minutes, Mr. Morgan?" an assistant asked. Although he looked hale and hearty, she seemed concerned about his recently sustained injuries.

"Yeah, I'm fine." At his charming smile, the assistant gave him an awed look as she finished what she needed to do and stepped back.

Kenzie sat on a stool the assistant offered her at the back of the room, behind all the equipment. The news anchor promised he would be back after the commercial and the camera panned to Tate who beamed a dimpled smile, waving before they went to a break.

The anchor hurried over to Tate, shook his hand and offered a word of welcome before disappearing into an adjacent room.

Tate looked at Kenzie and winked. She blew him a kiss he pretended to slap on his cheek as the anchor reappeared.

"Who's the pretty girl?" the man asked as he positioned himself next to Tate.

"My girlfriend, Kenzie Beckett." Tate grinned at Kenzie again.

She couldn't hear what they said, but when both men looked at her, she blushed and waggled her fingers at them.

"You want her on the show with you?" he asked as he got the signal the break was nearly over.

"I think she'd prefer to stay behind the scenes, but I'm happy to have her join me if she wants to." Tate looked her direction.

"Miss Beckett, do you want to stand up here with Tate?" the newscaster asked, speaking loudly so she could hear him across the room. When Kenzie shook her head, the man glanced at his assistant with an unspoken request.

He turned back to Tate, gave him a ten-second rundown on the interview, and then smiled as the news went live again.

After welcoming Tate with a friendly on-air greeting, he asked about his career, how he felt about finishing the finals in third place for saddle bronc riding, and his injuries. They discussed his plans for the coming year. The man threw Tate a curve ball when he asked about the new love in his life.

Surprised, Tate quickly replied that he'd finally met the woman who could tame his wild ways and looked forward to spending the holidays with her.

Before Kenzie quite knew what happened, the assistant divested her of the coats in her arms as well as her purse and shoved her next to Tate. He draped his good arm around her shoulders and smiled encouragingly.

Drawing on her own experiences of being a leader and trainer with Dew, Kenzie stood to her full height, smiled confidently, and answered the questions asked of her about Tate's career.

"He's too good at what he does to stop now," Kenzie said. Her voice filled with pride while her eyes glowed with love. "He'll be back on the circuit in no time, giving everyone a run for their money."

The newscaster thanked them both and then went to a commercial break. As soon as the camera was off, Tate hugged her and whispered apologies in her ear. "I'm sorry, Kenz. I had no idea he planned to interview you as well. You did great, though. I think you may have a little experience with this sort of thing."

"A little," Kenzie admitted. She'd been interviewed many times as a representative of Dew. "Don't worry about it."

The newscaster came back and thanked them again for being on the show. He apologized for adding Kenzie at the last minute, but said they made such a nice-looking couple he wanted to include it in his segment. He wished them a happy holiday season before they went outside and carefully worked their way across the parking lot to the pickup.

Tate drove them to a nearby restaurant where they lingered over a leisurely breakfast. He ordered biscuits and gravy with hash browns and bacon while Kenzie indulged in pumpkin pancakes with link sausages.

As they ate, they chatted about plans for the next few days.

Monte had everything under control at the ranch. Tate had passed out the Christmas bonuses before he returned to town the previous afternoon. There was no reason for him to hurry back, especially with the roads in their current condition. With his suitcase at Kenzie's apartment, it was easy to decide to stay there a while longer.

While the streets thawed, they decided to go back to Kenzie's place. They planned to take Kent out for lunch and then to the mall to see the Christmas decorations and displays.

Tate paid for breakfast then held the restaurant door open for Kenzie when someone stopped him to see if he'd sign an autograph.

Quickly shooting Kenzie a questioning glance, she took his keys and quietly told him she'd warm up the truck while he did the fan thing.

Only a few steps beyond the door, a force hit her from behind, knocking her flat on her stomach on the frozen sidewalk. A weight dropped on her back and she heard someone screaming above her head.

"He's mine! All mine! I'll kill you before I let you have him!"

Chapter Nineteen

Panic welled inside her, but Kenzie refused to give in to hysteria as she assessed the situation.

She attempted to move her arms so she could push upward and dislodge the crazy person on her back. Instantly, the woman sitting on her jerked her hair with such force it made her gasp in pain.

From the corner of her eye, she saw something shiny glint against the ice and realized the woman wielded a knife. Frantic to roll away from her attacker, Kenzie suddenly felt the weight shift from her back and heard the woman scream.

"No! No! I'll kill her! You love me, Tate! You love me!"

Swiftly rolling over, Kenzie watched in horror as the lunatic slashed the knife at Tate while he tried to grab her wrist before she could do harm anyone. As she lunged at him, she buried the tip of the blade in his arm.

The man who requested Tate's autograph knocked the woman's feet out from under her and held her face down on the sidewalk.

Tate pulled the knife from his sleeve and dropped it. He engulfed Kenzie in his arms as he sat on the icy pavement next to her and held her close.

"Are you okay? Did she hurt you? I'm so sorry," Tate uttered over and over. Kenzie felt him trembling as he held her, his fear and shock as great as her own.

"I'm okay. What happened?" Kenzie asked when she regained the ability to speak. She buried her face against the wool of Tate's coat and breathed in the comfort of his familiar scent.

"It's Darcy, the woman who's been stalking me," Tate said. "I was signing the autograph and looked up in time to see her land on top of you. I've never been so glad for an ice storm because her feet slid out from under her right before she hit you. By the time I got outside, she was waving that knife around. I pulled her off, but you were already down. I've never been so scared in my life."

Tate kissed the top of her head, holding her tight as they both tried to regain their mental balance.

Darcy continued to sob and scream. The man who'd asked for an autograph held her down while a burly man dressed in a chef's uniform used an apron to tie her hands behind her back. Tate got to his feet and pulled Kenzie up with him, toeing the knife well out of reach of the crazy woman.

Sirens signaled the arrival of the police. With the restaurant so close to the news station, a crew quickly arrived and started filming, asking questions while an officer handcuffed Darcy and put her in the back of a police car.

After giving their statements and answering questions, Tate took a step back from Kenzie and noticed blood on his coat sleeve. Since the knife didn't penetrate through his cast, he spun her around and discovered a gaping tear in the back of her coat where blood trickled from a wound on her shoulder. Warily pulling apart the ragged edges of the ripped fabric, it looked like a superficial cut. He pointed it out to the officers, who agreed she should go to the emergency room to have it checked.

After thanking those gathered around them for their help, Tate drove Kenzie to the hospital where they declared her clothing beyond repair, but her wound just in need of bandaging. Thanks to her heavy coat, her attacker didn't do much more than give her a deep scratch.

She insisted the doctor check Tate to make sure he hadn't done any damage to his healing injuries. Other than his ribs being a little tender, he wasn't any worse for wear.

Assured he was fine, they left the hospital, both quiet and subdued.

Silently huddled against the pickup door, Kenzie stared out the window while Tate drove them home. The doctor said she might be in a state of shock for a while and if she seemed worse, to bring her in.

When Tate parked near her apartment door, Kenzie didn't seem to be aware she was home. He walked around the truck and opened her door, giving her a hand down. She moved on autopilot, following him to her apartment.

With a spare key she'd given him, he unlocked the door and led her inside then helped her take off her coat. He turned on the fire in the living room and watched as she looked around without really seeing anything.

Concerned by her behavior, he gave her another hug and asked if she wanted to change her shirt. At her slight nod, he took her hand as they walked to her bedroom.

She opened the door of her closet and pulled out a sweatshirt while kicking off her shoes. While she changed, Tate picked up a quilt from the foot of the bed, covering her with it when she sank onto the mattress and closed her eyes.

"I think I'll rest awhile," she whispered as Tate kissed her forehead.

"Rest as long as you like," he said, his voice raw with emotion. "I'll be right here."

"Thanks, Tate."

He carried in a chair from the kitchen and placed it close to the bed, watching her sleep. When her breathing evened out, he went back to the living room and sank down on the couch. If it hadn't been icy out, Darcy could have really hurt Kenzie, or worse.

It was the thought of worse that made Tate's blood turn to ice and his gut tighten with fear. He couldn't fathom a day without Kenzie in it. He loved her completely, from the very depths of his soul.

Anger unlike anything he'd ever known washed over him, making him clench his fist.

He was angry with Darcy for the harm she inflicted to Kenzie and putting her in danger. He was also angry with himself for putting Kenzie into a vulnerable position. Although he knew Darcy was crazy, he never imagined she'd go to such lengths to try to be near him.

Thoughts of how close he came to losing Kenzie made him feel sick to his stomach. Tate took a deep breath, then another, and another until he calmed down.

In hopes of finding a distraction, he turned on the television. Instead of some happy holiday show, he watched a scene from his morning nightmare replayed on the national news. He stood holding Kenzie against his chest while people from the restaurant poured outside.

The camera panned to police dragging Darcy to a car and placing her inside. It showed him and Kenzie answering questions then the look of horror on his face as he discovered the bloody slash on the back of her coat.

The final shot showed him helping Kenzie into his truck. The reporter dubbed him a hero, highlighting how he'd pulled the woman away from Kenzie and put himself in harm's way to keep her safe despite his recent injuries.

Not feeling at all like a hero, Tate wondered how the news clip had spread so quickly. The whole thing happened only a few hours ago.

He hoped his dad wasn't watching the news. Or his friends. Or anyone they knew.

What if Kenzie's mom saw it?

The immediate buzzing of his phone assured him someone he knew had definitely seen it.

"Tater, are you okay? Is our girl fine?" his dad asked, his voice sounding surprisingly strong and commanding for a man in his nineties. "What happened and how come I had to see it on the news?"

"We're both okay, Pop. I was going to call you later and let you know then I turned on the news and there it was." Tate explained what happened and that Kenzie had fallen asleep.

"You give her a hug for me and take good care of her, Tater. I've told you before and I'll tell you again, that girl is a keeper."

"I know she is, Pop."

Kent disconnected the call.

Tate stared at his phone and nodded his head in agreement to his dad's parting statement. Kenzie's home phone and Tate's cell began ringing at the same time. He let his phone go to voice mail and picked up her phone. "Beckett residence."

"Who is this?" a panicked voice questioned.

"I might ask the same." Tate wanted to know the identity of the caller before he divulged any information.

"This is Susan, Kenzie's mother." The voice suddenly went from frightened to annoyed and demanding. "I'll ask again, to whom am I speaking?"

"Sorry, ma'am. This is Tate Morgan, Kenzie's boyfriend. She's sleeping right now." Tate wanted Kenzie's mom to like him, or at least not be irritated with him.

"I just watched the end of a news report and couldn't believe what I saw. What in the world happened? Is she okay? Are you okay? What's going on?" Susan pelted him with questions faster than he could answer them.

"She's fine. The stab wound is really just a scratch, and the doctor said some antibiotic cream and a bandage is all she needs to treat it. She's a little out of it from the shock but the doctor said that is normal from trauma," Tate said, realizing he probably told Susan more than Kenzie would want her to know. "Really, the doctor said she'll be as good as new in a day or two."

"Stab wound? Trauma? Does she need me to come take care of her?" Susan asked. Before Tate could answer, she continued. "How did this happen? Who would want to hurt Kenzie? She's one of the sweetest girls in the world."

"I agree." Tate took a deep breath, admitting Kenzie's injury was his fault. "I've had a problem with a fan turned stalker. She somehow found out I live near the Tri-Cities and has been hanging out here trying to find me. When the news aired a promo about me being on their morning show today, she waited in the parking lot and followed us to the restaurant where we had breakfast. Kenzie walked out of the restaurant and Darcy attacked her before I could even get out the door. I'm sorry. I had no way of knowing Kenzie was in any danger. I'd have done everything in my power to keep her safe if I'd known Darcy was in the area. Evidently, she's done this before, but with the jail time she's facing she won't be bothering us anymore."

"What about the next stalker? What then?" Susan asked, sounding near hysteria. "Would you keep putting my daughter in danger?"

"Never. I had no idea she was in danger here, of all places." He started to wonder if anything he could say would calm the distraught woman on the other end of the line. "This is an isolated incident. Not something that is going to keep happening. I promise I won't let anything happen to Kenzie. I love her too much to let her be in harm's way."

"You love her?"

Tate tipped his head back and stared at the ceiling before answering. He certainly didn't plan to share that news with Kenzie's mom before he told Kenzie.

"Yes, I do. More than life itself. If something had happened to her today, I don't think…" Tate needed a moment before he could finish his statement when emotion burned fiercely through his chest. Clearing his throat, he went on. "I don't think I could live with myself if anything happened to your daughter, ma'am. She's everything to me. If keeping her safe means giving up rodeo, I'll do it in a heartbeat."

"Oh," Susan said. From the sound of things, Tate really was in love with Kenzie and had her best interest at heart. When he revealed the depth of his feelings, it went a long way toward calming her. "I'm sure that won't be necessary, but I appreciate you sharing that with me, Tate. Now, are you certain Kenzie doesn't need me to care for her? My husband can take care of the girls for a few days if she needs me."

"I'll have her call you when she wakes up, but I'm pretty sure she'll be fine." He hoped he had properly assured Kenzie's mother. "She did mention your invitation for New Year's and if the weather cooperates, I look forward to meeting you all then."

"We're looking forward to meeting you as well. The twins have researched all sorts of information about you online. They're quite excited to have you visit. They've been referring to you as Kenzie's Christmas cowboy."

Tate could almost detect a smile in her voice.

"They sound like they're as much fun as their big sister." Tate pictured the twins as younger, shorter versions of his beloved Dewdrop.

"Almost," Susan said with a genuine smile in her tone. "I'll let you go for now, but please have Kenzie give me a ring when she's up."

"I will." Tate liked Kenzie's mother from their conversation. "I'm truly sorry this happened, Susan. If I could make it all go away I would."

"I'm sure you would, Tate. Bye."

Tate didn't have time to mull over the conversation before the phone rang again. He snatched it up to find one of the neighbors on the line, asking if they were okay. He answered a few questions and thanked them for the call. Kenzie's cell phone rang in her purse but he let it go to voicemail while he answered her home phone again, this time finding her boss on the other end of the line. After assuring the man all was well, Tom said he'd let the rest of the company know Kenzie was fine.

Unable to handle all the incoming calls, Tate unplugged the landline from the wall. He answered his phone when it rang again. He spoke to Cort and then Huck, thanking them for their concern and letting them know they both were okay. The next call was from Megan and he guaranteed her Kenzie was going to be fine and promised to have her call later.

Finally taking Kenzie's cell phone from the outside pocket of her purse, he turned off the volume so it would quietly go to voice mail and answered three more calls on his phone from friends.

He shut off his cell and went into Kenzie's office. After turning on her computer, he wrote a short comment about what happened on his blog and thanked everyone for their concern. He posted the same information on his Facebook page and left a brief statement on all his social media sites.

Tired, he went to the kitchen, took a bottle of Mountain Dew out of the fridge, and realized he was hungry. A glance at the clock told him the afternoon would soon be gone.

Although he wanted Kenzie to rest, he hadn't meant to leave her alone so long.

Hurriedly setting the pop back in the fridge, he walked down the hall to her room and peeked in her door to see her moving restlessly on the bed. He sat in the chair he brought in earlier and brushed his fingers lightly across her forehead, smoothing her hair away from her face. She stilled then slowly opened her eyes.

Looking up at him, she pulled her hand from beneath the quilt and grasped his.

"Hi," she said quietly.

"Hi," he whispered, his heart suddenly climbing to his throat as he thought again how close he came to losing her.

"What time is it?" she asked groggily, not bothering to turn over so she could see the clock on the other side of her bed.

"After four." He didn't want her to be concerned about the time.

Swiftly sitting up, Kenzie glanced around the room, looking more like herself.

"I didn't mean to sleep the day away. Should we go get your dad and take him to dinner? Did you have some lunch? Did the…" Tate silenced her when he slid onto the bed and pulled her to his chest, softly kissing her lips then nuzzling her neck.

She could feel the hard form of his cast against her side where his arm encircled her. His other hand rubbed comfortingly along her arm.

"Everything's fine. I told Pop we'd see him tomorrow. I thought we could order something delivered for dinner or I can get some takeout." Tate held Kenzie like he'd never let her go. "Don't worry about anything."

Gently pushing away from his chest, she looked into his eyes. They gazed back at her with such love, it made her catch her breath.

"Tate, I'm fine, or at least I'll be fine." She sensed the need to reassure him. "Some knife-wielding crazy woman won't keep me down for long. Besides, it's nearly

Christmas, there's no whining, moping, or fits of hysteria. Santa's watching, you know."

Tate mustered a smile at her attempt at teasing. He rose to his feet and held out his hand to her.

"Come on. How about we order an early dinner and watch some Christmas movies? I might even be able to make hot chocolate by myself."

Kenzie flipped aside the quilt and stood. She looked down at her dress slacks and wrinkled her nose.

"You go ahead and make the chocolate. I'm going to change then I'll be right there."

Tate nodded and shut the door behind him when he left her room.

Kenzie changed into a pair of jeans and some fuzzy socks then went into the bathroom and washed her face.

She pulled up the sweatshirt she wore and looked at the bandage on her shoulder in the mirror. There was bruising around the cut, but she was very fortunate the knife hadn't done more damage. She was current on her tetanus shot and the doctors gave her antibiotics to make sure nothing nasty from the knife got in her system.

Fortunately, her long coat absorbed most of the fall and with gloves on her hands, she didn't even have scratches from the icy sidewalk.

Both her knees were a little stiff and her shoulder ached, but other than that, she didn't have any injuries.

Unable to fathom how someone could want to kill her and actually make an attempt at it, Kenzie struggled to wrap her head around the idea. Every time she closed her eyes, she saw the crazy woman slash at Tate and then viciously bury the knife in his arm.

What a blessing his broken arm turned out to be. Without his cast, there was no telling what kind of damage the knife would have done to him.

Determined to push those thoughts aside, she put on a fresh coat of mascara, spritzed on her favorite perfume and applied a coat of clear lip gloss. After fluffing her hair, she pinched her cheeks to add some color then went to find Tate.

After agreeing on Chinese for dinner, Kenzie called and placed the order while Tate warmed up his pickup. He gave her a kiss goodbye with a promise to be back soon with food.

In his absence, Kenzie called her mom and let her know she was fine and not to worry, reiterating Tate's promise to visit for New Year's if the roads were clear.

When her mother told her she'd seen the whole thing on the news, Kenzie couldn't believe anyone thought what happened was important enough to share on such a broad scale. Then again, Tate was something of a celebrity in the rodeo world, especially after his injury in the last round of the finals.

She called Megan and promised to let her know if she needed anything. One by one, she went through the numerous messages on her phone, returned calls, and let everyone know she was fine.

Kenzie was exhausted from repeatedly answering the same questions by the time Tate returned with bags of wonderful-smelling food. He took one look at her and shook his head.

"Decided to turn on your phone?" he asked, hanging his coat in the closet and setting his hat on the shelf above the coats.

"Yep. How'd you guess?" Kenzie gave him a tired smile. He went to the kitchen and returned with two plates and forks then went back to get them both something to drink. He removed the food from the bags and lined up the cartons on the coffee table.

"You mind if we eat in here?" he asked as he opened a carton of Mandarin chicken and passed it to Kenzie.

"Not at all." She slid off the couch to sit on the floor by the table. They both leaned back against the couch and

Tate pulled the coffee table closer. Kenzie started to give thanks for the meal but choked on her tears and couldn't continue. Tate squeezed her hand and finished, emotion making his eyes moist as he looked at her and kissed her cheek.

"Sure you're okay?" he asked, concerned not so much about her injury but the thoughts tumbling around in her head. Although she tried to act as if everything was fine, he could tell the whole situation unsettled her.

"I'm fine, but thanks for asking and taking care of me." She picked up her fork and waved it at Tate. "No chopsticks for you either?"

"Nope. Never learned how to use them and I'm usually too hungry to waste time trying to get the hang of it."

Kenzie laughed.

They watched some old Disney Christmas cartoons as they ate while the fire blazed merrily and the lights twinkled on the tree.

They finished eating, did the dishes, then returned to the living room where they watched a Christmas comedy. Kenzie relaxed as she rested against Tate's side with his arm around her shoulders.

She laughed at the funny parts of the movie and visited with him on the commercials. When it ended, she asked if he wanted some more hot chocolate. He volunteered to make it so she let him.

As he walked into the room trying to balance the mugs and a plate of cookies, she grinned at him and took the plate, setting it on the coffee table.

A holiday romance movie held their attention for a while. Tate enjoyed the time spent stretched out on the couch with her beside him. Her head rested on his good shoulder and he wrapped his arm around her as they watched a couple overcome their challenges to admit their love for each other in a dramatic Christmas Eve scene.

Although Tate had planned to tell Kenzie he loved her Christmas Eve, he couldn't wait that long, didn't want to wait a moment longer to tell her how he felt. If he'd lost her today, she would never have known she completely captured his heart, made everything brighter and better in his world.

He loved everything about her — her laugh, her smile, and the way her eyes turned warm and liquid when she looked at him. He could never get enough of the sound of her voice, the feel of her hand in his, the smell of her perfume.

Then there was the way she cared about the people at her company, her family, and friends. She was loyal, gentle, loving, witty, and perfect for him. He loved every little detail about the beautiful, smart woman, especially the way she fit so wonderfully in his arms and his life.

As the movie ended, Kenzie rolled over to look at him. A magnetic pull drew him to her lips.

After kissing her tenderly, he whispered the words that had been on his heart for so long. "I love you, Kenzie. So, so much."

"I love you, too," she whispered, putting a cool hand to his warm cheek and fastening her gaze to his. "I've loved you since the day you sat by me at the airport and asked me if our consultants went door-to-door peddling goo."

Tate laughed and kissed her again. "You are the best thing that's ever happened to me."

"Same here, cowboy." Eagerly tugging his head down, she kissed him passionately.

Tate pulled her more firmly against his chest, trying to absorb her very essence. Her heart pounded against his and he suddenly found himself consumed with her. Before he got too carried away, he kissed her reverently and pressed his cheek lovingly against hers.

"Since we've both had a pretty exciting day, and since I'm about to lose my ability to think rationally where you're concerned, I think we better turn in for the evening."

She processed the fact Tate seemed to be having as hard a time as she was at keeping her wits about her. After taking a deep breath, she sat up and smiled at him. "You're right. It has been a rather interesting day."

"I think I could do without any more interesting days for a very long time." He unplugged the tree lights then turned off the TV and the fireplace while she checked the front door to make sure it was locked.

Tate walked her to her room, kissed her softly, telling her to have sweet dreams.

As she got ready for bed, Kenzie was sure all her dreams would be of Tate.

Chapter Twenty

Startled out of a deep sleep, Tate attempted to figure out what woke him. Intently listening in the midnight quiet, he heard a whimpering sound that drew him from the warmth of his bed.

A nightlight glowing in the hall provided enough light he kept from bumping into walls as he rushed to Kenzie's bedroom. In the dark shadows of her room, he could see her thrashing beneath her covers.

Quietly approaching the bed, he shook her arm, trying to wake her. She continued fighting something in her dreams until he placed a hand on her forehead and brushed back her hair, whispering her name.

Abruptly, she stilled and opened her eyes.

"Tate?" she whispered, reaching out a hand and connecting with the cast on his arm.

"I'm here, baby." He fumbled to turn on the bedside lamp. When it illuminated the room, tears glistened on Kenzie's cheeks. "What's the matter, Dewdrop? Having a bad dream?"

"Oh, Tate," she said on a sob as he sat on the bed and gathered her against his chest. Unable to stop the tears rolling down her cheeks or the fear gripping her, threatening to squeeze the air from her lungs, she clung to him.

"Shh, Kenz. Shh. It's okay. I won't let anything happen to you." He rubbed her back and held her close. "Everything's fine."

Once her tears subsided, he handed her a tissue from the box on the nightstand and she mopped at her face.

"Thank you," she whispered, studying the blankets covering her lap. "I'm sorry I woke you."

"There's nothing to be sorry for." He used his forefinger to nudge up her chin until she looked at him. "Do you want to talk about it?"

"Not really." From her dreams, Kenzie recalled Darcy coming at her with the knife and then stabbing it into Tate again and again.

Horrified and chilled, she slid back down in bed.

"Want me to stay here with you for a while?" Tate asked, moving the kitchen chair back to the edge of Kenzie's bed from where she'd set it against the wall.

"Yes, please." Kenzie rolled onto her side so she could see Tate and hold his hand. She gripped it like a lifeline. He turned off the light and leaned forward in the chair, awkwardly stroking her forehead as best he could with his broken arm. The edges of the cast brushed against her skin, but somehow she found it comforting.

"I love you, Kenzie. I promise to keep you safe," Tate whispered. Anger that anyone would try to hurt her and frustration he couldn't make the incident go away seeped through him.

"I know. I love you, too," she said, fighting to keep her tears from erupting again. "Sing to me, Tate. Please?"

"Sure."

It took him a moment to decide on a song. He quietly sang all the verses to *Silent Night* then started to sing *The First Noel*. He made it through the first verse when the sound of her even breathing let him know she slept. For a while, he listened to her breathe, praying for her safekeeping, before going back to his room and falling into an exhausted sleep.

The next morning, Tate awoke unusually early, but got up to check on Kenzie. She slept soundly so he went back to bed and let himself relax.

Daylight peeped around the edges of the blinds in his room the next time he opened his eyes. After stretching his good arm, he rolled out of bed and wandered back toward Kenzie's room.

She opened the bathroom door and nearly ran into him, wrapped in a big fluffy bath sheet with a matching towel encasing her hair.

"Tate!" she said, blushing from her head down her neck to where the towel covered her chest. "I… you…" she stuttered, backing toward her door.

"Don't you think I better take a look at the cut?" Tate searched for any excuse to keep her from running into her bedroom and shutting the door. He liked seeing her flustered, fresh from the shower, with her skin glowing like smooth satin.

His hands itched to run up and down her arms and along her shoulders. Instead, he kept them at his sides, forcing himself to remain relaxed in posture. Every nerve ending in his body stood tense and alert, zeroed in on the beguiling woman before him.

"Oh, I suppose." She turned around so he could look at her cut. Scabbed over, it appeared clean so he offered to dab some antibiotic cream on it for her. She stepped back into the bathroom. He carefully rubbed in the ointment then covered it with a bandage before kissing the back of her neck.

Slowly backing out the door, he grinned when Kenzie turned around appearing even more rattled than she had earlier.

"How about I go take a shower and then we can decide what we want to do today?" he asked, moving down the hall toward his room.

She nodded her head, trying to recall if Tate singing her to sleep had been real or a dream. Quickly returning to her room, she dressed in dark-washed jeans and a peacock blue sweater before drying her hair then applying minimal makeup.

In the kitchen, she made oven pancakes for breakfast then whipped thick cream. She rinsed a bowl of fresh raspberries, pleased the grocery store had some decent produce when she'd gone the other day.

Plenty jittery without coffee, she opted for tea and made two cups. She stirred sugar into hers when Tate sauntered into the kitchen looking as handsome as always. His hair was still damp on the ends and his cheeks looked utterly tempting after his shave.

The deep breath she inhaled filled her nose with his enticing scent, making her stomach quiver as she handed him the cup of tea with a shaky hand.

"Hope you don't mind, but I don't need a caffeine jolt this morning," she said, carrying her tea to the kitchen table then setting down plates and forks. Tate carried the berries and whipped cream while she took the puffy baked pancake from the oven.

"What's that?" he asked, watching as she cut it into slices and put one on each of their plates.

"A Dutch baby. It's a baked pancake," she said, glad she'd gone to the effort of making it. Her repertoire of breakfast recipes was limited and she'd gone through about all she knew in the time Tate stayed with her.

He eyed the golden, crusty slice on his plate and followed Kenzie's example of spooning whipped cream and berries on top. Eagerly taking a bite, he closed his eyes and savored the delicious flavor and rich egg texture.

"That's good. Thanks." He took another bite then drank from the cup of tea.

"You're welcome. I'm glad you like it." Distracted, she took a few more bites before setting her fork on the edge of her plate and staring at Tate. "Did I wake you last night?"

"Yeah, but don't worry about it." He ate another bite, enjoying his breakfast treat.

"Did I really cry all over you and then ask you to sing?" Kenzie asked, focusing on the snowflake pattern on her plate.

As he studied her beautiful dark head bent over her breakfast, love swelled in his heart. "You did." The strength of his feelings last night was just as real and heartfelt this morning. He'd do anything to make Kenzie feel safe and protected.

Determined to lighten her somber mood, he tried to make her laugh. "Apparently my rendition of holiday favorites puts you to sleep in no time at all."

"I'm sorry." Embarrassed at having bothered Tate, she shoved her food around on her plate. He was still healing from his injuries and required uninterrupted rest. The last thing he needed was a panic-stricken female forcing him out of bed with her sobbing and ordering him to sing.

"There's nothing to be sorry about, Kenzie. I'm glad I was here. You can cry on me any time you want or insist I sing. Well, at least where there aren't witnesses to the singing." When she ignored his teasing grin, he pushed up her chin so she'd look him in the eye. "Okay?"

At Kenzie's slight nod, he kissed her cheek and returned to eating his breakfast. He asked her about all her goodie tins. They decided to deliver some that morning before going to pick up Kent for lunch then heading to the mall to look at the decorations.

Quickly rinsing the breakfast dishes and putting them in the dishwasher, Kenzie and Tate both took a few moments to respond to voice and text messages as well as emails before bundling up to head outside. The temperature climbed high enough the previous afternoon to melt most of the ice and the streets looked clear.

After delivering several tins of goodies that morning, they arrived at the assisted living center in time to take Kent to lunch at his favorite restaurant.

Throughout the meal, the three of them enjoyed one another's company. When they finished eating, they left the restaurant to do a little shopping. Tate drove them to the ranch supply store where he bought a new coat, since his was covered in Kenzie's blood and one sleeve was slashed.

Rapidly yanking off the tags, he put on the new coat, stuffing the old one behind the pickup seat then drove to the mall.

As they gawked at the colorful decorations, Tate tried to cajole Kenzie and Kent into sitting on Santa's lap. She and the elderly man refused, but they stood and watched a few anxious youngsters and screaming toddlers take turns on the red-suited man's lap before wandering through some of the stores.

Tate insisted on buying Kenzie a new black dress coat when she happened to see one she liked.

"You don't need to buy my coat." She carried it to the cash register to pay for it.

"Yes, I do. It's my fault your other one was ruined." He pulled out his wallet as the sales clerk looked from one to the other.

"Let the boy pay for it, Kenzie. It'll make him feel better," Kent finally said, patting her on the arm and giving her a wink. "Fellas like to buy things for their girls, you know."

Kenzie smiled at Kent and nodded her head. "Fine. I can't win with the two of you conspiring against me, but it wasn't your fault, Tate. Just keep that in mind."

Tate paid for the coat and tried to take the bag from Kenzie, but she shook her head and walked ahead of him, looking back over her shoulder with a sassy grin.

"Tater, are you going to marry that girl or not? If you don't snap to it, someone else will snatch her up, like that neighbor of hers who lives upstairs," Kent said as he strolled beside his son. Kenzie ducked into a gift shop while Tate stayed with his dad outside.

"I'd sure like to if she'll have me," Tate admitted, guiding his dad to an empty bench where they could sit and wait for Kenzie. He chose to ignore the comment about Kenzie's neighbor. Tate knew his dad was just trying to goad him.

"Have you asked her?" Kent pinned him with a questioning gaze.

"No, but before you give me step-by-step directions on how to do it, I've got plans. Just cool your heels, Pop." Tate grinned at his dad, patting him on the back.

Kent slapped Tate's leg and laughed.

"I was starting to wonder if you were as all-fired smart as I give you credit for being. It wouldn't take a genius to see that girl is head-over-heels in love with you." Kent relaxed against the bench. He could almost picture a grandbaby bouncing on his knee. "When are you going to pop the question?"

"Christmas Day and that's all I'm saying." Tate watched people hurry by, arms loaded with bags and packages.

"Good enough, son. What time are you heading back to the ranch?" Kent dug in his pocket for a piece of hard candy. He'd been sucking on peppermints for so many years, he couldn't remember why he started the habit. He offered one to Tate and grinned when his son shook his head then took one anyway.

"I'm not. I'm staying at Kenzie's." As the full force of his dad's disapproval hit him, Tate battled the urge to squirm under the older man's scrutiny.

"Young kids today don't hold with what you see as old-fashioned values, but I didn't raise you to be a trifling kind of man, Tater. What do you mean you're staying at Kenzie's?"

"Monte has everything under control at the ranch and we're supposed to get another storm. I don't want to drive back and forth to town when it isn't necessary. Besides, it's not what you think." Tate looked his dad in the eye, feeling like he was twelve again, caught trying to sneak out to join Cort in some mischief. "I stay in the guest room, just like I have been since we came back from Las Vegas. In case you forgot, I'm not back at one hundred percent and even if I were, I'd still behave myself. You did raise me better than that and I haven't forgotten what you taught me."

Kent slapped Tate on the back and smiled. "Glad to hear it, boy. You are both adults and can do as you please, but I'm still not sure it's a good idea for you two to spend so much time together unsupervised. As long as I've got your word you'll act like a gentleman, I'll leave it be."

"I promise, Pop. Now you better hush because here she comes." Tate stood then helped his dad up as Kenzie approached carrying several bags.

"You boys ready to go or did you have more shopping you wanted to do?" She asked as she approached, giving Tate a kiss on his cheek. He tried to take some of the bags from her hands, but she shook her head and took a step away from him. She smiled in smug victory as Kent leaned on Tate's good arm.

"I'm about tuckered out." Kent glanced at Tate as he nodded his head. "When you get to be my age, a daily nap is pretty much required to function."

"A nap sounds good." Kenzie walked to Tate's left, trying to protect his injured side from the jostling crowd while he helped his dad navigate through the throngs of people.

After taking Kent back to his room at the care center and their packages home, Tate asked Kenzie if she'd like to go to the movies. She agreed and they hurried to catch a new holiday film.

Surrounded by the darkness in the back of the theater, Tate spent as much time kissing Kenzie as he did watching the movie. He did manage to help her eat a tub of popcorn and drink a large soda pop.

When they exited the theater, evening had settled in so they went back to her apartment where she made soup and grilled cheese sandwiches for dinner.

They sat for hours in front of the fire talking about childhood memories and things they'd loved about Christmas when they were kids before turning in for the night.

Tate had a hard time relaxing, listening for a sign that Kenzie struggled with another nightmare. Finally falling asleep, he awakened hours later when he heard her scream.

He raced to her room and found her sitting in bed with the light on. Terror lingered in her eyes as she clutched the sheet in both hands. Her chest heaved and her breath came in tight gasps.

"It's okay," he said, taking her cold hand in his. "It was just a dream and it's over now."

"Tate, it was awful. She was there… the knife…" Kenzie shuddered. She'd dreamed Darcy had come after them and stabbed Tate repeatedly. She knew the woman was in jail and likely would be for a long while, but she couldn't get past the feeling that Darcy was still going to hurt them, Tate in particular.

"It's over, Kenz. She can't get to us. We're safe. I promise to keep you safe, baby. I promise." Tate sat beside Kenzie on the big bed and wrapped his arm around her. "Let go of the fear that she'll come back. She can't. I won't let it happen."

Kenzie buried her face against Tate's bare chest, drawing comfort from him. When Tate shivered in the cool night air, she gently pushed against him until he got to his feet.

"Will you keep holding me for a while?" she asked, pulling back the covers so he could climb in beside her.

The innocent yet intimate proximity to Kenzie would push his willpower to the extreme, but he nodded his head. He turned off the light and got into bed beside her. After sliding down so his head rested on a fluffy pillow, Tate wrapped his right arm around her and kissed her temple.

Curling against his side, Kenzie rested her head on Tate's shoulder and listened to the steady thumping of his heart.

Tate felt her relax as he quietly hummed. Eventually, her even breathing told him she slept. Afraid to wake her if he moved, he let his eyes drift shut and fell asleep.

Kenzie awakened slowly, feeling more secure than she had in years. As she moved her hand beneath her cheek, she realized her pillow had suddenly grown extra firm. Unusually hard.

Her hand trailed downward and she popped open her eyes. Tate's bright blue orbs gazed at her with love and amusement as her hand caressed his bare stomach.

"Happy Christmas Eve, Kenz," he whispered, placing a kiss on her forehead.

"Happy Christmas Eve," she said, disoriented. What had happened last night? Why was Tate in her bed and why was she using him as a pillow?

Frantically sorting through her memories, she recalled going to bed early because they both were so tired. She remembered having a nightmare and Tate coming in to comfort her.

In the vague recesses of her sleepy mind, she thought she may have asked him to hold her, heard him humming as she drifted off to a peaceful sleep.

Would she be plagued with nightmares from now on?

Tate's presence not only drove away her midnight fears, but also made her feel cherished and loved. It would be so easy to get used to falling asleep in his arms but they couldn't let it happen again.

Even if all they'd done was sleep, she couldn't keep sharing a bed with Tate. It pushed the limits of her willpower far too close to the edge.

She would just have to banish her fears and get over what had happened with the stalker.

Kenzie placed a light kiss on Tate's strong chin then sat up and stared at the man who had won her heart.

In the light from the bedside lamp, she could see his hair pinwheeling around his head. A day's growth of beard accented his scruffy cheeks along with creases from the pillow, but he looked wonderful to her.

Tate reached out and playfully flipped the collar of her blue flannel snowman pajamas. "Now that's what I call sexy nightwear, Dewdrop. You get those at Victoria's Secret?"

Kenzie glared at him and scooted further away in the bed. "Snarky comments from a man who's wearing red and green plaid pajama bottoms? If you aren't careful, I'll tell Cort and Huck you've got a pair of Spiderman pjs."

"You wouldn't dare." Tate grinned wickedly as he reached for Kenzie. She backed away from his grasp.

"Yep. I'll tell them that you suck your thumb, too," she teased. Laughter spilled out of her as Tate lunged for her and grabbed her leg before she fell out of bed.

"You, Miss Beckett, are a complete tease and a terrible liar." He pulled her to him. Wrapping his arms around her, he gave her a warm hug while his lips brushed across her neck.

Sparks flew between them while heat flooded through Kenzie. In another minute, those sparks would ignite into inextinguishable flames.

"Guilty as charged." If they didn't get up, it was highly likely they'd spend their entire Christmas Eve in her bed. Forcefully pushing her thoughts toward the day ahead, she pulled back from Tate and got to her feet on the opposite side of the bed. "What would you like for breakfast?"

"Anything's fine. We can just have cereal or toast." Disappointed she'd ended his attempts at cuddling so speedily, he knew it was the right thing to do given the circumstances. Leisurely climbing out of bed, he helped Kenzie make it.

"Did you decide on your plans for this evening and tomorrow?" Kenzie asked as she followed Tate down the hall as far as her bathroom.

"Yep. I'd like to spend them with you." He grinned as Kenzie rolled her eyes in exasperation.

"I know that. What I'm asking is if you want to spend the time here or at the ranch?"

"If it's all the same to you, I think we should stay here. Since I wasn't home, I didn't put up a tree and with the threat of another storm coming in, I don't want to get stuck out there with you here." Tate wondered how Kenzie could look any more adorable than she did at that moment in her snowman pajamas with her hair all mussed and not a speck of makeup on her face. "I'll be closer to Pop as well. Do you mind if we have dinner with him tonight?"

"Not at all. If you want, he can spend the night here. I can sleep on the couch." It would be fun to have Kent with them all evening and in the morning.

"I think he'll sleep better in his own bed, but we can keep him out as late as he can stand it tonight then go get him early tomorrow." Tate cupped her cheek with his right hand. "Thank you for being so good to my dad. He thinks the world of you."

"I'm pretty fond of him myself." She turned her face to kiss Tate's palm. "And I like his son a little, too."

"Just a little?" He asked, taking a step closer to her with a menacing look on his face.

"Yeah. Unfortunately, he thinks enough of himself without anyone else joining in the efforts," Kenzie teased then ran into the bathroom, shutting the door behind her. Tate's chuckles echoed down the hall as he made his way to the guest room.

They spent the morning delivering the rest of her goodies and made it home just as Megan and Owen arrived. Over a simple lunch, they visited and laughed, talking about plans for the New Year.

"What did you do with the baby?" Kenzie asked as the two women put away leftovers and cleaned up the dishes while Tate and Owen talked cattle, horses, and ranching in the living room.

"He's with Owen's folks. It's a little hard to shop with him along and his grandparents thought it would be fun to keep him today." Megan wiped down the counter and rinsed off her hands. "I've never seen your apartment look so festive, Kenz. I'm glad Tate helped you find your Christmas spirit."

"I know." A dreamy look settled over Kenzie's face. She'd worn it more often than not since deciding to give her heart to Tate. "He's really special."

"You think?" Megan laughed and gave Kenzie a playful shove. "I'm pretty sure I tried to convince you of

SHANNA HATFIELD

that about a hundred times last fall and multiple times before you ever met him."

"I had to arrive at that conclusion all by myself." Kenzie grinned. "And I'm really glad I finally arrived. He's the best."

"So what are you two doing for Christmas? You know you're invited to our house. That should go without saying." Megan linked their arms as they returned to the living room.

"Tonight we're going to take his dad to services at church then come back here for dinner and maybe watch a movie. Kent will come over in the morning and open presents and just hang out for the day. I'm planning to make a turkey with all the works."

"Really? You're doing a full-on turkey dinner?" Megan asked, surprised. It would be a first for Kenzie.

"Well, don't sound so surprised. I am capable of cooking, you know," Kenzie said as they rejoined the men. She sat down on the arm of the couch next to Tate while Megan took the rocking chair by the fire.

They visited for a while longer before Megan and Owen decided they needed to finish shopping and head home. It had started snowing and the roads would soon be slick.

The afternoon passed quickly with visits and phone calls from neighbors and friends.

As evening approached, Tate and Kenzie hurried to change so they could swing by the care home for Kent then head to church for the Christmas Eve service.

Kenzie breezed into the living room where Tate waited and caught her breath. Dressed in a new black sports coat with a bright blue shirt the same shade as his eyes, he looked devastatingly handsome.

Quickly standing, he pushed at the legs of his jeans as the hem stacked around his polished boots. He nervously twirled his black Stetson in his hands as he looked at her.

"Wow!" Mesmerized by Kenzie's appearance, he drank in the sight of her. The teal green dress she wore outlined her curves to perfection. Although modest, it looked sleek and sexy. He could hardly wait to run his hands over the smooth fabric. A finger-tempting jumble of curls adorned her head and her eyes, those gorgeous dark eyes, glowed with an inner light. "You're so beautiful."

She blushed then walked over and kissed his cheek. "And you, cowboy, are quite possibly the most handsome man I've ever seen." As an excuse to touch him, she brushed at imaginary lint on his shoulder. "Where did you get this jacket? I know it wasn't in your suitcase."

"I picked it up when we were shopping yesterday." He wanted to pull the pins from her hair and bury his face and hands in the fragrant tresses. "I suppose we better hurry or Pop will think we've forgotten about him."

A short while later at church, tears stung Kenzie's eyes, as they did every year, when the pastor spoke about the most precious gift the world ever received. Something else he said caught her attention as she sat between Tate and Kent thinking about a sweet baby in a humble manger.

"Why wait to accept the gifts God has given you, my friends? They are there before you for a reason. Accept them gratefully, graciously, and with thanksgiving in your hearts."

Kenzie swallowed back the tears threatening to spill over her cheeks. Tate was such a beautiful, precious gift. One she'd pushed away, scorned, and ignored. If he hadn't been persistent, if he hadn't been so kind and forgiving, she'd still be sad and alone, mired in the misery of her past without hope for a happy future.

Still contemplating the pastor's words hours later after they left Kent at his room, Kenzie waited until they sat on the couch in front of the fire at her apartment to tell Tate what was in her heart.

"Tate, this has been the most wonderful Christmas Eve, Christmas season, I've ever had." Kenzie set down her hot chocolate and took his hand in hers. Gently rubbing it, she savored the warmth as well as the strength of his hand against hers.

"It's been the best for me, too." He lifted her fingers to his lips before turning over her hand and pressing a hot kiss to her palm. "You've made everything so special and fun, Kenzie. I appreciate you opening your home and your heart to me. I... well... I..."

Kenzie didn't let him finish. "Up until you got hurt I was awful to you. I ignored you, pushed you away, believed the worst about you instead of listening to the truth and I'm so sorry. I want you to know what a gift you've been to me, a blessing. I don't ever want to take you for granted again. I love you, Tate, with all my heart, and I can't see a future without you in it. You mean everything to me. I'm so sorry I wasted all that time we could have been together."

Caught off guard by Kenzie's statement, Tate stared at her for a long moment trying to decide if he was dreaming or if the woman he loved was saying she couldn't live without him. When tears slipped down her cheeks and she began to pull away, his heart melted in his chest.

"It's okay. Don't cry, Kenz. Don't cry." Tate gathered her to him and kissed her wet cheeks.

When she calmed down, he slowly pulled the pins from her hair and set them on the coffee table, then ran his hands along the smooth fabric covering her back. It looked so cool, yet felt warm to his touch. Warmed by Kenzie.

Tate's insides heated as he dug his fingers into her hair and gave her a flirty smile. "I don't want to spend any more time fussing about the past. From here on, let's focus on the future. Our future." He kissed her until they lost the ability to think about anything except each other.

Mindful that they needed to say good night, Tate lingered at Kenzie's bedroom door, holding her close, breathing in her fragrance, thinking things he knew he shouldn't.

When he couldn't stand it any longer, he pulled back and took a few steps down the hall, away from the gorgeous girl who stirred his emotions and tugged at his heart.

"Dream of sugar plums tonight, Dewdrop." Tate fused his fervid gaze to hers as he backed down the hall. "Merry Christmas, Kenzie."

"Merry Christmas, cowboy." Kenzie felt overwhelming gratitude for how special Tate had made the holiday season for her. "Love you."

Tate caught the kiss she blew him with a grin and turned away from her before he gave in to the temptation to go back to her room and spend the night wrapped in her arms.

After a peaceful night of sleep, the two of them awakened early, sitting beneath the tree, sharing kisses and laughter as they sipped hot Christmas tea.

Finally deciding to open their gifts, they soon sat amid pieces of discarded paper, bows, and ribbons.

When Kenzie opened the stand mixer Tate bought for her, she couldn't believe he remembered she said she wanted one. The fact he got her a hot-pink model was an added bonus.

After exchanging some frivolous and practical presents, they each had one gift left under the tree.

Kenzie handed Tate a heavy box, covered in red plaid paper with a big green bow.

The paper fell to the floor in a shredded mess and Tate stuck the bow on Kenzie's head as he opened the box. Lifting out an album, he turned the pages, enthralled with the scrapbook Kenzie created.

She spent hours online searching for articles and photos about Tate's rodeo career and assembled everything she found into a leather-bound book. Kent contributed photos and news clippings he kept over the years and Kenzie added the few photos she'd taken of Tate in Santa Fe and Pendleton to make it more complete. Some blank pages at the back left room to add details from the coming year.

"This is probably the best Christmas gift I've ever received," Tate said, awed by the effort Kenzie put into his present. "Thank you, Dewdrop."

He set the book on the coffee table and wrapped his arms around Kenzie, giving her a tight hug. When he pulled back, he got to his feet and picked up a box from beneath the tree.

"Why don't you open this?" Tate set the box wrapped in western paper featuring bucking broncs and brands topped by a red bandana bow on her lap. Barely able to contain his excitement, he wanted to bounce off one foot to the other as he waited for Kenzie to open her gift. "Go on, open it."

Eagerly ripping away the paper, Kenzie opened the box to find a pair of hot pink boots, almost identical to a pair she had worn and loved as a young girl. Swiftly taking one boot out of the box, she ran her hand over the smooth leather and smiled.

"Tate, I don't know where or how you found these, but they're perfect. I love them," she said, still holding the boot as she gave Tate a one-armed hug.

"Try them on. I want to make sure they fit." He watched as Kenzie removed her slippers and tugged on the first boot.

She held out her leg to admire how it looked.

"I bet they'll look even better with jeans instead of your reindeer pjs."

A happy grin curved her lips upward as she started to put her foot in the other boot. Something wedged in the toe prevented her from pulling it on. She tipped it up and a small box fell into her hand. She dropped the boot and opened the box, revealing a beautiful diamond ring.

Tate took the ring and slipped it on Kenzie's left ring finger then kissed her hand. Unable to get down on his knee, he made up for it with the look of love that filled his face.

"I love you, Kenzie Amelia Beckett, and I can't wait to start a life together. I promise it will always be filled with laughter, love, and more than a good share of Christmas cheer." Tate kissed her cheek as she stared at him, utterly surprised. "Will you make this the best Christmas ever and agree to marry me?"

Kenzie laughed and wrapped her arms around her Christmas cowboy, kissing each of his dimples before lingering on his lips.

"Yes, I'll marry you. Just name the time and place, and I'm there." Kenzie lavished his cheeks with kisses before returning to his mouth for another passionate exchange.

"How about today?" Tate's lips moved tantalizingly against hers.

"What?" Kenzie asked, sure she'd misheard him.

"Let's get married today," Tate said, pulling back and looking into her eyes.

"Today? Are you insane?" Kenzie only half-objected to the idea. "Your dad will be here for lunch and there are more gifts to exchange and where would we possibly find someone to marry us today anyway? We don't have a license or anything."

"It's Christmas. Miracles happen all the time." He shoved aside all the trappings of gift opening so he could lean back against the couch cushions. After tugging on her arm until she sat across his lap, he gave her the smile he knew would make her agree to most anything. "I've never wanted a single thing as much as I want to be with you, Kenzie. Please, Dewdrop, end my misery and marry me as fast as humanly possible. Just say yes. I'll figure out the details."

"Yes…" Kenzie managed to whisper before losing all ability to speak as Tate kissed her with a passion, a bone-deep longing she'd never dreamed of experiencing.

Chapter Twenty-One

Impatiently glancing at his watch, Tate shifted from one foot to the other. Cort nudged him and gave him a teasing grin.

"It's not like she's gonna run off, you know. She's the one who planned all this." Cort waved his hand around the elite Las Vegas wedding chapel filled to overflowing with guests.

Tate and Kenzie agreed to a large ceremony the day after the rodeo finals so all their friends could attend. With the help of Kenzie's mom and stepdad, Kent traveled to Las Vegas. Together, they watched the last night of the rodeo competition. They also escorted him to the wedding.

At that moment, Kent sat in the front row across the aisle from Kenzie's family, beaming at his son.

Red and white carnations, red roses, and a profusion of poinsettias decorated the chapel. Tate glanced down at the red rose boutonniere fastened to the lapel of his black tuxedo, inhaling the faint floral scent. Cort and Huck wore matching rosebuds on their jackets as they stood beside him.

As he looked out over the sea of faces, Tate noticed Kenzie's boss and her friends from Dew, their friends from back home, several of his ranch hands including

Monte, many of his rodeo friends, and extended family members.

The opening chords of the processional pulled his gaze to the back of the room where Kenzie's twin sisters and her friend, Michele, walked down the aisle followed by Megan.

When the wedding march began, Tate smiled as his wife of nearly a year floated down the aisle on the arm of her stepfather.

Their gazes connected and she shot him a wink. His heart skipped a beat, like it did every time he set eyes on her.

She looked stunning in a simple ivory satin gown that draped around her curves and fell into a short train. Kenzie's glorious dark hair rested in a profusion of curls on top of her head, surrounded by a crown of ivory roses with baby's breath. He couldn't wait to pull out the pins and run his fingers through the silky tresses then undo the many buttons marching up the back of her dress.

Tate smiled at Kenzie, flashing his dimples. He watched her eyes widen in response to him, felt her squeeze his arm, breathed in her familiar intoxicating fragrance that never failed to remind him of a field of flowers on a warm summer afternoon.

More in love with this beautiful woman now than he'd been on the day they wed, he thought he had loved her then with an all-consuming passion. He assumed after a year the magic of their love would have dimmed, but it seemed to gain intensity and depth with every passing day.

While they turned and listened to the words of the minister who performed the ceremony, both of them thought back to the day after Christmas last year when they drove to a little town in Idaho just a few hours from the Tri-Cities where they could get married without delay.

After running by the courthouse for a marriage license, they exchanged vows in a private ceremony at a tiny wedding chapel. Tate's arm was still in a cast and Kenzie wore a bandage on her shoulder from the attack by his stalker, but it was what they wanted to do.

Neither of them could bear the thought of being apart any more than absolutely necessary. Then there was the fact they couldn't keep away from each other.

Kenzie and Tate had no regrets about their quiet union. If anything, it made them feel more connected.

Deciding not to tell anyone about their hasty wedding, they instead spent a year planning a big celebration in Las Vegas to take place the day after the rodeo finals.

Their secret marriage became something special just between the two of them. Kenzie didn't know how they'd managed it, but no one seemed to be the wiser.

She glanced over at Tate and smiled. Light gleamed off the gold champion buckle he received the previous evening when he'd taken the title in saddle bronc riding. Cort and Huck both wore similar buckles, having earned the titles in their respective events.

They'd all worked so hard the past year and she was proud of all three of them, but she was especially proud of her husband.

Although he had an eight-week late start in the circuit after the holidays due to his injuries, Tate put everything he had into each ride and managed to finish the year on top.

He squeezed her hand and she looked at him with all the love she felt for him shining in her eyes.

The past eleven months presented numerous challenges to them as they both agreed to pursue their careers for one final year. Kenzie let her boss know early on that after the finals in Las Vegas she would no longer be able to travel for the company.

Not wanting to lose a great employee, Tom offered her a position as a program developer. She could work from home creating trainings and would even present some of the programs online.

Tate and Kenzie remodeled a room in the old farmhouse at the Morgan Ranch into her office space, complete with a video area for her to record training presentations and do live video feeds.

Efforts to coordinate their schedules paid off since Kenzie attended many of the rodeos where Tate competed throughout the season. Sometimes it meant she picked up an extra training opportunity to be in the same city as Tate, but she hadn't minded the additional work when it let her be close to him.

In the end, it was worth it.

There were no regrets of the year spent secretly married, but she was thrilled everyone would now know they were committed to making a happily ever after together.

Her husband, the most handsome man she knew, looked movie star gorgeous in his tuxedo, his smile wide and his heart in his eyes.

His unforgettable scent enveloped her and his warmth surrounded her. Her heart tripped in her chest as she thought about the future they could now openly plan together.

As they turned to each other and exchanged vows, Tate couldn't believe they finally arrived at the place they'd worked so hard to reach.

Winning the championship title the previous night was the icing on the cake. Regardless of how he placed, he knew going into the year it would be his last on the rodeo circuit. He and Kenzie were eager to settle into ranch life and pursue their dreams together, as a family.

With both of them home and not on the road, there was no reason Kent couldn't live with them in the house he'd always known.

As soon as they got back from their honeymoon, they planned to move him into a newly remodeled room at the ranch. Then they'd get to work on making one of the many grandbabies he continued to insist they needed to have sooner rather than later.

The minister pronounced them husband and wife and Tate gave her such a steamy kiss, many of the guys in attendance whistled and clapped until Kenzie's face turned a bright shade of pink. Once they turned to the crowd, they smiled and waved before hurrying down the aisle to the adjoining ballroom for the reception.

Hours later, as they retired to the honeymoon suite at their hotel, Tate grinned as he carried Kenzie over the threshold.

"Just sticking with tradition, Mrs. Morgan," Tate said, liking that he could actually call her that now. There had been so many times in the past year when he almost let the cat of the bag by saying something revealing in front of family or friends.

Trips to visit her family had been torture since they slept in separate rooms. Rodeo travel with Cort around had been nearly as bad. Tate and Kenzie engaged in covert maneuvers trying to sneak him into her hotel room too many times to count.

Overall, their clandestine meetings added an element of intrigue and excitement to their marriage, keeping them going toward their December goal.

"You are a traditionalist," Kenzie agreed, removing Tate's tie while he used his elbow to close the door behind them. "I know for a fact you've got an entire holiday season filled with plans of caroling, cutting down our Christmas tree, and every other traditional activity you can possibly squeeze in between now and Christmas Day."

"Yes, I do," Tate agreed, letting her slide down the length of him until her feet touched the floor. As his hands rested on the soft satin of her gown, heat licked up his arms, making his temperature spike.

Tate removed the crown of flowers on her head followed by her hairpins. A sigh of contentment fanned her warm breath across his neck as she leaned into him. Nibbling her earlobe, his fingers moved to the back of her gown.

While he worked at the buttons, he thought of spending the holiday with his bride — their first together as husband and wife.

He could hardly wait to take Kenzie home and show her what Christmas was all about at the Morgan Ranch.

Not that he hadn't enjoyed spending the holidays with her last year at her apartment, but Christmas at the ranch was about to become a spectacle to behold.

First, though, he had other, more pressing plans requiring his full attention.

"I do have a bunch of Christmas plans, Kenz. But I've got even more important plans. Plans of a more immediate, intimate, urgent nature."

"Do tell, Mr. Morgan." Her sultry voice made Tate's blood zing through his veins. She removed his tux jacket, followed by his shirt. Lazily kissing her way across his muscled chest, she moved to his face and paid particular attention to each dimple in his cheeks before trailing her lips down his firm jaw. "Am I involved in those plans?"

"You most certainly are, my beautiful Dewdrop." He finished unfastening the last button on her dress and watching in delirious joy as her gown fell to the floor, revealing bits of silk and lace. He ran his callused hands across the smooth skin of her back, down her arms, across her sides. "Every plan I've got includes you. Christmas plans, New Year's plans, ranch plans, family plans, but most importantly, love you forever plans. Love you completely and thoroughly plans. Starting right now."

Kenzie's willing gaze connected with his and they both smiled.

"I like those kinds of plans, cowboy."

Epilogue

"Hey, Dewdrop," Tate called as he shut the back door behind him. Quickly leaving his outerwear in the mudroom and removing his boots, he washed his hands at a deep sink and hurried into the warmth of the kitchen.

The January wind was bitterly cold and he felt half-frozen as he poured himself a cup of coffee. "Are there any gingerbread bars left?"

Kenzie slid a plate of cookies toward him from her seat at the counter, trying to swallow back her tears.

Tate set down the cup in his hand and wiped away a glistening drop from her cheek. He looked at her with love and concern in his bright blue eyes. "What's wrong, Kenz?"

"It's in today's paper." She handed the newspaper to her husband and wrapped her arms around his waist as he moved closer beside her. Slowly opening the paper, Tate read his father's obituary.

~*~

Kent Gideon Morgan, 94, died peacefully at home with his family around him.

A long-time rancher in the area, Kent loved the outdoors, his family, and his Lord.

Marrying late in life, he and his beautiful wife, Caroline, had one son. Tate filled his father's heart with much joy and brought a beloved wife to the family. Kent loved her like a daughter.

His greatest delight, in his last year of life, came from time spent with his grandson, especially during the recent holiday season.

Preceded in death by his wife, his parents, two brothers, and many friends, Kent is survived by his son, Tate, and daughter-in-law, Kenzie, along with their son, Gideon David...

Gingerbread Bars

Years ago, I embarked on a quest to find a gingerbread cookie recipe that was flavorful, soft and delicious. I finally came up with what I thought was the perfect cookie, but they were so much work.

One magical day, I went to a cookie exchange party and some wonderful person brought Gingerbread Bars. What a concept. Instead of rolling out dough and cutting what seemed like hundreds of cookies, I could make the most delicious gingerbread bars in a third of the time with half the work!

This easy recipe has become a holiday staple at our house and Captain Cavedweller somehow always manages to lay claim to the last one.

Gingerbread Bars

2 3/4 cups flour
1 1/4 teaspoons baking soda
1 teaspoon salt
2 teaspoons cinnamon
1 teaspoon ginger
2 1/2 sticks butter
1 1/4 cups packed light-brown sugar
1/2 cup plus 2 tablespoons granulated sugar
3 eggs
1 1/4 teaspoons vanilla extract
1/3 cup unsulfured molasses
Cream Cheese Frosting
Glazed Pecans (optional)

Preheat oven to 350 degrees. Coat a 17 x 12 inch rimmed baking sheet with non-stick cooking spray.

Line bottom with a piece of parchment, cut to fit. Coat parchment with cooking spray.

Whisk together flour, baking soda, salt and spices. Set aside.

Soften butter and then beat on medium-high speed with sugars until pale and fluffy. Add eggs, one at a time, beating well after each addition. Add in vanilla and molasses. Reduce speed to low and gradually add in flour mixture, then beat just until combined.

Spread batter into prepared pan. It seems like you won't have enough batter to fill the pan, but you will, keep spreading. Bake until edges are set and golden, about 25 minutes. Let cool completely in pan.

Remove from pan, frost with cream cheese frosting and cut into 2-inch squares. Top each square with a glazed pecan, if you desire.

Justin Cowboy Crisis Fund

In *The Christmas Cowboy*, Tate's injuries leave him sidelined from competing in the rodeo for two months. While he had good insurance and the family ranch to fall back on for income in the story, many cowboys in the sport of rodeo aren't quite so fortunate.

In reality, when these professional athletes are faced with serious injuries, it often results in financial hardship. They don't have a guaranteed salary or provisions for income upon injury.

While injuries are part of the business of rodeo, financial worries don't necessarily have to be.

The Justin Boot Company formed a partnership with the Professional Rodeo Cowboys Association (PRCA) and the Women's Professional Rodeo Association (WPRA) in 1989 to establish the Justin Cowboy Crisis Fund (JCCF). The fund was granted 501-C3 status as a non-profit charity organization in 1991.

The idea behind the JCCF is to assist professional rodeo athletes and their families in the event of catastrophic injuries resulting from professional rodeo activities. The fund helps lift the burden of financial hardship when a serious injury interferes with the careers of those who have dedicated their lives to the sport.

To find out more about the Justin Cowboy Crisis Fund or to make a donation, please visit their website: http://www.justincowboycrisisfund.com/

Thank you for reading Tate and Kenzie's story. Now that you've finished the book, won't you please consider writing a review? I would truly appreciate it.
Reviews are the best way readers discover great new books.

Also, if you're interested in discovering more details connected to the story, visit *The Christmas Cowboy's* board on Pinterest.

Never miss out on a new book release!
Sign up for my newsletter today!

http://tinyurl.com/shannasnewsletter

It's fast, easy, and only comes out when new books
are released
or extremely exciting news happens.

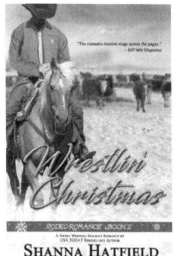

SHANNA HATFIELD

**Wrestlin' Christmas** _(Rodeo Romance, Book 2)_ - Sidelined with a major injury, steer wrestler Cort McGraw struggles to come to terms with the end of his career. Shanghaied by his sister and best friend, he finds himself on a run-down ranch with a worrisome, albeit gorgeous widow, and her silent, solemn son.

Five minutes after Cort McGraw lands on her doorstep, K.C. Peters fights to keep a promise she made to herself to stay away from single, eligible men. When her neighbor said he knew just the person to help work her ranch for the winter, she never expected the handsome, brawny former rodeo star to fill the position.

Ready to send him packing, her little boy has other plans...

Turn the page for an exciting excerpt!

Chapter One

The raspy, slobber-laden tongue scraping across his cheek combined with the malodorous scent of dog breath rousted Cort McGraw from his drunken stupor.

"Down, boy. Get down." Blindly, he reached out to Frito, the family dog. His hand connected with the back of the animal and he nudged the friendly beast away then struggled to sit upright.

Cort grasped his head between his hands in a feeble attempt to keep it from pounding and sucked in a gulp of morning air. Unwillingly opening one eye, the other gradually followed.

The effort required to gain his bearings from his sprawled location on the sidewalk, steps away from his parents' front door, made him groan.

Frito lapped his face again, accelerating the queasy roiling in his belly.

He clamped his lips together and lumbered to his feet. If he lost the contents of his stomach in his mother's pot of geraniums, the pain ripping through his head now would be nothing compared to what she'd deliver later.

Frantically grabbing the crushed Stetson that served as his pillow, he staggered around the house, rushed through the back door, and into the small bathroom located near the kitchen.

The hat landed on the counter as he splashed cold water on his flushed face and drew in several deep breaths.

Once his stomach settled, he glanced in the mirror and grimaced at the bloodshot gray eyes and haggard appearance reflected in the glass. Bright streaks of blood-red lipstick blazed along his jaw, across the dimple in his chin and encircled his mouth, marring his face as if creative inspiration struck a macabre artist.

Warily wading through his fuzzy memories, he tried to remember which girl he'd been flirting with at the bar the previous evening before he had one too many drinks.

Disgusted with himself, Cort rubbed a hand over his cropped black hair in frustration. He'd promised his dad he wouldn't do this again, yet he started the day with a hangover and no idea where he'd been last night.

Quietly opening the bathroom door, he snagged his hat off the counter and started down the hall, hoping to make it to his room undetected.

"Cort? Is that you?" his mother's voice called to him as he sidled past the kitchen doorway to the back stairs. His boot stopped mid-air above the first step.

Busted.

Turning back to the kitchen, he stuck his head around the doorway.

"Hey, Mom." He pasted on a cheerful smile while holding his breath. The normally inviting aroma of the bacon she fried for breakfast made his stomach resume its disgruntled churning. He swallowed twice, doing his best to ignore the nauseous feeling threatening to swamp him.

"Are you just getting in? Again?" Jana McGraw glared at her only son and oldest child.

Cort didn't need to see the scowl on her face to recognize her disappointment in him. His parents hadn't raised him to be a drunken, womanizing loser although the last few months that seemed an apt description.

"Yeah. I'm gonna go grab a shower." He hoped she'd let the matter of his nocturnal activities drop without commentary.

"You just do that." Jana pointed her fork his direction. "But when you no longer stink like…" She wrinkled her nose as she got another whiff of him. "When you're clean, get yourself back down here. Your father and I want to talk to you."

"Mom, just leave it alone," Cort said, unable to keep the irritation from his voice.

"We've left it alone far too long as it is."

"I don't want to talk about it." Deliberately ignoring her summons to return to the kitchen, he hurried up the stairs.

Angry and despondent, he tromped into his room, shut the door, and sat on his bed staring at the photos and trophy buckles lining his walls.

For three years running, he'd been a world champion steer wrestler. On track to make it to the finals again, a freak injury in April blew out his knee and left him unable to compete. More than one doctor assured him if he tried to bulldog a steer again, odds were high he'd end up permanently crippled.

After spending the last dozen years competing in pro rodeos, Cort didn't have a clue what to do with his life. Between rodeos, he always returned to his parents' farm where they raised hay, sugar beets, and beef cattle in the small community of Star, Idaho, near the state capital of Boise.

He assumed someday, when he was ready to retire from the rodeo, he'd buy his own place nearby or work fulltime with his dad. Now, he rebelled against the prospect of farming the rest of his life.

Cort wanted to be back on the rodeo circuit, bulldogging and raking in the prize money like he had the last several years.

In truth, nothing had been the same since his best friend, Tate Morgan, gave up riding saddle broncs to marry the love of his life. He retired from his career a few years ago as a world champion, happily settling into domestic bliss on his ranch near Kennewick, Washington.

Cort visited Tate and Kenzie, and their baby Gideon, several times, but he missed the days when he and Tate were travel partners, on the road to the next rodeo.

The Big Four Rodeos would kick off in a few weeks in Kennewick. He hated to miss the events and wished his dreams hadn't ground to an agonizing halt.

The moment his foot hit the dirt on that April night, he knew he wouldn't walk out of the arena. Instead of scoring, he ended up in the hospital. The doctor assured him he'd never steer wrestle again if he had any hope of being able to walk and move normally for the rest of his days on earth.

On mornings like this, hung-over and maudlin, Cort sometimes thought it would have been better if he'd landed on his head and ended his misery. He hated grappling to get through one day, then another, as a washed-up former rodeo star.

Much to his annoyance, he had to agree with his mother as he removed his clothes. He did stink - like stale beer, cigarette smoke, and tacky perfume. The cloying fragrance most likely belonged to the girl who'd smeared her garish lipstick all over his face.

Cort stepped into the shower in his bathroom and stood with the warm stream spraying over him, wondering what his mom and dad planned to say. It wouldn't be anything they hadn't said multiple times in the last few months.

Once he regained the ability to walk without a crutch or cane, Cort had helped his dad farm during the day then ran off at night to drink away his memories.

His behavior appalled his parents, but he couldn't muster a sufficient amount of shame to care. No one, not even his sister, Celia, seemed to understand the accident had robbed him of his career and destroyed his hopes for the future.

In no hurry to listen to another lecture from his parents, Cort took his time drying off and getting dressed. A quick check of his clothes hamper showed it was empty, so he took the clothes he'd worn last night downstairs to the laundry room. He dropped them into the washer and turned it on before sauntering into the kitchen.

Celia sat at the table with their parents. The look she gave him carried a mixture of sympathy and displeasure that set him on edge.

Regret stung his conscience, but not enough to check his attitude as he poured himself a cup of coffee and sank onto a chair next to her.

"What brings you out here, Miss Fancy Pants?" Cort asked, taking a piece of toast from a plate on the table and buttering it.

Celia tossed back her mane of red hair and narrowed her green eyes his direction. "You, unfortunately." She sipped from a glass of cold orange juice while continuing to glower at him.

"Me? What are you talking about? Why don't you mind your own business, Celia, and stay out of mine." Cort bit into his toast, glaring at her then his mother.

His dad thumped his hand on the table, forcing Cort to turn his glance his direction.

"Look, Cort, things haven't turned out like you hoped, like you wanted, but you're thirty-three years old." Trevor McGraw fought the urge to shake some sense into his son. "You've still got a long life ahead of you and we can't watch you throw it away. We've encouraged you, supported you, done everything we can to help you get back on track, but we're through. We didn't raise you to be the kind of man you've turned into since your accident. We refuse to stand by and watch you destroy yourself because you can't get over the past and deal with the present."

Cort tossed the remnants of his toast onto his plate and rose to his feet. "I don't have to listen to this."

"Sit down!" Trevor stood so fast he knocked his chair over. His firm voice made it clear he expected Cort to obey his command. Every bit as tall and burly as his son, his presence demanded attention and respect. "So help me, if you don't sit your butt in that chair, wipe that snide sneer off your face, and listen to what we have to say, I *will* take you outside and pound some sense into your thick skull."

Shocked by both his father's words and the look on his face, Cort slowly returned to his chair. His father had never laid a hand on him in anger and he seriously doubted he would now. Nevertheless, the fact he even made the threat gave him a moment of pause.

"Cort, please, try to understand." Jana reached out and took Cort's big hand in her small one. "We just want to help you."

"Your mother and I can't watch you do this to yourself." Trevor righted his chair, sat down, and crossed his arms over his chest. "If you don't drink yourself to death, you're going to kill yourself or someone else driving home drunk as you do most every night. We've told you a hundred times not to drive if you've been drinking." Trevor released a sad, broken sigh. "We're done with this, Cort. As of today, you are on your own."

"What?" Cort's head snapped up, shooting a questioning gaze to his dad.

"You heard me." Trevor nailed him with a steely glare. "After breakfast, you're leaving. Celia has graciously agreed to escort you to Tate and Kenzie's place. Some time away from here will be good for you."

"Just like that, you decide what's best for me without considering what I want?" Unable to stop his anger from bubbling over, Cort's voice increased in volume while his face flushed an angry shade of red.

Celia glared at him, her own temper flaring. "What you want is irrelevant. You've become a selfish, self-centered pig and we're done tiptoeing around you." She wanted to reach out and smack him. Through the years, she'd gone many rounds with Cort and didn't shy away from a verbal sparring match. "You've had plenty of time to get your act together and instead, you wallow in self-pity. It's time for you to grow up and start acting like a man instead of a pathetic pile of garbage."

Jana put a warning hand on Celia's arm, but the girl paid it no mind as she squared off with her only sibling.

"Is that right?" Cort asked, getting to his feet again and curling his hand into a fist. He desperately wanted to punch something.

Celia stood then climbed onto her chair so she would be taller than Cort. She shook her finger in his face, refusing to back down from the defiant stare filled with hate and loathing he aimed her direction.

"That's right. If there's anything you want we didn't already pack, you better run your lazy, worthless backside upstairs and get it because we're leaving. Now." Celia jumped down and stomped out the back door.

After giving his parents one last surly look, Cort thudded up the stairs and slammed his bedroom door for good measure.

Empty hangers and a few remnants of clothing from his high school days were all that hung in his closet.

Although he hadn't given it a thought when he dressed after showering, he'd found the clothes he wore neatly folded on the counter in his bathroom. A glance in his dresser drawers revealed they stood empty. His family hadn't left a hat or spare pair of boots in his room.

Heedless to what he broke, his hand swiped across the length of the bathroom counter, dumping his toiletries into a leather travel bag. A fleeting look around his bedroom served to reaffirm he didn't need to take any reminders of his rodeo days with him.

Livid, he crammed his keys, wallet, and cell phone into his pockets. Yanking on the boots he'd removed before his shower, he tugged on his crushed hat and clomped down the stairs.

Cort returned to the kitchen, leveling a furious stare at his parents. "If you wanted me to leave, you could have said so. You didn't need to plan this little intervention or whatever it is you want to call it." He stalked across the room and lingered in the doorway.

"We've tried everything possible to get you to snap out of this funk you've been in," Jana said, placing a gentle hand on his arm. "Please, Cort, let us help you."

"I don't need your help and I don't need any of you. Just remember, you're the ones who kicked me out." Cort pushed the kitchen's screen door open so hard it banged against the side of the house.

Footsteps echoed behind him as he strode across the yard to where Celia waited with his pickup and horse trailer. At least they were letting him take his horses.

"Don't leave like this." Trevor put a restraining hand on Cort's shoulder, drawing him to a stop.

"How am I supposed to leave? Get down on my knees and thank you for kicking me out? Or maybe I should be eternally grateful that you went behind my back carrying tales to my supposed best friend." Cort couldn't believe his family had betrayed him. He thought they'd always have his back, always support him when he needed it.

Instead, they'd abandoned him.

"That isn't what happened. We're worried about you, son. You need to get over this and move on with your life." Trevor wished he could make Cort comprehend they wanted to help him, not hurt him.

"Whatever, Dad." Cort jerked away from the hand his father still held on his shoulder and continued toward his truck.

Incensed, he opened the driver's side door and grabbed Celia's arm to pull her out. She swung her foot around and kicked him soundly on the thigh before wrenching the door shut and locking it.

"You don't seriously think I'm leaving here with her driving?" Cort inquired of his mother as she stood beside his dad at the edge of the yard.

"Cort, honey, just get in. No need to make this any worse." Jana closed her eyes against the pain radiating from her son's.

"I'll never, ever forgive you for doing this." He slid into the truck and slammed the door.

"We love you, baby," Jana called as Celia put the truck in gear and started out the driveway. She turned to Trevor and buried her head against his chest as tears rolled down her cheeks. "Will he ever speak to us again? Will he forgive us?"

"Someday." Trevor blinked at the tears stinging the backs of his eyes. "We're doing what's best for him, honey. He'll realize it eventually."

"Pull over. I'll let you out and Mom can come get you." Cort jerked his thumb toward the side of the highway.

Celia kept her attention focused on the road.

"At least let me drive." Cort growled at his sister, putting his hand over hers on the steering wheel. She shoved it away and ignored him, entering the freeway heading west toward the Oregon border. In about four and a half hours, they'd be at the Morgan Ranch where, she hoped, Tate and Kenzie could work a miracle and help Cort find himself again.

"The first time you stop, I swear I'm kicking you out and taking over the wheel." Cort speared her with a cold, threatening glare across the cab of the truck.

"You try anything, buster, and you're going to rue the day you were ever born." Celia shot him a warning look.

Cort remained silent for a few miles then gave her a sidelong glance. "What are your plans, exactly?"

Celia shook her head, turned up the radio, and kept driving.

Three hours into the trip, Cort desperately needed to find a rest stop and thought he might die of thirst.

"How about you stop in Pendleton for a break?" he suggested as they drove out of the Blue Mountains. "Don't you need to stretch your legs? Find a restroom?"

"Nope. I'm good." Celia watched as Cort moved restlessly in his seat. Served him right. If he'd behave himself, she'd gladly pull over at the next rest area. Despite her assurances she didn't need to stop, she drank one too many cups of coffee before they left and desperately needed a break. After his threats, though, there was no way she'd give him the opportunity to escape until she arrived at Tate and Kenzie's. "We'll be there soon."

"Right." Cort stared out the window, trying to think of anything other than his full bladder, empty stomach, and boiling anger at his sister and parents.

"Here, chew on this." Celia handed him a package of bubble gum.

He took a piece and tossed the pack onto the seat between them. It didn't take long before he began loudly snapping the gum. Each time the earsplitting pop echoed through the truck's cab, Celia's shoulders inched closer to her ears. The more it bothered her, the more enthusiastically he blew and popped bubbles.

After several more miles of him smacking the gum and her cringing, she rolled down his window and jabbed a finger his direction. "Enough! Stop acting like a spoiled brat!"

Cort spit out the gum and frowned at her as she pushed the button and the window closed. The weather outside was unbearably hot and stifling for mid-August. It made him grateful to be inside the cool air-conditioned cab of his truck even if he didn't want to be in it with Celia.

He removed a cinnamon-infused toothpick from a box in his console, stuck it between his lips, and returned his gaze to the passing scenery.

Celia followed the freeway around the outskirts of Pendleton while Cort recalled all the years that he participated in the Pendleton Round-Up. The first thirteen years of his life, he faithfully attended the Pendleton rodeo as a spectator, and it remained one of his favorites. He'd won the steer wrestling event half a dozen times over the years he participated as a contestant.

As memories flooded through him, he closed his eyes and leaned his head back against the seat.

"I'm sorry, Cort. I truly am, but this is for the best." Celia voice carried a hint of empathy, aware of his memories and internal struggle to come to terms with the loss of his career.

"Best for whom? Mom and Dad? You? It certainly isn't best for me, not that any of you care." He kept his eyes closed, unwilling to see the compassion or concern on his sister's face, although it filled her voice.

"We care. More than you can imagine. If you weren't out drinking and carousing every night, you'd know that Mom spends her evenings praying you'll come home in one piece. Dad paces the floor, frantic with worry. How can you not see what you've put this family through?" Celia asked, both her tone and temper on the rise. "You aren't the first person to have to give up something you love and find a new path. You certainly won't be the last. However, you are, quite possibly, the most pitiful. It wasn't like you could be a steer wrestler forever, anyway. Why is your forced retirement throwing you for such a loop?"

"You wouldn't understand."

"Then enlighten me. Help me understand so I can explain it to Mom and Dad."

Cort mumbled something and shook his head.

"What did you say?" Celia kept one eye on the road and the other on her brother.

"I said if I knew maybe I could explain it to you."

"Well, be sure and share the details when you figure it out." She snapped her mouth closed before she said something further to irritate Cort.

They rode in silence until she turned off the freeway onto the road that would take them to the Morgan Ranch. Cort flicked his toothpick out the window and studied his friend's well-tended fields.

"Looks like they're done with wheat harvest," Celia observed, nodding toward the vast acres of harvested wheat fields.

"Yeah. Tate said they had a bumper crop this year." Cort had always liked the look of the rolling hills covered in golden wheat. He missed them when his family moved to the Boise area. While the ground there was fertile, it was flat where his parents farmed.

"I'm glad for the farmers around here, then. Dad isn't sure how the sugar beets are going to turn out this year since water has been so scarce. Good thing the hay and beef market is strong." Celia turned down the driveway to Tate and Kenzie's house.

"Dad's worried about the beets? Why didn't he say something to me?" His dad never mentioned any concerns over the crops or a lack of water. Then again, he'd tuned out most of what his father said, too wrapped up in his own thoughts to care.

"Maybe you weren't listening," Celia suggested as she waved at Kenzie and braked to a stop in front of the big farmhouse.

Before she could get out of the truck, Tate opened her door and lifted her out into a big hug. He'd always been like another older brother. When he wed Kenzie a few years ago, Celia felt like she'd gained a much-loved sister.

"Hey, stranger, great to see you." Tate set her on her feet then they walked around the truck to where Kenzie hugged Cort. "Can you stay long?"

"No. I have to leave this afternoon, if someone can give me a ride to the airport. As much as I'd like to leave him stranded, Cort's truck stays here." Celia smiled at Tate's handsome face.

Dimples danced in his tan cheeks while his sapphire blue eyes twinkled in the early afternoon light. Nearly as tall as Cort, it was no wonder his beautiful wife was head-over-heels in love with him. He was good-looking, good-hearted, and a great father to their young son.

She hoped some of his maturity and kindness would rub off on her brother.

"Where's Gideon?" Celia asked, expecting to see the baby in his mother's arms when they pulled up at the house.

"It's nap time." Kenzie smiled as she hugged Celia then looped their arms together as they walked into the house. She glanced over her shoulder at the two men standing at the end of the walk. "I'll pour the iced tea while you two take the horses to the barn."

"We'll be in soon." Tate nodded to his wife before slapping Cort on the back. "Let's get them unloaded."

Cort climbed behind the wheel of his truck, wanting to pull out on the road and keep driving. Instead, he drove up by Tate's massive barn and unloaded his horses into an empty corral. Tate tossed hay over the fence and checked the water tank while Cort ran into the barn to use the bathroom.

He returned to the corral as Tate gave Stoney, his favorite horse, a good scratching on his neck.

"Surprised he remembers me," Tate said as the horse bumped his head against his chest. "I haven't seen him for a while."

"How could he forget you after all those miles we traveled together?" Cort's memories tugged uncomfortably at his thoughts. He quelled them before they overwhelmed him again and plastered on a fake smile.

"Where should I park the trailer?"

Tate pointed to an empty space next to one of his trailers near the machine shed. Cort expertly backed into the spot he indicated.

His friend helped gather his belongings from the back of the pickup before they walked to the house.

"Just leave your stuff here, for now." Tate motioned to a bench by the back door. Carefully wiping their boots on the doormat, they entered the mudroom then the sunny kitchen where Celia and Kenzie sat at the table, consumed with giggles.

"What's so funny?" Tate washed his hands before joining them at the table. He accepted the glass of iced tea his wife handed him.

"Celia was telling me about an impossible bride she worked with last weekend." Kenzie grinned at her husband, dark brown eyes sparkling with humor.

"How's your photography business going?" he asked.

Celia had a talent for taking photos of weddings and family portraits, as well as rodeo photography.

"Great!" Celia took a cookie from the plate Kenzie handed her. "I'm booked solid through the holidays."

"That's fantastic!" Kenzie motioned for Cort to join them.

After sitting for so long, his knee ached with a brutal force. He refused to limp as he made his way to the table, hoping his stilted walk came off as an arrogant swagger.

Cort accepted a cookie and an icy cold glass of tea from Kenzie then sat back and studied the orderly, homey kitchen. No wonder Tate traded in his rodeo career for staying at the ranch full time. From the many meals eaten around their table, Cort knew Kenzie was a remarkable cook. She was also hard-working, funny, and completely dedicated to his friend.

Their baby, Gideon, was almost two. From what Tate shared, the little guy was turning into quite a handful. Like father like son, no doubt.

Kenzie and Celia carried the conversation with Tate throwing in an occasional comment while Cort sat in sullen silence.

"Will that be okay with you, Cort?" Kenzie asked, looking at him.

"Sorry, Kenz. I missed what you said." Cort didn't sound particularly apologetic.

"Do you have any requests for dinner? I'll pick up something when I drive Celia into town to catch her flight. Would barbecue be okay?"

"Anything is fine." Cort helped himself to another cookie. Between no breakfast and Celia not stopping for so much as a bottle of water, he was famished and thirsty. When he drained his tea glass, Kenzie refilled it and slid the cookie plate closer to him.

"I hate to ask, but can I please see Gideon before we leave? I won't wake him up, but I'd love to see him for a few minutes." Celia stood and rested her hand on Cort's shoulder, giving it a squeeze. Uncertain what she wanted to convey, he shrugged off her fingers. She scowled at him then turned her attention back to Kenzie.

"Gid will be up from his nap soon, anyway. Come on." Kenzie hurried up the back stairs with Celia following close behind her.

The two women returned to the kitchen with Celia carrying Gideon in her arms. The baby rubbed at his sleepy eyes while his golden brown curls danced around his head in a tousled mess. He inherited Tate's dimples and smile, but got his molasses-colored eyes from his mother.

Gideon glanced around the faces in the kitchen. He grinned and reached out his arms to Cort with a happy squeal. "Tort!" he exclaimed. "Me, Tort!"

Tate and Kenzie laughed as Celia handed the wiggling toddler to her brother.

"Hey there, Gid." Cort took Gideon from his sister and patted him on the back. "How are you?"

"Good." Gideon launched into some fast-spoken babble none of the adults understood.

Kenzie picked up her purse and smiled at Celia. "Now might be a good time to go, while he's occupied."

"Okay." Celia bent over and kissed the baby's head. "Behave yourself, big brother. Don't make me have to come back here and kick your sorry backside into next week for acting like a jerk."

"Like to see you try, sister, dear." Cort's smile lacked both warmth and conviction.

"Anything you want me to tell Mom and Dad?" Celia asked at the door.

"Nope."

"Okay." Celia hugged Tate and whispered something in his ear. Tate nodded his head, kissed Celia's cheek, then gave Kenzie a hug and kiss before she opened the door and the two women rushed outside.

"Me go wif Mama." Gideon slid off Cort's lap and hurried across the floor toward Tate.

"No, Gid. You're staying home with the guys." Tate picked up his son and tossed him in the air. "How about a cookie?"

"Tookie?" Gideon asked.

Tate handed the baby a cookie then settled him in his highchair. "That will keep him busy for a few minutes." He grinned at Cort as he poured milk into a sippy cup and set it in front of Gideon. "Let's talk about what sort of work you feel up to doing."

"What have you got in mind?" Cort asked. It would kill him to tell his lifelong friend he didn't want to be there, didn't want to be part of the sweet, loving family Tate and Kenzie created.

"We've got another cutting of hay to put down, cattle to work, and I've got two new horses to train. If you're up for it, you can…"

Cort wondered just how long he'd be forced to depend on Tate and Kenzie's hospitality before he could hit the road. He didn't know where he'd go or what he'd do, but he certainly had no plans to make his visit at the Morgan Ranch an extended one...

Wrestlin' Christmas
Rodeo Romance, Book 2

Available on **Amazon**

Rodeo Romance Series

Hunky rodeo cowboys tangle with independent sassy
women who can't help but love them.

__The Christmas Cowboy__ *(Book 1)* — Among the top
saddle bronc riders in the rodeo circuit, easy-going Tate
Morgan can handle the toughest horse out there, but trying
to handle the beautiful Kenzie Beckett is a completely
different story. As the holiday season approaches, this
Christmas Cowboy is going to need more than a little
mistletoe to win her heart.

__Wrestlin' Christmas__ *(Book 2)* — Sidelined with a
major injury, steer wrestler Cort McGraw struggles to
come to terms with the end of his career. Shanghaied by
his sister and best friend, he finds himself on a run-
down ranch with a worrisome, albeit gorgeous widow,
and her silent, solemn son.

__Capturing Christmas__ *(Book 3)* — Life is hectic on a
good day for rodeo stock contractor Kash Kressley.
Between dodging flying hooves and babying cranky bulls,
he barely has time to sleep. The last thing Kash needs is
the entanglement of a sweet romance, especially with a
woman as full of fire and sass as the redheaded
photographer he meets at a rodeo.

Barreling Through Christmas *(Book 4)* — Cooper James might be a lot of things, but beefcake model wasn't something he intended to add to his resume.

Chasing Christmas (Book 5) — Tired of his cousin's publicity stunts on his behalf, bull rider Chase Jarrett has no idea how he ended up with an accidental bride!

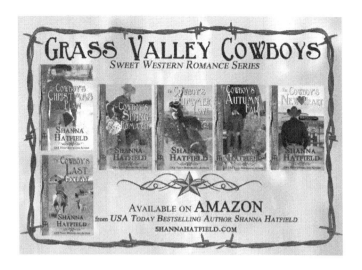

Grass Valley Cowboys Series

Meet the Thompson family of the Triple T Ranch in Grass Valley, Oregon. Three handsome brothers, their rowdy friends, and the women who fall for them are at the heart of this sweet contemporary western romance series.

The Cowboy's Christmas Plan (Book 1) — Cadence Greer's plans for a happy-ever-after are quickly derailed when her fiancé runs off with his secretary a week before their wedding. Homeless, jobless, and jilted, she escapes to Grass Valley, Oregon, where she takes a job as a housekeeper and cook to seven cowboys on a sprawling ranch.

The Cowboy's Spring Romance (Book 2) — Trent Thompson has carried a torch for the new schoolteacher since she moved to Grass Valley more than three years ago. Instead of asking her out, he's dated every single female in a thirty-mile radius, giving her the impression he's not interested in her at all.

The Cowboy's Summer Love (Book 3) — Always the wild-child, Travis Thompson doesn't disappoint as he rolls from one adventure to another in his quest to keep his adrenaline pumping. He needs a release for the tension constantly building inside him, especially after he discovers the girl he's loved his entire life just moved back to Grass Valley.

The Cowboy's Autumn Fall (Book 4) — Brice Morgan thought love at first sight was some ridiculous notion of schoolgirls and old ladies who read too many romance novels. At least he does until he meets Bailey Bishop at a friend's wedding and falls hard and fast for the intriguing woman.

The Cowboy's New Heart (Book 5) — Years after her husband died unexpectedly, Denni Thompson can't bear to think of giving her heart to anyone else. With three newly married sons, a grandchild on the way, and a busy life, Denni doesn't give a thought to romance until she meets the handsome new owner of Grass Valley's gas station.

The Cowboy's Last Goodbye (Book 6) — With his siblings and friends all entangled in the state of matrimony, Ben Morgan is more determined than ever to remain blissfully single. Despite his vehement refusal to commit to a relationship, he can't help but envision a future with the sweet, charming woman who unknowingly captures his heart.

Hardman Holidays Series
Heartwarming holiday stories set in the 1890s
in Hardman, Oregon.

__The Christmas Bargain__ *(Book 1)* — As owner and manager of the Hardman bank, Luke Granger is a man of responsibility and integrity in the small 1890s Eastern Oregon town. When he calls in a long overdue loan, Luke finds himself reluctantly accepting a bargain in lieu of payment from the shiftless farmer who barters his daughter to settle his debt.

__The Christmas Token__ *(Book 2)* — Determined to escape an unwelcome suitor, Ginny Granger flees to her brother's home in Eastern Oregon for the holiday season. Returning to the community where she spent her childhood years, she plans to relax and enjoy a peaceful visit. Not expecting to encounter the boy she once loved, her exile proves to be anything but restful.

__The Christmas Calamity__ *(, Book 3)* — Arlan Guthry's uncluttered world tilts off kilter when the beautiful and enigmatic prestidigitator Alexandra Janowski arrives in town, spinning magic and trouble in her wake as the holiday season approaches.

__The Christmas Vow__ *(Book 4)* — Sailor Adam Guthry returns home to bury his best friend and his past, only to fall once more for the girl who broke his heart.

__The Christmas Quandary__ *(Book 5)* — Tom Grove just needs to survive a month at home while he recovers from a work injury. He arrives in Hardman to discover his middle-aged parents acting like newlyweds, the school in need of a teacher, and the girl of his dreams already engaged.

The Christmas Confection (Book 6) — Can a lovely baker sweeten a hardened man's heart?

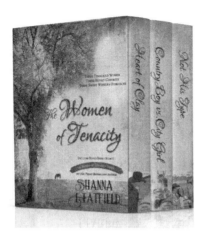

The Women of Tenacity Series

Tenacious, spunky women give the wild, rugged men who love them a run for their money in this contemporary western romance series.

Heart of Clay (Book 1) — Easy-going cowboy Clay Matthews is the man family and friends turn to for help, or when they need a good laugh, since he's a huge tease and practical joker. Life would be almost perfect, except for the mysterious woman he calls his wife... (*Available* **FREE** *for electronic downloads.*)

Country Boy vs. City Girl (Book 2) — A confirmed city girl finds herself falling for a wanna-be country boy. Sparks fly as a battle of stubborn will ensues.

Not His Type (Book 3) — Tired of living life in the shadows, Anna Zimmerman steps into the light, unprepared to handle the attention of the charming, handsome cowboy who works across the street.

ABOUT THE AUTHOR

SHANNA HATFIELD spent ten years as a newspaper journalist before moving into the field of marketing and public relations. Self-publishing the romantic stories she dreams up in her head is a perfect outlet for her lifelong love of writing, reading, and creativity. She and her husband, lovingly referred to as Captain Cavedweller, reside in the Pacific Northwest.

Shanna loves to hear from readers.
Connect with her online:

Blog: shannahatfield.com

Facebook: Shanna Hatfield's Page

Pinterest: Shanna Hatfield

Email: shanna@shannahatfield.com

Made in the USA
Columbia, SC
24 September 2018